WHERE *the* FIRE BURNS

The Hidden Harvest

Bread Upon the Waters

Where the Fire Burns

WHERE *the* FIRE BURNS

A Novel
by
Anne de Graaf

BETHANY HOUSE
PUBLISHERS
MINNEAPOLIS, MN 55438

Where the Fire Burns
Copyright © 1997
Anne de Graaf

Published by Bethany House Publishers
A Ministry of Bethany Fellowship, Inc.
11300 Hampshire Avenue South
Minneapolis, Minnesota 55438

Printed in the United States of America.

Library of Congress Cataloging-in-Publication Data

CIP Data applied for

ISBN 1–55661–619–8   CIP

To Erik

ANNE DE GRAAF is the author of twenty-seven children's books published in more than thirty countries. Nearly three million of her books have been sold worldwide. Her first novel, *Bread Upon the Waters*, has been published in six countries, including Poland and Germany. She has also worked as a journalist and economics translator for the Dutch government. She lives in The Netherlands with her husband and their two children.

A Word From the Author

⎯⎯⎯⎯⎯⎯ ✑ ⎯⎯⎯⎯⎯⎯

To start with, thank you to all the many friends and family around the world who are *not* mentioned below. You come first, all of you who continue to encourage me and have helped me tell this story. And I want to say a special word of thanks to my parents.

My prayer for those who read this is that they will be touched as I was by the endurance and inspiration of the true-life stories on which the book is based. I thank God for the privilege of writing them, and I hope the Lord will use these stories to deepen others' faith as He has mine. These real men and women, those who have endured and whose lives continue to inspire—those people know who they are and have asked to remain anonymous. I thank you all for trusting me with your stories.

I want to stress, however, that while this book is based on true-life stories, it remains a work of fiction. I have woven the stories of several people together into a novel, not a documentary. I have also embellished the stories I heard and invented a few characters of my own. Although many of the events described actually took place, the characters and their relationships are purely fictional, as are certain persecution events described in the concluding chapters.

As with the first book, my deepest gratitude goes to Elżbieta Gajowska, who read the final text with Polish eyes, looking for misspelled Polish verbs and historical inconsistencies. As much as was possible, these have been corrected. Elżbieta has translated and interpreted, sought out people who were willing to talk about painful periods in their past, submerged herself in archaic archival systems, and looked at the same hundreds of old photos I have. More important, she has provided me with a lasting friendship, a shared love of art and travel, and a circle of friends I'm honored to call my own.

I also want to express my deep appreciation and admiration for Anne Christian Buchanan. She is that rare editor with vision, who sees the beauty of a story where others see only words. Without her patience and encouragement I could never have finished this book. She has been my guide and mentor, a precious friend.

I owe a special debt of gratitude to everyone at Bethany House who have watched the deadline come and go as we all struggled to bring the project to a close. I did not make your jobs any easier, and I deeply appreciate your patience and understanding, not to mention your occasional tactful silences. You are a terrific team of people to work with, and I'm honored to be part of the Bethany House family.

I am very grateful to the entire Van der Stelt family. The eldest generation gave me a place of peace where I could write the final chapters undisturbed. The youngest generation are friends of our children, a gift in itself. And the one in between gave me their prayers and deep friendship while introducing me to the richness of trekking through Central America and Africa and getting Erik to finally go on vacation.

Thank you Julia and Daniël. Your love and insights and laughter and discoveries continue to bring me only joy.

And without my anchor in the storm, I could never have brought these thoughts onto paper. Once again, Erik, this book is dedicated to you.

Contents

EUROPE IN 1970

Moscow ✪

(R U S I A)

R.

Katyń
Smolensk

I A)

S.

S.

Stalingrad ●

Artemovsk ●

U K R A I N E)

D)

(GEORGIA)

Black   Sea

T U R K E Y

✪ Ankara

"I will bring the third part through the fire,
Refine them as silver is refined,
And test them as gold is tested.
They will call on My name,
And I will answer them;
I will say, 'They are My people,'
And they will say, 'The LORD is my God.'"

—Zechariah 13:9, NASB

1

Gives No Light

Job 18:5

1952

Where could he go to hide? Jasiu knew deep down that he could never forgive himself. He was the one who had sent his father to prison.

He ran on deeper into the woods, his seven-year-old legs pumping hard. Tears forced their way out of his eyes. Jasiu held up his arms, as if waiting for some tree to bow down, pick him up, and bear him away. Instead he tripped over a root and stumbled, sobbing.

The night before there had been frost-cold darkness when the men pounding on the door woke Jasiu up. He sat up and pulled the blanket under his chin. Jasiu slept on a couch on the other side of the same room where his parents slept behind a curtain. He heard his mother suck in her breath as his father called out, "Yes, yes, I'm coming," and made his way across the room.

Through the door burst light and men's forms, bringing strange smells with them, sweat and cigarette smoke. And then the lone light bulb in the room flared to life. Two of the three men grabbed his father by the elbows and forced him to stand spread-eagled against the wall. Jasiu's mother swung her black eyes over to Jasiu, locking onto him. Her warning was clear: he should say nothing, do nothing. Then she stood, smoothed her nightdress, and asked, "What is the meaning of this?"

"Tadeusz Piekarz?"

"Yes." His father's voice sounded muffled against the wallpaper. One of the intruders had jammed his face against the wall and now held him there with one hand clamped at the back of his neck.

"Then you are under arrest for having contraband in your possession." The man nodded at the other two, who kicked Tadeusz's feet farther apart. Then they dragged him toward the door.

Before they reached it, Jasiu's mother had knotted her hands into fists, lifted her chin, and asked, "What contraband? We have nothing."

While the other two men stopped at the door with Tadeusz between them, the man who had spoken glanced around the room. A cruel sound came out of his throat as he strode over to Jasiu. Jasiu saw his father twist in the men's grasp. The look he shot Jasiu was like his mother's, but it also warned him of something else, something Jasiu didn't understand.

The man's eyes grazed over Jasiu, discarding him. Then his hand reached out and snatched the half-hidden Bible off the table beside Jasiu's couch. He raised the thick, coverless volume high in the air, swirled to confront the woman who had challenged him, and sneered, "Is that so?" Then he dashed it against the wall, where it fell with a thud, loose pages fluttering onto the floor.

Then the door opened, and Jasiu heard only the soft timber of his father's voice saying once, "My Hanna." The door closed, and the room became heavy with silence and fear.

Jasiu tried to breathe again, but it seemed all he felt were the sharp bits of his shattered world piercing his heart. The pain swelled as slowly, over the eternity of a few seconds, a realization of why this might have happened crept over him.

"*Mamusiu?*"

Hanna let out a long, shuddering breath. She had gone to the window and was closing it. Then her hands flew to her face, and now she began to shake so violently that even Jasiu could see it. She turned her glazed eyes onto him.

"When will *Tatuś* come back?"

Hanna held out her arms. "Come, Jasiu, I . . . don't know."

Jasiu suddenly discovered he could move, and he flew into his mother's arms. But the ache of fear would not let him go. And he could not bring himself to tell his mother about it. If what he

16

feared was true, then putting it into words would only make it worse.

Jasiu tried to stay awake long enough to hear the familiar sound of his mother's steady breathing, the sound he was used to hearing whenever he woke up early and read. But that sound did not come. And her soft body next to his never slackened.

When he woke up the next morning, he forgot for a moment what had happened. He looked over at his mother and wondered why he was in his parents' bed, and where was his father? Only then did he remember the night before. His mother's eyes were closed, her lips moving. Jasiu lay a small hand on her shoulder and asked, "Are we praying for Tatuś?"

"Yes, for your father. Close your eyes now and pray with me." She pulled him into her arms and began praying out loud. "Our Lord, You are with him now, and for that we thank You. Please bring him home soon."

Jasiu could tell from his mother's voice that she was almost crying. He had never seen her cry, and he didn't want to now.

It was a shorter prayer than he was used to hearing, but even before he opened his eyes, the drowsiness had lifted. In its place fell fear. Fear of why this thing had happened. As Jasiu caught his breath, remembering all, he felt his little-boy confidence swept away finally, like a house of cards in a hurricane.

The day of his father's arrest had been Jasiu's first day of school. Proud of his new backpack and the blue shorts his mother had sewn for him, Jasiu had walked by himself to the big building at the end of the street. The teacher was a young woman. She had assigned him a place on one of the benches. And he had spent most of the day trying to sit still and learn the names of the other children in his class.

When it was almost time to go home, the teacher had sat down on the edge of her desk and crossed her legs. Jasiu thought it looked as though she wanted to act less like a teacher and more like an auntie. She crossed her arms across her chest and smiled at the children.

"I wonder who can tell me a little bit about their homes."

"I can." A small girl with a big white bow in her hair stood up. "I have three big brothers and one little sister. Both my parents work in the fish factory."

"Yes, Dana, that's very nice. But I was wondering more about the things in your homes. What are the most important things? What do your parents value most?"

One by one the little hands went up. As the teacher nodded at them, children called out, "A picture of *Babcia*, Father's mother."

"A sword."

"Three silver spoons."

"The violin."

"Money in the jar."

"The amber necklace."

"Our cat."

As Jasiu listened, he felt more and more unsure. What could he say? What would be a clever answer that would make the teacher smile at him as she was smiling now at the boy next to him? Then he knew, and he knew he was right. Jasiu felt proud that he had something different to offer.

The family Bible was the most valuable thing in their home. Hadn't Tatuś told him the story of his time in camp with Jasiu's grandfather and how God had worked a miracle to bring the Bible to that place, how Tatuś had made a pair of shoes from the Bible's leather cover for another man, how grandfather had been killed on the very day that Tatuś was set free, so he had carried the Bible home with him, their own Bible with no cover?

Jasiu smiled. He felt a little bit smart to know what he and his parents valued most. *"Proszę pani?"* he pointed his finger toward the peeling paint on the ceiling as he had seen the others do.

"Yes, Jasiu. You have been very quiet today. What did you want to say?"

Jasiu didn't think he had been so quiet. Besides, he had just been trying to sit still. He swallowed. "It's our Bible. That's what's most valuable to us."

His teacher uncrossed her arms and legs and leaned forward. She waited a moment before looking up. When she did, and when Jasiu saw her eyes, he knew something was wrong.

"Yes, Jasiu, tell me about this Bible. Why is it so important?

Does it have a special place in your home?"

He had to think about this a few moments. What was the right answer? "No, it stays on the table, which isn't so special. But Father says our treasure is stored in heaven. That's in the Bible. So maybe the Bible helps us get that treasure, and that's why it's worth so much."

He was still waiting for the teacher's smile, but the more Jasiu talked, the more sternly she looked at him. Finally, in a small voice, he said, "We read it every day."

"And tell us, Jasiu, what does your father do? What kind of job does he have?"

Jasiu hoped to score better here. Speaking with renewed confidence, he said loudly, "He is a teacher at the Polytech University in Gdańsk."

"University? Now, class, listen to me. These are bad people, Jasiu's parents. They think they are very smart, but really they are very dumb. Before the war they probably thought they were special, but now they must make room for workers. People like Dana's parents who work in a factory—these are the people who will build Poland into a great land. Jasiu has taught us an important lesson here today, class."

Jasiu looked up hopefully, his face still smarting from the insults about his parents.

"Only silly people went to university before the war. And this was a silly story Jasiu Piekarz has told us today about that book in their home. Very silly, don't you think?" She looked over Jasiu at the other children and smiled at them, nodding.

"Yes, miss, very silly," one of the girls called out. Then slowly, like a storm at sea, their laughter rose and rolled over Jasiu, nearly drowning him as he realized he was certainly the one they were all making fun of.

He made himself small and looked down at his feet. Their voices cried, "Silly Jasiu, silly Jasiu!" Jasiu felt as if someone had played a game with him but had not told him the rules. He glanced again at his teacher. Now that she was smiling at him, it wasn't really a smile.

After a very long time the teacher clapped her hands. "All

right, children. Now I hope all of you had a nice first day of school."

"Yes, miss!" the voices chorused.

"Good. Then I will see you all again tomorrow."

"Yes, miss!" The children stood up and filed out of the room in a line, bench by bench, as they had learned to do earlier that day.

Jasiu thought of only one thing. *I won't cry. They won't laugh at me about that, too.* As soon as he was outside, he did not wait to see what the other children said or did or if the boy who lived in the same block of apartments as he did would walk home with him. No, Jasiu started running. He ran the whole length of the street to his home, then he ran up the stairs. And when he ran through the room that belonged to their neighbors and into his parents' room, he saw that his mother was just setting the pot of tea on the table.

Jasiu stood there for a moment, too out of breath to say or do anything.

"Jasiu." His mother stroked his soft hair, bleached blond by the summer. As she combed the part to the side with her fingers, she said, "You look like you've seen something terrible. What is it?" His mother came down to his level and took both his hands into hers.

The tears caught up with him. He flung himself into her arms and sobbed into her shoulder. "I hate school! I hate the teacher! I hate the other children!"

"Oh, Jasiu," she said softly. "What happened? The first day is always a big step, but you're more than ready for school. Why, you can already read. What's the matter?"

So Jasiu told her what had happened, and he watched her face change as quickly as his teacher's had. But his mother's face didn't have that smile that hurt. Instead, she looked away from Jasiu, up out of the window. She moved her mouth and blinked hard. When he finished talking, she sighed and folded him back into the safety of her arms.

"All right. Listen, Jasiu. You did the right thing. You told the truth. Remember what we always say—never be ashamed of be-lieving in our Lord Jesus. He has special rewards for His children who hurt like you do because you believe in Him. It's just . . ." Her voice trailed off.

"What, Mamusiu? What did I do wrong?"

"It's just . . . I had hoped you wouldn't be earning these rewards at quite such a young age."

That night when Jasiu's father came home from work, Jasiu heard his parents whispering in the other corner of their room, behind the curtain around their bed.

All he had heard his father say at that time were the words, "Now, Hanna, you know as well as I do that it would only attract more attention and bring more trouble on his head. Let it go. They will forget about him soon. Who listens to a child of seven?"

At the time he hadn't connected those words with what had happened at school. But later he would have the chance to go over and over the events of that evening. And then he would realize it was all part of the same disaster.

The family ate their evening meal at four o'clock. Then, as on every day Jasiu could remember, his father read out of the Bible and they held hands and prayed. When Jasiu opened his eyes, he saw his parents smiling at him.

"Son, your mother tells me school did not go so well today." The skin around his father's eyes furrowed. "She says you don't want to go back tomorrow, is that right?"

Jasiu nodded, the hot shame of the other children's laughter still stinging in his ears. But he had a plan. "*Tatusiu*, you are a teacher. If I stay home, you could teach me. I would do all my homework and could help Mamusia."

His father shook his head. "Ah, my clever son, I can see you have been trying to solve this problem. But I'm afraid this will not be easy." His father reached across the table and took Jasiu's hands into his own. "Son, listen to me. You will have to go to school tomorrow. Tomorrow and all the other days—do you hear me?"

"But, Tatusiu. It wasn't fair. The teacher and the other children—"

Jasiu's father held up a hand. "Son, you are right. You are so young to learn such hard lessons. But things in this world are rarely fair, and almost always, someone is getting hurt. Now you are being hurt, and we hurt with you. I wish with all my heart that we could change the way your teacher is doing this."

"You could go and talk with her."

Jasiu watched his father look up and stare at his mother for a moment, then his father said, "Very well. Maybe you both are right. I'll go with you tomorrow morning, but then you must promise me you will go to school every day after that, no matter what—unless you're sick, that is."

"Yes, Tatusiu, I promise." Jasiu held out his hand and felt the warmth of his father's smile lift the weight of his worry. His father would go with him to school the next day. That would make everything all right.

"And now, Jasiu, we have some news," his mother said.

"Good news or bad news?" Jasiu asked.

"Good news, my little man. Come here." As Jasiu came around the table, his father pulled him onto his lap.

"Yes," his mother continued. "You see, in a few months you will become a big brother."

Jasiu held in his breath. A big brother. He looked at his parents, not sure what they expected of him.

His mother said, "We were saving the news until we were sure, but we thought that after what happened to you this afternoon, you could use some good news. You see, Jasiu, this new baby is a gift from God. You were a very special gift, and now the Lord has blessed us a second time."

Jasiu knew the story of his own birth by heart. It was one of his favorite things to ask his parents about. Then they would sit on his couch with him in the middle and take turns telling about the time at the end of the war, about their separation, about his mother's travels to Czechoslovakia and his father's to a Soviet camp, about how God had "taken Tadeusz by hand" and miraculously led him to Hanna just in time for Jasiu to be born with both his parents there, waiting to welcome him into the world. Jasiu loved to hear about his parents' adventures, but he loved most of all to feel the warmth this story never failed to bring to rest on them. His mother said that good feeling was a gift from God, the gift of gratitude.

His mother continued, "Jasiu, God has given us so much love. When you were born, He gave us even more love. Can you understand this? The baby will take nothing away from you, but only add to our love." His mother leaned over and touched his cheek.

"Yes, Mamusiu." Jasiu got off his father's lap and stood as tall as he could.

"Your mother and I will need your help with the baby. And we know you will be a big boy, a real helper. Most babies have brothers who are still quite young. But your baby brother or sister will be lucky to have a brother who is almost eight years older. What do you think about this news, Jasiu?"

Jasiu felt proud. "I think this is good news. Mamusiu, I will go to school every day. And then I can help my little brother when it's time for him to go to school."

"And if it's a little sister?" his mother laughed.

"Then I will help her, too."

"Ah, Jasiu." His father folded him into his big arms.

———— ∽ ————

The morning after his father's arrest, Jasiu wondered at the safety he had felt in his father's arms the night before. That time had seemed so far away, it was almost impossible to imagine it. As he lay beside his mother, trying to pray with her, all he had been able to think about was the teacher, his parents' conversation, and what had happened that night. When his mother finished praying, he waited a few moments in the silence of the dawn-lit room. He waited for the fear to lift, but Jasiu could sense that somehow it was there to stay.

"What are we going to do?" Jasiu asked.

He could see tears trembling in the corners of his mother's eyes. Maybe if he asked questions and she talked, she would feel better. His parents always said he was good at asking questions. He took a deep breath. "Where do you think they've taken him? When will he come back? Mamusiu?"

"—Hmm?" She turned to look at Jasiu as if hearing him for the first time.

"Mamusiu, who will go with me to school now?"

"Oh, Jasiu." She sighed. "Oh, Jasiu," she said again, not answering his question. Hanna sat up straighter. "You want to know where Tadeusz is. Well, you know that was the secret police last night, don't you? The Security Office?"

He nodded. "The UB."

She gazed at him as if sorry he knew the name. "Yes, the UB," she repeated. "So that's where he is. And when he will come back? I wish with all my heart that I knew. It will probably be only a few days. The same thing happened to a few of our friends who come on Tuesday nights, and that was just for a few days. It could be . . . now listen, Jasiu, and listen closely. It's important that you not talk to people about what happened here last night."

"Why?"

"Because not everyone can be trusted. I need you to do as I say, now. I know it's hard. Tatuś is gone, but we will pray it's only for a short while. And we will believe that the Lord God will keep him safe."

Jasiu thought his mother was talking more to herself than to him. "Yes, Mamusiu, God will keep him safe." He slipped his small hand into hers. He had an idea. The fear in him told Jasiu that the teacher was somehow connected to his father's arrest. "Would it . . ." He swallowed. "Would it help if I went to school by myself?"

Hanna glanced at him sharply as he continued, "I mean, the teacher is one of the people you don't want to hear about Tatuś, right?"

"Oh, my little prince. How is it possible? You do understand. Yes, it would help. If I go, there could be even more problems. Can you do this? Do you remember what Tatuś said last night?"

"Yes." Jasiu nodded solemnly. He felt as if he had made a very hard promise to keep. "Yes, I'll go every day."

"That's my brave boy. Now, let's get ready for school, shall we? You don't want to be late."

Hanna stood up, then sat down again. "Mamusiu, what is it?"

"I just feel a little . . . oh." Hanna hugged her stomach and swallowed hard. "I'll be all right. I just have to lie down for a moment. You get yourself dressed, all right?"

Jasiu left her bed and crossed the room to his own couch. He stripped the mattress and folded up the blankets and sheets. As he put them away in the drawer beneath the couch, he could hear his mother throwing up. When she came out from behind the curtain, looking pale and teary-eyed, he said, "You're sick."

"No, I'm not." She smiled weakly at his disbelieving look. "Well, not really. This is what happens to women when they're going to have a baby. It's the first time I've been sick this time. It's all right; it will pass. Now let me see what you've done."

Jasiu was having some difficulty. He did not want to go to school. He did not want his father to be gone. He did not want this stomachache that made him want to join his mother and throw up. He did not want to feel as if he might start crying any moment. He wondered if his mother knew all this. He looked up at her back as she bent over the couch, his eyes pleading for some sort of order to be brought back into his frightened world.

Jasiu stood in the middle of the room and caught sight of his reflection in the mirror. He saw his short legs, his long body, freckles on his nose, and he saw his eyes, different somehow. He did not want to feel the panic that threatened to engulf him if he took his eyes off that reflection.

His mother turned toward him and cupped his chin in her hand. "I think you and I need to keep busy today. Standing still won't be good for either of us. Come on, show me how good you are at setting the table, Jasiu."

He broke the gaze and looked up at her. "It's all right," she said. "You're not alone, and neither am I. I want you to pray today every time you have this empty feeling. Pray in your thoughts to God and then try to find something to do. Can you do that?"

"Yes, Mamusiu."

So Jasiu and his mother busied themselves with tasks that, because of their very everyday nature, brought comfort. She made breakfast in the corner of the room where they had a one-burner stove and pots and plates, and he set the table. Neither said anything about Jasiu's father until Jasiu looked at the two places he had just set and went back to the cupboard for another plate.

His mother watched him without a word. When Jasiu had finished setting the third place, he looked up at her and asked, "It's all right, isn't it? I mean, he could come home this morning?"

His mother sat down hard on one of the chairs and looked at

him with her dark eyes. "Yes. It's a good idea. He could walk through that door any moment."

Jasiu watched his mother slice the small dark loaf he had placed on the table. She held it under her arm with one hand and sawed with the knife in the other. When she had placed several pieces on the plate, she put the bread down and took Jasiu's hands.

"Close your eyes. Lord God, we call on Your angels today to protect our Tatuś. Send Your own army to keep him safe, just as You did during the long months we were separated the last time. Lord, I trust . . ."

Jasiu heard his mother's voice crack. He opened one eye and saw her rocking back and forth, even as her eyes stayed tightly shut. When she spoke again, her voice sounded like Jasiu's father's when he had just made a decision.

"Lord, I trust You. Lord, I can feel Your hand on myself, my son, and my husband. Hold us there in Your palm today, and all the rest of our days here on earth. Lord, thank You for this food, precious as it is. Amen."

Jasiu had heard often enough of how difficult it had been just after the war, with so little food for so many, so many people lost and without homes. He closed his eyes quickly and said, "Yes, thank You, Father God." Then he waited a few moments, as his parents had taught him. It was a time for saying prayers to himself, or just for listening to see if God had anything to say. When he heard his mother straighten her chair, he opened his eyes.

"*Smacznego*," she said.

"Smacznego," Jasiu replied. He took a slice of bread, covered it with cheese, cut it into quarters, and lifted a corner up to his mouth. The food tasted like dust. He put it back down on his plate.

"You must eat, Jasiu. Here, try some herring; you always like that."

Jasiu fished out a side of pickled herring from the jar reeking of vinegar and onions. His mother's herring was better than any other recipes made by aunties he knew, or by the friends and neighbors they visited on Name Days or christenings. "Yes, Mamusiu." He put a chunk of fish on the bread and managed to swallow it down. After he drank his tea, he said, "I think I'm just not hungry."

"It's all right. You can go wash up and put your shoes on. I'm not hungry either. I'll clear up here."

Jasiu started to stand up, then remembered and sat down. "*Dziękuję*, Mamusiu."

"Thank you, Jasiu," she replied.

When Jasiu was ready, he went to put on his coat and boots. Then his mother joined him, and they left the apartment together. She walked behind him through the other family's room and down the stairs of the apartment building. Then she stood at the main entrance, fastening his coat. "Are you sure you'll be all right?"

Jasiu nodded. He didn't feel so sure, but he thought maybe his mother needed him to be the man of the house now. He stood on his tiptoes and kissed his mother goodbye. "Tatuś will be home when I come home from school, yes, Mamusiu?"

"I hope so. Now, you go and be brave. Don't let anything anyone says hurt you. I'll be praying for you today, Jasiu."

He nodded again and headed down the street that led to school. Jasiu couldn't help but notice the difference between what he felt today and what he had felt yesterday. Then he had been a little boy on his way to his first day of school. Now he had grown so much older, his father had been taken away, his mother was going to have a baby, and Jasiu was scared as he had never, ever been.

He entered the schoolyard and headed straight for the open door. He was hoping the children might forget what had happened the day before. That's what had happened during the summer when he had a fight with a boy who lived downstairs from them. Jasiu was sure the boy would never talk to him again. But the day after their argument, the boy had come upstairs and asked Jasiu's mother if he could come out and play.

The door to the classroom was locked. He had forgotten that he couldn't go in until the teacher opened it. So he went back outside and sat down in a corner of the schoolyard and pretended to be busy with his books and his wooden pencil box. Only when the bell rang and the other children began filing into the room did Jasiu stand up to join them.

The teacher entered the room, following the children. He stood with his classmates, waiting for her to tell them to be seated, then he sat down and folded his hands on the desk. The breakfast in his stomach felt like a heavy lump. Would the teacher say anything about what happened yesterday?

But the teacher said nothing. She simply opened her notebook and school started just as it had the day before. They had their reading lesson and their arithmetic lesson and they drew pictures. By the end of the morning, Jasiu had relaxed somewhat. Despite everything, he managed to get excited about all he was learning; a little of the anticipation he had felt all summer about finally being old enough to go to school came back.

When the bell rang for the break at noon, the teacher asked Jasiu to pass out the salted bread and the whale-fat drink they received every day. When he had finished, Jasiu brought the plate back to the teacher's desk.

And then her hand clamped down over his thin wrist. "So tell me, little Jasiu. What happened at your home last night?" The fear slammed down on him just as her hand had. Jasiu looked around the class and saw that none of the children had heard the teacher's whispered question.

He said in a weak voice, "I'm not supposed to talk to you anymore about what happens in our family." This was not altogether true, but Jasiu had to find out something for sure, and this was the only way.

"Oh, you're not, are you? Why? Did the police come and visit your parents last night?"

Although Jasiu had prepared himself for this, the sure knowledge that the teacher really was connected with his father's arrest still startled him. He blurted, "Yes, they took him away."

The teacher let go of Jasiu, leaned back, and breathed loudly out her nose. Then she made her eyes small and said, "You sent him there."

The four words were like nails driven one by one into Jasiu's soul. "No," he said. Then louder, "No, I couldn't, I didn't!" The tears had come back to betray him, but Jasiu didn't care. He looked up and saw now that the other children were staring at him. The teacher looked away from him.

"No!" he screamed this time, slamming the plate onto her desk.

"Get out," she said, still not moving her head. "You're spoiled and just as arrogant as your parents."

"No!" Jasiu said one more time as he tripped toward the row of jackets hanging on the wall, grabbed blindly for his coat and school things, and ran out of the room.

Once outside, Jasiu kept right on running. Down the street, past his home, down more streets, up into the hills outside *Gdynia*. The tears blurred everything. His heart felt as if it would burst right out of his chest.

Jasiu had never been this far away from home alone before, but he didn't care. If he kept on running, the horrible certainty growing in him with every pounding step might somehow be left behind.

But the teacher's words would not let him rest. "You sent him there. You sent him there." He could hear her with every pounding step. While he ran on streets with buildings, Jasiu tried to block out the sound with the same rhythm, "No, I didn't. No, I didn't." By the time he reached the woods beyond the hills, though, Jasiu could no longer keep from hearing it. Despite his mute resolve, Jasiu's answering rhythm became, "I sent him there. I sent Tatuś to prison."

He ran blindly, veering off the road and diving into the deep woods. Their early autumn colors had already turned the ground into a path of gold and red. Jasiu needed somewhere to hide. The weight of guilt seemed to push him down into the very summer-dried dirt beneath his feet. Jasiu could not breathe. He threw his arms up high as if even his body wanted to flee and fly.

Then Jasiu fell. He panted into the dust, watching his tears scar the leaves beneath his hands. "Why?" he cried out loud. Then he held his breath for a moment, trying to be still. Suddenly a stick broke somewhere beyond those trees, and he swung his head to the left like a hunted animal. It sounded as if someone were walking toward him.

Jasiu had no idea what was hidden in these woods. He had

been near here only one other time. That had been on his birthday, a month earlier, just before they went camping at the lake. He had come here with his parents to search for mushrooms.

As he lay panting, Jasiu let the warmth of that day wash over him again. He heard his mother laughing as his father chased her between the trees, her dark hair dotted with the daisies she had pushed between the curls during their walk. His big, strong father, his blond hair falling in his eyes, had grabbed his mother just as Jasiu ran up to them both and curled his arms around their waists.

"Such a happy family we are"—he remembered his father's deep voice. The smell of his mother's skirt, the feel of her soft hand against his cheek, the taste of the peppermints she always had in a pocket somewhere, the loving looks he saw his parents exchange when they thought he was not watching, were all like secret jewels passed in the dark. Jasiu hugged himself. How had he come back to this place so alone?

To his left, Jasiu thought he heard a sound again. He picked himself up and staggered onward, not even sure anymore of what he was trying to escape. Exhausted, he slowed to a walk. In front of him he thought he saw more sun, a clearing of some kind. He pushed his way through the berry bushes and emerged on the edge of a wide expanse of fields. To his right and left stretched the border of the woods.

Jasiu whimpered and wiped his eyes with the backs of his hands. He took a deep shuddering breath and looked behind him. He heard and saw no one.

Then Jasiu raised his eyes and followed the line of the horizon. Before him rolled the stubble growth of freshly harvested grain. And even now, the fields were not empty. Like giant snowflakes, hundreds of white storks moved with bent necks, bathed in the light of Indian summer. Jasiu had never seen so many of the great birds in one place before. This was something different than the pairs of birds nesting on farmhouse chimneys.

He opened his eyes wide. Why wouldn't the feeling go away? "No, please," he moaned softly. He knew now that there was no running away from it. He would have to go back home, to a home without his father . . . for how long? He would have to go back to school, every day as he had promised, no matter what the teacher and children were like. He would have to carry the guilt of what he had done.

"Father God . . ." His voice shook. It was all he could say. The words died in his throat as he collapsed to the ground. Then Jasiu pushed his arms upward. Again, it was a gesture of supplication, but this time there was something more, an attempt to push off the invisible burden that would not let him go.

Jasiu's anguish poured out of him, hot with the fear and anger and betrayal that had brought him to this place. A little boy on the edge of a field, Jasiu cried out loud, in sounds that knew no words, as even then the light began to bathe his face.

At the same moment the cloud of storks lifted upward. Like his prayers, a gift from heaven, they turned and circled once above him, returning home from a sea of sunshine.

2

Baptizes

Matthew 3:11

1952

Amy Baker wondered what she should do next in the few hours she had left before the party.

She had just finished hanging balloons from the trees around the barnyard. Before that she had tied bows around the goats' necks. Now she headed for the stables. She would give Blackie a good rubdown, then braid his mane and tail with the little red bows her mother had given her on his birthday.

"Now we're both thirteen," Amy whispered in the animal's ear. It was true. The big day had finally arrived. Amy hummed as she worked.

She had been born in Boston on St. Patrick's Day, so that had to mean she was lucky. That's what her friends told her, anyway.

Amy had many friends. Every year she had a birthday party, and every year more and more children came. This year Amy had planned a slumber party with all the girls in her class. Her parents would take them on a hayride, and then the fresh hay would be dumped inside the barn where the girls would sleep, all snug and warm against the icy March wind.

Amy finished with her Blackie and ran into the kitchen to see if the cake had arrived from the baker's yet. Her mother had said that this time it would be more beautiful than ever, in the shape of a heart and covered with sugar-frosting roses.

Amy burst through the kitchen door to find her mother talking on the phone. "Yes, yes, of course we understand," she said with a tight voice. "Thank you for calling." She set the receiver down and sighed. "Amy, you'd better come here."

Ruth Baker's carefully colored hair gleamed a discreet silvery blond; her figure was trim and petite. The diamonds on her fingers blinked in the sun as she motioned Amy to come sit next to her at the kitchen table, but her blue eyes were tender as she gazed at her dark-haired daughter.

"That was Joyce's mother," she said gently. "Joyce can't come to the party."

"Oh." Joyce was Amy's best friend.

"And, Amy," her mother continued, "neither can anyone else, I'm afraid. Joyce was the last one of the group to call. All the rest called and canceled while you were outside."

Amy felt tears of disappointment sting her eyes. "But why? They can't all be sick."

"No, honey, they're not sick." Ruth sighed again and rubbed the bridge of her nose.

It was a motion Amy had seen her mother make often lately. It reminded her that both her parents were older than those of most of her friends. John had turned sixty that year and Ruth was fifty-eight. Only in recent weeks had they begun to look their age.

Amy had a feeling now and took her mother's age-flecked hand in her own smooth one. "What is it, Mom? What's wrong? Why aren't they coming? You know why, don't you?" she asked through smarting eyes.

"Yes, honey." Ruth pushed a lock of hair out of her eyes with the back of her hand. "It's your father. John is in trouble, and that trouble is spreading. There are some people who are trying to hurt him."

Amy blinked. "Dad has enemies?"

"Yes, you could say so. The company has done very well for some time, and there are some men who would do just about anything to get their hands on it. Now one of these men has found out that John and I were members of a discussion group in our old neighborhood in the city, and they're using this against us, trying to take the company away from us."

Amy had no idea what all this had to do with her birthday party, but she had never seen her mother look so distraught. She was happy that her mother was talking to her like this, like she was an adult. She was, after all, thirteen. Amy squeezed Ruth's hands. "They can't do that, though. There are laws against people saying bad things about you and trying to steal something like a company."

"Yes. There are laws. But that's just the problem. There's a senator in the government, Joseph McCarthy, who has been getting new laws passed that let this kind of thing happen. He says he wants to find all the communists in America, but what he's doing is ruining people's lives."

"Communists? You and Dad aren't communists, are you?" It was a dirty word. Amy had heard it often enough at school lately. Her history teacher talked about The Red Threat. The kids called one another "dirty commie." It was the latest bad name.

"No, of course not. But we did belong to this sort-of club, and there were other people there who later became communists. And now John has been singled out by this government committee, and they're going through all the company records and talking to our friends to see if they can find a reason to arrest him under these new anticommunist laws."

"Arrest Dad? Oh, Mom, this kind of thing doesn't happen in America. It's a free country; you can belong to any club you want."

Ruth gave Amy a strange look and sighed. "Yes, that's what I thought, too."

But something had dawned on Amy. "You said they've been talking to our friends. Is that why . . . ?"

Ruth nodded. "Yes, that's why no one's coming to your party. It seems our friends are scared that our trouble might somehow spread to them."

"But . . ."

"In all fairness, Amy, it could very well be that the same government people who are trying to hurt us have frightened or threatened our friends somehow."

"But if they were really our friends . . ." Amy didn't have to say any more. She could see that her mother had been thinking the same.

"I know. But let's not judge too harshly. And you will have your party, but it will be with just your old dad and mom. How's that for a disappointment?" Ruth smiled at her daughter.

Amy smiled back. "That's not so bad," she said. But she

thought something else. *What can I do to help them out of this?*

Her father came home that evening looking tired and old, his tie at half-mast and his expensive suit sagging. Ruth told him that Amy knew what was going on. "She's growing up," Amy heard Ruth saying as she walked into the room.

"Ah, my girl, what a disappointment your birthday turned out to be. Give your old dad a hug from the birthday girl."

"No disappointment," she said. "But you and Mom have to spend the night with me in the barn—that's the deal." In this way Amy managed to make both her parents laugh, and she was glad she could give them that at least.

It was a special evening, cold and blustery with the latest storm front. Amy and Ruth hugged one another in the back of the wagon, sweet-smelling hay in their hair and on their shoulders. John drove the wagon back to the barn. There they unrolled the sleeping bags, and Amy fed pieces of the huge birthday cake to her pony and her parents until no one could eat another bite.

Then they blew out the Coleman lantern and whispered ghost stories to one another in the dark. The animals snuffled and grunted. The wind blew rain through the cracks in the wood. Amy had never felt safer.

Lying there in the friendly dark, she didn't want to think about her friends not showing up. She didn't want to think about Monday morning when she'd have to face them all and pretend everything was all right.

But some things she just couldn't help thinking about.

She looked over at her parents. Even in the dark she could see them lying close together, each with an arm around the other.

"Why are you looking at us that way, birthday girl?" her father asked.

"I . . . was thinking." She had been thinking something she didn't often want to admit, that maybe being born on St. Patrick's Day wasn't so lucky after all. "I want one more story."

"Well in a half-hour it won't be your birthday anymore, so you'd better speak now or forever hold your peace."

Amy laughed. It was an old catch phrase between them. The familiarity of the humor gave her the confidence she needed to say, "Tell me again about when you and Mom adopted me."

It was a request Amy used to make often as a little girl, whenever she was feeling unsure of herself. Certainly now, Amy was uncertain about the luckiness of her birthday. If St. Patrick's Day was so lucky, why had she lost a father she never met to a war that began the same year she was born? And why was her mother killed in a car accident before that same war was even over?

"Ah," her friends had said then, "but look at the family who adopted you—they're nice and they're rich! And they love you. Of course you're lucky."

Amy pushed that voice out of her head and listened instead to John Baker's as he began the story she knew so well.

"You were six when we adopted you. You changed everything for us. It was because of you that we bought the farm. We used to live in a penthouse in Boston's downtown district. Now I drive an hour to work, but it doesn't matter. We wanted these three acres of forest and meadows to become a child's paradise—and that child was you.

"During the war I was sent home from the navy after I lost my leg fighting on a small island in the Pacific. Before the war your mother and I had tried for years to have a baby, but it wasn't meant to be. By the time I came home, I was already fifty."

Ruth interrupted him. "I was so relieved to have John home. But at the same time, we both knew the time for having children had passed us by. But you changed that."

John said, "When the Catholic adoption agency we had registered with called and said they had an older child, we jumped at the chance."

Amy could fill in the blanks. Her father didn't mention that they had given Amy everything money could buy—the farm and the animals, the topnotch private education, the private art lessons. But they had also given her love, and their family name.

Amy's original name had been Skrzypek. The difference between the complicated sounds of that name and Baker were just as extreme as her life before adoption and after.

She could still remember her natural mother, Barbara. Amy remembered her every time she looked in the mirror and saw her mother's pale skin and dark hair. But unlike her mother, her hair was straight, and so black it shone almost blue when the sun hit it a certain way. Amy knew these things because she still had a photo of her mother holding Amy just after she had been born.

Amy could also remember the way her mother smelled, like roses in the autumn, and the soft, drawling sound of her voice. And she remembered Barbara holding her in a rocking chair and telling her that her father had died in the war, so far away you had to ride a boat for weeks to get there.

"He died near the end of the war," her mother had said in her soft drawl, "fighting with other American soldiers in France."

Amy could not remember saying goodbye to her mother the day she died. And this had always bothered her, as if she should remember, as if, if that last hug had been memorable, it might have saved her mother somehow.

When the accident happened, Amy had been with a neighbor, the same woman who had baby-sat Amy all her life whenever Barbara had to work. And then some lady in a hat had taken her to stay with a couple who put her in the top bunk in a room with three other children. And then the Bakers had come to that house and talked with her while she sat on the top bunk, dangling her legs over the edge, and then she was packing and moving into their house. And then there was the farm.

It was after the move that Ruth had sat down with seven-year-old Amy and asked, "Do you know why you've come to live with us?"

Amy had thought it was because her mother didn't want her anymore. But she didn't say this. She just shook her head.

Ruth said, "Your mommy was in a car accident, honey. She's died and gone to heaven. She didn't want to die. I think she would much rather have stayed and taken care of a special girl like you."

"Is she coming back for me?" Amy asked.

"No, sweetie, she's not. She's dead. But I know she loved you. Do you think you could let us love you for a while?"

It was the first time in the whole nightmare that anyone had asked Amy what she wanted. She had been told her mommy wasn't coming back, but no one had told Amy why. Ruth's words had released a tremendous relief in Amy.

It wasn't that she felt glad her mother was dead, but she was glad to finally *know* what had happened. Amy felt guilty about that gladness. And she felt bad about loving Ruth for telling her the truth like that, as if, if she didn't, that too might have kept her mother from being killed. And to make things worse, Amy called Ruth *Mom* from that moment on. John was the only father she had ever known, so she had no problem calling him *Dad*. But she later thought maybe she should not have done this so easily either. Maybe it was a bad sign.

So it was complicated. And the sisters who taught her at school didn't seem to help much. They taught her about confessing her sins and saying her prayers every day, but they never seemed to address her exact situation. How could you say confession about something you didn't even understand yourself? Amy found herself confessing all kinds of sins, real and imagined, all the time aware that she was not getting close to the real source of her guilt—that she might never belong to this new family—and that she wanted to so much.

Amy wanted to belong to the rows of pious little girls wearing hats and white gloves on Sunday mornings. She closed her eyes at the right times and held her hands correctly pointing upward. She said the Latin responses in time with the rest, letting her voice rise and fall to the same cadences, even as she sat with John on one side and Ruth on the other. She wanted to belong because she was afraid that if she didn't try her hardest to be the daughter they so loved, maybe something would happen to them, too.

Every morning at school, Amy stood with the other children, put her right hand over her heart, and saluted the flag. *"I pledge allegiance to the flag of the United States of America. And to the republic for which it stands, one nation . . ."* It seemed a normal thing to do, since everyone else did it.

Now all her puny efforts at belonging had been eliminated, thanks to Senator Joseph Raymond McCarthy. His gift to Amy was teaching her to look differently at the people who claimed to be her friends. This day was to have marked the beginning of her own adolescent search for what was of value in her life. Now, at an earlier age than most, Amy had discovered the worthlessness of certain types of trust. Financial security, friendships, even the respect her father had enjoyed in his circles, they could all be swept away with one angry hand.

The result was the tired voice of her father speaking to her out of the dusty dark.

3

Is Offered

Numbers 3:4

1952

Jacek Duch sat beside Marshal Konstantin Rokossovski, the Vice-Premier, Minister of Defense, and member of the Political Bureau. Together they surveyed the regiments as they marched by, their red flags fluttering in the summer sunshine. Jacek inhaled the smells of the crowd, the trees and flowers blooming in the park. He glanced over at Rokossovski; the Marshal was visibly sweating in his dress uniform.

The day was July 22, 1952. The celebration was in honor of the inauguration of the Constitution of the People's Republic. It also happened to be the eighth anniversary of Soviet rule in Poland. Jacek knew, as did everyone else on the podium that day, that the so-called constitution and the "People's Democracy" it initiated was nothing but a farce. But it sounded good.

Rokossovski stood up and surveyed the crowd from behind the microphone before beginning to speak. "This fine sight of so many Polish youths marching before us today is crucial for the survival of the People's Republic of Poland." The crowd roared, and Jacek clapped. As Rokossovski's right-hand man, he was obligated to look enthusiastic.

"Our comrades in Moscow have confirmed that the forces of American imperialism, armed with the H-bomb, are preparing even now to attack this part of the world. Will we let them?"

"Nie! Nie! Nie!" came back the chant.

Jacek nodded his agreement even as he tuned out the rest of

the speech. His face impassive in his official mask, he let his eyes and mind wander, aware as he did so of the danger that ever lay in being less than alert. Idly he surveyed the shouting faces, the stiffly arrayed soldiers, the bunting and flags decorating the platform. The Polish flags, so familiar but different since the war.

Jacek allowed himself a wry half-smile. *Just like me.* For Jacek likened himself to the eagle emblem of Poland, still flying, but without the crown of its true loyalties.

In the seven years since the end of the war, the communist government in Poland had been carrying out policies dictated to it by the Soviet Union. The process had already begun back in 1944, when the communist arm of the Polish army had decided the emblem for the new Poland should be the same white eagle as before the war, but without the crown that symbolized self-sovereignty.

Jacek's own story was not that different from Poland's. He, too, had labored for one occupying force, then another. But what were his true loyalties? He had lived for so long under conflicting layers of allegiance that he was no longer sure why he did it. Because he was good at it—very good. Perhaps. Because it was the life he had chosen. Because he had been doing it so long that he could no longer imagine another life.

Born in *Gdańsk*, emigrated to America as a young boy, raised in a series of orphanages, he had been recruited for U.S. military intelligence before the war. His first assignment had been to work for the Polish cause as an underground officer with the goal of making his way into the postwar Polish government. When it appeared that the communists would be controlling Poland after the war, he had changed sides. And then after the war, when Poland had been forced to remain in the realm of Soviet influence, the need for well-placed covert agents behind the newly fallen Iron Curtain had become imperative. There had never been any question of bringing Jacek Duch home. Until recently, that had been fine with Jacek. Until recently. Until the ghosts started appearing.

The speeches took a long time. Afterward, more soldiers marched past the podium, their unison movements perfectly timed. When the parade was over, Jacek was only too glad to join the Marshal and the rest of his staff at a picnic reception in a closed-off area of the grounds. Pretty girls carrying trays of Iranian caviar wove in between the guests, who were all Party officials or army generals.

Jacek couldn't help but notice the conspicuous absence of navy uniforms. *Thanks to me*, he thought.

He had just returned from a long assignment in Gdańsk, sent by Rokossovski for the purpose of weakening navy leadership. Professionally speaking, Jacek had completed his mission. Personally, however, he had not weathered the trip well, and now he was glad to be back in *Warszawa*. *Very glad*, he thought as he stood quietly and listened to the Marshal joke with one of the Party officials.

The girl serving the vodka on ice had a sweet smile. The drinks went down smooth and easy on such a hot day. And with them came a loneliness, a longing, almost a nostalgia. Suddenly he was struck by an overwhelming need to talk to someone, anyone who knew who he really was. What he really was.

Even as he thought it, a warning sounded in the back of his brain, somewhere behind the vodka-induced sentimentality. That he ignored it was a mark of how badly the trip to Gdańsk had upset his usual balance.

But it wasn't just Gdańsk, he realized. It had started long before that.

It had started that day in 1949 when the photo of Ina finally reached his desk. . . .

———— ∽ ————

The only part of her he had recognized were her eyes.

They had stared back at him from a stranger's face—blistered lips, scars under the eyes, a crookedly healed nose. The brown hair had been shaven short. *For the lice or the typhoid*, Jacek thought, already trying to distance himself from the memory of the woman who had made the war bearable for him.

The picture was already four years old, taken in 1945 while she was still a prisoner. He was surprised it had taken this long to show up. In his position as special aide to the Marshal, he had been able to place a standing order for any information regarding her whereabouts.

The Soviet Union's secret police, the MGB, had been in the pro-

cess of hunting down members of the Polish Resistance movement and the Polish Home Army since 1944, when Home Army
members had emerged from hiding to help the Soviet army's offensive against the Germans.

Just one more little betrayal, Jacek mused, *among many.* For the
Soviets had immediately declared the Home Army an illegal
movement and then arrested the same men and women who had
fought alongside them to drive out the Nazis. The Soviets had labeled members of the Home Army as "reactionaries" and "Fascist
collaborators," charging them with opposing Allied policy, then
shipped them off to prison camps. But they hadn't captured Ina.
The Nazis had already gotten Ina—as the picture staring back at
him from the immaculate desktop graphically testified. All the secret police had been able to secure was this picture, which verified
her death at the Oświęcim concentration camp at Auschwitz.

Jacek was very, very glad that Ina's photo had reached his office in Warszawa first. It was absolutely crucial that no one find
out about his own wartime connections with the Home Army. If
such news ever got out, he could kiss his cushy Party job goodbye,
as well as the confidence he had worked so hard to earn from Konstantin Rokossovski.

Jacek was a different man now from when he and Ina had
worked together in the Home Army. During the war, the two of
them had planned the assassination of a Gestapo officer named
Koppe in *Kraków,* but someone had tipped off the Nazis, and their
entire team had been arrested. Everyone, that is, except Jacek. As
the only one to escape, he had been awarded Ina's rank and re-
sponsibilities, while she had been sent to Oświęcim.

The Soviet army had liberated Oświęcim on January 27, 1945.
Ina's date of death, scrawled hurriedly on the back of the photo,
had been January 20. *So she had only six months of suffering,* Jacek
calculated. He didn't want to think about the fact that if she had
lasted one week longer, she might still be alive.

Not that it would really matter, Jacek thought. For that same week
when Ina lay dying had been the week that Jacek had turned his
back on the Polish cause. Those dates marked the precise time
when he had sought out Marshal Rokossovski and accepted his

first assignment to spy for the Soviets. Jacek had been working for the Soviet Union ever since.

Or pretending to work for the Soviets, just as he had first pretended to be a student and then a mathematics professor and then pretended to fight for the Home Army.

Jacek looked down at Ina's photo. *No*, he thought, *it wasn't all pretending*. . . . But she belonged to another world, one of his other worlds. One thing he had learned; it was never a good idea to entertain ghosts.

Jacek scraped the chair back from his desk. "Wiktor!"

A huge bear of a man filled the doorway of Jacek's office. "Yes, boss."

"I've got to get out of here. I'm going for a walk."

Wiktor said nothing and stepped aside as Jacek walked past him. Jacek liked the bulk of this particular bodyguard. He had chosen to save Wiktor from a firing squad when he had been set up by other Russians in the Soviet secret police. Jacek had told him it was because he had shown he was smart enough to learn Polish. Wiktor had never let on if he got the joke. He didn't have to as long as he did his job well. Now the two of them went down the stairs and out of the ministry building.

Ah, sweet Warszawa, Jacek thought grimly as the stink of the city's brown coal and questionable sewage system struck him. "Where are we going?" he asked Wiktor. It was an attempt at Polish humor. Jacek considered it his hobby to try to get Wiktor to show some sort of emotion.

"Crazy," Wiktor answered, not cracking a smile.

"Good man." Jacek headed for the park. He had to clear his head. Seeing Ina's image had shaken him more than he liked to admit. "Wiktor, have you heard anyone at the ministry asking questions about my orders for Home Army information to cross my desk first?"

The big man shook his head. Jacek felt uneasy, and he had long ago learned to trust his instincts. Something was wrong. Was it just the guilt he felt over Ina, or had his watching for news of her allowed some of his enemies to get a little closer to his myriad of secrets? He still cared, still missed her, or he wouldn't have wanted so badly to find out about her.

43

Jacek sighed. Enemies. It was all relative. Especially when he had as powerful an ally as the Marshal. Besides, the war had been over for four years.

He followed the perimeter of the lake. On the opposite side stood the outdoor theater where he spent evenings with other Party men listening to Chopin concerts. *Never Wagner*, he thought. *God forbid that anything so German be thought beautiful.*

Jacek stopped. Ina's photo *had* spooked him. He looked at Wiktor, who walked his usual five paces behind Jacek. Their eyes locked, and Jacek knew Wiktor could read the fear he was feeling. *What's wrong?*

Many at the ministry had let Jacek know they thought his employing a bodyguard extravagant. But Jacek had noticed how many of the Marshal's aides seemed to disappear. Their bodies had the strangest way of turning up in the *Wisła* River. He suspected the secret police. They hated the military, and although the Marshal was too big a target to hit, his aides seemed fair game.

Jacek heard two crows making a racket in the branches above his head. He was just tipping his head backward to look up at the sound when it happened. Jacek had shifted his weight to take another step when out of the corner of his eye he caught sight of bark flying off in little bits from the tree trunk to his right. Without even thinking he leapt to the left, rolled, and landed behind a fallen tree trunk. When he came up, his gun drawn, Jacek saw that Wiktor had been hit, but was not down. Wiktor was holding his gun in his left hand, pointing toward the direction from which they had just come. Blood dripped quietly down his limp right arm and off his fingers, coloring the gravel he knelt on.

The two men waited in the November dusk. It was barely five and already almost dark. The sky was dark with storm clouds. They were predicting the first snowfall of the season that night. Jacek could see his breath. Thoughts ran through his brain in a staccato rhythm as he evaluated the situation with military precision.

Whoever it was, they had a silencer. The light was bad. Both he and Wiktor had heard nothing; he had only sensed the pending attack.

Why only two shots? Maybe there had been more, but probably not. Had it only been a warning? Not the Marshal, try his aide. Not his aide, try his bodyguard.

In the moments that passed, Jacek watched the sweat drip off Wiktor's chin in an alternating rhythm to that of his blood. Then Jacek made a decision. As he stood, Wiktor took the cue and crossed over to him, his gun pointed toward the sky in readiness.

"What did you see?" Jacek asked him.

"I saw nothing. I heard nothing. That's what bothers me."

"I know. I was thinking the same. Whoever it was, he missed me on purpose. But not you. Come on. Let's get you taken care of."

"We were easy targets," Wiktor said as the two men moved quickly for the nearest exit. "He could have injured me worse than he did. He chose not to."

They passed a huge statue of Lenin and were out on the street. Jacek didn't need to say they should walk to his limousine rather than hail a taxi. When they reached it, he climbed in behind the wheel.

"I'll drive. You get in the back," he ordered Wiktor. They headed for the main hospital, running red lights on the way. The Party limousine would get him in anywhere.

———— ✑ ————

The crash of a tray falling startled him back to awareness. One of the servers had stumbled; she and another girl were scrambling to pick up broken glass. A few officials were watching, and more than one stared appreciatively at the bent figures of the two girls in their miniskirts. While the head waiter looked mournfully at the spilled caviar, most of the party had resumed their conversations.

Jacek looked around. Everyone was talking to everyone else. No one even looked up as he set his glass on an empty table, walked to the edge of the park, and strolled casually away from the gathering. Once he checked behind him, but no one had noticed his leaving.

Izzy's place was only a few streets away from the park.

It had been more than two years since he last climbed the steps leading up to the door from the alley. Two and a half years since he'd given her a report, received his orders while inhaling her musky perfume.

Almost three years since he had any face-to-face contact with anyone who knew who he was.

He had never met his contact in Gdańsk. They had only an arranged drop point with two alternatives, where Jacek left his reports, written in a code of his own making.

Now, unconsciously he quickened his pace, his face still impassive, but feeling more excited than he liked to admit.

———— ❦ ————

The last time he had seen her was the night Wiktor was shot. Jacek had driven himself home from the hospital where Wiktor lay resting. He remembered feeling vulnerable, unused to being alone. The only consoling thought about that afternoon's episode had been the fact that Wiktor was left-handed. He would still be able to shoot when he got out of the hospital.

Jacek knew his house was bugged; it was standard practice for the secret police to spy on government leaders, especially those connected with the military. The only way any of them got ahead was by scrambling over the backs of dead or ruined comrades. Jacek had lied and cheated, in short, done everything he could, to get into a position of leadership after the war. Now this afternoon had proven it was his turn to act as target.

As he climbed from the car and paused on the front steps to fumble for his keys, Jacek could almost feel the eyes of someone watching him. Once inside the three-story chalet, Jacek drew the drapes before turning on the lights. Only then did he pour himself a glass of Remy Martin. Something had spooked him, and it wasn't just the shooting. He couldn't get the proof of Ina's death out of his head.

Jacek lit a cigarette and reached for the ashtray. It was filled with charred snippets of paper.

"What the. . . ?" The English words had formed in his mind before he could stop them. He could not remember the last time he had sworn in English or even spoken the language. Why?

Then he remembered. The yellow bits of paper had made him remember. He was thinking of a similar sight four years earlier when he had burned the letter telling him of Barbara's death, burned the news that he had no more ties "back home." *That was written on lined yellow paper, too*, Jacek thought.

More ghosts.

Even as Jacek tipped the ash into the wastebasket, he knew his housekeeper would not have missed a full ashtray. Someone was trying to tell him something.

Was it a threat or a warning? It couldn't be from the Company's station chief. He wouldn't dare contact Jacek so overtly.

After the war, only a trickle of American agents had been sent into Poland. Jacek had been told he was too high profile to risk exposure through the usual activities of others in his branch. There would be no sabotage or photography assignments of naval bases along the Baltic coast for Jacek; he was far too valuable in the position he held. For years already, his only order had been, "Ears open." And that activity alone had proven immensely fruitful. As Rokossovski's inside man, Jacek was privy to Josif Stalin's long-term plans for Poland even before the ministries had been set up to harness those particular yokes onto the country: an extravagantly large conscript army, the Command Economy based on central planning, the passion for heavy industry, and the monopoly power of the Polish United Workers Party.

Jacek crossed the living room and unlocked the glass doors leading to the back garden. Then he unlocked the padlocks on the wrought-iron gates that covered every window and door of the house. As he stepped out onto the back patio, he inhaled the crisp scent of autumn-turned-winter. The apple orchard stood stripped of leaves, its bony branches reaching up to a moonlit sky. A dog barked in his neighbor's garden farther down the street.

Jacek walked over to a lone pot of frostbitten geraniums and lifted it from its position. His form blocked the light, throwing his searching motion with his hand, palm downward, into darkness.

Jacek replaced the pot and walked back inside the house, locking the gate and door, then redrawing the drapes. Only then did he uncurl his left hand. A single cigarette butt lay in his palm. It was Jacek's cue to make contact.

So the paper in the ashtray was to get my attention. Jacek was annoyed that they had entered his home like that. They had to know it was watched. He had been thinking for some time that his housekeeper Gabi might be on the Company payroll. He knew she was on someone's payroll besides his own because she did far too good a job at cleaning his house. He had no doubt all his garbage was scrutinized, as were the envelopes of any mail that arrived at the house.

Well, this could be confirmation of Gabi's true loyalties. One thing for sure, the issue must be urgent for them to go outside the usual channel of his monthly reports, left in different places and at new times agreed to and changed every year. Something must be wrong.

Jacek poured himself another drink and rolled the glass in his palm as he checked the refrigerator. The meals Gabi prepared for him were as nondescript as Gabi herself, with her limp, mousy hair and her quiet ways. Today she had put together a simple dish of sauerkraut and sausage that he normally would have wolfed down without thinking. But Jacek had eaten a heavy lunch with the Marshal that afternoon, and his stomach still burned with indigestion. He gulped down the cognac, grabbed his hat and coat, and left his house, for once glad that Wiktor would not be accompanying him.

Jacek drove toward the city center to a boardinghouse behind the train station. The sign out front read simply *zajazd*, or inn. Inside lived Jacek's only U.S. contact.

"Madame Isabella" ran an unofficial brothel, complete with officially registered prostitutes. This way, Jacek's visits to her establishment were made in the guise of a customer. Any of the usual secret-police agents assigned to tail him would assume he was just taking advantage of his many Party privileges.

She conducted what she liked to call his "semiannual checkups." Twice a year he had a verbal debriefing with her, always in her "safe" room or outdoors. But her other function, far more crucial to Jacek, was just to be there. Her very presence in Warszawa, or rather the knowledge of her presence, was a balm on the raw wounds Jacek willingly inflicted on himself when doing his job.

It was highly irregular, however, for Jacek to visit Izzy outside of their scheduled visits. He knew this, but he went anyway. He had to.

Jacek walked around to the back entrance by way of a narrow alley. Izzy was waiting for him. She was in her thirties, small and blond, with brown eyes and eyebrows that gave away her true hair color. Izzy's most striking feature was her cheekbones, high and pronounced, so that Jacek thought she must have some White Russian blood flowing in her.

She met him with one of her dazzling smiles. "Darling, it's been too long." Then in one movement as they stood in the doorway, she wrapped an arm around him, kicked the door shut, and used the other arm to slip a piece of paper into his breast pocket. "I won't be a minute. You caught me by surprise." As she led him into the debugged anteroom, she added for the sake of anyone who might hear them through the open door, "Let me slip into something more comfortable," then left him alone with his communiqué.

Jacek smiled at her professionalism. Izzy wasn't head of station, but she was close enough—high enough in command to make some of her own decisions. And he imagined her clientele slipped up often enough for her to glean her own set of gems for the "folks back home," as she liked to call the Central Intelligence Agency.

He sat down and pulled out the paper. As he read, the knot that had been twisting in his gut all day tightened another notch.

> Witnessed evening's incident. You have a situation. Perp is from within Polish special-service branch. Suggest request outside-Warsaw job from Rok until we isolate and resolve.

Jacek sighed. As he had suspected, the Marshal's enemies had targeted him. He left the room and headed down the hallway to the communal bathroom at the end, ignoring the sounds that leaked from one of the closed doors he passed. In the bathroom, he ripped the paper into a hundred little pieces. Only then did he notice that the bits he was flushing down the toilet were yellow and lined. As Jacek left the building, a curtain on the first floor falling into place was the only sign that anyone had witnessed his departure.

———————— ∽ ————————

It had taken Jacek a while to get himself reassigned outside of Warszawa without drawing undue attention to himself. But the opportunity finally presented itself when Rokossovski announced a staff-relocation project—part of the recently announced Six-Year Plan for industrial development.

"Sir," he began carefully, "I think I can best serve your interests if I get out of Warszawa. . . ." But the Gray Fox was one step ahead of Jacek.

"Yes, I heard about the shooting."

Jacek thought it odd that he hadn't said anything when it happened a few months earlier. But that was all right. Now at last he had a good excuse to get out of the capital.

Rokossovski continued, "I've had some of my people following you to make sure it doesn't happen again." Rokossovski glanced sideways at Jacek, who was trying to mask his reaction to the news that his stalkers had been stalked. His life had become a hall of mirrors.

"As it happens," the Marshal grunted, "I have a particularly, eh, challenging job that needs to be done in Gdańsk. And I think you're the only one I can trust with it. It will do you good to get out of the hothouse this city has become. I envy you." Then he clapped Jacek on the shoulder with a force that, Jacek had learned, meant he was being sent into yet another sticky situation.

"Back to Gdańsk, where we first started working together," Rokossovski added.

"What do you want me to do?" Jacek asked foolishly, already knowing that Rokossovski enjoyed keeping him in the dark.

The Marshal grinned. "To keep an eye on them and us."

———————— ∽ ————————

Izzy's place still looked the same now, even after more than two years. The stairs still creaked. The door still opened on its own when he pushed it. The heavy perfume still hung in the air. He moved forward, lulled by the sense of familiarity, beginning to feel like himself again. But the moment he crossed the threshold into the dark hall, he felt the cold bite of steel against his neck, and the throaty voice was tight and angry. "In the little room, and don't breathe."

Instantly, Jacek was focused. Inside the anteroom, Izzy kept the gun at his throat and whispered, "It's been a long time since you've felt this kind of danger, hasn't it? The head of station thinks maybe too long."

Jacek began to turn but felt the nose of the gun grind into his skin. *She wouldn't dare*, he thought.

"I have orders to eliminate you the *second* you get out of line. Do you understand? You were followed here today, did you know that? I didn't think so. You see how far it's gone. You're back in the lion's den now. You have to watch every word, every breath. Why do *I* have to tell *you* these things?"

When Jacek said nothing, she hissed the word again, "Why?"

"The drink." He coughed, choking the words out. "I had some drinks at the reception. They made me careless."

Even as he said the words, the enormity of his mistake broke into his consciousness, dispelling the alcoholic haze. He had broken his own cardinal rule and was out of control. Worse, he had enjoyed drawing attention to himself, signaling the black-haired waitress each time for another drink. A good agent was so nondescript he had trouble getting a waiter to notice him. "All right. I get the message."

"Word from above is, there won't be another warning."

Suddenly the pressure was gone from below his earlobe. He turned and saw nothing, no one. As he returned to the busy city streets he stared at everyone looking into shop windows or reading newspapers. Which one had followed him? Jacek felt his personal anguish mix with anger.

He started walking across the city, heading toward his house in the suburbs near the airport. With each step, Jacek's head pounded as cramps seized up his stomach. He had thought the walk would help him relax, but instead the tension only seemed that much more likely to explode inside him. As Jacek approached his house, the cool shade of his trees welcomed him like an old friend. He opened the gate and let himself inside, then headed straight for the bathroom. There he threw up his guts.

That night Jacek slept without waking up once. *For the first time in how long?* he wondered. The answer was easy.

Two years, since he had left Warszawa for Gdańsk.

———————— ∽ ————————

As the train pulled into the Gdańsk station, Jacek found himself wondering how much of the city had changed. He saw one answer as soon as he stepped out onto the street. It seemed the Hotel Eden had been renamed the Hotel Monopol. *A sign of the times*, he thought to himself.

Back in March of 1945, inside the men's room of the old hotel, Jacek had passed on information to Rokossovski's messenger about just where and how Gdańsk could best be taken. Then he had waited and watched while the Soviets first routed the Germans, then looted the city and set block after block afire.

Now, five years later, his job had become one of securing the city, *against "them,"* he thought.

"I'm convinced the Party is behind your attack," the Marshal had told Jacek just before he left Warszawa. "I want to hit back at a certain segment of the military that has chosen to side with the Party against the military's leadership of the government."

Your own leadership, you mean, Jacek thought.

"What's the weakest part of our military machine?" the Marshal had asked him.

Jacek did not have to think twice. He was speaking, after all, with the head of the army. "The navy," he answered quickly.

"Right. And I have reason to believe the navy has been disobeying the Home Army directive set up by the government. I want you to go north and teach them a lesson. You may even pay back the same people who were after you here."

Jacek understood the connection. The Marshal needed someone discreet, yet effective, to get the navy into line by eliminating all the former Home Army officers still taking refuge behind their navy commissions. The Soviet-run communist government had dictated the policy of rooting out Home Army officers; now Rokossovski could turn the witch-hunt to his own ends—solidifying his power over both the navy and the Communist Party.

Having arrived in Gdańsk, however, Jacek could tell it would be no easy job singling out navy victims. The city thronged with men in big caps and sailor's uniforms. The biggest port in the Baltic was open for business, and Jacek was there to shut down part of this well-oiled machine.

Jacek spent the next months familiarizing himself with the Gdańsk naval and Party hierarchies. He worked out a foolproof tactic, one Jacek intended to put into practice with every man he went about arresting. And only then, a year after his arrival in Gdańsk, did Jacek pounce.

———— ✍ ————

"Wiktor, send him in." Jacek had sat behind a black wooden, hand-carved desk of massive proportions. He had requisitioned the Gdańsk-style piece as soon as he saw it in someone else's office. His own office overlooked the harbors.

He had taken particular care with his appearance that morning. He wore baggy pants. His dark hair was cut short, above the ears. And hanging on the coatrack was a long coat of the finest cashmere, which he preferred to the latest men's fashion of furs.

Wiktor showed a young man in uniform into Jacek's office and closed the door soundlessly behind him. *Good*, Jacek thought, *the boy's already sweating*. He did not invite him to sit down, but made him stand erect in his double-breasted navy whites, unable to keep from twisting the flat hat with the dark band around and around his fingers as Jacek pretended to finish his reading.

"You are the admiral's personal aide?"

"Yes, sir."

"To start with, you have done nothing wrong. But you can set a great wrong right. I understand you have a wife and young boy." He paused. "And your wife is pregnant?" Now Jacek looked at him.

The boy could have been nineteen, his face covered with pimples. He blushed as he answered, clearing his throat first, "Yes, sir."

"You are eager for promotion, I imagine. The navy does not pay well at the entrance level." Jacek wondered if the sailor was smart enough to catch his meaning. Surely the admiral had chosen him as aide for a reason.

Now the boy returned Jacek's gaze. *So he does understand*, Jacek thought.

"Very well, now that we know what is at stake, tell me a few things about the admiral."

It was standard procedure, and it had never failed to yield up yet another ex-officer of the Home Army, someone who had managed to stay hidden since the end of the war, protected and screened from scrutiny by the navy brotherhood. All Jacek did was play on the fears running rampant at the time. These young sailors were much more interested in getting on with life now that the war was over than in protecting former Polish patriots. The number one priority was protecting one's family and whatever shelter had been assigned to them as a home. Jacek chalked up this boy as yet another recruit in his intricate web of informants from within the navy office. Often the youngest and most zealous were the most resourceful.

Within days of his little talk with the admiral's aide, Jacek was ready to issue orders for the officer's arrest. "Send a message to our admiral," he told Wiktor, "that he should report to the Gdańsk train station so he can pick up new orders and travel on to War-szawa. Then get some of our Russian comrades to wait for him. Dress them in Polish navy uniforms. It's an old trick, but it always works." Jacek faked a wry chuckle and saw Wiktor nod.

He continued, "In Polish uniforms, no one can accuse our men of being responsible. Have your men carry out the arrest, then we'll have the official trial with the usual evidence in Warszawa. We'll make it look legal, but the admiral will be eliminated in prison in Warszawa." Wiktor knew the routine. Jacek liked him for that. With Wiktor, he didn't need to spell out every detail, es-pecially about something he did so often.

For the sad truth was something Jacek had already started run-ning from. This was just one more in what was fast becoming an endless stream of deaths with Jacek's name on the order form.

A few months later, Jacek had walked the quay back and forth between the harbors below his window, his hands jammed deep inside his pockets. Under his breath he swore repeatedly, hotly. It was a private struggle, and the simple fact was that he had no one, not one person with whom he could share the burden of the conflict raging within him. Daily he battled the voices, the knowledge, deep inside, that he was murdering his former compatriots. The knowledge had taken its toll. For reasons of self-preservation, Jacek was only now realizing he had to silence the voices before they pushed him to say too much.

He returned to the office and signaled Wiktor with a nod. When the two were back outside, Wiktor asked, "Where to?"

"Back to my place. You and I are going to get drunk tonight, my friend."

Wiktor raised an eyebrow but said nothing.

In the comfort of the stately home overlooking the *Sopot* beach, Jacek carried the tray of glasses and frozen vodka onto the porch. He had hired no servants here in the north and wasn't about to now, even though he was easily one of the most powerful men in the area. No, Wiktor was his only luxury, a necessary one.

The two men sat outside, pouring the clear syrup again and again into their glasses until the moon rose. Jacek had been watching Wiktor slug down two shots for every one of his. When the bottle was empty, he figured Wiktor was finally drunk for him to ask the question that had been bothering him for some time.

"So, comrade, tell me. Do you know who is reporting back to the Marshal about me? Is it you, Wiktor?"

He was counting on the element of surprise to unmask the truth. Jacek sent the Marshal regular reports, but he knew Rokossovski would also have his own sources for hearing all about his operations in Gdańsk. The Marshal would not condemn Jacek for playing king in the particular empire Rokossovski had granted him. What Rokossovski would never forgive was weakness.

And yet.

And yet this was precisely what had been surfacing in Jacek during the last months. Despite his resolve, he caught himself sentencing more and more of his victims to fates other than death.

Jacek fought it. He could not afford to blow this cover. Not now. Nor could he afford to return to Warszawa. Not yet.

And all the while, he was still reporting back to Washington, moving like some vague apparition down the corridors of two worlds, passing through the walls at will, never being seen, never being questioned. His Company contact here was sight unseen, so he had no touchstone like Izzy. So Jacek played at being invincible, an enigma.

And yet.

The yets piled up as Jacek drank more, ate less, and retreated into a private world. The deaths of those he had condemned would not let him go. Jacek walked the streets of Gdańsk a haunted man. He knew Wiktor was witnessing the changes, and he did not want the Marshal finding out about them.

"Well, my friend?" Jacek thought he must really be drunk to even be expecting a straight answer from Wiktor.

"But of course!" Wiktor answered, slurring his words together. "*Na zdrowie!*" He said it the Polish way and not the Russian. And for that Jacek could have loved him.

Jacek had been walking down a street, but no one saw him. He spoke out loud but could not hear his voice. When he reached out to ask a man where he was, his hand passed right through the man's shoulder. He turned a corner and saw a woman on the street, her sweater pulled over cotton pants, bobbed curly hair with a side part, and large costume jewelry clipped over the ear. She turned slowly. Jacek stepped closer to see, but her face was in shadow. Then she looked up and Jacek recognized her, even as he saw she had no eyes.

Jacek woke up screaming. He could still hear his voice ringing in his ears as he sat up in bed. The linen was drenched, and he could feel every muscle in his neck and back knotted tight. "Thank God no one else is in the house," he mumbled. If he had been back in Warszawa he would have been afraid the hidden microphones would pick up whatever he had called out in his sleep. But no, this was still Gdańsk.

As Jacek stumbled to the sink in the bathroom to throw cold water over his face, he suddenly thought back to another time during the war when he had called out loud unconsciously. He had been delirious. He had never been sure, but thought at that time he might have actually spoken in English. Luckily the man who had attended him, nursing his gunshot wounds, was not in a position to know the significance of Jacek's words.

He tried to steady his breathing. Wiktor was not downstairs. Wiktor was in Warszawa. Jacek had sent him there with his latest report for Rokossovski—and with a separate agenda of checking out the climate among the Marshal's other aides. The longer Jacek stayed in Gdańsk, racking up points in the name of the Party but really for the army, the more solid his position would be when he returned.

He swore to himself. The dream had been too real. He returned to the bedroom. His hand shook as he reached for the glass beside the table, knocking over the bottle that stood on top of the clock. But there was no mess to clean up. The bottle was empty.

He collapsed into the chair and turned his back on the street. He cupped his face in his hands and rocked back and forth in the agony of memory.

There had been a woman in Gdańsk during the final days of the city's bombardment by the Soviets. Monika, the landlord's daughter. She had walked into his life for a few brief moments, her departure all the more horrific by the brightness she had taken with her. And now Jacek could not let go of his final memory of her, somehow now balled up together with those he had been condemning since his return to the city. She lay curled up on an old mattress where countless Russian soldiers had raped her, where he had abandoned her and later returned to find only her eyes alive, open with hate, while the rest of her lay dead.

Even now that image burned in his mind, a final haunting in this city of ghosts. And Jacek knew he could not allow this.

He knew this about himself. There had once been a time when the memory of a woman had kept him sane. He knew his mind was capable of grabbing on to an image and not letting it go until it had changed him. This change he could not have.

Gdańsk had become a dangerous place for him. Jacek knew it was just a matter of time before the city and its ghosts dragged him down and broke open the many masks he hid behind. He stared at his hands, well-manicured, ringless. He clenched his fists and took a deep breath, the emotion of taking control feeling foreign where it had once felt familiar.

———————— ✑ ————————

The next morning in the office there had been an unexpected knock on Jacek's door. He looked up and was surprised at how glad he was to see Wiktor enter—the broad, familiar face his only constant. "You're back. I'm glad," he said gruffly. "Sit down. Tell me about Warszawa."

At the end of Wiktor's report, Jacek said, "Well, it's just as well. I've made a decision. It's time for me to go back. Now listen closely: I want you to watch for others who watch me. Oh, and bring in our friend the Minister of Economics. It's time to tighten the noose one last time before we leave this godforsaken place. We're going out with a bang."

Jacek didn't want to know how Wiktor and his men went about the final details, but his last coup in Gdańsk would be the arrest of the man who had promoted small-business enterprise in the area. The communist Party strongly disapproved of individual initiative, not to mention entrepreneurship. This final arrest would be conducted solely for the benefit of the Party.

Jacek knew his assignment in Gdańsk was limited to the military, specifically the local navy office. He was overstepping himself by going after a civilian, an enemy of the Party and not the army, but felt he had to take that chance, to hedge his bets by winning the Party's gratitude. So Jacek quickly organized a group of informants willing to condemn the minister for a variety of reasons.

Then, within a week of the minister's departure, Jacek had applied for a return to Warszawa. Another two weeks later, he was home.

———————— ✑ ————————

And now it was morning. Jacek made a cup of tea and carried it out onto the patio. The reflection off the white table almost blinded him. Birds sang in the orchard. The city noises seemed a long way off. As he sipped from the steaming glass in its silver holder, he felt he had made a narrow escape.

Even Jacek could recognize the danger he had enveloped himself in during the last two years. A psychological fault that had first opened after his days in the Soviet prison camp had shifted again, threatening to crack open his cover. The alcohol, the sleepless nights, the incessant headaches had all been warning tremors. His exposure to the ghosts of Gdańsk had split open a fissure in his mental health. Jacek had managed to climb out just in time to retain his cover, just in time to salvage his sanity.

Just in time to remember what he really was.

Jacek shook his head as a chill ran up his back. Tiny daisies dotted the grass in his orchard. The summer sun had disappeared behind a cloud, and the breeze rustled through the leaves above him. He squinted up at the sky and made a promise to himself. Izzy was right about too many things. No matter how long it took, he would take back control. He would stop drinking, and he would spend the next years getting back to doing what he did best.

And what did he do best?

He survived.

Jacek had survived when Ina was arrested. He had survived while a city was falling down around him. He had even survived his own weakness. And he would survive Rokossovski; arresting the Minister of Economics would see to that.

For Konstantin Rokossovski was but one of the masters Jacek had served, just as Ina had been but one of the women he had loved. He had turned his back on her as easily as he had on Monika. And before that, on Barbara. But turning his back on Barbara had never been his intention.

Jacek sighed. Even now, after so many years, that ghost had the power to move him.

Barbara had been his wife back in the States. He had loved her so much that Jacek had even made her a part of himself. Thoughts of their young love had been all that kept him alive in the Soviet prison camp near *Smolensk*. The memories of her face were all he could remember from that terrible time in Russia. But he wasn't even sure if he was remembering her face correctly. It had been too long.

Too long. That was the problem.

Jacek had left Barbara alone for too long, and during the war she had divorced him, to the relief of his controllers back in Washington. They had let him know they wanted him free to do his job without anyone back home having a hold on him.

At one time he had kept a photograph of Barbara, but that was long gone, along with all the paperwork that could tie him to his former life. Now he carried only one photo after all the years—almost fourteen years—since his departure from America. That was the picture Barbara had sent him back in 1939.

That September after she sent that picture, Hitler had invaded Poland and Jacek had been trapped by the war. What information he had managed to smuggle out through the intelligence network was too valuable to the war effort to sacrifice for personal reasons.

He had left a sign, though, just in case something went wrong and he disappeared without a trace. When he first visited Gdańsk in 1939, Jacek had entered his real name in the Gdańsk city registry. Jacek Skrzypek, not Jacek Duch. After he had done it the first time, it became almost an act of superstition to do the same again and again, each time he moved on to a new city. Afterward, it had been impossible to go back and erase the trail without drawing attention to himself.

Had he done it for Barbara?

He couldn't say. All he knew is that the years had dragged on. And then she was no longer his, and then it was too late.

The last report he ever received about Barbara had also been typed on lined, yellow paper. It stated that she had died in a car accident, together with his daughter.

Jacek had burned the report back when he first started working for Rokossovski in Warszawa, but he had kept the photo that came with it. It too must have belonged to Barbara.

4

LEADS

Nehemiah 9:12

1972

I was born nineteen years ago when my father was in prison. When my mother talks about the past, she uses that as the indicator. "Before your father was arrested" and "after your father was arrested" is how she begins most of her stories. This is how I learned about much of what happened in the early years of my life. And what she didn't want to tell me, I heard from my big brother, Jan.

One of my first memories is of him. It's not a good memory. I was five years old. A friend of mine and his mother were walking home with me. I was carrying a loaf of bread under my arm. I remember how it smelled. When we passed Jan's school, something made me run ahead of my friend and look behind the wall at the edge of the schoolyard. My friend's mother could not see where I was; she was busy talking to her older son. It must have been during one of the breaks because all the children were out and there was a lot of noise.

I rounded the corner and saw my brother standing in front of the statue of Mary that marked the main entrance to the school. I heard the boys laughing, and I remember feeling a little bit proud that Jan was with them, so I could join the big boys. As I came closer, though, I could see this wasn't the case. The other boys were laughing *at* my brother, not with him.

"Get down on your knees, Devil-Boy!" The boys waved their forefingers behind their ears, imitating sets of horns.

"You can pray to Mary just like God. She's just the same! What's

61

wrong with you that you won't get down on your knees and pray to her like we do? You're a Devil-Boy!"

"No, we don't believe in Mary like that. . . ." But before Jan could say anything else, two of the bigger boys knocked him over. I stood by and watched. Well, I did worse than that. I hung around the corner so they couldn't see me, and then I watched.

These same two boys—they were fourteen and from the highest class, a year older than Jan—they held him face down in the dirt. Then one of the boys kicked him and rolled him over. "Get on your knees, freak. Now you can be like us and pray to Mary." When Jan still shook his head no, they both kicked him again and left him lying there.

My friend's mother was calling me, and I didn't know what to do. Jan still wasn't crying, but I didn't want to attract attention his way. I didn't want anyone to see him like that. So I ran back to my friend and walked the rest of the way home. You're the first person I've ever told about what I saw that day.

That's how it is with us. Everything seems to revolve around my parents being different, and this was always reflected back onto Jan or me. Well, Jan more than me, since he's the one who lived through the worst years, during the fifties. During the Stalin times teachers worked at creating fear at a child's level before any crime had even been committed, because then there was simply too much fear to let it happen. I was too small to really notice what he and Tatuś call the persecution period, when people were singled out for being different from the so-called working class in any way. During the Stalin years, seeds of betrayal were planted that took root in all levels of the society and later could not be weeded out.

For us, it wasn't just growing up under the stigma of having a mother with a German background and living in a country where both the Poles and Russians hated the Germans. My parents were Protestants in a Catholic country, Christians in an atheist State, believers in truth in a land of lies.

You can't know what it was like to read history books and memorize dates but know that half of what you are being taught had been made up. And the worst part was not knowing which half. As the new history was being taught, the teacher would ask, "What do you think of this?" This was a way of fishing for the boys who knew the truth from their parents, like Jan and I did.

If a boy made the mistake of telling the version of history his own parents had lived through, then he was laughed at by the teachers, who encouraged his classmates to make fun of him as well. Then the parents were paid a visit by the secret police—the Urząd Bezpieczeństwa or UB for short—and questioned about their patriotism. Didn't they like the People's Republic of Poland? And then one or both parents would be demoted at work . . . or worse. It was not flagrant persecution by the time I was growing up, but people were still segregated on the basis of trusting or not trusting the government.

One time a boy in my class asked why there was no mention in the history book of when Poland defeated Russia in 1922. Immediately the teacher attacked him verbally, explaining away his claim as nothing but imperialistic propaganda. We were also only taught those things about the prewar period of Polish independence that the communists thought suitable for us to learn. The rest was ignored because, supposedly, it didn't glorify Polish history, Polish communist history, that is.

There was also no mention of a Soviet invasion of Poland; that date was never taught in school. But it is embedded in my memory, thanks to a rhyme my parents taught me. Sometimes my friends and I would gather on the playground and sing secret songs against the Soviets using dates like the third of May, 1791, when our constitution was written—something else the communists didn't want us remembering. Singing those songs was a little bit risky in the sixties and less so now, but not nearly as dangerous as it was in the fifties.

I believe that the stories my family tells are important because they're one of the few places in my world where I've found truth. Most of what I know from the fifties was whispered to me in bits and pieces. After my father was arrested late in 1952, many Christian men were taken from their homes; it didn't matter if they were Catholic or Protestant. (It was different later, when the government decided to court the Catholics.)

My mother tells me that Tatuś was not there when I was born. She doesn't talk about that time much, but because she doesn't, I know it was hard. She talks about the time she and Tatuś were separated near the end of the war, when she was pregnant with Jan. And that was hard. But I think the time she was pregnant with me was even worse.

All Jan tells me is that she was so happy when I was finally born healthy and that right away he knew I was going to be a brave boy. I still don't know what he meant by that. Only once has he told me the whispered story of what it was like when they took Tatuś away.

My uncle Marek has told me that Jan had a hard time at school during that time, when he was still very small. Knowing what I did about the beating he had when he was thirteen, I believe Uncle Marek. He is an old wartime friend of my parents. After the war he found them again in Gdynia, and now he is also a pastor of a church near my father's. Jan has told me that Marek helped Mamusia take care of us in the years when Tatuś was gone.

Tatuś was never really healthy after he came home. I don't know what he was like before prison, but when I was growing up, even though he was big and strong, he was often coughing, and he always needed more sleep than any of us. Always after preaching or praying with the church, he would collapse into bed for at least four hours if it was during the day.

My father took over the care of several other denominations, since their pastors had been arrested later and so were also released later. In the years when Tatuś was in prison, they arrested many church leaders, Catholic and Protestant. Even the Catholic Primate was imprisoned then because of his political influence on the clergy and the whole of the country.

Our church is really just a group of people who come to our house or our small church building at least once a week to pray and read the Bible. My father will say a few words and then ask questions that are neither too general nor specific. He will sometimes talk about ways we can put into practice what we have learned that evening, but the applications are never too narrow. Sometimes Mamusia adds a word or two, naming examples or leading the prayers for thanksgiving. They're an unbeatable team—but you know that already.

The security police are always watching our home. This is because of the church. Since Tatuś came home they've had a stakeout at the neighbor's across the street, and they watch us from there. All these years the police have been there. That's another reason we're different. They're still watching our home on and off.

I'm sure they also keep track of who comes and goes, but we have always found ways of sneaking people in and out. We can't fit more than thirty people into the two rooms. Whenever we are having a Bible study, Mamusia always makes sure there are cakes and sandwiches, and Jan and I help her pass them out with cups of tea. This is because it's against the law to meet as a church and read the Bible and pray together. But we are allowed to have purely social gatherings. It's crazy, really, but thanks to Mamusia's sandwiches, we've always had an alibi whenever the police burst in on us.

And they did that often. For a long time, Bibles were almost impossible to find. Members of the church had handwritten copies of certain chapters. But even if they had had Bibles, no one could ever have carried one with them to the meetings here. It's way too dangerous. We have our big one, and Tatuś reads from it, but we always had people posted by the window and at the entrance to the main door. So if the police came in to raid us, we had plenty of time to hide the Bible inside the hole in the wall Tatuś had made behind the sofa. And when the police showed up, Mamusia would offer them pieces of her poppyseed cake and say we were just having tea.

Tatuś is famous for his Bible teaching. I've heard other pastors call him a radical genius. What he preaches is simple, really: reliance on the Word, reading the Bible, and prayer. This is his message for everyone he comes in contact with. It doesn't matter to him that he spent nearly two years in prison because of that message.

I know another story from the Stalinist time. It was something that took place at the university where Tatuś works, and Uncle Marek told me about this. It was rumored that a certain group of girls were working as prostitutes on the university grounds. The administration called a meeting, and a Communist Party man led the discussion of how to solve the problem.

Evidently, when my father was asked for his opinion, he stood up and said, "There is only one answer, and that is to live as God commanded." There was a terrible silence. Such a thing said at such a time—just a few months after Tatuś's release from prison—was very dangerous. But even though that man from the Party was there, no one ridiculed Tatuś. His words were weighted with authority, and the Lord's name was still respected, even then. My father's courage at this time touched many different people.

I can remember him often reminding us that Satan is the enemy. It is Satan we hate. But people we love, no matter who or what others might have done to us. Then he would cite Jesus' command to love our enemies.

I could never believe this. I wanted to. I wanted to be like the others in our room, nodding their heads in assent while my father preached. More than anything, I wanted to be like my big brother, Jan. He could believe in everything Tatuś and Mamusia taught us. He had what Tatuś *called the gift of faith. No one gave me such a gift. We read the Bible as a family every day, and then would talk about what we had read. Jan was always the one who said the things that pleased my father. I just could not believe. Was it the same with you?*

---------- ✺ ----------

How else can I help you understand who I am, how it was?

I have three photo albums Mamusia put together for me and Jan, which she gave to each of us when we turned eighteen. Maybe they will give you a better idea of what it was like when I was growing up. The first book begins with a baby picture of me and has my birthdate written in Mamusia's flowery handwriting.

Here is one of the few pictures of Mamusia—she was the family photographer, so she was rarely in front of the camera. She's pushing my pram, which is very low to the ground, has small wheels and a high handle, and is covered in wicker. There's an open seat on top of the pram for Jan. Mamusia hadn't cut her hair yet, and it looks so pretty here.

On the next pages, marked 1954, you can see our visit to the Warszawa zoo. There are photos of me wearing tiny shorts with suspenders and white knee socks and waving at the seals. There's a big brown bear and a baby elephant. Why am I telling you these things?

Here's a picture of me playing with my toys. I can remember this; yes, it was when I was six. I can remember these toys so well. Tatuś had carved me a set of wooden blocks, and somehow I had a Pan American airplane model. This was all I really had, but at the time it seemed enough. Mamusia has told me I used to play for hours with these things.

And then there was my tricycle. Tatuś had put it together out of boards and welded bars and old wheels. This was the only bike Jan and I had for the longest time.

One Easter Sunday we were searching for the sweets and eggs our parents had hidden from us. Tatuś had a very good sense of mischief. The older we got, the more difficult the hiding places became. On that particular Easter, after we had combed the apartment and found every one of the eggs we had decorated and more chocolate than we had ever had before, Tatuś had said, "There's still one more present."

Well, we looked and looked. But now that I think back, Jan must have been sixteen, since I was eight. So maybe Jan knew where the hiding place was, and he just let me be the one to find it. Anyway, when we still couldn't find it, Mamusia made a soft clucking sound. We looked at her as she folded her arms, then nodded toward the other room. We went back to where we had just searched and still saw nothing. Then we looked behind the curtain, and that's when I finally found it. A bicycle. A real bike. We jumped for joy. We were so amazed, for the truth was, Tatuś didn't have much money. There was no way we could afford such a thing.

This bike meant freedom and independence to us boys. I still to this day don't know how Tatuś paid for it. I know that despite his doctorate in engineering and all his teaching experience during that long decade of the fifties, Tatuś received hardly any compensation, let alone recognition, for the research he conducted. It had been made clear to him by the communist-run university administration that only those teachers who joined the Party could hope for tenure. So that meant a very low salary over the years.

Even this could not make my father into a two-faced man. He continued to pray for his enemies, like these men at the university who wanted to keep him down. He often said, "Don't forget he's a poor sinner. Jesus hated sin, but not the sinners."

How can you answer something like that?

This was again something I could find no place for in myself. I lived a split life as a child. Our homelife was so different than that of my friends. They were all Catholic, and they went to church, but it was a church the State did not dare challenge.

The reason for this was that after 1956, when Władysław Gomułka became First Secretary, the government eased up on its atheist line and decided to try to make certain concessions to the Catholic church. Perhaps you know that already. Yes, it would have been part of your training. The Party had decided it did not need to fight the church head on.

This was true even though in 1950 the government had confiscated all church property and priests had been arrested. Under the auspices of a separation-of-church-and-State slogan, the communists limited the powers of the church. The State even wanted to control clergy selection. The Catholic church officially said no, but there were plenty who said yes.

Among Protestant believers during that time, people said we have as much freedom as we have courage. It is absolutely amazing to me the power of saying such a thing with conviction. Fear and lies are the communist weapons, but they become impotent when challenged openly. Nonetheless, our small Baptist church suffered repeatedly from informers and bad pastors who visited our home and then betrayed us to the UB and, later on, to its successor the SB. Still our parents said we should welcome strangers as Jesus calls us to.

My parents had no false illusions—even after 1957, when the government started to give back some of the church buildings to the Protestants. I remember one time when Mamusia was praying with us for the faithful in the church. Afterward she said, "Even in non-communist times we were called to be the light for the world. Now should be no different."

There was a difference between the way they taught me and Jan Bible stories and the way they told other stories. "This is God's Word," they would say. "Don't listen lightly."

I remembered this when I was in school and the rest of the class recited their Hail Marys. Then I would close my eyes and say another prayer. Sometimes the other children would see me and tease me. Then the teacher would single me out and call me nasty names, especially when I wouldn't go to Mass.

They may not have been able to make me go to Mass, but they made all of us learn Russian, starting in the fifth grade. And it was compulsory in the secondary school. There might have been fewer Russian soldiers around than just after the war and when I was very small, but they left a mark in other ways.

Take sports, for example. All sports events were obligatory. Everyone had to take part in every competition. It was strange how this became mixed up with patriotism and being a good communist. As the Russian presence in Poland lessened, you would have thought their influence on our daily lives would have lessened as well. It didn't. Somehow sports achievements became a sign of how good a Pole you were. And every time there was an Olympics, we talked of nothing else. It was good when Russia beat the United States, but it was even better if a Pole beat a Russian.

There were other more subtle signs of the Russians' influence. Little things, like the repeatedly ordered city clean-ups on Sunday mornings, gradually changed the atmosphere. People started realizing that the Russians were here to stay, seen or unseen.

Another example was the list of illiterates. One way for the authorities to humiliate non-Party members was to post a list of names of people who were illiterate, adults as well as children. The teachers said this was a form of motivation, when in fact it was yet another means of pointing the finger at people who dared to remain different. I know because my father's name appeared regularly on these lists. Can you imagine, a university professor on a list of illiterates?

I can remember that in my second year of school the Gdańsk opera gave concerts for one hour a month with a real orchestra. When our school was invited, that performance opened up a new world for me— my first taste of real music. We could also visit cinemas and see films, but the only non-Eastern-bloc movies were American cartoons like Mickey Mouse. We thought these were really great.

I have been told that many people in the West define themselves in terms of things—their jobs, their car, their homes. If I did that, I would be nobody. I can remember that whenever I complained about the lack of something, Mamusia would respond by saying, "We are rich in other things." Our parents taught Jan and me about integrity.

When I was six they started teaching me French and English, that is how I am able to write you like this. A brother from England left us tapes and books to continue where my parents left off. And thanks to Mamusia, I speak fluent German. She made it a game to keep this a secret from everyone except Uncle Marek and, later, my teacher Paweł, since it might have meant more persecution. At school there were also some foreign-language classes, but I learned more at home.

This lesson about intellectual faithfulness which my parents taught me was something I could believe in. It had to do with asking questions and searching. My parents always encouraged me in my need to search for the truth.

But my parents also taught us that suffering is part of experiencing the kingdom of God. This was something Jan could embrace, but I still cannot. "What God would want His people to suffer?" I asked Tatuś. He said I was asking the wrong question.

So I went to Mamusia and asked the same thing. She said, "You can only learn to know Jesus if you suffer. He suffered for us, but it is not that He wants us to suffer. It is not even a question of want. It simply is so. You can only get to know Jesus if you suffer. Which is why we believers who are privileged to suffer in His name are thankful. This is treasure stored in heaven." Her eyes shone so bright, I could not argue. And I have never forgotten that look. Even now as I try to describe these things to you, I feel almost jealous of her conviction.

Shortly after this a very strange thing happened, as if someone had been listening to us. I think of that now because I'm looking at a photo of me wearing a white sailor outfit and cuffs, standing next to some little girl with a big white bow. Behind us stands a four-door Mercedes with a luggage rack. My father is looking very sharp here. I can remember this well. I must have been six, so Jan was fourteen. I was obsessed with all kinds of cars and was constantly pretending that my wooden blocks were cars of all shapes and colors.

I will never forget it—on that particular afternoon I was lining up all my blocks into a sort of parking lot in Jan's half of our room. Jan had a real model of a red Volkswagen, which was on the shelf above his bed, together with his reading lamp. His part of the room had a tapestry hanging on the wall. I remember the details of that day so well. There was even a Christmas tree with ornaments in the room.

Jan was reading on his bed when I looked up and caught him staring at the wall. Then he suddenly said, "Piotrek, collect your blocks and go play in the next room." He gave no reason at all, and it was all very strange. He picked up the book he had been reading and that red VW, then we went into the next room, and Jan did something even more unusual. He locked the door to the room we had just left.

A few moments later there was a huge explosion. Then Mamusia burst into the living room. She had been visiting next door and now ran into the apartment, screaming our names. She stopped when she saw Jan and me standing there, staring at the door to our room.

She walked over to the door, looked at Jan again when she found it locked, unlocked it, and walked into our room. On the floor by my sofa bed she found a bullet. I ran in after her, looking for more, but there was only the one. Shards of glass covered the floor by the window.

Mamusia put the bullet in a small box and held out her hands for Jan and me like she used to do when we were small. We each took one hand, and then she squinted into the cold wind that blew in through the broken window.

"Someone must have shot it from the apartment building across the street." She picked up the broken lamp, then turned to Jan. "You and Piotrek were in this room when I went to Iwona's. Why did you leave?"

Jan shook his head. "I don't know. Something told me to take Piotrek into the other room."

Tatuś said later that it was one of my angels. "Jesus said that the angels of the little ones are the closest to the Father."

It's hard for me to believe that I had my own angels at that time, but maybe my family's God gives children the benefit of the doubt.

5

ILLUMINES BY NIGHT

Psalm 105:39

1952–1958

Jasiu had no idea how he ever found his way back home from the forest. He stumbled up the seven flights of stairs and knocked at the door of the apartment. Auntie Dorota, the lady who lived with her family in the first room of the apartment, let him in just as Jasiu remembered he had a set of keys. Tatuś had given the keys to him just yesterday morning, on his first day of school.

"Jasiu, you're home early. Your mother is still running errands. I have to go out, but you can be alone by yourself, can't you? You're a big boy, going to school now."

He would not look at her. Something in the way she said "big boy" made him think she was laughing at him. "Yes," he said. He dragged himself to their door, unlocked it, and let himself in the room. Then he climbed up on his sofa and fell fast asleep.

Jasiu woke up to the feel of bright sunshine warming his face. He stretched. There were two men talking loudly to someone in the room next door. He heard Uncle Henryk and probably Uncle Henryk's brother. Then he heard his mother's voice. "No. You cannot decide whether we stay here anymore. I have the papers to prove we have as much right to our room as your family does to theirs. No."

Her last *no* had sounded like she was being hurt. Jasiu jumped off the sofa and ran to the door, opening it slowly. He saw bread on the floor, and Uncle Henryk standing near his mother. The other man was holding her with one hand like he wanted to

72

dance. With the other hand he was taking out the pins that held up her hair. "Mamusiu?"

All three grown-ups turned to look at him. Jasiu felt as though he had done something wrong again. Uncle Henryk reached up, pulled his brother's hand away, and said, "No. Not with the boy watching."

"Mamusiu, have you found out where Tatuś is? Have they hurt him?"

The brother was angry. He said, "We don't want those meetings you have on Tuesdays. We don't want those foreigners walking through our home to get to yours. It's not right. This is the only warning you'll get."

In no time she had crossed the room and was on her knees, swooping Jasiu into her arms, gathering up her spilled groceries and pushing open the door with her foot. Their room was bathed in autumn sunshine.

"Jasiu, I was worried." She turned around to lock the door behind her. Then she looked very carefully at him and touched his face.

Jasiu knew he had been bad. "Mamusiu, I ran away from school. I had to." He would not look at her.

"Where did you go, my little prince?" Her voice was soft.

"I went," he swallowed hard, then said, "I went to a field that was full of storks. And later I felt better."

"And why did you feel bad?"

Jasiu wouldn't answer her. He couldn't.

They did not leave their room again that night. When he heard the family come home next door, Jasiu and Mamusia were eating the simple supper she had brought home. After that, they both went to bed early. She told him she would empty the bedpans in the morning. Jasiu had gone ahead and set the extra place at the table again, but his mother had said nothing about it.

The next morning, when she told Jasiu she would walk with him to school and have a talk with the teacher, he felt the panic rise up in him. "No, Mamusiu. There's nothing wrong. Really."

"Now listen to me. I think I know what is happening. You're not my happy little boy anymore, and it's about time I did something to change that. Come on."

He heard his mother take a deep breath as she unlocked their door. "You have your keys?" she asked Jasiu. He nodded. Mamusia knocked first, as she always did, then entered the outer room. Uncle Henryk was there, along with Auntie Dorota, but he did not look up.

"Good morning, Dorota." Jasiu wondered why no one answered his mother. Mamusia looked down at Jasiu and smiled at him. Once outside on the stairs, she said, "It's all right. They're just afraid because Tatuś was arrested."

Jasiu looked up at her, thinking, *So am I.*

They walked the rest of the way to school in silence.

Jasiu saw the teacher going through the door as they arrived. They had come early, ahead of all the other children. "You stay outside and play," Mamusia said to Jasiu. She quickly bent down and gave him a kiss on his forehead. He turned away.

"Excuse me," Mamusia called as she ran after the teacher. She went through the doorway and called out again at the woman.

Jasiu didn't know what to do. This would make things much worse; he knew that after the events of yesterday. Still, some small part of him knew his mother could do special things sometimes. Maybe now was one of those times. He waited under a tree and did not play with the others when they arrived.

Finally he saw his mother coming back out the door. She looked around, then headed toward him. Jasiu could tell by how she walked that whatever she had done hadn't worked.

He looked up at her hopefully. "You didn't talk to her?"

"Yes, I did." Jasiu shuffled his feet back and forth.

"Jasiu, I know you think you sent Tatuś away because you told the teacher about our Bible. Am I right?" He nodded, still not looking back at her.

She knelt beside him. He only half heard the children playing jump rope behind them. She cupped his chin in her hand and turned his head so they could look straight into each other's eyes.

"Jasiu, this was not your fault. Do you hear me? Tatuś was arrested because of the prayer meetings we have in our home and because we sometimes have people from other countries praying with us—like Brother Hans, remember? Many people knew about this, people who saw them enter and leave our home. There were

even people at the meeting who could have talked about this to the police. We don't know why Tatuś was arrested, but *you did not send him there.*"

"Then we should stop the prayer meetings." He looked up at her finally.

"No, we shouldn't," she said softly. "Jasiu, you can always tell when you're doing what God wants because people who don't know Him will try and hurt you for it." She closed her eyes for a minute, then opened them again. "It's a hard lesson, but those meetings are exactly what the Piekarz family is supposed to be doing. And we won't let anybody make us too afraid to pray."

"And the Bible?"

Mamusia said, "If the police knew about the prayer meetings, they knew about the Bible. They didn't need to hear about that from your teacher."

But Jasiu looked down again. "But they did, and that's why he's gone now. That was what did it."

"*No.*" Mamusia sounded almost angry. Just then his teacher emerged in the doorway and started clapping her hands. She looked over at their corner, but her eyes passed right over them. Mamusia stood. "All right, you go on now. The teacher's calling you. It will be all right. And I promise you, *Tatuś will come home.*" As Jasiu left her, Mamusia called out, "I'll meet you here when school is out."

As the children filed into the building, the teacher said to Jasiu, "So you're not even big enough to walk home alone."

———— ❧ ————

In a few weeks it would be Christmas. Jasiu fell asleep praying that the police would let Tatuś come home for Christmas. When he woke up in the morning he discovered to his great shame that he had wet his bed. Again. Lately he was doing it almost every night.

Mamusia wasn't up yet, so he got up and very quietly stripped the bed, wadding the damp sheets into a ball. To his surprise he discovered a rubber sheet as a bottom layer. Mamusia must have put it there the night before. She hadn't mentioned it, but he was relieved now that he hadn't ruined the sofa mattress.

When his mother got up, Jasiu was too embarrassed to say anything about his problem. Her stomach was getting bigger. When he noticed her look at the sheets in the corner and not say anything to him, he felt like hugging her.

"Did you have more bad dreams last night?" she asked.

"No, why?"

"I heard you calling out in your sleep. When I came to check on you, you'd fallen back asleep again."

Jasiu shook his head. "I . . . I don't remember."

"Is everything all right at school?" She asked him this almost every day.

"Yes, fine," was always his answer. But this time he added, "It's just . . ."

Hanna looked up from the sandwiches she was making. She came over and sat down next to where he was putting on his shoes. "Tell me."

"It's just that I told a lie yesterday." He sighed. Things were *not* going well at school.

"Yes?"

"Every morning the teacher asks us who is speaking German at home. Well, it's not really a lie maybe because I don't say anything. I don't say yes or no. I just don't say anything."

"It's all right, Jasiu. I speak German, and I'm teaching it to you. But at home our first language is Polish. And unfortunately, your teacher is the type of person we cannot tell everything to. So you did the right thing. Do you understand?"

"Yes." But he didn't. Not really.

———— ✑ ————

Jasiu liked holding his baby brother. "Piotrek." He said the word very quietly whenever he had the little dark-haired bundle in his arms. "He's a little bit my baby, isn't he?" he asked his mother.

"Of course. And you will help me give him baths and keep him clean."

"Oh not that!" They both laughed. Jasiu liked it when his mother laughed. She was very pretty then. She hadn't looked so pretty since Tatuś was arrested.

Jasiu could feel the difference little Piotrek made in their home. He also felt better, especially when he held Piotrek like this. Jasiu could not get enough of the little fingers that would grab on to his and hold with such strength. And already, when Jasiu stroked Piotrek's chin, he smiled. Then when Piotrek woke up and looked straight at Jasiu, it was almost as if he recognized him.

That made Jasiu feel important. He promised his little brother in his thoughts that he would always take care of him.

Mamusia reached over and squeezed Jasiu's shoulder. "My boys," she said, and Jasiu couldn't tell if she was happy or sad, "my two beautiful boys."

———— ✑ ————

The day began like any other. Jasiu was nine. He walked home from school and let himself in the apartment. By then, the neighbors had moved away and no one had come to take their place. But even though they no longer had to share their two-room apartment with another family, Jasiu and his mother and Piotrek still continued sleeping together in the one room.

When Jasiu came in, the first thing he saw was Mamusia standing in the doorway to their room. She was crying. But why?

He thought there must be something wrong with the baby. Then he heard little Piotrek giggle like he did whenever Jasiu tickled his toes. A man's voice in the next room was counting, "*jeden, dwa, trzy. . . .*"

He took two steps toward his mother and was almost too afraid to ask, "Mamusiu, are you hurt?"

She turned and smiled through her tears, shaking her head no. "God has answered our prayers," she said.

Jasiu didn't know what she meant at first. But slowly a feeling came over him as he thought about her words, thought about the man's voice he had just heard talking so gently to Piotrek, thought about his own prayers. And then all at once he felt so warm and good and excited. He felt like a bird who had just been let out of his cage.

He ran first to Mamusia and hugged her. Then he pulled her by the hand to their room. He opened the door and stood there holding Mamusia's hand and saw little Piotrek on Tatuś's lap.

Tatuś looked up slowly, and his eyes rested on Jasiu. Jasiu thought it was like watching somebody wake up from a long sleep. Tatuś stared at him, but in the first few seconds he didn't really see Jasiu. It was like he had expected someone else to walk in. Then he saw who Jasiu was, and Tatuś's whole face changed. He looked like he suddenly knew where he was.

———— ↬ ————

At school, all the classrooms contained three portraits: Stalin, Bolesław Bierut, the Polish First Secretary, and Marshal Rokossovski with his black hair and square, clean-shaven chin. There was one boy in Jasiu's class who committed the terrible sin of painting a Hitler mustache on Stalin's portrait, even after his death in 1953. Some members of the Young Pioneer Club told on him, and the boy's parents were sent to prison for two years. He was Jasiu's age, only eleven.

In December of 1956, Jasiu overheard his parents talking about Polish workers who had gone on strike in *Poznań*. Uncle Marek was visiting.

"Tadeusz, this marks the end of the madness, I'm sure of it. The cult of Stalin is finally over."

Jasiu's parents had looked at each other the way they did whenever Piotrek got carried away with one of his plans. But they had shared in Marek's excitement. He had brought over a bottle of Bulgarian wine and poured it into four glasses. "Come, Jan, will you join us and drink to the demise of the cult of Satan?" Marek asked him.

Jasiu liked being called by his grown-up name, Jan. But he remembered the boy in his class and was a little afraid. He looked at his father, who winked at him.

His mother said, "Really, Tadeusz, he's only eleven."

"Almost twelve," Jasiu said.

"Well, Hanna, we're drinking to his future. A future without Rokossovski and all the rest of them. A future where the curse on this country has finally been lifted."

"We can start hoping again," Marek said. "To Gomułka." They all clinked glasses, and Jasiu felt very important.

Piotrek came running up to him and pulled on his pants leg.

"Me too! Piotrek, too." Everyone laughed.

Then Mamusia said, "It's almost like it was just after the war. Remember? When we felt like we could build something up again?"

———— ∽ ————

After 1956, Rokossovski's portrait as well as those of Stalin and Bierut were taken down from Jan's schoolroom wall. In the unfaded space they left behind on the wall the teacher hung a cross. This meant that the religion classes that had been discontinued in 1949 would start up again now eight years later. Jan wished he had never given the letter from school about the religion classes to his parents. His father had written a note that since these were Catholic religion classes, he did not have to attend them. It was yet another reminder that he was different.

When Mamusia and Tadeusz wrote the note asking that Jan be excused from these new classes, they wrote that he already received religious training at home. This meant that Jan was free to play in the playground. On the first day this happened he was alone with nothing better to do than kick all the dead leaves into a pile in one corner.

Then two boys snuck up behind him and started to taunt him.

"You're supposed to be in school," Jan said.

"And so are you. We told the teacher we had to go take care of some business," the first boy said.

"Yeah, so she said we could go to the bathroom. But the business we wanted to take care of was *you*. Why aren't *you* in religion class? Don't you believe in God?"

Jan said, "I believe in God. If you did, you wouldn't make fun of me."

The boys leapt at Jan and threw him onto the ground. One sat on his back and pulled his shirt up, while the other grabbed a stick. "Hurry! We don't have much time before the teacher comes looking for us."

Jan started to yell, but the one boy hit him on the back of the head with the stick. Then he began cutting into Jan's back with the stick, covering it with scratches.

Jan struggled as best he could, thrashing his legs and arms. He could taste the dirt, and his eyes were watering with pain and the dust. He yelled again, and they hit him one more time.

"You Jew!" the first boy yelled.

"You German!" said the second boy.

Then they threw the stick away and ran as fast as they could back inside the school. It had taken less than ten minutes.

Jan lay in the dirt, sobbing. He would have to go back inside when the hour was up and pretend nothing had happened. Those two boys would be sneering at him. He saw it all happening even as he lay there with the smell of the rotting leaves in his throat. It would do no good to report what had happened; he would just get blamed for it. The last four years had taught him that much.

Jan struggled to his knees, then stood up. His head throbbed where he'd been hit. He rubbed the spot as he walked back inside the building and headed for the boys' bathroom.

Inside, he lifted his shirt and turned around to look at his back in the mirror. Inscribed on his back was a crude face with devil's horns coming out of the top of the head.

It wouldn't be the last time such a thing would happen.

———— ∽ ————

Tadeusz stood at the front of the crowded room. Jan stood beside his mother. Everyone was listening to his father so carefully that there was no other sound in the room except his voice.

"Look around you," Tadeusz said. "Have we ever seen these numbers before? If it keeps up, we might actually have to go find a church somewhere."

Everyone laughed a little. Jan looked down at the street. It was his and Uncle Marek's job to keep watch.

Tadeusz continued, "You feel the disappointment; we all do. It seems to make no difference who's in charge. Bierut, Gomułka—they're both the same. The government is still obeying the Party line, still bowing to what the Soviet Union dictates. So yet again, our hopes have been disappointed."

He paused, then said, "I think we should give thanks for that. In a strange way, the act of neighbor being turned against neighbor, the distrust encouraged in our society, the betrayal, the lies by the government, the dashed hopes—these are precisely what is forcing this population into the churches and onto their knees for answers and relief, as well as a sense of order."

Jan was fascinated by how his father's voice seemed to gather more power as he went on. He leaned forward as Tadeusz said, "And that sense of order can be found in only one place—at the side of our Lord Jesus Christ. He is the only . . ."

Jan felt a finger poke his shoulder. He looked up and saw Marek. He was a miniature, chubby version of Tadeusz, blond but balding. *They could be real brothers*, Jan thought fleetingly. Then he noticed that Marek was pointing out the window. On the street below, a police van had just pulled up. He looked at Marek, who nodded.

"*Przepraszam*. Excuse me, Tatusiu." Jan's face burned with embarrassment when everyone turned to look at him.

"Yes, Jan, what is it?" His father sighed. "I think I know."

"The boy's right," Marek said. "We have visitors."

Whenever this happened, Jan always felt sick to his stomach. He couldn't help it. Mamusia said it was left over from when he was a boy and they took Tatuś away. He swallowed hard and followed his mother through the crowd toward the kitchen corner.

"Everyone be calm now. This has happened before. It's quite simple, really. You're all here for tea. Now, please don't panic. You might even want to pray."

As he spoke, Tadeusz picked up the altar Bible that had no cover and collected the various sheets of handwritten Bible pages around the room. He carried these into the other room where Piotrek and the younger children were asleep.

Jan, meanwhile, took the trays of sandwiches and sponge cake his mother handed him and started passing them around the room. Mamusia and two other women were pouring cold tea and coffee—anything they could get their hands on—into cups and mugs, while Jan put these on trays and passed them around as well.

Then came the expected knock, loud and commanding. Everyone grew silent. Jan was nearest to the door. His father moved up next to him and started undoing the locks. "Keep talking," Tadeusz whispered loudly to the people staring at his back. It was all Jan could do to keep from snatching his father's hand away from the door and telling him not to open it. He stepped back against the wall as the fear nailed him up against it.

"Let us in!" Another rap on the door.

"Yes, yes," Tadeusz replied. Just before he opened the last bolt, he looked over at Jan, pale and shaking. Tadeusz winked. Then he said to the men at the door, "What is it now? Can't you see we're just . . ."

But the three agents pushed him aside and shouldered their way into the room. The number of people present seemed to take them by surprise.

"What is this?" They were dressed in uniforms with black boots. The one with a burly black mustache looked around the room, and his eyes settled on Jan. "You, boy, what's going on here?"

Jan couldn't stop blinking. The terror he felt had risen from his stomach into his throat. "I . . . it's—"

"It's my Name Day today, sir. And all these people are friends and family," Tadeusz said and stepped forward with a plate of cake. He positioned himself between the agent and Jan. "I don't suppose you and your friends would like a piece of cake?"

The man narrowed his eyes. "Have a look around," he told the other two. The men turned over cushions and opened books, flipping through the pages. When they reached the other side of the room where the door was, they started to push aside Marek, who was standing there with Mamusia.

"Excuse me," she said to the youngest of the two. "There are babies asleep in that room. I don't think you want to be the one to wake them all up."

The man looked over at his superior, who shook his head in disgust. "Forget it. I want these *friends and family* out of here in ten minutes, do you hear me? Or we'll do more than wake your babies." Then he turned around in the doorway and spat on the door.

When the other two had followed, Tadeusz quietly closed the door behind them. All eyes were on him as he said, "Let us pray."

Jan closed his eyes and bit his lip. He felt so ashamed of his fear. He hated the tears that started running down his cheeks and hoped everyone else had their eyes closed, too. Then he felt his father's hand on his shoulder.

"Let us pray," Tadeusz repeated. "For Poland, for her people, against the enemy. We pray for those three men tonight, for Jesus taught us to do so. And we give thanks. For our being together tonight." He squeezed Jan's shoulder and paused. "And for the seven flights of stairs leading to our humble home."

6

Is Unquenchable

Matthew 3:12

1956–1959

Jacek had been expecting the invitation.

With Marshal Rokossovski's expulsion from power, there would be a great deal of reshuffling within the corridors of the ministry buildings. He was down for the record as a Party man, but he still had to prove himself. And there was no better way than with a gun in his hand.

Jacek drove himself to the lodge address given on the invitation. He had been there before. Ironically, it was one of Rokossovski's favorite spots, and Jacek had gone hunting there with the Marshal more than once. *That's probably why they chose this place*, he thought grimly.

It was indeed fortunate, he mused, that his own relationship with Rokossovski had cooled during the years after he returned from Gdańsk. That Rokossovski had disapproved of his targeting the Minister of Economics and authorized surveillance of Jacek. That Jacek, in turn, had worked to distance himself from the military and pander more to the Party.

And then it had happened. In June of 1956 workers had rioted in the city of Poznań, chanting, "Bread and Freedom!" It had been obvious to everyone but the generals running Poland that enough people had come to resent the suffocating measures introduced in the last ten years. The Party had feared an uncontainable "situation" and moved quickly to head it off by electing a new First Secretary.

But the Soviet Union couldn't help but notice such an independent action. An enraged Nikita Khrushchev had flown immediately from Moscow to Warszawa. It had not mattered to the Soviet First Secretary that the Polish Communist Party had initiated the action; what had mattered was that it had acted without consulting its Soviet counterpart. Khrushchev had mobilized the Soviet army, and the Soviet fleet had appeared off the coastline of Gdańsk.

Around that time, Jacek had heard rumors that Rokossovski was plotting a coup. Had the Marshal remembered his Polish roots, after all? So Jacek had made sure that a few of the other higher-ranked aides overheard him saying that Poland would be nothing without its Soviet big brother. Then he had written some memos explaining the special relationship that the two countries' Communist Parties should enjoy.

In the agreement reached by Gomułka and Khrushchev, Poland had pledged continued subservience to the USSR in exchange for its own autonomous, national brand of communism. The Polish Communist Party would run the country, and this time the military would answer to the Party. In turn, the Party would answer to the USSR. Rokossovski had been expelled.

But Jacek had been in the fortunate position that he had never exactly belonged to Rokossovski's military world. He was not a soldier. In fact, he was listed in Rokossovski's file as being a professor of mathematics who had happened to be good at spying on the Germans—and, more recently, someone not to be wholly trusted by the military. This looked much better to the Party than the records of his colleagues, who were members of the military elite. They were by definition part of the problem that had just been solved.

Jacek had known instinctively when to jump off the train and take another track. He was still fulfilling his prime directive from the CIA, to position himself among the leadership of the new government. And this weekend in the mountains would help determine exactly where he would fit.

It promised to be a lovely weekend. The *Bieszczady* Mountains also happened to have some of the best hunting in all of Europe. If certain aspects of being a leader in a centrally planned government ate away at Jacek, this particular perk was a saving grace. He had spent many autumn weeks roaming between mountain villages in this southeast corner of Poland. In that secret part of him he still cherished, Jacek saw the beauty in these hills as inherent to Poland's own.

"Look around you!" The loud voice was the first thing he heard after he slammed the car door shut. "Now I ask you, are the Bieszczady not more beautiful than making love to a virgin?"

Jacek looked down at the letter inviting him. It had been signed by the number-three man in the Polish Communist Party, a man he had never met. *A good sign*, he thought. *They want to check out my loyalties. And this loudmouth must be my man, since everyone is fawning up to him.*

"Comrade." Jacek extended his hand and strode straight into the circle of admirers.

In the middle stood a small, fat man who was now enjoying the licentious chuckles his comment had caused. He turned his attention to Jacek and took in his leather breeches and the gold lettering on his rifle case. "Comrade Duch, I assume."

At that moment Jacek realized he was the only one on trial that weekend. Every other man present was there to test him. *If I can make it past his pack, I'm in until the next workers' strike*, he realized in a flash of prescience.

The fat man continued, "I like your gun. Shall we trade for the weekend?"

"Of course." Jacek extended the case to his host. "I have a better one in the back of the car."

This caused each one of the group of about fifteen men to grow silent. They looked to their leader, who slowly, very slowly, saw the joke Jacek had made. He grinned, showing a broad expanse of yellow teeth. "Ah, good man, good man. You may call me Roman." He clapped Jacek on the back and led him toward the lodge. "Zenon, fetch that other gun of Comrade Jacek's, will you?"

Jacek knew he had one foot in already.

The next day as they crossed a high ridge they could hear church bells ringing in the valley below. "Ever been to church, Duch?" Roman asked him.

For once, Jacek didn't have to lie. "No." The truth was, Jacek had never set foot in a church of any kind. Even when he and Barbara were married, it was at the office of a justice of the peace. He had never seen the need.

"You know I've read your file, so I won't mince words with you."

Jacek checked himself from looking too interested. Had he found that rare bird, a forthright communist?

"So, what do you think of Gomułka sitting down at the negotiation table with those *priests* on both sides of him?"

From the way Roman had said "priests," Jacek knew what opinion he was supposed to have—that the Party and the Roman Catholic church would never make good bedfellows. But perhaps the question was a measure of something else.

"I have to admit," he replied carefully, "in light of recent events in Poland, I too have been wondering just what the source of power for that institution might be."

"I told you I don't like fancy words. Talk to me in the people's language."

Jacek pointedly refused to switch into the guttural tones of the accent Roman used. But he did stop speaking formally. "No, I mean it," he repeated. "In the deal that Gomułka cut with the Soviets for Poland's survival, the power of the Church took on a surprisingly significant role. Of course it will never prove an even match for the Party, but you have to admit it has managed to push through a few key concessions."

"Go on."

He had Roman's attention now, but Jacek was not sure if that was a good thing. "Well, you asked me. Look at the major players left after the downgrading of the military's status. Was it the intelligentsia? Was it the workers' movement? No, as you said yourself, bishops and canon lawyers sat in seats beside Gomułka's own."

"And on the other side of the table sat the Soviets."

Both men were aware enough of the true events to know that in the previous year Poland had come heartbreakingly close to chiseling out its own independence.

Jacek sensed Roman's disappointment was as deeply felt as his own. He thought, *If this is my new boss, it will be a pleasure working for a Pole who believes in his country instead of one who's sold out to the Russians.* The nature of the game was changing.

The two men had broken off from the others. They stopped speaking as the climb up the ridge steepened. Eventually they had no choice but to scramble up loose bits of shale, using their hands for balance. At the top, Jacek was surprised to hear himself panting harder than Roman.

"I will tell you why Gomułka made concessions for these men of the cloth," Roman said, unscrewing the cap to his water jug. He took a long drink and handed it to Jacek. "It seems when we plotted out a communist-based destiny for Poland ten years ago, someone forgot that ninety-six percent of the country was Roman Catholic. That's still more or less true, so we need the Church now. But in twenty years the demographic trends will swing in our favor. Look at the rest of Europe. Do you really think that young people growing up in an atheist country will want to go to church?"

"Look!" Jacek had been scanning the ridge as Roman spoke. Now he pointed and said reverently, "Elk." A magnificent stag stood exactly where the undergrowth ended in rock.

Jacek handed the binoculars to Roman, who whistled softly, "He has at least six points. Listen, you saw him, but I outrank you."

Jacek grinned.

"What do you say we both try for him?"

"Of course," Jacek said, and both men released the safeties on their rifles and set their scopes.

Jacek knew that half the art of hunting was patience. Second came timing, and only then accuracy. He wondered who would choose to shoot first. Roman did not fit into any of the generalizations Jacek had of Party men. He certainly was more to the point than most men of power Jacek had to work with.

The wind shifted and Roman swore softly. The elk had picked up their scent. Jacek tensed his shoulder. Slowly he let out his breath, focusing on the broad chest of the animal. He could almost see its pulse through the hide. He squeezed the trigger, and a terrific blast cracked through the canyon.

As he lowered his rifle, he saw Roman looking at him in surprise. "What is it?" Jacek asked, suddenly concerned. Had he just stolen his host's prize? If so, that shot could have jeopardized the entire weekend, let alone whatever post he was in line for in the new government. He could feel the sweat beading on his forehead.

"I think," Roman said slowly, "I think we both shot at exactly the same moment. Ha! Well done! Did you hear that echo? Tell me, where did you learn to shoot like that?"

Jacek's heart raced with excitement, but he would not be caught off guard. For all his easygoing manners, Roman knew exactly what he wanted of Jacek.

"You've read my file," he answered, wondering what details Roman did know.

"A mathematics teacher?" He laughed scornfully and started sliding down the scree at breakneck speed.

When he finally caught up with the fat man at the side of the fallen elk, Jacek said, "I can't believe that someone with your, er, profile can move so fast."

Roman squinted up at him and said in the same soft voice he had used when he sighted the elk, "I could say the same about you, my friend." He paused, then turned back to the animal and pointed. "Look." The two bullet holes were so close that only one of Roman's fingers fit between them.

———— ✍ ————

Later that night when the lodge owner presented the two men with the trophy, Jacek insisted that Roman accept it. Roman accepted, although he laughed at the chivalrous gesture. "You're not an aristocratic gentleman under all that proper speaking, are you?" Roman jabbed Jacek in the ribs.

"God forbid," Jacek said, and both men broke out laughing. The lodge was white with cigar smoke. Inside the huge fireplace, stew pots bubbled around a roaring fire. All the men around him seemed to be laughing and drinking and telling dirty jokes.

Why do I have the feeling I'm on a stage, that it's not real? Jacek caught himself asking.

"Comrade Duch." Jacek squinted his eyes in the smoke. Who was this man standing next to him? If he wasn't mistaken, the speaker was Roman's right-hand man. "I've been meaning to ask why it is you don't join us in drinking? That's what these weekends are all about. Bragging about impossible feats and drinking until we are all too sick to brag."

Jacek heard the joking tone in the man's voice but saw no sign of it in his eyes. His feeling of wariness intensified. Confused, he said, "I don't mean to be rude. I've just had some health problems, and my doctor says I should tone it down a bit."

"I see."

The party was moving outside. Seven of the men had lifted the lodge owner onto their shoulders and were threatening to throw him into the pond. Jacek followed behind the crowd, wondering where all the women had come from. They didn't dress like local girls. Roman must have imported them from the city. By the way they were hanging on the rest of the hunting party, Jacek figured them for prostitutes. He didn't want to stand out, so he put his arm around one woman and started cheering with the others. Everything was a mass of color and movement, until he felt a hand on his shoulder.

"Come with me." Jacek knew Roman must have had at least half a bottle of vodka, but his tone was steady and sober.

Jacek looked down at the girl in his arms. Her lipstick was smudged. "Off you go," he said, giving her a pat and pushing her into the ring of dancers swinging by them.

Jacek remembered the elk and waited as he walked behind Roman. When they were outside earshot of the others, Roman said, "I heard what my aide asked. It's none of his business. But *I* want *you* to know I prefer a man who knows his own weaknesses. You know, I should give you the trophy."

"Why is that?"

"Your bullet was closest to the heart," Roman continued. Then he asked, "Where is your heart, Jacek Duch?"

He had a sense this was what the whole weekend was about, that his post-Rokossovski future hinged entirely on what he now replied. Summoning up all the honesty he felt in his answer, Jacek said, "My heart belongs to Poland."

The two men stared at each other for a long moment. Jacek knew he was expected to look away first, but he did not. He would not. Finally Roman broke the silence.

"Someday, Poland will be free of the Soviets, but for now our only hope of surviving as a nation is to work with them. They will crush us otherwise. At least thanks to those workers in Poznań, we have eliminated the military's stranglehold on the country. Now we need to tighten our grip and be wary of the next enemy from within. Our security forces are still in the hands of the KGB. I need a Party man to work with them but still be loyal to Poland's interests. I know more about you than you think, Jacek Duch. Is this job for you?"

Jacek was truly taken aback. He had never dreamed, never ever thought he would be handed something like this. He swallowed hard and could barely get the words out, words that had to be asked if only because they were expected of him. "What do you know about me?"

"That you played the chameleon with the Marshal, but that your heart was never with the Soviets. I know what you must have undergone in their camps at the beginning of the war. I was in one of them, too. I was in Anders' army, though, and I know you, too, must have been biding your time for the opportunities that are ours now after all that happened last year.

"I need someone with your abilities to work with the security service, *but not be one of them*."

Jacek knew that the dreaded Security Office coordinated a labyrinthine security apparatus that reached far into the homes of every Pole. It was the head office for a maze of groups, the sole purpose of which was to police the people and discourage any independence or freedom of thought and movement. It kept the people down. The UB was everywhere and had files on everyone. It exercised a humiliatingly petty control over all levels of Polish society.

"I can do that," Jacek answered. Smiling inwardly, he repeated, "I cannot be one of them."

—————— ∽ ——————

The irony was not lost on Jacek. Acting as an agent for the Polish Communist Party, he was to work with none other than the Polish underling of the KGB, the newest incarnation of the Soviet secret police. Izzy's folks back home were delighted to have an inside man so close to the KGB. It had all occurred so naturally that the CIA hardly knew what to do with the gold mine Jacek began excavating for them.

Jacek forwarded briefs describing the absolute control of the population, the turning of neighbor against neighbor, and incessant spying, not to mention night raids and arrests. In 1957 the UB became the SB, or Security Service, the *Służba Bezpieczeństwa*. With the new name change came an intensification of pressure put on the population.

And then in 1959 Jacek received instructions from Roman to check out a Polish intelligence officer named Michał Goleniewski. Jacek had run into Roman at a cocktail party for the wife of one of the other Party bosses. Roman dragged him into a corner and told him, "We don't want the SB getting too powerful, now do we? Targeting this man might be a way of bringing them down a notch or two."

Jacek started running the usual checks. He pulled Goleniewski's file. And that same day when he went home and was eating some of Gabi's soup, he noticed a cigarette butt sticking out from under the geranium pot.

When it was past midnight, he drove himself over to Izzy's. Only once before had he ever seen her so mad. Now her anger made her cold and tight.

"Do you remember the last time you felt the steel of my gun against your neck?" she hissed.

Jacek said, "Izzy, I have absolutely no idea what you're talking about. We're on the same side, remember. You're my touchstone."

"I'll be your gravestone if you don't stay away from my mark."

"Your what?"

"He's mine, I tell you. *I* turned Goleniewski. He's much too dangerous for you, Jacek. We wouldn't want someone like him jeopardizing your precious position, now would we?"

"I . . . I had no idea." Even as he spoke, Jacek wondered if Roman had set him up.

Jacek was remembering, this was not the first time. In 1954 Józef Światło, a colonel in the UB, had also defected. But again the process had completely circumvented Jacek. It wasn't his job to turn agents. "What's he given away?" Jacek asked.

"Only the names of several hundred Soviet bloc agents hidden in the West," she whispered in his ear.

"And he's exiting?"

"That's for me to know and you to find out. I'm rather proud of myself about this one." Izzy flashed one of her rare smiles.

"It'll rock the entire security network," Jacek said by way of congratulating her.

"Tell me about it."

"I'll have to report back to Roman that I couldn't find anything suspicious about Goleniewski. Then I'll just have to hold on tight and outride the storm. You know what this means, don't you?" Jacek was just starting to realize it himself.

"When my mark defects—if my mark defects, that is—the SB will jump into paranoia gear and begin immediate investigations within its own corps. Why do you think we're having this meeting? I'm supposed to warn you of a pending mole hunt so you can take the necessary precautions."

"I'll have to lie low." Jacek was thinking of the project he was currently working on for the SB. They knew him as a Party man, and as such he was not really welcome in the Security Service's inner circle. But that suited him just fine. A low profile meant there was no one place where he belonged. And his security clearance was still high enough to get his hands on information the U.S. was desperate for. The package Jacek had handed over to Izzy that night had not only contained film of top-secret documents, but even a few originals.

"Listen up, Duch," she was saying. "Your orders are simple: *Do nothing*. This isn't wartime. There are others who can cover for you while you go under. Do you know the chances of ever getting someone like you so high up in the government again? Do nothing."

7

Takes Hold of Itself

Exodus 9:24

1957–1960

The same year Senator Joseph McCarthy died, Amy Baker had announced to her parents that she would not be going to college. "I just don't know what I want to do," she explained, knowing how much she was disappointing them. She knew they wanted nothing more than that she go on with her education. But she couldn't see the point.

"It's not enough reason for me to go just because that's what everyone else is doing. The sororities and parties, I don't know, it's not for me, I guess."

Amy was fighting an all-too-familiar dread of not feeling at home. She was already so different—branded, as it were, by the years her family had no longer been welcome in Boston's elite. *What's the use of fighting to get back in where I never belonged in the first place?* she wondered.

Ruth and John did not push. "Whatever you choose to do, you will do well," Ruth told Amy. "Wait a while. We're behind you, no matter what you become."

"Even if it's a bum?" Amy could still make her parents laugh.

John nodded and looked Amy in the eyes. "Go get 'em, Tiger. Be the best bum you can be!"

So Amy spent most of the summer of 1957 sailing alone in her new Laser, a graduation gift from her parents. The wind whipped through her glossy black hair, and she willed it to blow away all that was dark and bad inside her. All her life the course had been set for her. Now Amy was struggling to find her own stars to steer by, trying to get her own bearings.

"Maybe you could learn the ropes in the business," John suggested hopefully as they sat companionably on their dock. Amy leaned against the pier, her sketch pad propped on her knees, while he reeled in his line for another cast. Already she had more drawings to show for their afternoon than he had fish.

"Even though I'm retiring," he went on, "I've still got some clout. I bet I can get you in at a lower management position, and you could learn the business from the ground up."

She added another level of shading to her sketch, trying to capture the way the reflected light from the water played on his face. "Thanks, Dad," she said, "but can you really see me as an executive in a steel firm?"

"Like me, you mean?" he asked, turning to face her.

"You know that's not what I mean. And turn around. I still don't have this right."

He sighed and returned to his previous position. "You're probably right," he said. "But I just want you to find something you love."

"I do have something I love," she said, standing to slip an arm around his waist. "Now all I need is to find something I want to do."

That half year after graduation had seemed to last a long time. By the time she turned nineteen, Amy was ready to face up to the fact that all her former classmates had headed off for their freshman years at various colleges. Feeling restless, she finally enrolled in an evening art class at the local junior college. She thought, *I might be aimless, but at least there's one thing I know I enjoy doing.*

So this is what Amy did as she waited for life to happen. She figured the fewer chances she took, the safer she would be. She drove back and forth to town in her Corvette convertible, a gift from her parents when she had gotten her driver's license at sixteen. She listened to her father complain about the new management of his company, in which he still played an active role despite his recent retirement. And she went out a few times with the boy who sat across the aisle from her in art class.

His name was Ron, and he was about as interested in a serious relationship as Amy was. But she thought he was cute, and he liked art and he was someone to go to movies with and dance with and kiss in her car at night when the top was down and they were watching for shooting stars.

Amy lived this way for the next two years, until March 17, 1960. On that day she turned twenty-one.

She had invited Ron over for dinner, and they had a small family party to celebrate. When she sat down at the table, Amy found a long envelope under her plate. Inside was a round-trip ticket to Paris with no dates written in.

"Oh, Mom, Dad, this is too much!" She stood up and gave them both hugs and kisses.

"You're old enough to see the world," John said. "And anyone with your talent should see the Masters." He added, "It's something I always wanted to do with your mother, and we never had the time."

"Well, come with me then!" Amy said.

Ruth laughed at the look on John's face. "See, I told you she'd say that. No, of course not, honey. This is your adventure."

"We've always said your education comes first. Now just because you're not going to college like the others, that doesn't mean you can't keep learning. This way you'll end up with a fine art education—with or without a university degree."

Amy was deeply touched. *How could they know me so well?* she wondered. "I don't know what to say," she murmured.

"I do." Ron laughed. "Ask if your boyfriend can come along and carry your bags!"

They all laughed, and Amy made a face at Ron. "Any idea when you'll go?" he asked.

"Nope."

After the party Ron and Amy walked out to the porch and down to the barn, where he had parked his motorcycle. He had to get up early the next day to work at the construction job he had in town.

"Listen, I have something for you, too," he said. "I was thinking about those sketches you showed me of the lake in the woods. You know, where your father always goes fishing? Well, I may not be able to draw flowers like you do, but at least I know what they're called. So ... happy birthday, beautiful." He shoved a package into Amy's hands and roared off before she could even give him a thank-you kiss.

Amy stood in the dark and heard the old pony and her horse whinny at her. She tore open the wrapping and found a small handbook to wildflowers. On the overleaf were written the words, *To Amy. Now you can call the flowers to you by name. Love always, Ron.*

She turned toward the sound of Ron's bike roaring down the lane and whispered, "Thank you." This romantic side of Ron always took her by surprise.

———— ◊ ————

The sound of her parents' voices floated down to her from the porch as she walked slowly back to the house. She looked up and saw they were waiting for her. "Were you two spying on us?" she joked.

"No, we just have another present for you, and we thought it best to wait until Ron was gone," John said.

Amy squinted in the darkness as she climbed the steps to the porch. An unwrapped shoebox lay on the table next to the tray with hot cocoa. It was tied with a dirty piece of string.

"What is this, matching luggage so that Ron can come along after all?"

"No, darling. Here, come sit down."

Amy shivered; she did not like the sound of Ruth's voice. She turned up the collar of her coat against the blustery March wind. "Wouldn't it be better to go inside first? I don't want you two to get sick."

John snorted. "We're not that old! No, we're out of the wind here. Come sit down." As Amy did so, he continued, "This is a box containing your mother's personal belongings. I'm talking about Barbara Skrzypek now. The box was given to us by your old baby-sitter. She said Barbara gave it to her with the instructions that if anything should happen to her, these things should be given to you on your twenty-first birthday."

He paused when Amy gasped. *Had she known she would die?*

Ruth picked up where John had left off. "Here, Amy," she said softly. "The woman who was taking care of you at the time of your mother's accident waited until she knew we would definitely adopt you before she gave the box to us. We've never looked inside. I hope . . . Well, it's just that your father and I have always thought it better not to talk too much about the accident. We wanted you to get over it as soon as possible. I hope we made the right decision. Here, I've turned on the porch light, and we'll leave you alone. Good night, honey." She stood, then bent over and kissed Amy's cheek.

Amy left the box where it was while she stood to hug Ruth hard, then John. "You know I could never have had better parents than you two." She felt so torn inside, as if she were a six-year-old all over again.

When her parents had left her, Amy sighed and slipped the string off the box. The lid was worn and almost flattened. Inside lay a sheaf of yellow papers.

She took the box onto her lap and scooted the chair over closer to the lamp. Then Amy picked up a paper and held it to the light so she could read it.

She whistled softly, then read out loud, "A certificate of divorce 'filed by Barbara Skrzypek on the grounds of desertion.' This is dated 1943. But nobody ever told me they were divorced."

Amy picked up an empty envelope. It bore a 1941 postmark. The stamp on the envelope was from Poland.

"Not France," Amy said to herself. "And there's nothing here about veterans' benefits or my father being killed in the war. Poland?"

And then she felt it, like a little shiver of recognition, the quiet knowledge that the life she had been waiting for had finally begun. This was real. This was her. At twenty-one, she had finally come into herself.

Poland. . . .

———— ❧ ————

The next morning Amy showed the documents to Ruth and John and watched them exchange glances. "Did you know?" she asked.

John shook his head. Ruth looked her straight in the eyes and said, "Can you still remember that evening when I sat you down and told you that Barbara had died? Do you remember what a relief that piece of truth was to you? Believe me, Amy, if we had known your parents were divorced before your mother died, we would have said so."

"Your mother's right," John said. Amy looked deep into his dark blue eyes and saw he was telling the truth. It was not their fault that these secrets had been kept from her. "We were tempted to look in the box," he was saying, "but every time we discussed it, we knew we couldn't. This is probably the only valid piece of your blood past you will ever have. It was not our place to explore it for you first."

Amy nodded. They had protected her from so much, but they couldn't protect her from who she was. She thought about the plane ticket they had given her the night before. All night she had been struggling with how she would say the next sentence.

"I want to find out if he's dead."

She saw Ruth's and John's eyes meet again. "What does that mean?" Amy asked. "That's twice you've given each other that look."

"It's the look two parents give each other when they're afraid they might lose their only child, but they know that if they don't let her go, they may never get her back." Ruth's voice cracked, and John came and stood behind her, holding her shoulders.

"Ah, Mom, Dad." Amy went to hug them both, each time again shocked at how frail they felt.

"It's okay," she repeated as she replaced the papers in their box. "You won't lose me." Softly, so that her parents almost didn't hear her, she added, "But I . . . I might find myself."

A few seconds later, John pulled away. "Your mother and I will help you in any way we can. Of course, it's hard for us to think that your father might still be alive."

"And that I want to go looking for him."

John swallowed. "And that you want to go looking for him. But as I said, we're behind you. There's one thing—I don't understand why Barbara would tell you he was dead if he wasn't."

"I know I didn't dream it," Amy said, but she was thinking how much she didn't know, and wondering how much she didn't want to know.

"No you didn't. Your baby-sitter said the same to us," John continued.

"Your baby-sitter," said Ruth, "maybe that's the place to start—if you're sure you want to do this. . . ."

Amy looked at them both, so old, so eager to be there for her. "No one, no one will take your places," she said again. "This is just something I have to do."

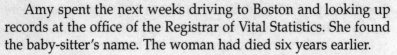

Amy spent the next weeks driving to Boston and looking up records at the office of the Registrar of Vital Statistics. She found the baby-sitter's name. The woman had died six years earlier.

Amy figured that the reason there had been no VA benefits was that her mother might have died before she was able to claim the money. The first time she had ever even read her father's name was on that night of her birthday. The divorce document described him as *Jacek Skrzypek*. Now she started hunting for the name in military records.

She had thought it would be easy—first the list of killed-in-action near the end of the war, then the list of total war casualties from the Boston area. There was no "Skrzypek" on either list. Amy racked her brain. The name had to be on a document somewhere. "Enlistments, greater-Boston area"—nothing.

John offered to try his connections with the Veterans Administration. There were national lists of the personnel sent to France and master lists of all Americans sent to Europe during the war. Again, no Jacek.

It was as if the name Jacek Skrzypek had never existed. There simply was not and never had been any such person by that name.

Amy made one last trip to the city. She had invited Ron to come with her. "Bring your sketch pad," she told him.

"Which office are we visiting now?" he asked. The two walked down the street on a warming spring day, just barely not holding hands.

"The office where we register you as a luggage carrier."

"Oh, so you're giving up and going to Europe." His square-jawed face was poker-straight. Amy could not tell if he was teasing her.

"No, I haven't given up, but yes, I am going on that trip. I don't know what else I'm supposed to do."

"You are giving up, or else you'd stay here until you found him," Ron said.

Amy was surprised at his stubborn tone. "You just don't want me to go."

"You wish." Now he was smiling.

She wondered if maybe they weren't caring more for each other than they had planned on. *He's my only friend, but the last thing I need is to fall in love*, she thought.

"So which is it?" Ron stopped her by putting his hand on her arm. "If you're not giving up, why are you going away, and why now?"

Amy squinted her eyes at him. "Look, I'm going away *because* I'm not giving up. I'll still be looking, but I'll just be over there looking."

"Ah, the Polish stamp." Ron nodded.

She didn't know what else to do. "He's not on the list of the dead, and he's not on the list of the living," she told Ron.

"You'll find what you're looking for, one way or the other," he said.

Amy didn't answer. At that moment they had turned into the Department of Health Services' Office of Records. She filled out the form applying for a copy of her birth certificate. The woman behind the counter said to take a number and wait. Amy and Ron sat drawing the people they saw around them. After about an hour Amy said she'd be right back. "Little girls' room." She winked at Ron.

While she was gone the lady called Amy's number. Ron went up to the counter. "She stepped out for a moment. I can take it for her."

"There's a fee." Ron paid, and the woman handed him a small rectangle of paper with the official seal of the Commonwealth of Massachusetts stamped on the back. He quickly read the document and thanked the woman. As he was walking back to the chairs, he saw Amy coming toward him.

"Your Jacek Skrzypek," Ron said.

"My Jacek Skrzypek, I can't find his name anywhere. And

what a name it is," Amy said. "I don't even know if I'm pronouncing it right."

"Well, I found him for you."

"What?" Amy took her birth certificate from Ron and read the details. "So he exists in two places—on my mother's divorce papers and on my birth certificate. He's out there somewhere. I just know it," she said. "Come on; with this I can get my passport." As they started to leave, Ron suddenly stopped and grabbed Amy's arm.

"Show me that thing again. Look, are *his* parents listed on the birth certificate? Your grandparents? No. Well, look, you've got his name and age plus his birthplace and 'present or last occupation' at your time of birth. This is a lot more than you had before."

Amy looked down at the slip of paper, as if seeing it for the first time. *Certificate of Live Birth* was written in bold capitals across the top. "You're right, Ron. He was or had been a student when I was born in 1939. And we know he was born in . . ." She sucked in her breath.

"In *Poland*. I told you we were getting somewhere." Ron looked as excited as Amy felt.

The space under "kind of industry or business" was blank. But Amy could see the birth dates. "Barbara was five years older."

"And he was born in 1909."

"And she was born in Lafayette, Louisiana."

"And he was white."

"And I was born in Boston."

"So what have we got?" Ron asked.

"We have a birthdate of a Polish immigrant who was a student—but where? Just because I was born here and they were divorced here—that doesn't mean he studied here. Besides, do you know how many colleges there are in Boston?"

"No, but we're going to find out. First, let's try the list of naturalized citizens for say, 1909 through 1919, the first ten years after his birth."

So once again Amy made the rounds of government statistics offices. She made several more trips, and Ron went with her on his days off. But once again she found nothing. This was, she thought, suspicious in itself.

Once she had her passport in hand, she told Ruth and John of her plans to leave for Paris at the end of the summer. "Paris in the autumn—it will be lovely," John said.

But she still hadn't figured out a way to tell them she wanted to use their plane ticket to continue her search. Later that evening, when she and Ron went on a walk to the lake together, she did manage to tell him that she wanted to go to Poland. "It's where all the clues point," she said.

"All two clues, you mean. Have you figured out how you'll get into Poland?"

"It's not that hard, as long as I can get a visa here and pay up front for each day I'll be there. Although I don't know how many days it will take. . . ." Her voice trailed off.

"Well, what's the problem then?"

"Oh, Ron, it's hopeless. How will I get into people's homes? I have to be free to talk. And I can't speak Polish."

"I don't know, Amy."

"I know I'm half Polish."

"That won't be enough."

Amy didn't like the look Ron was giving her. "You're going to have to let me go," she said softly.

"I've been thinking just that. I hadn't counted on feeling this way. But now that you're talking about leaving and I'm about to lose you, I've finally seen what I had these last two years. I was a fool." He turned away, but Amy pulled him back so he would have to face her.

"You were a good friend. And that's what we'll always be, friends. That means so much to me—it's enough, it really is! You're really the only friend I've got; you know that, don't you?" She wanted him to smile.

"And you are so beautiful. You know that, too, don't you?"

"Hmm." She gave him a hug. "And here's a friendly kiss for my friend."

"Okay, okay, I get the hint." But he wasn't laughing.

Amy had only the one problem. How to get into Poland and be with people who could help her find some information about this Jacek Skrzypek. She could not even think of him as her father. But there was a connection, for she would not let this thing go.

When Amy went home, she decided to finally tell Ruth and John that she wanted to continue the search for her father in Poland. Amy was surprised to see John pale on the spot. "A communist country."

Only then did Amy remember. "Poland *is* communist, isn't it?"

"Of course it is; didn't you think of that? You can't just go behind the Iron Curtain and start asking questions. I mean, they're calling it the Cold War, but it's a war, all the same, and it's not one I care to fight a second time. This country still has a rampant fear of anything labeled 'communist.'"

Amy didn't know what to say. All the years of uncertainty and distrust came crashing back down on her as she saw the suffering resurface in her parents' faces. *Have I done that?* she asked herself.

"Amy," Ruth asked her softly, "what brings this on all of a sudden?"

Amy told them about the birth certificate. Ruth said, "Of course. We haven't looked at it since we filled out the adoption papers and John put them all into a safety deposit box." Ruth paused. "But, Amy, you can't just go to Poland and start asking questions."

Then Amy looked over at John; he had sighed so deeply. He raised one hand as if he were about to say something. Before the hand could open, his entire body seemed to crumple and curl. His face turned purple, then gray, and he began to groan.

"Oh, Mom! No, Dad!" Amy flew to John's side and tried to support him, keeping him from falling onto the floor. "Mom!" Amy called again. She looked over her shoulder and saw Ruth was already on the phone, calling for help. *How long will it take?*

By the time the ambulance arrived, Amy and Ruth had slid John down onto the floor and put a pillow under his head. He was unconscious, but breathing regularly. As the attendants took him away, Amy knew nothing would ever be the same again.

8

In the Midst Without Harm

Daniel 3:25

1960–1966

By the summer of 1960, Jan had already completed his first year at the four-year secondary school *liceum ogólnokształcące*. For Jan, it had been a good year. At this new school he knew no one and could begin with a clean slate. In addition, he found that the teachers were less likely to harass teenaged students. Jan learned that if he minded his own business and simply showed them what he knew, he would be left in peace.

What worried him now, however, was that Piotrek would soon be starting at Jan's old school. And Jan was afraid for his brother.

For seven long years in primary school, Jan had felt hunted, as if the teachers were always watching the corridors for him, and he had been constantly afraid of being publicly ridiculed. Often he had been punished for imagined infractions, and these punishments had always been physically tiring. Sometimes Jan had been forced to sit with his hands behind his back on benches made for small children. And his teachers had yelled at him repeatedly for using his left hand to write and then for holding his pen incorrectly in the less-coordinated right hand.

Would the early school years be like that for Piotrek?

But Piotrek was more daring than Jan had ever been. He didn't seem afraid of anything. And things were changing; the atmosphere at school and on the streets seemed less tense. Maybe, just maybe, the fear would circumvent his brother.

Piotrek came home from his first day at school with a black

eye. Jan was there when he came in the door. Mamusia was not pleased. "Piotrek, you can't start off like this. All summer your father and I have been hauling you out of fights, and it can't continue when you're at school. You're a big boy now, act like one. Why can't you be more like your brother? Jan never came home with a black eye." Both boys looked at her in surprise.

When she left to run some errands, Piotrek came over to where Jan was sitting, polishing his shoes. He sat down next to him and said nothing for a few moments. Jan waited, hoping Piotrek had not discovered the same hell he had known.

"Jan?"

"Yes, Piotrek."

"Mamusia doesn't understand."

"What doesn't she understand, Piotrek?" Jan held his breath and prayed, *Let him be spared.*

"Well, the boys fight in gangs, the boys from here against the boys from other parts of Poland that have moved here."

"Is that why you got in a fight?"

Piotrek nodded. He wiped his nose with the back of his hand. "There was a boy who talked funny, and Edek downstairs and some of his friends started beating up on him. So I went to help."

"You helped the boy?"

"Of course."

Jan looked at his little brother blinking up at him and thought about how he had tried so hard to stay out of trouble for his parents' sake. He thought maybe there was a chance his prayer would be answered.

"And, Jan?"

"Yes."

"What am I supposed to do when the others are praying to their God Mary?"

"No, Piotrek, she's not a god. She's Jesus' mother, remember? But it's all right. You can pray in your thoughts, quietly. That's what I used to do. Can you do that?"

Piotrek sniffed and nodded. "Did you like school?"

Jan looked at him. Before he could answer, Piotrek said, "I do. I like the teacher and I like the books and I like having my own box of pencils. Do you want to see it? I carved my name on it today."

"Yes, Piotrek. Show me your pencils."

———— ❦ ————

In 1963, when Jan was almost eighteen, he graduated from secondary school. Yet even though he had passed the exams that made him eligible for the university, he was not admitted. There were only so many places, and the system was set up so that workers' and farmers' children with the same qualifications as Jan—not to mention the children of Party members—were admitted ahead of him.

Jan resolved to reapply every year for the next decade if that's what it took. He wanted to become an engineer like his father.

It was Tadeusz who came up with the idea of tutoring Jan at home. That way he could continue his studies and, once admitted, perhaps complete his degree early and make up for the time he had not been allowed into the university.

So Jan settled into a routine of working mornings at the cannery and studying at home the rest of the time. One day in the early spring, he came home from work smelling like fish and was nearly bowled over by his eleven-year-old brother.

"We're going to *Zakopane* for a week!"

Jan laughed and asked his parents, "Is it true?"

Hanna laughed. "I think so. Your father has decided this family needs a vacation. And it's been a few years since the last time we went skiing. I don't want you boys to forget how."

Piotrek had unfolded the map of Poland. Now he pulled Jan down onto one knee. "See, Jan, here. It's in the southernmost tip of Poland, as far away from *Gdynia* as you can go and still stay in the country."

"Well, right you are," Jan laughed. "Somebody's been paying attention at school," he looked up at his parents.

Piotrek was unfazed. "I always pay attention," he said, and then, "When are we leaving?"

———— ❦ ————

That was a week of long walks and much laughter. Sometimes

Jan would take Piotrek for hikes in the woods behind their cabin. Every day the two boys joined their parents skiing. Often the four of them would picnic high in the hills.

Then late one afternoon Jan and his mother volunteered to walk to the village and do the shopping. Jan could hear the bells in wooden churches echoing from valley to valley. Dark clouds cloaked *Giewont*, the peak that looked like a sleeping knight. These were the *Tatry Zachodnie* and *Tatry Wysokie*, the Tatra Mountains. Jan breathed in the biting air. It would snow again that night. To his left the day's last shafts of sun cut through the pines.

In the village they walked by the wooden houses, so different than the endless rows of concrete apartment buildings in Gdynia. "Mamusiu, had you been here before you started coming here with us?" Jan asked.

She stopped in front of the little graveyard and nodded softly. "You ask the strangest questions, my Jasiu." Jan smiled. She hadn't called him that in years. She seemed to be listening to the wind blowing through the pines. "Come, this is a quiet place." She took him inside the graveyard where there was a little bench overlooking the statues and gravestones, all outlined in snow.

"Yes, I passed through here on my way home after the war. It was summer then and there were a thousand shades of green in these mountains." Jan was staring with fascination at the wooden crosses and granite rocks around them. Some newer stones had *Więzień Hitlerowski* carved on them. He knew it meant these had died as Nazi prisoners. He pointed. "Some of these other gravestones are four hundred years old."

Afterward they visited a small café, and Jan ordered *rożki orzechowe*, his favorite pastry in the world. Mamusia sipped her strong coffee, seemingly silenced by her memories.

———— ∾ ————

Jan turned twenty-one in the summer of 1966, almost two years after Tadeusz had finally been awarded his chair at the university. To celebrate, the family decided to invite neighbors and friends from church to a party. Thirteen-year-old Piotrek invited a friend who had taken violin lessons from the same teacher. And Jan asked a few young men and women from his secondary-school days. They all gathered at the shore of one of the lakes out-side Gdynia.

Hanna had been working on the food for their picnic barbecue for more than a week. Marek's *Polski Syrenka* did double duty as catering van and transport from the city for those who couldn't catch the bus. Back and forth the little car went all morning, bring-ing yet more food and friends of the family.

That afternoon there was a point when Jan glanced up from his post at the barbecue, where Hanna had put him to work turn-ing over the sausages and keeping an eye on the potatoes baking in the embers. He looked up and down the beach and saw only people who knew and loved him. He felt that. He saw it in the laughter and the looks, the smiles and jokes. The sunshine spar-kled off the water. Jan had to laugh as he watched his father being pushed off the pier by two five-year-olds.

"Still sorry we made such a fuss over you?" His mother had come up behind Jan and put her arms around him.

"I told you not to. There's no reason."

"And since when do I do what you tell me?" she teased. "Here, give me that fork; you're burning the meat. Go down there and have some fun. It's your birthday. Go on now." She gave him a shove, and Jan gave her a kiss on the cheek. Then, feeling just a bit reluctant, he made his way over to the place where his friends had gathered.

The truth was that all this attention did make him feel a little uncomfortable. He preferred being in the background; the more supportive, silent, and strong role suited him just fine. A part of him balked at the idea of being good enough or interesting enough or noble enough to warrant this kind of attention.

Piotrek was different. Jan looked his brother's way and saw that Marek must have brought Piotrek's violin with the last ship-ment of salad and sausage. A group of some of their neighbors were urging him to play. "It's no different than the noise we hear coming from your home every evening!" they joked. They pulled their towels and blankets a little closer, and soon a little ring of people surrounded Piotrek as he stood tuning his violin.

Jan drew closer with a strange mixture of feelings. The child part of him, so recently set aside, wondered how his little brother always managed to overshadow Jan's few moments in the sun. As he watched Piotrek open his violin case and resin his bow, Jan conceded to himself he did envy Piotrek. He envied his talent on the violin, his easy manner on stage, his good looks and sense of humor, his charm. Surely it was a sad state of affairs for a twenty-one-year-old man to be envious of a thirteen-year-old boy!

And yet, as Piotrek began to play, Jan felt a familiar surge of pride. This was the part of himself he usually acknowledged, the big brother who looked out for the younger boy and delighted in his achievements. Jan firmly believed that no one could bring forth music that touched the soul like his little brother could.

Jan knew the piece. Piotrek had been practicing it for months, eight measures by eight measures. He would not play it now if he did not think he had mastered it.

Jan watched the faces of their friends. The music moved them all; even the children had stopped playing in the water to look toward the group on the beach.

And suddenly Jan was seeing himself—standing there, observing the scene, caught up in the music but still far away. *It's what I always do*, he realized. *I play the role of bystander. I'm the watcher in the family*. And whose choice was that? he wondered.

As Piotrek finished the last movement, Jan moved toward the group. He waited until Piotrek had finished, then joined in the applause as he reached his brother's side. "Thank you. It was beautiful. You couldn't have given me a better gift."

Then Jan turned to the others. He looked them in the faces one by one. *"When I was a child, I thought as a child."* He spoke out loud, for the first time assuming the role of host, "Let the neighbors complain, little brother. I never get tired of hearing you play." When the laughter died down, Jan asked, "Now, who wants to see if they can swim with me to the other side of the lake?"

The crowd cheered, and Piotrek smiled up at him. Jan was thinking, *I might not be able to play the violin like an angel, but I can outswim him any day.*

Jan looked up from his books. They covered the table in the

kitchen corner. He stroked the blond mustache he had been growing for a year.

"What's wrong, Jan?" Hanna stood on the other side of the room ironing. The radio played classical music.

"I don't know. I was just thinking ... wondering...." He asked his mother, "What's wrong? I'm meeting no resistance."

Jan was working days to make some money, continuing his studies in structural engineering with Tatuś's help, and doing independent study to become a pastor.

"Tell me what you mean," his mother said.

"Well, remember when for a while there it seemed so many things were going wrong—misunderstandings among certain members of the church, the secret police harassing us, Tatuś's job, Piotrek's fighting at school. I mean, we almost got used to things going wrong."

Mamusia nodded. "I remember."

"Well, I thought then, as a sort of preventative medicine, that I should start reading twelve pages of the Bible each day instead of six. And now, for the first time in years, no one is bothering me. Being out of school helps, maybe. But it's also true, for the first time in a long time, no one is harassing Tatuś."

He was quiet for a moment. "I mean, I don't want to sound proud. But I do believe in what Tatuś preaches so often, about the gems God gives as a result of trials. So ... what am I doing wrong?"

She came over and stood beside him, gently fingering his hair. Jan was struck by how small she seemed. Even sitting, he was taller than she.

Mamusia said, "Jan, I want you to look at what kind of man you've become. You are deeply rooted in your faith in God. You have been blessed with a willingness to trust, no matter what. That is gift enough. Don't worry about those gems. You have your studies to concentrate on. And believe me," she added, "the resistance will come."

9

RAINS

Genesis 19:24

1960–1969

The stroke had been massive. When John Baker finally came home after his stay in the hospital, Amy and Ruth turned the picture-window corner of the living room into his space. They ordered a new bed, one that could be raised, and they established a daily routine of washing, feeding, and massaging John, according to the doctor's orders. A physical therapist came to the house once a week with new exercises. A nurse came twice a week. Either Amy or her mother were always in the house. They read to John and talked with him and brought him flowers. Together they could lift him out of bed and into the wheelchair. They took him for walks around the farm and left him outside on the porch to enjoy the sights and smells and sounds of the farm.

Ron came over and built a ramp up the stairs of the porch. He said he wasn't going to stop seeing Amy just because she had made a career change from art student to nurse. In fact, he was almost thankful for John's illness.

"I shouldn't be glad," he admitted to her one afternoon when they were finally alone. They had gone for a walk and stopped at their favorite place by the lake. The trees had turned, and above them hung a rainbow of reds and yellows.

"I would never have wished what John is going through on anyone," he added. "But I am so grateful that you're here instead of over in Europe. I'm so very glad that I can keep on holding you in my arms and staring into those pools of dark light that are your eyes."

Amy felt uncomfortable. She didn't think she should be enjoying this. "Since when are carpenters poets?" She tried to make light of the caresses he was giving her and started to pull away.

But Ron would not let her. "I told you I had been a fool not to see sooner what I had." He pulled her even closer.

"I thought we were 'just friends,'" Amy said.

"We can be that and more, if that's what we want. I'm just saying I won't be blind to you a second time."

Amy looked up at his kind face, so tan, so young and caring. He wasn't anything like the boys at her parents' country club. The hands massaging her neck were hard with callouses. She leaned backward, into his arms and sighed. It would be good to love this man, to be loved by him.

Ron is a good man, with a good heart, she told herself, almost as if she needed convincing. Maybe it would be enough.

———— ✑ ————

There was no question now of going to Europe, although Ruth urged her to. "Your father wants you to go," she said, her own mixed feelings clear on her face.

"Right," Amy said. "Well, I don't want it. I don't want to be on the other side of the world in Paris when you need my help." She didn't even mention Poland. That had become a forbidden subject to both of them. Nor did she say what she and Ruth both were thinking. *What if John has another stroke?*

"In fact," Amy said, "I want to give the ticket back."

"No, I won't hear of it," Ruth said in that tone of voice that meant there was no arguing with her. "Cash it in, if you must, and keep the money for something special later on. But we won't take it back. It was a gift, honey." Ruth turned away, and Amy went up to her.

"Don't cry, Mom. Sometimes things don't turn out the way we had planned, but that doesn't mean it can't be good. We're together as a family and that counts for something." Amy was surprised at the comfort her words seemed to bring Ruth.

So autumn became winter. Ruth and Amy worked to take care

of John. And Ron came around more and more often until he, like John, was a focal point in Amy's life. She found herself looking forward to their times together. And slowly she felt herself letting go of fears and doubts and insecurities as Ron's love washed over her. He accepted her, and he wanted nothing more than to love her.

It was Ruth's idea at Christmas that Ron should move in with them. "I daresay the two of you have been very creative in finding ways to get some privacy. But Ron is here so often, maybe it would be a good idea if he gave up the room he rents in town and took one of the upstairs rooms."

Amy could not believe that this was her proper, Boston-raised mother speaking. "Mom, I don't know what to say. Thank you."

Ron almost choked on his steak. "Yes, Mrs. Baker. It's very generous of you and Mr. Baker."

"On one condition, that you call us John and Ruth. And that you have your *own* room. You'll be paying rent." She arched an eyebrow at Ron.

"Yes, of course."

Amy laughed. It would be so good having Ron in the house. It would be good for her and good for Ruth. He could help them with lifting and turning John.

Ron turned into a better nurse than them both. He knew just how to talk to John, who could only respond with his one good eye and grunts. They worked out a system of one- and two-grunt messages so that John could communicate more easily.

That winter Ron was laid off his job, so he kept busy repairing things around the farm. Amy thought more than once that her mother had known exactly what she was doing when she invited him to stay on. He was Amy's boyfriend and Ruth's strong man around the house. Ron didn't seem to mind being either.

By the end of that winter Amy knew she loved Ron deeply. But she also knew she did not want to marry. She hoped he wouldn't pressure her. Her friends at college came home at spring break and told her about the parties, but also about the new dances and rock music. "Everyone says it's okay to just live together. No one is getting married these days," Amy said to Ron.

"Don't be so nervous. I told you I would take you any way I

could get you. I'm just glad we've had these few months together on the farm with your mom. Anything extra is a bonus."

————— ∽ —————

It was Ruth's idea to get Ron a job at John's steel company. All spring he had been looking for work and nothing had materialized. So why shouldn't they use their connections to help get him established in a good job?

Amy had mixed feelings about the offer. It was as if her parents were trying to make Ron into the typical son-in-law, working at the family business. But as long as no one mentioned the *W* word and suggested they marry, Amy kept calm. Besides, Ron liked the idea and after a few weeks, it was obvious to everyone that he had a good head for the business, especially for structural design. He had just never had the training.

The family settled into a routine, with Ruth and Amy continuing their nursing duties, John making painfully slow progress, and Ron working nine to five in the city. Evenings and weekends, he kept himself busy making repairs around the farm. They lived in an easy rhythm, and Amy felt safer and safer in Ron's love.

Every now and then whenever she experienced little twinges of guilt that they were living like man and wife under her parents' roof, she reminded herself that they didn't seem to mind the arrangement. The one time Amy hinted at it, Ruth looked her in the eyes and said, "You're an adult now. Times have changed. That's what *they* say, anyway; these are the sixties. The important thing is that you're happy, even though you're tied down here. I know you could leave anytime you wanted, but you don't. If Ron's presence here makes this period in your life, this decision you've made to stand by us, any easier to bear, who am I to send him away? Besides, he's a good boy."

So in a way, Amy had the blessing she so craved.

There was something else Amy was doing, though, for which she doubted Ruth would give her a blessing. Amy had not discontinued her search for the elusive Jacek Skrzypek. Just because she was tied to home didn't mean she couldn't keep looking for him. Once Ron started working in Boston, Amy gave him shopping lists of offices where he could inquire about her biological father.

They did it together. At first they found nothing, and then as 1961 wore on, Ron started coming home with bits of information. His odd afternoons off were paying off. Slowly both he and she had learned all there was about the city, state, and military bureaucracies.

Their break came when they found Jacek's name on a list of immigrants who had arrived at Ellis Island from Gdańsk, Poland in 1912. Once they had that, they continued the paper search and discovered that Jacek had been a ward of the state until he was eighteen. After that, there were no more records of him. Nothing. Not a high-school diploma, not a social security number, not even any student identification. Despite his description of "student" on Amy's birth certificate, they never once found his name on any list of enrollment belonging to any of the colleges or universities in the Boston area.

The little they found out about Jacek's parents, whose names had been on the immigration forms, told them next to nothing. The mother had died in some accident when her son must have been very young. The father had gone to prison, convicted of manslaughter, and the boy had been shipped out to an orphanage.

There was no listing of where Amy's grandmother was buried, no record of where her grandfather had served his time, no addresses of the foster homes where Jacek had been raised. This absence of information actually told Amy and Ron more than the bits and pieces they *had* managed to find out. It told them that someone in the government did not want Jacek found.

When Amy realized this, it only made her hungrier for an explanation. But there was none. There was nothing. She talked with Ron endlessly about what the possibilities might be. They fantasized about secret missions and cover-ups, but the fact remained: they could move no further.

———— ⌒ ————

They all were waiting. Amy didn't like to think of it, but John's stroke had put them all on hold. *Are we waiting for him to die?* she asked herself. No, but the attention and care he needed was what kept Amy and Ruth at home with him. Ron came and went, bringing them news of the outside world. And Amy noticed that Ruth was not getting any younger either. Privately she decided that no matter how much time her parents still had on this earth, she would make sure it was as pleasant as possible, spent on the farm they both had grown to love so much.

They had given her so much. She loved them so much.

Poland had waited this long. It could wait a little longer.

So another year slipped by, and then another, and nothing seemed to change about Amy's life, although she was aware that things were indeed changing in the world outside. Walter Cronkite told them in the evenings that the nation was undergoing a tumultuous transformation, that the campuses all over America were broiling with discontent. Amy heard from her college-going friends, who were now beginning to graduate, that students were no longer accepting everything that was being taught.

And then the television news started showing them maps of an obscure part of the world called Southeast Asia. Where was Vietnam? That was where the United States was sending her boys.

By this time Amy and Ruth felt so removed from the rest of the world, it seemed unreal that America could be fighting yet another war. Korea was settled—why this now?

In the past year Amy and Ruth had discussed getting more nursing help for John, but both women had decided they would rather just spend the time with John. They needed it. On the two afternoons per week when the nurse was there, Amy and Ruth went shopping or met with friends. But their world revolved around, really, John and his health, his slow progress of recovery, his aging.

And then the Vietnam War reached out its hand from halfway across the world and touched them in a way that took them totally by surprise. Some of Amy's friends from high school were drafted. Soon it seemed that more and more young men were being called to serve in the armed forces overseas.

"They won't want Ron, will they?" Amy asked her father once when they were alone. "You know how the military works, Dad. He's too old, right? And he's working his way up your company.

It's not like he's a student or what they like to call an aimless youth."

John did not grunt an answer. But his eyes told Amy enough.

The notice arrived at their home in 1966: Ron was to report at the local recruitment center. Amy could not believe it. They had spent the last five years loving each other in an easy routine that she had assumed could last forever. John's painfully slow progress had been the focal point of each of their days. Amy had found such relief in Ron's arms, the comfort of every night.

And then he was gone.

Amy didn't understand any of what was happening. She saw one thing on television and heard another from her friends in town. Ron wrote her, but she could tell he was not being honest about what it was like at boot camp and, later, overseas. She knew that because he said nothing about his surroundings, only about his love for her and his fond memories of the farm in autumn.

He came home once in three years. That one visit had been to let her know that he was signing on for another term of duty. Amy could feel the change in him. He was evolving, hardened and hurt by what he had seen and done in Vietnam, distancing himself from her. She was staying in one place, caring for an invalid father and an aging mother, while he was being trained for a world of killing and being killed.

And so it was that when the man stood on their porch, calling through the screen door that he had a telegram. Amy knew what it was.

She had known what it would be when Ron came home so changed and distant.

She knew that he was never coming back.

10

❧

Consumes

Deuteronomy 9:3

1972

I have been looking through these three photo albums as I wrote this. It has taken me several weeks to get my thoughts together enough to share these things in some kind of order. It is the order my own mind has made of my life. The things I remember, the stories I've been told—these are the things that are important to me and so make up who I am.

Here we must have gone to Warszawa on a family trip. There's Stalin's gift to Poland, the great ugly gray tower that my father used to say was a miracle of Stalinist architecture. I'm standing in front of the Palace of Culture and Sciences, holding my father's hand and wearing a sleeveless wool vest.

Mamusia has told us that during the fifties it was not so much the lack of materialistic comforts that disappointed people. They had become used to deprivation during the war. What everyone ached for was a chance to start over. Gomułka had promised them prosperity, but the backbone of the economy was slowly being broken. Even the most basic market principles, such as "those who work hard, get ahead," no longer applied. Poland was slowly waking up to the fact that it didn't matter who the First Secretary was. For the country was being run by forces that had turned the ladder of society upside-down.

Mine workers made more money than office workers or teachers or, for that matter, university professors. Children of laborers received special preference when applying for university or apprentice jobs. Anyone who worked harder or knew more—or anyone who did anything that could be labeled as Western—was the object of discrimination. The rewards went to the ones who only did their jobs, nothing more. The State promised to take care of them with free medical care and a guaranteed pension. But what price did they pay?

Here is a photo of me when I was three and Jan was eleven. I'm dressed in a sailor suit, and he's wearing dark shorts, a jacket, and knee socks. Here he is in the winter with lace-up leather skates, a wool coat with a wide, dark collar, and a thin belt.

The following summer, and this time we're sitting outside with sunglasses on. Tatuś was already balding by then. We're playing with a multicolored beach ball and an orange blow-up lifesaver. Jan has a metal scooter with small wheels.

Here is one of my favorites—Tatuś holding Mamusia, his arms around her, grinning with the waves behind them. It must have been taken at the beach at Sopot.

That was the summer Jan taught me how to write. He made me hold the pencil in my right hand. He said that if I didn't, the teachers at the school would get mad.

"Did they get mad at you?" I asked.

"Yes."

"Did they hit you?" I almost didn't want to ask, but I had to. And Jan nodded.

Then I asked Jan why he didn't say anything to our parents, and he looked away.

"I did once," he said. "Tatuś believed me; he would not believe the lies the teacher told him. Tatuś told me, 'Don't be afraid of people if you have right on your side.'"

Jan said that when Tatuś went to his school, the teachers were afraid of him. That makes sense to me, since most of the teachers were only a few years older than Jan; the older ones had retired or had been fired for not teaching the way the State wanted them to.

"Did the beatings stop after Tatuś went to school?" I asked him.

"The physical beatings did." That was all he said, but his eyes were sad.

I realize now that hypocrisy is hard for a child to understand.

———— ✣ ————

Tatuś always encouraged us to notice what was going on around us, to look at developments. I was looking at developments all right. My *world was changing fast. In 1960 I turned seven, and that autumn I started school. The year earlier, Jan had graduated, something I hadn't counted on. I thought that he would always be there, ready to protect me. Instead, I was seven and very much on my own. Somehow I ended up in a lot of fights. And almost right away my differences with the other boys were highlighted when they all dressed up for their first Holy Communion in white pants and white cassocks and I didn't go.*

During my second year at school, the teacher told us about a giant wall that had gone up that summer and ran right through the middle of Berlin. She said that now there were two Berlins, and that East Berlin was the only good one. The Soviets had liberated the good Germans from the bad Germans in West Berlin. These, according to the teacher, were the Germans who had started the war.

I didn't want it to be so, but in spite of everything, school was important to me. There was one reason for that: music. The schools took care of musical education, and for me this meant the violin. It had been love at first sight when I saw my first violin at the opera in first grade. I begged my parents to let me study the instrument, and they agreed.

I think Tatuś was especially pleased. He loved music, and he could sing a song for any subject, but he had never studied an instrument. Never had the chance to, he said. So he was very happy for me to have the opportunity. He always said jokingly that I got my talent from him.

I began my music studies when I was eight with a quarter-sized violin, learning the scales and the placement of my fingers. Lessons were twice a week for forty-five minutes. In addition, I had lessons about types of music and composers for another forty-five minutes twice a week. We studied Vivaldi and Dvořak, and later we could study composers like Mozart—all the German and Austrians except Wagner. I practiced a minimum of five hours a week and, as I grew older, sometimes fourteen hours. I never complained. This is what I loved best.

It did not take long for me to learn most of what the school teacher knew. Then Tatuś found me a new violin instructor, a man named Paweł, who had invented what he called violin gymnastics. *Paweł had been raised in a privileged background and, as a result, was shunned by the State music schools and worked as a milkman.*

Paweł spoke French and German. Before the war he studied in Germany with the best. He happened to be on scholarship in England when the war broke out. His family was in Vienna at the time, and his sister managed to get out of Austria and join him in London. There she told him about what they feared was happening to the Jews. He said he thought it was terrible, and then she told him that he was a Jew. It sounds crazy, but he had never known this. They were not practicing Jews, and he had just assumed they were nonpracticing Catholic Poles. He felt anything but Jewish. During the war, Paweł converted to Christianity at an English country church after being invited to the altar by an elderly woman. He also joined the British air force, teaming up with other Poles in the RAF and flying to Arnhem instead of Warszawa as they all had dreamt of.

After the war Paweł returned to Poland, but he was immediately blacklisted because he had fought for England. Well, Paweł learned to live with his blackballed status. By the time he became my teacher in 1961, he was working actively in Tatuś's church. He also free-lanced as a translator. He translated everything, even a nine-volume set of Bible commentary. And he was a milkman.

Paweł taught me that to memorize music I had to think in eight-bar sentences. "Play the music until you can hum it without looking, then play it without looking. Then move on to the next eight-bar sentence, then practice, and only then can you play the music." Through this method I can still hum all the notes to the opening movement of Mendelssohn's violin concerto.

This was a man who used to turn bad students into gems. He could practice his magic on anyone but the tone-deaf. I once heard him say to a tone-deaf student, "You had better go play football instead."

I'm telling you about this man because I would say he had the greatest influence on me. He would take the violin into his arms and cradle it like a baby. Then he would begin to play, and it was as if the angels Tatuś was always talking about had come into his small and shabby ninth-floor room. More than anything else, I wanted to play like that.

Paweł told me that the violin was a selfish mistress. "She demands that you stand naked and completely vulnerable before she is willing to surrender her secrets."

In my home, at my parents' prayer meetings, I never took my eyes off of Paweł. He always prayed for the wounds of Poland. And sometimes he played for us. Sometimes he was invited to play at private concerts, despite his lowest status. Then he always ended the concert by requesting no applause, since the song had been dedicated to his Savior, Jesus Christ.

———————— ✑ ————————

I am looking at the photos of a skiing holiday as I write this. There were several times that we went skiing as a family. During one trip, when I was eleven, we went to spend a week in the mountains around Zakopane. I had wooden skis and leather boots with laces. Mamusia is standing proudly next to me. She was a talented sportswoman and, at that time, could ski even better than Tatuś.

That was such a wonderful week. I remember listening to birds and mountain streams, discovering small waterfalls and a huge lake, Morskie Oko, that reflected the changing sky. I remember our family being happy together, with no dark clouds of sickness or fear hanging over us.

And then, when I was thirteen and preparing for my audition to enter the music academy, still a year away, Paweł became so sick that he could no longer play. He gave up teaching but had to continue delivering milk bottles in order to live. I would meet him in the dark dawn, and we would talk together about my preparation for the composition part of the entrance exams for the academy. It was highly unusual they were even allowing someone my age to audition. Students almost always had to complete secondary school and become eighteen or nineteen before they were allowed to try for a place. But Paweł was convinced I had exceptional talent, and the academy was allowing me to compete in my last year of primary school. This was all thanks to Paweł.

But one morning he was not there to meet me. I ran to his block of apartments and up to his room. The door was not locked. I found him bent over plans for a new church building he and Tatuś had been working on. He was dead. Gone.

At his funeral Tatuś spoke about Paweł's life being like a bright flame that burns out after a short time. "Better that," he said, "than a smoldering flame like the lives of some Christians, which only produce a lot of smoke." And then I think he looked at me. I don't know.

That was a hard time because of Mamusia's sickness. I think it was about two years earlier, during the summer when I was eleven, that Mamusia first became very ill. My favorite photo in all three books was taken just a few short weeks before that. It is one of Tatuś and Mamusia during the summer of 1964. His gray tufts of hair are sticking out above his ears. *They're staring at each other, laughing. Looking back as I can now, it seems so unfair that they had no idea what was ahead of them.*

Later that same summer Mamusia left for Germany to visit a cousin there. This was somebody she had grown up with in Kraków and who used to belong to her church there. It was still quite special at that time to be able to leave Poland. My parents had heard that the government was granting passports to people who could produce an invitation from someone in the country they wanted to travel to. They had to state where they were going and for how long. There was also the condition that the one traveling leave immediate family behind, a good incentive to return to Poland, and carry only the equivalent of ten dollars. Mamusia decided to apply for such a passport. She was thrilled when she was granted it, even though it arrived with the stipulation that she turn it back in to the government upon her return to Poland. Travel was limited, but at least it was becoming possible.

So Mamusia went to Germany. You have to understand that this was 1964, and we were only just starting to hear about the differences between our side of the Iron Curtain and yours.

Well, Mamusia was thoroughly shocked by what she encountered on that first trip out of Poland since the end of the war. To start with, she had expected East Germany to be much better off than Poland. That's what our news programs had told us, anyway, that Poles should strive to be as patriotic as the East Germans. In other words, our neighbors the East Germans were supposed to be better communists and, as such, were enjoying greater rewards.

But this wasn't at all true. As the train traveled through East Germany, Mamusia was lucky enough to sit next to a woman who was willing to talk as long as they were the only ones in the compartment. This woman told her how jealous many East Germans were of the Poles. "At least you are allowed to travel out of your country now. I will never live to see my brother in München." When Mamusia told her how difficult it was to trust anyone back home, this woman sighed and said it was the same in East Germany. "I think half the country must be working for the Stasi." And she knew nothing of the so-called rewards she was supposed to be enjoying as a citizen of East Germany.

When Mamusia crossed the border into West Germany, it was not the heavy border security with watch towers and soldiers walking everywhere with guns over their shoulders that shocked her. No, it was the affluence she encountered on the other side. She felt privileged enough to be traveling abroad at all. But when she finally arrived at her cousin's, she could not believe that they had not one car, but two! And a television, and a washing machine, and a large house with two gardens, front and back, all for themselves.

When Mamusia asked her if all this was normal, her cousin said yes. When Mamusia went with this cousin to their church, she was shocked at the prayers for prosperity she heard. She told me all this later, when she was in the hospital. She said that she was so upset by this trip that she did a stupid thing on the train trip home; she tried to lift down her heavy bag from the luggage rack alone. Her arm gave way, her leg gave way, and she crumpled to the ground, where another passenger found her.

When Mamusia came home, she went into the hospital for tests. And she didn't come out for another half-year, just before my twelfth birthday. When she came back, she was never the same. She never could ski again like she did the times we went to the mountains. After my twelfth birthday, I never saw Mamusia do any sport but swimming again.

When she came home from the hospital, she was paralyzed on one side. Yet it wasn't a stroke. There was a lot of talk about an unknown disease and wrong treatments. Mamusia accepted it all, and I just became more and more angry. How could she be so weak not to fight this thing? How could her God let her be struck down like that?

She used to say, "I'm so thankful for this hand because, before long, it will go to sleep like the other." And this would make me so mad. But I couldn't let her see my anger because it would only upset her worse, and she barely had enough energy for getting up and moving around the apartment every day.

Now, seven years later, I can see that all that time she was fighting— she was actually battling for her life. This is something I still don't completely understand, although I'm getting closer. You see, after that attack in 1964 and all those months in the hospital, the doctors finally decided what was wrong with Mamusia. She told us what she had one day soon after she came back from the hospital. With the radio blaring I heard the words multiple sclerosis, and I didn't know what it meant.

Already at twelve, I was taller than she was. Tatuś was kneeling at her feet with his face in her lap, and I've never seen him looking so weak. She held out her good arm for Jan and me and said, "We should give thanks and not discuss everything so much, see the positive side more." I think she could see my rage, and it used to frustrate her. She didn't know what to do with me.

"Listen to me," she said. "We will keep on going for our walks. We will keep on swimming. We will keep on living as we have been, with the Lord's strength keeping us going from day to day. Can you do that for me?" Jan and I nodded, but I was too mad to believe her promise that acceptance would bring peace.

Sometimes when Mamusia didn't know what to do with my moods, she would say, "You children should not have as many choices, and no rewards. That way you can learn about the power of acceptance." This acceptance is something I still have not mastered, as you well know.

In some ways this period in my life was even stranger than my childhood. Outwardly things seemed to be going better for us. Tatuś was finally granted his own chair at the university in 1965. I did well at school whenever I chose to study, but it was the violin that had stolen my heart. I spent those years exploring the challenge of playing well, under the demanding tutelage of Paweł.

But inwardly we were suffering with Mamusia, and I was restless. Tatuś insisted that we live in a disciplined way, with set times for our chores and homework and my hours of practicing the violin. He's not a strict man, though, and has a soft heart. He used to cough whenever it was time for me to stop talking about what I wanted and listen to him. There are many people who come through our home talking about Christianity, but Tatuś is a man who actually does something by caring for the people who need it most. Whenever he sees dishonesty, he is sharp and not afraid. When he sees need, he is tender.

I spent most of my last year of school dreaming of my future life as a concert violinist. I had sworn to myself after Paweł's death that I would honor his name. When he died I was already working on the piece I would perform for the entrance concourse for the music conservatory. It was a piece by Beethoven, his Concerto Number 9 in D Minor. This was my ticket to fame.

I did nothing but practice during those months. The audition was set for January of 1968. I was due to turn fifteen a month later and then graduate at the end of that school year. At that time I was conducting the school orchestra. I worked too hard, slept too little, and fought too often. I was a loner, with no friends. Yet despite the fact that I was often laughed at for, among other things, my dream of making it as a violist, I was the one my class elected as president. And I was also voted best student of the graduating class.

It was quite something to win that prize. My parents said I was being rewarded by the Lord. They said they had enjoyed similar rewards despite the persecution that still hung over us in the form of surveillance by the milicja. "Cast your bread upon the waters," they said to me, "for after many days you will find it again."

I took this to mean that we should all take a chance. I have tried to learn this lesson.

Later that same year the students rioted in Warszawa. Of course, the state media only referred to it all as problems caused by "revisionists," "Zionists," and other "troublemakers," but Jan was working there, and when he came home he would tell us about it. We did hear on the news, though, about the student protests and riots in America. The radio announcers said this was because young people in America could no longer stomach the imperialist system. Jan, though, had heard other things about America. He told us words we had never heard, like flower power and hippies.

America seemed like another planet at the time. But looking back I can see that the tremors going through your land actually did reach out and touch us.

Those spring riots marked the end of Tatuś's persecution at the university. The rioting actually accomplished something. It brought about the very changes my parents had been praying for so long with no results. To me, that said something important.

It was becoming easier for Western missionaries to visit us, and they did, sometimes (as you know) bringing the Bibles Tatuś had spent so many years praying for, but too often bringing worthless things and even more worthless advice about how Polish Christians should solve their problems and live according to the Western ways.

Something new that did appeal to me was what we called the tape ministry. Some of these missionaries brought tapes of sermons and lectures, Christian music, and recorded parts of the Bible; we translated them and made countless copies. These were especially useful for people who were cut off from our meetings, either by the milicja or by distance.

So I did my part, you see. I spent countless hours recording the Polish version of American sermons in my back room.

And all this time I kept on practicing. I wanted to live up to Paweł's memory and to better myself. I was taking my chance, casting my bread upon the waters, hoping it would return to me something better than this life we have lived so long.

Tatuś insists on believing that this persecution we have all grown so warped under is actually treasure in disguise, given by God during trials. When I was little, I used to believe there was a treasure chest with my name on it in heaven. But I have seen my brother beaten in the name of that God. My family has suffered too much for what they believe, so I do not believe as they do, even though I love my brother and my parents. I would die for them.

Dear, dear Paweł was important because he taught me about vision and discipline. He brought out the talent in me, something everyone who heard me agreed was tremendous. But then, a little over a year after Paweł died, I auditioned for the conservatory. I seemed aimed at a target I could not miss, one of fame and fortune, concerts and recognition. There was no stopping me. Despite the four-to-five-year age difference between me and the other contestants, I won first place. I could see my life unfolding.

And then we received a letter stating that my place would be given to a student of more deserving background. There were only so many openings.

I got the message. Because my father had gone to prison, because my parents were not Party members, because my family was different, I needn't apply again.

Paweł gave me a dream. My father's God took it away.

11

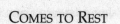

COMES TO REST

Acts 2:3

1968

Jan had not wanted to leave. He tried his best to shrug off the fear, the worry. But the sight of his parents waving good-bye with Piotrek standing between them haunted Jan all the way to Warszawa.

Piotr, not Piotrek, Jan reminded himself. His brother had turned fifteen just a week earlier and didn't want anyone calling him Piotrek anymore. Jan had to smile. His baby brother was finally growing up. The entire family was charged with the excitement of what this year might bring Piotr. He would graduate from school—quite possibly as head of his class. Best of all, he played the violin like an angel, and a month ago he had auditioned for the conservatory, where he was almost guaranteed a place, despite his young age. *He deserves it. Piotr's worked so hard.*

Jan thought of when his parents had prayed with him that morning, back in Gdynia. His father had laid hands on him, a new sensation for Jan. "We're sending you off as a sojourner, not in a strange land, but to a strange city. Be open to the vision God gives to young men." His father's blessing still rang in Jan's ears as he looked out the window, watching the frozen farmland roll by.

A few weeks earlier he had argued with his parents about this trip, and now that the time had come, he still did not feel right about going. It was not often that they disagreed with each other.

"Jan, it's time. You know that. You're twenty-two, and it will be good for you to get out on your own. Except for a few camping

129

trips with boys from the church, you've never been away from home," his mother said.

"That's not true," he objected. "What about the summer when I went to that secret youth camp outside of Moscow?"

"When I was one of the counselors? I don't think that counts," Tadeusz said. "No, Jan, every man needs some time away from his parents in order to better know who he is."

"I *know* who I am," Jan answered quietly.

His father took his hands and said just as firmly, "I know. But this is still something that needs to happen, especially now that the opportunity has presented itself. Besides, you'll be doing Marek a personal favor. The pastor of the church you're going to help in War-zawa is a friend of his. Your mother and I have been wanting you to get some time living by yourself, and now you'll have the chance to work as an assistant pastor for someone other than your father."

"Someone else can help him," Jan argued. "You and Mamusia need my help here. Neither of you is as strong as you used to be."

His father coughed, and Jan knew that signaled the end of the discussion. But he still wasn't finished. "You tell me I'm twenty-two and that you're concerned for me. Then listen to me as an adult. *I cannot leave you two.* Not now, not when you're building the new church building—there's too much happening this year. And not the way your health is deteriorating." He hated saying it. His father never would admit he was growing weaker, but maybe hitting them over the head with the truth was the only way to convince them.

His father's steely gaze gripped Jan as he said slowly, "No. You go."

End of discussion.

Now that he was finally on his own, all Jan could think of was how fragile Mamusia and Tatuś had looked next to healthy young Piotr. Jan had tried repeatedly during the last week to change their minds as he packed his things, but they would not listen. How could he enjoy this so-called independence they had forced upon him when all he could do was worry about how they would man-age to run the church and their household without his help.

There was one area he hoped he could still help them in and that was financial. Jan counted on finding a job in Warszawa that paid better than his cannery job. Then he could send money home and at least not have to worry how they would make ends meet. In addition, Jan hoped to spend some time in the engineering library of the university, doing some research to supplement his studies with his father.

When the train pulled into Warszawa, Jan was already waiting at the door, his trunk on his shoulder. As he disembarked, Jan caught sight of a middle-aged stranger approaching a little hesitantly.

"You are Jan Piekarz?"

"Yes. You must be Reverend Otak."

"Please, call me *Krzysztof*." A cheerful smile lit the round, weather-chapped face with its grizzled mustache. "I am so pleased you have come to join us. Marek tells me you are quite capable." They shook hands, and Jan noticed the cracked, reddened hands, the patched clothing. What had Marek told him? That the man had a big family and an even bigger congregation. And also that the secret police harassed Krzysztof and his family much more than they had Jan's own family, probably because this was Warszawa, and the SB was even more active in the capital than in Gdynia.

"I've found you a room," Krzysztof said as they walked out of the station. "It's not much, but the price is quite reasonable. It belongs to a brother who had to take care of a sick mother in the south. It's quite close to here, so we can walk."

Jan was relieved. This took care of item number-one on his list of things to do—a place to stay. Jan sidestepped a pile of coal in the middle of the sidewalk. The city hadn't changed much since the last time he had visited with the family. When they reached the building, Krzysztof nodded at the old woman sweeping the sidewalk in front of the door. She bent over her bundle of twigs as if she had never done anything else in her life.

The building was old and the staircase stank. He shared a bathroom with the rest of the hall, but his room was clean, though shabby, with a bed and a table and no room left for anything else. And it was heated.

He took the key from Krzysztof with a bow of thanks. "You will have to tell me what you expect of me, how I can help. Then I will try to find a job that does not take away from the church's needs."

The pastor's kind face took on a worried look. "Jan, I'm afraid it won't be that easy. Half the country seems to have moved to Warszawa with the hope of finding work. Do you have enough to live on for a little while?"

Jan nodded, and Krzysztof's face again lit up with a smile.

"Good. Now, don't worry, my boy. Tonight, you'll come to my home for dinner. And we will have plenty of time to talk about what you can do and how you can help."

———————— ⌒ ————————

The hot water steamed. Jan noticed as he poured it into the old dishpan that the rust color came from the water, not the pan. And it smelled curiously more like the toilet than water from the tap. Jan didn't want to think about it. He had boiled the water and that should make it safe enough. Jan gingerly worked his aching feet into the hot water, then sighed and wiggled his toes.

"Poor feet," he said with a wry smile. "You are the ones who work the hardest these days."

For it was on foot that Jan was learning his way around Warszawa. He walked to restaurants and hospitals applying for cleaning jobs, he walked to the homes of church members who were sick or lonely, he walked to lessen his homesickness and concern for his family in Gdynia. And he walked to ease his troubled heart, for as the days became weeks and he still had not found work, he realized he might have to return to Gdynia a relative failure, unable to support himself.

He was living on boiled water and potatoes—hardly a soup, but he could not afford anything else. Food prices had gone up yet again. In the lines where Jan stood to apply for work and buy his meager groceries, Jan often heard discontented grumblings and whispered arguments.

Jan's restlessness had little to do with the food supply, however. He was more concerned with finding the work God had sent him to Warszawa to do. Daily he prayed and searched in himself for the vision his father had spoken of, but no answers seemed to come.

He knew that helping others often distracted from more pressing problems, so he threw himself into the parish work Krzysztof showed him. He took over half the preaching and did more visiting than Krzysztof, who had his large family to care for.

Jan had learned that Krzysztof worked most nights as a dish-washer in one of the finer hotels. The money, together with his wife's wages from her job as a switchboard operator, was enough to support their four children. That's what Krzysztof claimed anyway.

The government claimed zero unemployment; supposedly, there were jobs for everyone. It was even obligatory for men to work. Jan knew the propaganda as well as anyone. But the reality of earning enough to live on was different.

Krzysztof was lucky. Many others were not so fortunate. And Jan was haunted that he had almost nothing to share. Everything in the city seemed more dilapidated than in Gdynia. Some of the elderly he visited lived in run-down apartment buildings like his own. The rooms were clean as far as they could make it so, but the buildings were infested with cockroaches and rats and cursed with bad plumbing.

As he familiarized himself with the city, Jan began to notice that at night there were always certain women standing in the doorways of the more expensive hotels. Their empty eyes haunted him. He asked Krzysztof about these women one night as he walked the older man to the hotel where he worked.

"Those are the prostitutes, Jan, waiting for the Western businessmen or Party elite. They at least have found work," Krzysztof said.

Jan felt foolish, naïve. He should have guessed. And yet those empty eyes would not let him go.

"Has anyone tried to reach out to them?"

"From our church? No. Ah, Jan, you can see for yourself we have a hard enough time taking care of our own. Now, what was it you wanted to talk with me about? Have you had any luck finding work?"

"No, and I'm afraid if something doesn't come up in the next week, I will have to go back to Gdynia."

"It's a pity, I need your help. In the month since you've arrived I've started feeling like a father to my children again, and not at the expense of my congregation. You truly are a born pastor; half the old ladies in my church are in love with you. I'm sure your father misses you. If you do go back, I will miss you terribly. . . ."

Krzysztof stopped abruptly and clapped Jan on the shoulder.

"We'll give it a week, then," he said briskly. "By then we should have a better feel for whether the Lord wants you here or back home." His voice softened. "And I will continue praying for you, Jan."

Setting a deadline seemed to help Jan's anxiety. He woke up the next morning with a renewed vigor and anticipation. *What you need to do*, he told himself, *is to act on your prayers. Act as if you'll be staying in Warszawa, and let the Lord tell you otherwise if that's the wrong course of action.*

If he couldn't find a job, he reasoned, he would study. Studying to become a pastor, studying for an engineering degree he would never be granted, looking for a nonexistent job—they all seemed equally unlikely to yield results and so equally worthy of his time. He set out for the university to inquire where the engineering library was.

Three days later Jan was coming out of one of the libraries when he ran into a group of students carrying banners and signs.

"It's happening around the world!" They didn't even seem to notice the rain.

"What do you mean?" He fell into step with one of them. He turned up his collar and tucked the books inside a plastic bag to keep them dry.

"Students are protesting all over the world. In America they've been demonstrating for four years already. And in Czechoslovakia, they're throwing the Russians out of Prague!"

Jan stopped still, the rain pouring down his face. A tiny shred of hope tickled at the back of his mind. Was it possible? Was the time of persecution coming to an end? Was this how his parents had felt at the end of the war and again in 1956, hardly daring to hope?

He ran to catch up with the students. "Wait! Tell me more." Jan came alongside the same young man, a lanky fellow with a wisp of a beard. "How come I haven't heard about any of this?"

"You think they'd advertise this in the State media? But it's true. Haven't you noticed the nervous tone of the commentaries in *Trybuna Ludu*? The official newspaper wouldn't give it so much attention if it didn't pose such a threat. They can't jam all the foreign stations. Most of the time Radio Free Europe gets through. Don't you have a radio?"

"No!" Jan shouted over the crowd. They were picking up more people as they went, and not just students either. The excitement enveloped them all.

"I'm Jan," he said.

"Bogdan. Today we're going to change history, Jan. If they can do it in Prague, we can do it in Warszawa. You wouldn't believe what's happened there. Free press, freedom of speech, people speaking out against the government openly, criticizing the Party, proposing democratic measures. We can do it here, too."

"Freedom of worship," Jan said softly, almost wonderingly, but no one heard him.

The crowd was laughing and clapping. Jan turned around and saw a woman hanging out of a top floor window behind them, waving a Polish flag. She had carefully painted a crown over the eagle's head. Some people beside Jan began singing the Polish national anthem, and others joined in. Soon they were walking and singing with one voice, certain lines ringing out above the others:

> Poland is not yet lost
> So long as we still live,
> *Jeszcze Polska nie zginęła*
> *Póki My żyjemy.*

> That which alien force has seized
> We at swordpoint shall retrieve. . . .
> *Co nam obca przemoc wzięła*
> *Szablą odbijemy. . . .*

Jan had never felt this way before. He was buoyant, almost lightheaded, swept forward by the power of the emotions around him. *Is it true? Is it really true?* he kept asking himself.

They turned down a corner and met another group of students marching. Another cheer went up as their numbers doubled. They marched down streets lined with women and children, and everywhere Jan looked people were smiling and waving at them, hanging out of windows, standing in doorways, children clapping their hands. Even the rain had stopped.

And then, so far away that it seemed almost to come from the back of his mind, Jan heard an explosion of some kind. He ignored it until another just like it went off again, this time closer and louder.

The people around him looked as puzzled as he felt. "What was that?"

"Did you hear it, too?"

The cheering was not so loud now, and they walked more slowly, as if waiting for something.

"Bogdan, what do you think?"

"I don't know." He hesitated, then said in a quieter tone, "We were warned not to protest, but no one took it seriously. . . ."

Screams came from farther up in the crowd, then from behind them, then another explosion, closer this time. Bogdan grabbed Jan's arm and pulled him toward the edge. "C'mon, my room is close by here. There's trouble. Follow me!" he called to the students around them.

"Bogdan has a place to hide!"

"Hurry!"

And then Jan heard the word he knew too well already. "ZOMO!"

Since the early 1960s, the heavily armed Motorized Detachments of the Citizens' Milicja, or ZOMO squads, had acted as an iron fist for the all-pervasive Security Service, the SB. The ZOMO squads were first on the scene of surprise arrests. They were also in charge of roadblocks and patrolling the streets for illegal meetings. To Jan, their appearance at this time could mean only one thing. The SB had a special interest in crushing the student underground.

"There are ZOMO up ahead with guns!" The crowd panicked and turned, running into itself. Jan and a few other men and women dashed after Bogdan as he flew down a side street and up a flight of stairs. When the last one entered the room, he locked the door.

As spontaneous as the joy of a few moments earlier was the dark fear that now clutched their hearts. Jan looked around the cramped room and recognized the face of fear in the expressions of the strangers around him. "Everyone," Bogdan said, "this is Jan. You are, uh, a graduate student?"

Jan smiled inwardly. "Yeah, sort of."

"Does anyone have a camera?"

"I do," one of the girls said.

"Then get over by the window and see if you can get some shots of what's going on out there," Bogdan said.

A leader, Jan thought. Bogdan was trying to haul a shortwave radio out of its hiding place under the bed. Jan hurried to help, and Bogdan had it set up and running in a moment.

"Can you understand English?" Jan nodded. "RFE has a Polish broadcast, but it's only at certain times. The English news is more detailed. Last night they said that NATO would defend the cities of Eastern Europe; all we had to do was protest like we did today. They said they had saved Berlin, and they pledged to protect Prague in the same way. Students in Prague called out to their brothers and sisters in Warszawa and Budapest for solidarity. They said, 'Rise up, fear not; you will be remembered.' They said, 'Unite!'"

What had begun as an explanation for Jan ended as a rousing speech addressed to the rest of the room. Bogdan fiddled with the dials for a few moments, then said to Jan, "Now you can hear for yourself how we're all part of the same movement."

The announcer's voice filled the room, a strong American accent singing out the names of nations:

> America, France, and Great Britain call on the brave men and women of Prague, Warszawa, and Budapest. All the world joins you in hoping the day has finally dawned when the Iron Curtain will be shredded to pieces.

Bogdan held up a hand, but the room had already grown quiet. Slowly, as if he didn't believe the words himself, Bogdan translated them for the rest in the room, his voice a faint echo of another world, home to ideas so foreign it was hard to find the matching phrases:

> We repeat, throughout all of Eastern Europe students are rising up in protest against the Soviet aggressor. Claim back your freedom! Freedom to choose your own government, freedom to speak out, freedom to meet in the open, freedom to protest, freedom of the press. Claim back what is rightfully yours! The downtrodden people of Poland, Czechoslovakia, and Hungary will not be overcome! The Prague pro-

test will spread across the whole of Europe! Your Western brothers and sisters salute you!

Bogdan had stopped translating. Despite the ongoing radio voice, a silence seemed to hang in the room. Then some began to murmur, "What has happened to our protest?"

"Why are we hiding like this?"

"Where is the military support they promised us?"

Fear became indignation, became anger. Bogdan turned off the radio and stood up. He waited until he had everyone's attention, then began quietly, "We all tasted it today, my friends. We tasted freedom. You heard them. They're waiting for us to initiate the change. What our parents were too weak to do, our generation will achieve. We must throw the communists out! Throw the Russians out!"

His voice had risen quickly and now reached a pitch as the others joined in. And only at that moment did Jan realize he was in the presence of a professional. Bogdan was no ordinary student, and he was probably more than a student leader.

Some of those in the room were nodding with Bogdan. Most were just caught up in the chant. Jan took a good look around as the hair along his spine began to tingle.

Give it a name. Hatred. That was what filled the space. Jan realized suddenly that these people were venting a hatred so real he could smell it.

"Leave Poland for Poles!"

"No more Russians!"

"Down with the communists!"

He stood quietly and made his way through the crowded room toward the door. Bogdan broke off and nodded at one of the other men, who took over the chant without missing a beat. "You're leaving us?"

"Yes, I have to get to work." Jan had promised a certain old woman whose eyes were cloaked by cataracts that he would read to her that afternoon. But that wasn't the reason he had to get out of that room.

Bogdan grabbed his arm again. His grip was far more powerful than his scrawny arms would indicate. "Jan, I'm glad we ran into each other. We marched yesterday, and they tried to stop us. We marched today—you were there. We'll march tomorrow. They won't be able to stop us. Join us again, will you? You know where I live now. You're welcome anytime. By the way, what are you studying?"

Caught off guard, mesmerized by Bogdan's charisma in spite of himself, Jan answered simply, "Engineering."

"Okay. We'll see each other again, then. Be careful out there." Then Bogdan raised a clenched fist in a silent salute. As Jan descended the stairs to the alley, he could hear the students singing the anthem again. How were the words different now than when he sang them on the street?

Once outside, Jan was struck by the emptiness and the silence. He saw no one. The shop doors were closed. The only sign of the demonstration that had passed through here a half hour earlier was a pile of broken placards heaped against a wall. Jan went to find his old lady, not quite sure what had happened that day. They had heard no gunshots as they hid in Bogdan's room.

———— ⌒ ————

"Jan, Jan—are you in there? Wake up now. . . ."

Jan woke to the sound of Krzysztof's voice calling his name from the other side of the door. He was knocking softly, and as Jan shook himself he understood why. The sliver of sky he could see through the edge of his window was just turning blue with the dawn; daylight was still an hour or two away. Krzysztof didn't want to risk waking any of the neighbors.

As soon as he let the older man in, Jan could see his face was flushed. His clothing smelled like cigarette smoke, and he had rings under his eyes, but he was stroking his mustache fast and furiously. "What is it?" Jan asked.

"Today's your deadline."

After a confused moment Jan remembered. It had been a week since they had talked about the possibility of Jan's leaving Warszawa. With the previous day's events, he had forgotten. "Yes?" he asked tentatively.

"Oh, it's quite a story, but I've come here to tell you our prayers have been answered, and just in time! You know about the student demonstrations this week?"

"Yes."

"Well, a man I work with was arrested last night. He was one of the leaders of the protest. Anyway, his job is open, and tomorrow there'll be a line as long as this street to fill it, but my manager says if I say a good word for you and bring you back with me now and you can start work this morning. . . ." His smile said the rest.

Jan was suddenly very awake. "I can be ready in ten minutes!" For once, seeing as it was 4:30 in the morning, he didn't have to wait for the bathroom.

It was dirty, sweaty work, standing hour after hour in the steaming hotel kitchen and scraping the greasy leftovers from other people's plates, but Jan was thrilled with his job. For the first time in his life he would be earning a living, his own. He didn't know how Krzysztof could possibly support a family on such a wage; he knew he would only manage to send half back to Gdynia. But he would be able to send something. He would have enough to eat, to pay his meager rent. He could stay in Warszawa and continue his work and his study.

The only news on the television about the student unrest blamed it on "Zionists" and "counterrevolutionaries." Jan joined the rest of Poland in praying that the Czechs might be more successful than the Poles had been. Just the fact that Moscow's *Pravda* was running articles about events in Czechoslovakia showed that the Czechs had the Russians' attention. But when the paper's commentaries started denouncing the Czechs' continued reclamation of freedom, Jan knew the Russians were getting nervous. In Poland, meanwhile, the shouts of protest had weakened and, with the arrests, finally been wiped out.

During that first week of work, Jan could not get the sights and sounds of the demonstration out of his mind. Over and over again, standing at his post in the noisy kitchen, he remembered details of that afternoon—the faces in the crowd, the sound of many marching feet, the panic as the gunfire sounded, Bogdan's heroic leadership, so naturally assumed. He remembered what Krzysztof had said about how Jan's job had come to be open, and he felt a twinge of guilt about having a job at the expense of someone now condemned to a cell inside the Warszawa *Mokotów* Prison. Had Bogdan been caught as well? he wondered.

One thing became clear to Jan over the next few weeks. There were no more open protests, but the murmurs continued. In the kitchen Jan often heard people mumbling about the Russians, and the same sense of hate rose up and hit Jan in the face, the power of the emotion often overwhelming him. Obviously, you didn't have to be an educated protester to hate the Russians. This had become Poland's national pastime.

Jan thought on these things as he stooped over the stainless steel sink. His days were now overfull. He worked four days, trading off whenever necessary with Krzysztof for the night shift. On Saturdays, if it was especially busy, the waiters shared their tips with the dishwashers, and then he had more than enough to send home and still give a few anonymous gifts to his favorite old ladies. Their widows' pensions didn't cover the cost of food, let alone their other expenses.

All this time, Jan had been following his father's instructions, praying for vision. He was here, and he was working, but there had to be more. Krzysztof told him there couldn't be more, that he was already carrying a heavier load than most pastors. He also said Jan had a way with the elderly; he called it a gift, the way Jan could listen and make them laugh during these difficult times.

It was through the words of his almost-blind friend that Jan first caught a glimpse of the vision he had been searching for. She was telling him about the war, and he had told her the story of how his parents had found each other in the midst of war-torn Kraków in time for him to be born. So they had shared secrets, and then she said, "It is strange how difficult I find it to forgive the Russians. When the war was over, I could forgive the Germans, even with all the terrible things they did. But when I heard what happened here last week, I . . ."

Not for the first time, Jan felt that it was not he who was doing the ministering. He searched for the right words, a warmth of understanding connecting him with the nearly blind woman sitting across from him.

He reached for her hands, and she clenched his tightly. He said, "It is hard to forgive the Russians perhaps because . . ." he paused, and the words came of their own accord, "the war isn't over." Then he thought about what he had just said. It was a dilemma that gripped the entire country. "Yes, it is a war, isn't it?" he asked.

"Ah, Pastor Jan, you ask *me* these things? If it is a war, what are we to do with our enemies?"

Pray for them. The answer rang through Jan's consciousness as sure and pure as a church bell across mountain pastures. "Shall we pray, Sister Emma?"

They prayed then, and as they did so, Jan remembered the many, many times his own parents had taught him to pray for his enemies, to pray as Jesus had. It was strange how he had never thought to apply that lesson since arriving in Warszawa.

This began the process. Jan began trying to pray consistently for the Russians—first as a people, then as individuals, for the mothers, the poor, the men wanting to provide for their families, the sons like him who were searching for vision. It was easy to pray for the Christians in Russia, some of whom he had met at camp when he was young. It was harder to pray for the politicians, for the police, for the work camp commanders who had killed his grandfather and caused his father so much suffering. But even these, in time, Jan began to see with new eyes, as lost men in need of Christ. Sometimes he was amazed to see how much his thoughts were changed by the very act of praying.

Months passed as the Prague protest became the Prague Spring. As Poland waited and watched, the change that had eluded its own student protestors seemed miraculously within the grasp of its southern neighbor. The anticipation gripped the entire country. Jan never mentioned any of this, however, when he wrote letters home or made his occasional calls from the main post office.

It was during one of his phone calls that he heard the deep disappointment in his mother's voice when she told him about Piotr's rejection from the music academy in June.

"Mamusiu, I'm coming up for a visit."

"What!"

As usual, the line was terrible. He threw his voice into the crackling static. "I'm coming up for a visit. It's been half a year. I'll be there for the weekend of my birthday!"

There was a sudden silence, then Hanna said, "Yes, dear, I

think that would be a good idea. Your brother needs you."

And so do you and Tatuś.

Then the line broke. But it was all right. He knew enough. *Something else to pray about.*

The day Jan was due to visit Gdynia, he noticed a crowd hovering around the kiosk outside the train station. He wondered what could be going on of such interest, so early in the day. As he stepped toward the group, a sense of foreboding stole over him as Jan noticed the shocked expressions on the faces coming nearer to him. Then Jan stopped and looked where they were looking, at the headlines of the morning paper. *Czechoslovakia aided by the armies of the five states of the Warszawa Pact.*

"This shame. Poland will never outlive this shame," he heard an old man mumble beside him.

Jan looked at him so sharply, the man must have thought he worked for the government. Jan could see regret for having spoken out loud pass over his face. He turned quickly and walked swiftly away.

In shock, Jan bought the paper and ran to catch his train. Only once he was sitting in the compartment did he dare to read the whole article. Even allowing for the State's distortion of the truth, the usual dose of misinformation, the fact could not be ignored: The Prague Spring had been crushed as tanks rolled in and occupied the city. And Poles had helped in this move to choke the movement for freedom in Czechoslovakia.

When Jan returned home, he could sense right away that the drastic changes in his family seemed to mirror the emotions of the nation. Hope and excitement had been wiped out by deep disappointment and frustration. Piotr refused to talk about the audition. His practicing no longer filled the apartment with music. A heavy silence hung over them all.

On his first night back home, Jan had a hard time avoiding Piotr's questions about the student protests in Warszawa. "Did you meet any of the leaders? What was it like? Did you march, too?"

It took all of Jan's self-control to lie to his brother as he lay in the dark room, again in his childhood bed. "No, I was stuck in libraries the whole time and didn't even know it was happening until I got my job and heard about the protests from one of the cooks." Jan had no doubt whatsoever that people like Bogdan were the last thing Piotr needed at this stage in his life. Their anger matched his too closely.

Piotr had enrolled in a three-year carpentry training center instead of the pre-university secondary school Jan had attended. When he finished, he would be able to find work as a carpenter. But he would never be allowed into a university because the carpentry course did not end with the *matura*, the final exam required for entrance into the university. And Piotr absolutely refused even to try applying again for a place at the music academy. He no longer practiced; in fact, he would not even look at his violin. He had ordered his parents to sell it.

Jan thought grimly that, against all odds, his brother had managed to limit his own future even more than others had. He knew Piotr. A school like this would only augment his boredom and frustration.

The morning after his arrival, Jan took advantage of Piotr's absence to see how his parents really felt about Piotr's disappointment.

"Of course we were surprised. . . ." his mother began.

"I never dreamed our ministry would exact such a cost from you boys. First your university degree, now Piotr's violin," Tadeusz said, burying his face in both hands.

Jan's heart broke for both of them. In a strange way, they seemed even harder hit than Piotr. "Don't. Don't blame yourselves. You can't do that."

"Whose fault is it then?" Hanna asked. "The communists, the Russians? Piotr blames God, blames the ministry, and perhaps he is right. . . ."

Jan was shocked. He had never witnessed his mother wrestle with her faith, although she had told them often enough that it was a healthy way of learning God's ways. Here, now, she would take on the regiments of heaven if it meant sparing one of her children further pain.

"No, Mamusiu," he said softly, summoning all the skills of giving comfort he had learned in his fledgling ministry, "no blame. I want to tell you about something I've learned lately. God has given me a heart for the Russians. It sounds crazy. He may even give us a way of praying for the Poles in the government who have done these things to us. But for now I think it's miracle enough that I *want* to pray for the Russians."

His father looked up now, and Jan could feel his eyes boring into him, seeking, questioning. He chose his words carefully. "Blame has no place here. How often have you both taught us that when we suffer in Christ's name, we reap His rewards? Piotr doesn't believe that now, I know, but he will. He must.

"It all works like a pebble in a pond. I *know* my prayers for Russia will cause something to go into motion, and that will set something else in motion, and on and on. I don't want to oversimplify what it meant for Piotr to have his music career wrenched out of his grasp. That is very terrible, so very unfair. But perhaps someday we can look back on this and see it as one ripple, the eventual outcome of which brought our Piotr finally to the feet of Christ."

Jan felt his cheeks burning. Sweat ran down his back. The words had tumbled out of his mouth unbidden.

"Go on," Tadeusz said.

"I have been reading Paul's letters to Timothy lately."

"You are like Timothy," Hanna said.

"No!" Jan laughed to cover his embarrassment. "Not like Timothy. I'm the worst of sinners." There was something, he wasn't sure; he felt so restless. His eyes darted around the apartment, taking in the details he had missed during the last half-year. He felt as if he should be searching for something. And then, "Those boxes. What's in them?"

Jan could feel both his parents looking at him curiously. Now Tadeusz swiveled in his seat and looked in the direction Jan was pointing. "Teaching materials from Aad and his mission in Holland. He was here earlier this year before, well, before Piotr got his news."

Jan didn't like them measuring time in terms of before and after the blow to the family. He stood, something drawing him toward the boxes. As he flipped back the flap of the carton and saw the children's Bibles, Jan suddenly realized what he was supposed to know.

"Tatusiu, this vision you prayed for me to see, do you remember?" He didn't wait for his father to answer. "I was sure it had something to do with this burden for the Russian people I was telling you about. It doesn't make any sense, so it must be from

God, wouldn't you say?" He grinned.

"What on earth are you talking about, Jan?" Hanna was shaking her head as if he had played a joke on them.

"I'm talking about this. I *know* what I want to do, what I *have* to do. It all fits, don't you see? I've been asking myself what I should be doing in Warszawa."

"According to your letters, you've been doing quite enough," Hanna said.

"No, I mean *why* I'm supposed to be there. Now I know." The quiet calm that descended on Jan told him he was right even as he said the words, "My main reason for being in Warszawa is to get backing for taking Bibles into Russia. Don't you see? Just like the poorer churches in Paul's circuit were called on to give gifts, so we should be reaching out. Aad and his supporters are helping us, but we should be helping somebody. It's that same ripple effect."

Tadeusz was nodding, and all Hanna could do was smile. It thrilled Jan to realize both his parents could catch the vision.

"It will be dangerous," Tadeusz said. "Aad and the others are from the West; they can't be arrested and disappear into labor camps. You can."

"But I won't."

There was a silence, then Hanna said proudly, "No, you won't." Then she added, "God will honor the vision He gives, my son. What is important is that we honor it, too."

12

---◆---

Is Cast Upon the Earth

Luke 12:49

1969–1970

I'm an orphan. Again, Amy thought. *An orphan and a widow. An orphan, twice.*

Irrationally, the words kept running through her mind as she walked out of the church. She was following a casket for the third time in two months.

John Baker had been seventy-nine when he died, finally silenced by the second stroke they had dreaded for so long. Not three weeks later, Ruth had died in her sleep, as if she no longer belonged on this earth without John at her side. She, too, was seventy-nine.

But Ron—Ron hadn't even made it to thirty.

That had been the real surprise. She hadn't counted on loving Ron. And then she hadn't counted at all on losing him.

Amy and Ruth had brought John to Ron's funeral. And the stroke had hit him a week later. And then Ruth was gone, too, and Amy had no one. No one.

A widow and an orphan. . . .

As Amy passed out of the church doors, her eyes needed something to focus on, something to keep her from crying. "You would think I couldn't do that anymore," she whispered to herself, simply to hear a voice.

The paper was tacked onto the church door with cheap tape, fluttering in the breeze: . . . *POLAND need your help*. She thought nothing of it as she followed the steps down to the parking lot and climbed into the black limousine.

147

Amy spent the rest of that day trying to feel something. There was the burial, with Ruth's casket being gently lowered next to two fresh mounds of earth. Afterward, friends and neighbors had gathered at the house, bringing dishes of food and words of sympathy. Amy talked and nodded and afterward struggled to remember anything that had been said.

A week later she had a meeting with her father's accountant. "I'm very sorry, Amy, but it seems that all the years of private nursing care for John have eaten up most of your parents' savings. You might not have known it, but your mother was quietly selling off all the stock to pay the bills. I'm afraid that once all the debts are settled you won't have much more than the farm. That'll be yours free and clear. And of course, you still have what is left of your trust fund. But beyond that there'll just be a little bit more than fifty thousand dollars."

Amy knew she should feel shocked—something—that so little was left. She had always assumed the stock dividends had replenished most of what her father lost while trying to clear his name during the McCarthy scare, that there had been plenty to cover the nurses and the therapists. But the stocks were gone. Almost all of it was gone. And instead of grief for this added loss, all she felt was numb.

She left the accountant's office and walked down the street toward her car, staring into shop windows but not seeing what they contained.

Then she stopped. Her reflection stared back at her, the black hair loose and long, her dark eyes ringed with fatigue, her lips tight and thin. Out of the corner of her eye she thought she saw something she recognized.

Again the word POLAND leapt out at her. It was another copy of the same announcement she had noticed at the church, this time taped to a corner of the shop window. She made the effort to read the entire headline: Christians in POLAND need your help.

Amy felt raw and on edge, certainly not in control. What had her father's accountant just asked her? "What do you plan to do with yourself, your money, your life?" He was an old friend of John's and had assured her that he would be glad to counsel and help her any way he could. She had thanked him but given him no answers to his questions. She knew nothing except that it was time to move on.

Amy took a closer look at the notice. The meeting was that night in the Lutheran church down the street from her own Catholic church. A missionary would be talking about smuggling Bibles into Poland. *No,* she told herself. *No, you don't need that now.*

Deep inside her, another voice seemed to answer, *But what else do you have? Who else is there? At least this is someone who's been there.*

Then Amy caught herself by surprise. Despite her indecision, she chose a direction. Left with no one, she turned to the one person still on earth with whom she had some sort of tie, a blood tie.

Sitting at the back of a church bare of statues, she let the man's words wash over her. Amy listened to a corduroy-clad Dutchman say "dis" and "dat" instead of "this" and "that" as he described conditions in Poland.

"Christians there often share one Bible among an entire village. They copy the Gospels over in longhand.... Up until Vatican II, it was only the minority of Protestants in the country who were trying to circulate Bibles. But now a growing number of Catholics also want to know what it is they believe."

Amy noticed that although he referred to the general acts of getting boxes of teaching materials and Bibles past border guards, he gave away no details about where or how it was done.

There were only about twenty people at the meeting. After they had dropped their money in a basket by the door and left the church, Amy approached the man. She made sure he saw her place a hundred-dollar bill in the basket.

"Excuse me, but I'd really like to hear more about what you do. You see, I'm ..." Amy hesitated. During the last hour a shred of a plan had formed in her tired mind. *Maybe it's just a way of escaping,* she warned herself. But she could not afford to think too carefully about all this. She plunged ahead.

"I want to go to Poland. I want to help you and your group. Maybe you could give me some more information."

Amy could feel the man's eyes looking right through her. He was of medium height and balding, a little overweight, perhaps around forty years old. Not really impressive, except for those intense blue eyes, both piercing and tender. Then he glanced away from Amy and looked at the church wall to their left. He said, "I appreciate your generosity. Yes, I noticed." Now, when he looked at her again, Amy felt embarrassed. He continued, "It's hard bringing Americans into Poland. They attract attention."

"What do you mean?"

"The way they talk, what they wear—they have a way of standing out in crowds—but most of all their passports. In Eastern Europe, someone from the U.S. is someone from the enemy. They'll be much more closely watched than someone from a small, seemingly insignificant country like The Netherlands."

"Why did you come here, then?" Amy asked.

"People here are very generous with their wealth. And the mission needs money." He paused, then said, "But I will admit that we are extremely short of help these days. It's something we've been praying about for a long time. You do understand, if you came to work with us, you would have to arrange your own plane fare and raise your own support."

"Support?"

"The money you need to live on, as well as a substantial contribution to the mission. But most important, you would have to believe in what we are doing." Amy could not face the man's eyes any longer. She had to look away. He added, "My name is Aad."

He extended his hand. It gripped Amy's as if he were trying to pass something on to her.

She said, "I'm Amy. Amy Baker."

"Well, Amy, I want you to think about dis. My speaking has been known to move people to do irrational things in the past." He laughed at his own joke. "Think about it and get back to me, all right?"

Aad gave Amy some folders with further information, as well as a newsletter about what the group did and a list of phone numbers where she could reach him in the coming weeks as he continued his fundraising tour. She tucked them into her purse, shook his hand, and walked out into the familiar streets, buoyed by an almost overwhelming feeling of being in the right place at the right time. Just to feel again, to be excited about something again, was like rediscovering a forgotten favorite place.

After so many years of waiting, Amy found herself moving a hundred miles an hour. During the next weeks she contacted the Polish embassy and inquired about the requirements for a visa. She learned that she would have to pay up front for every day she planned to stay in Poland. She could stay only at government-approved hotels run by the government-controlled travel agency. She held off on giving them exact dates until she spoke to Aad again.

Amy sent a check for twice the amount required to the address given in the brochure. Only when it had cleared did she call one of the phone numbers Aad had left with her. Now it was just a question of which lie she should tell.

"Yes, I would like very much to join your gr—" she corrected herself, "mission. I believe in what you do, and I want to help in any way I can. Money is no problem," she added quickly.

"Are you sure?"

"You have no idea," she said, thinking of her fifty thousand. Privately she thought, *All I need is this group's protection. These people will know how to get around and avoid the police. That's their business.* She continued, "I'm afraid I don't have many skills. I know about nursing, but I don't have a degree. I can draw pretty well, and I know a bit about livestock, but I've never had a job in my life."

"Can you look people in the eye when you know you're hiding something?" the voice on the other end of the phone line asked.

Amy caught her breath. "Yes."

"We need people, especially women, who can deceive border guards. . . .

"All right, Amy, you're on. But you'll have to be trained in Wien—no, you call it Vienna—by some of our staff. I'll send you the address and you can show up there when you want. One other thing. Are you a Christian?"

"Of course. I've gone to church all my life."

Aad paused. Then said quietly, "Welcome aboard."

Amy hung up the phone with shaking hands. She knew she had done a dangerous thing, making such a decision before she had even given herself the chance to grieve. But she felt driven. She had to get away. And this was really away.

She would be leaving New England for the first time in her

life. She would be leaving America. She was going to Poland to look for a dead father she had heard about for the first time nearly ten years earlier. She felt like some sleeping beauty, awakening to life after an age of dreams.

Maybe my luck has changed, she thought.

———— ✐ ————

The gargoyles leered down at her from atop of shop doorways, and Amy grinned back at them, happy to be in Vienna. The fine lines of Baroque architecture, the spires of St. Stefansdom—it all reached out to her, inviting Amy back to the land of the living. And pointing her east.

For although Vienna might have been the capital of a West-European country, it was farther east than all of East Germany and some parts of Poland, Czechoslovakia, and Yugoslavia. If there was a doorway from the West into Eastern Europe, it opened from this city. She really was on her way to Poland, but first she had to go through mission training. And that, she found, was a challenge in itself.

When Amy arrived at Aad's mission headquarters, she thought some of the volunteers there talked about being Christian as if they were selling a new type of Barbie doll. "Hi, my name is Cindy. Have you met Jesus Christ as your personal Savior?" Amy felt lifetimes too old for these enthusiastic collegiate types. She had practically been married, loving the same man for five years, and had just lost the three people closest to her. She put as much distance between herself and the younger set as possible, preferring the company of the few volunteers who were older and quieter. More often, she kept to herself.

During one of the morning prayer sessions, when one of the younger girls complained that Amy never talked about her faith, Aad shot Amy a look and then spoke gently. "For some people it's a private affair."

Amy liked the sound of that so much she used it often in the weeks to come to cover up her discomfort with the enthusiastic belief and devotion she discovered around her. Was Aad really going to turn all these bright young things loose on Poland?

As it turned out, he didn't. Most of the American students were there volunteering their office skills. Only Amy and two of the older recruits would be going with Aad during the various times he went east, and then they would only travel in pairs. Aad said he could only train one person at a time whenever he was "in-country."

This was another aspect of her training that Amy didn't like. Everything sounded so "them against us," almost as if "they" were part of some covert cover-up. She didn't like the group prayers, and she didn't like being treated like a child during the "culture-shock adjustment" seminars. In fact, the only part of the eight-week training she did enjoy were her language classes in German and Polish, which her teacher said she seemed to have a gift for, and her free times, when she could wander the narrow little streets of the old city.

She thrilled to the cold, the snow, the statues, the smell of roasting chestnuts in street-corner stands, the sight of frozen-over park ponds teeming with ice skaters. She could not get enough of the Dürers inside the *Kunsthistorischemuseum*, and she visited so often the guards nodded in recognition whenever she climbed the broad steps at the entrance. And every time she passed the statue of Marie-Therese, the former queen of the Hapsburg dynasty seemed to look down directly at her. Amy's sketchbook quickly filled during those weeks, and she had to find an art-supply shop to replace it.

During her training period, Amy even had to decide on a code name. In-country, this was what everyone would call her. This made little sense to Amy, since she would be traveling on her own passport. Amy thought the whole thing resembled a James Bond film, but she had learned to respect Aad's judgment. She chose her biological mother's name, Barbara Skrzypek.

Aad still did not seem to realize that he and his people were simply providing her with an innocent-looking cover to search for her father. She struggled briefly with a familiar sense of guilt, then laid it aside. She had been waiting nearly ten years to get into Poland, and this was her best opportunity. Besides, she would be doing some good while she was here.

Many times Amy had asked herself if she was doing the right thing, if chasing a man whose name did not appear in any of the right places was a wise thing to do. It had been twenty-five years since the end of the war. *Who knows what's happened to this Jacek by now?*

But that was exactly the question that now spurred her on, the reason she had to go. The reason why, at this moment, she had to pretend to be someone she wasn't.

———— ⌇ ————

Aad said, "Pack dark clothes, layered for the cold, wool, nothing acrylic or down. And leave your sketch pad at home, all right? You don't want to arouse suspicion by seeming to record conditions.

"The safety of our local contacts is paramount," he explained. "It's not that dangerous for them to talk and meet with strangers, but we're bringing in what the government considers to be illegal goods. And members of the mission have been accused of spying for the West, so when our contacts are arrested, it's for meeting with 'imperialist spies.' They can disappear for years. The worst that can happen to you is that you're held for questioning, then politely escorted to the border."

Aad and Amy were due to leave that night. She had learned how to act, how to meet contacts, and what to do if it looked like the secret police was following them.

They drove north to Berlin on the highways designated by the East Germans as transit routes. In Berlin they met briefly with an old friend of Aad's who was doing the same work for another group. The little old lady came from *Haarlem*, near Aad's hometown. When they were alone for a few moments, she squeezed Amy's hand and whispered, "Listen, my dear, the key in this work is prayer. Pray for the angels to blind the eyes of the guards. And keep your own eyes open for those angels."

"What did you think of Corrie?" Aad asked later.

"Interesting." Amy didn't know what else to say.

"Did you notice the numbers tattooed on the inside of her wrist?" Amy stared at him. "No? Well, you can tell the Dutch people who sacrificed the most in the war. They're the ones who don't talk about it."

As they left West Berlin on the transit route east, he explained how intimidating the East German guards could often be. "A lot of it is bluff. But never forget that these men have been ordered to shoot to kill anyone who acts suspiciously. So no matter what, just look them straight in the face and use those dark eyes of yours for all they're worth."

Even though she had seen photos of the border area, the high watchtowers and the guards walking around with Kalashnikovs over their shoulders still scared her. "Let me do the talking," Aad said as they rolled their way up the long line waiting to leave East Germany. "And you pray while I'm doing it."

When it was their turn, the East German guard asked Amy to take off her sunglasses, then pronounced the transit visa *in ordnung*. Aad was right about the border being so busy.

The Polish entry station at *Szczecin* proved even easier. The customs officer asked Aad what was in the boxes that filled every inch of the VW bus. Aad said they contained gifts for friends in Poland. Just then the phone rang in the official's booth and the man became agitated by whatever was said on the other end of the line. He waved Amy and Aad through with an impatient jerk of his hand.

Once into Poland, Aad turned and grinned at Amy. "I don't know what you prayed, but it sure worked." Amy felt guilty. She hadn't prayed anything.

Then they were driving past empty winter fields. A strange excitement came over Amy. She gazed out over the open countryside, unmarked by any sign of advertising or life other than scattered farms and horse-drawn wagons. "In the spring these are bright yellow with blooming rape plants," Aad said once to break the silence.

Amy settled back in her seat and sighed. It was strange, but Amy had the strangest sensation of having just come home. A few weeks earlier, when the mission celebrated Christmas, she had been one of the few not to complain of homesickness. She had thought it was because she had no more family in the States. But now she knew differently.

As the landscape changed from meadows to forest, Amy's excitement rose, and it spilled forth in conversation. She soon found herself telling Aad about her life—mostly about the last years, when she had been caring for her father and helping her mother and loving Ron. She hadn't intended to let it pour out of her like that, but Aad seemed to want to hear, and they still had half a day to drive over the rutted, bumpy roads to reach their first contact.

When she finished with a description of the three funerals she had attended, Aad reached over and took her hand. "You have my condolences for your parents, and for Ron." Amy was thankful he said nothing about their not having been married.

Aad continued, "Amy, I had a feeling about you from the first moment you stepped up to speak with me in that church. Anyone can see you are grieving; it shows in your eyes. You must give yourself time for the pain to be less." He paused. "But that you were so generous for so many years, nursing a dying father like that—that is a very special thing, Amy. God treasures hearts like yours."

With those words Amy's guilt returned. She had carefully avoided telling him the real reason that had brought her to Poland. And once again she felt she was simply using people who had been called to a higher purpose than her own.

Her guilt only increased in the next weeks as Amy and Aad crisscrossed the country and she saw and heard firsthand the risks people were willing to take for their faith. Amy had never witnessed such courage. The people who came out to meet them and take away a carton of Bibles always hugged Aad and welcomed Amy warmly. Few spoke English, and those that did spoke it very poorly. Most of the older people spoke German, which Aad spoke fluently, but Amy could only follow a few words of.

They met behind barns or in dark alleys. In the cities, only after taking circuitous routes to make sure no one was following them, they met in abandoned parking lots. Everywhere, the people they met spoke in hushed tones about the SB, the Polish secret police.

Some of the contacts were pastors in Protestant churches, some were Catholics. Among the Catholics were young priests trying to meet the needs of their parishes.

Amy thought all these people looked as if they had walked out of a film from the fifties. The baggy trousers, the caps, the women's hairstyles, the scarves tied under the chins—all these only increased Amy's sense of having stepped into another place in time. There was a general shabbiness to everything she saw, even though people were clean, their clothing was clean, their children were clean, their homes were clean. The cities lacked the color and creativity that marked Western cities, made them alive. It wasn't just the absence of advertising and merchandise in shop windows; it was also the architecture, the clothing. Everything seemed weary and faded.

Even the safety of the streets was simply a dubious benefit of the heavy police presence. Aad had told her she could walk the streets of any city in Poland at night alone and be perfectly safe. There were hardly any incidents of assault and theft; few acts of violence of any kind—except those inflicted by the government on its own people.

What surprised Amy, however, was that she didn't really mind the dirty streets and grimy public places. She didn't mind the discomfort of having to sleep on sofas instead of beds. She didn't mind carrying toilet paper in her pants pocket because no place she went ever had any. Nothing in her upbringing had prepared her for the austere conditions of the people they met, or for the language, or the culture. Everything she knew about Poland she had just learned a few weeks earlier during the training session in Vienna. And yet something in the land seemed to call to her, like horns in the distance, and something in her responded to that call.

For more than ten years she had waited for her chance to come here, but she had never expected to fall in love so completely with the land and its people. Amy fell in love with the hope and endurance of the people she met, with the timeless dignity of the buildings that had survived the war, with the tragic history that was still being lived out before her. Her artist's eye reveled in the beauty of the wild forests, the vastness of the rolling countryside, the stubborn hope etched in tired faces.

Why did it all feel so familiar? Why did it all seem so beautiful?

After a while she stopped wondering and contented herself with learning all she could.

When she and Aad didn't stay in people's homes, they often stayed in dirty motels. Aad would smile when Amy joked with him about the chronic lack of hot water or clean sheets in these places. "Just be glad it isn't summer," he joked back, "then, we would sleep in the van."

Finally, when the trip was coming to a close, Aad turned to her with an uncharacteristically solemn face and told her God had given her a heart for Poland. "It doesn't happen often," he said, "this special kind of gift. It means you've already lost something or someone. In your case that's certainly true. You have to be open to it. I don't understand the process very well, but it seems when we are broken somehow, God gives us something in return, a heart for something new. A new love to take the place of the old."

"Take the place of," Amy repeated softly. They had been driving for hours through wooded country dotted by lakes. The loveliness had mesmerized her.

"We only have one more stop in the north of the country. A pastor there has been waiting a very long time for those last two boxes of Bibles and tapes in the back. But we need to hurry. I try not to get caught over here late in February. The weather gets even worse than it is now. These roads aren't good in the best of weather, but when it freezes, they're deadly."

They were on the road to Gdańsk. *Where my father was born.* Amy wondered if she would be successful in finding out anything about Jacek there. She had been hoping to find some record of his emigration to America. And yet the more time Amy had spent in Poland, the less hopeful she had become about her secret search.

To start with, she had seen firsthand just how impossible it was to get anything done quickly in Poland, especially if it concerned civil servants or any type of bureaucracy. People were not in a hurry, and efficiency seemed a foreign concept, thanks to a system that guaranteed wages, pensions, and medical care but rejected all forms of incentive.

Second, even though she had picked up a little Polish in her training and on the trip, she knew her Westernness was obvious as soon as she opened her mouth. That in itself was enough to arouse suspicion, and there was a good chance no one would want to help her.

Aad interrupted her thoughts by picking up an earlier thread of conversation. "You know, we were talking about the way Polish society has been turned on its ear in the communist era. The more a family had achieved in the past, it seems, the less they're allowed to obtain in the present. Those who came from peasant backgrounds have been granted privileges. Many of the families we've met on this trip have children who can speak several languages or play musical instruments or who demonstrate leadership qualities. But because the parents categorically refuse to go along with the government leadership and join the Communist Party, they have hardly any professional careers. They are passed over again and again for promotion, and their children are often passed over when they apply to the best schools. Who you are has nothing to do with the things you have, with your car or clothes or job or house, since these people are forced to live in the most run-down housing. It's so different here than it is in the West. Any sense of personal dignity has to come from within, from the family unit itself.

"A real case in point," Aad added as he slowed for a curve, "is the next family you're going to meet. I've saved the best for last."

While they were talking, Amy noticed that Aad had driven right past the road off the highway leading to Gdańsk and continued north. Amy asked, "Where's the drop point?"

"The family lives in Gdynia; it's a port city just up the coast from Gdańsk. Our last contact got word to them that we'd meet them tonight. It looks like all our driving has paid off. We'll get there just as it gets dark."

Amy thought, *Great. Now I'll never make it to Gdańsk*. She sighed. She was just going to have to find an excuse to get away. She glanced at Aad; he looked tired. "Don't you need to rest? I could drive for a while."

"No, it's all right. But talk to me to keep me awake."

Amy said, "Well, tell me more about this family." It was a mission rule to communicate as few details as possible concerning the lives of the people they met. Amy knew no last names, no addresses, very few personal stories. This way, if she were detained by the milicja, she could not tell what she did not know.

But for some reason, perhaps because he was so tired from the long drive, Aad did as she asked and relaxed his usual reticence to discuss details. "These are special people. Well, they all are, of course, but this family has seen more than its share of suffering, and I have a feeling they haven't told me half of it. He's a pastor, and they have one grown son—two now, probably, it's been so long since I last visited. He teaches at the university in Gdańsk, and she has MS, but so far has managed to beat it."

Multiple sclerosis, Amy thought to herself. *It's not that far off from being paralyzed like Dad was.*

Aad continued, "As with a lot of the pastors, he was in prison for his beliefs during the Stalinist days, and he's never really been healthy since. He's not even sixty, but you'll see what I mean. The secret police might still be watching their home. They hold regular Bible studies and continue to meet with other Christians, even though they've been warned off several times and accused of being part of the underground. And yet . . ."

"Yet?"

"Yet you wouldn't know these people have any problems. I mean, sometimes we Christians act like everything is fine, but we don't really feel that way; it's a mask. But with these people you can feel their joy in the Lord; it's so palpable."

"Palpable." Amy was thinking about masks.

"Good word? Not bad for a Dutchman, huh? Ah, look, we're here already." The meeting point was an area behind the Gdynia train station where there were covered stalls. "In the morning we can buy some fresh herring here, as well as some pickled peppers that will make you breathe fire."

"I can't believe you think of food at times like this," Amy said. She tensed up every time they made contact with new people. *What if the secret police are watching? What if something goes wrong? What if someone gets hurt because of me—because I really shouldn't be here?* These were the thoughts coursing through Amy's mind as Aad parked the van.

A tall man, broad-shouldered but bent, appeared from the shadows between the stalls. Only one streetlamp was working, and Aad had parked so it didn't shine directly on them. As the man approached the van, Aad opened the door and stepped out. "Tadeusz, my old friend, *Cześć!*"

The man looked as though he could have been seventy, his face showed so many creases. Amy opened the door of the van to join them, and a blast of freezing air hit her in the face. "Oh!" she cried.

"Barbara, come here," Aad called over the wind. He used her code name, but Amy noticed he wasn't using one himself.

"It looks like one of our Baltic storms has come out to welcome you. Hello. I am Tadeusz. Tadeusz Piekarz."

It was the first time that a contact had told her his last name. Amy shot a look at Aad, and he shrugged his shoulders. To her surprise, Tadeusz knew exactly what she was thinking. "We try not to be afraid of too many things. Welcome, Barbara." Tadeusz reached out both his hands and took Amy's into them.

No one had touched her like that since her mother's death. The tears came completely by surprise. She glanced up into his eyes and saw bottomless blue. She also saw that he had seen her tears.

"This wind, it's so cold. Hello. Yes, thank you. It's good to meet you," she stammered, pulling her hands away and jamming them into her pockets.

"Yes, it is cold. Come back with me to our home, please. You must. Hanna has made some of her famous sandwiches, and there is a pot of soup on the stove. Jan is not home right now, so there is room. You must come and stay with us. We can park your car somewhere . . . safe. Aad?"

"And our friends?"

"Our friends have not been watching the house for several weeks now. Marek's garage is still empty, so we can put the van there, all right? Let's go before your lovely assistant freezes to death in this Polish winter."

The three of them climbed into the van and drove it down bumpy streets to a row of garages. Amy knew Aad didn't like standing outside on streets like they had. It was one of the rules—avoid loitering in public places. The van just barely fit inside, almost scraping the roof. Tadeusz and Amy had to get out before Aad could ease it inside. Then Tadeusz padlocked the door and led them across the street to a block of apartments that looked just as gray and lifeless as the endless rows of buildings Amy had seen all over Poland.

They walked up what seemed an interminable flight of stairs. As Tadeusz slipped keys into the three locks in the door and opened it, a glorious smell of yeast greeted Amy. She stepped inside and was greeted by a middle-aged woman with salt-and-pepper hair tied up in a bun. "Ah, you arrived safely. Our friends told us Aad had someone special traveling with him."

Amy could not help but smile. "Hello, I'm," she paused, "Barbara."

"Barbara, welcome. I am Hanna. Here it's not very large, but it has been a home to us for over twenty years."

Amy looked around and saw two sofas, a small wooden table, and a curtained-off corner where all the good smells were coming from. The sofas were backed up against the wall, so the room looked bigger than it was. There was no stereo, no pictures on the wall. But there were some plants in the window. And Amy saw a door to another room.

Hanna had been watching her with the same keen intensity as her husband. She said, "You must be tired. The bathroom is there to the right. And you and Aad will be sleeping in the other room. We have already made up the beds."

"Oh no," Amy protested, "we couldn't impose."

"Nonsense," Hanna cut her off. "This is the boys' room, and Piotr doesn't mind sleeping out here with us. Now come in, come in, and have something to eat. You must be so hungry after your long journey."

There was no arguing with Hanna; Amy saw that Aad already realized this. Evidently this was a familiar routine for his visits to Gdynia. *So this is what he meant by saving the best for last*, Amy thought.

They washed up and sat down around a table laden with food. The stiffly starched tablecloth with colorful embroidered flowers could hardly be seen for the array of dishes. It was much more than the soup and sandwiches Tadeusz had hinted at. Aad called the meal a feast fit for kings. Hanna had put together a four-course meal, starting with *barszcz czerwony*, a delicious beet soup, and including *grzybki marynowane*, a dish of mushrooms marinated in Hanna's own special recipe. There were also sandwiches, little squares of home-baked biscuits covered with cucumber and cheese or smoked salmon and dill. Amy could not get enough of the fresh buns, and she had two helpings of the soup, worried with each bite that she might spill and permanently stain the impeccable tablecloth.

Only when the meal was finished did they hear a key click in each of the locks. All heads turned as a tall young man entered the room.

13

FLAMES BY NIGHT

Isaiah 4:5

1970

"Ah, Piotr, our guests are here. Come meet them. Aad, you re-member Piotr. He's grown quite a lot since you were here, hasn't he? And this is Barbara, Aad's friend."

Amy saw a sullen, dark face, then a full head of dark curls. He did not look at Amy as he took her hand and kissed it. Amy was still not quite used to this Polish men's way of greeting women.

"Piotr," he mumbled.

When Amy heard his deep voice, saw the dark stubble on his strong jaw, she tried to guess his age. He could have been twenty. *I wonder if he's the older one who's not supposed to be home?*

Hanna was still talking. "So now Piotr is studying how to work as a carpenter." Amy looked up just in time to see Aad and Tad-eusz exchange glances. Piotr said he had already eaten and settled down onto one of the sofas. "Then you can join us for coffee," Hanna said.

Noticing that Piotr got up to help his mother clear the table, Amy did the same, only to be pushed back down in her chair by Tadeusz. "Guests don't work in this home," he smiled. Again Aad shrugged his shoulders as if to say this was ground already fought over and lost.

They drank coffee with the grounds still resting at the bottom of the glass. Aad and Tadeusz talked about mutual acquaintances in very general terms, not naming names. Amy recognized some of the allusions though and knew they were referring to pastors in other parts of the country, some of whom Amy had already met on the trip.

And Amy found she could not take her eyes off Piotr. He did not say much, but he missed nothing. Dark eyes burned like coals in the handsome face; long fingers seemed unable to rest. A discontent emanated from him in every move he made, and yet he seemed somehow pleased with himself. His muscled body reminded her a little of Ron's, and it occurred to her that Tadeusz might have looked like this years earlier—*maybe before he went to prison*, Amy thought.

As the conversation continued, she was startled to realize that Piotr was, in fact, the younger of the two brothers. The other one, Jan, was working in Warszawa. Amy wanted to learn more about Piotr, but he just sat there saying nothing. Somehow he didn't seem to fit in with what was going on around them.

After a while, Amy began to feel restless. Her whole purpose of coming to Poland had been to find a way to access information for her search. Time was running out, and all she had discovered was the fact that the government used countless petty rules and regulations to frustrate Poles on a daily basis and keep them down. This made it nearly impossible to find anything at all.

She sighed, and everyone around her laughed. "You haven't heard a word of what we've been saying, have you?" Aad asked.

Amy blushed and caught Piotr looking at her. A beautiful smile lingered on his face as he enjoyed her embarrassment. "I'm so sorry, you're right. I was thinking of other things, this trip mainly, and what I've learned."

"Well, we were just suggesting that maybe it was time for you to have a night off," Tadeusz said. "So I was asking if you and Piotr might like to go to the cinema tonight. There's an old John Wayne film on, so it would be in English."

"Oh yes." Amy was thrilled at the idea of going out, out somewhere, out anywhere. She turned to Piotr. "You don't mind taking an older woman on a date?" She had meant it as a joke, but right away his face clouded over again. To cover her confusion, she stood and thanked Hanna for the meal.

"Hasn't Aad taught you yet?" Hanna remonstrated. "Here the tradition is for everyone at the table to thank each other at the end of a meal. We are grateful for the company and the conversation, as well as the food."

Amy nodded. "I thank you, then," she said solemnly to everyone.

Piotr was standing with her coat. "I have a key, Tatusiu."

"Have fun," Tadeusz called after them. Amy caught Aad's eye, and he winked at her.

As soon as they were down the stairs and outside, Amy touched Piotr's arm. "I'm sorry. I didn't mean to embarrass you."

"You didn't."

His voice, the timber of it, the accent when he spoke English—it was the same as his father's. In an attempt to make conversation, she asked, "So how old *are* you?"

"What is this obsession with age?" he asked. "I'll be seventeen next month."

"You're only sixteen?" Amy couldn't help herself. Where was the innocence or insecurity that should have gone along with his age? "I just turned thirty."

"That's nice." Piotr obviously didn't want to talk about it. They walked the rest of the way to the cinema in silence. The cold wind made it hard even to breathe.

She was relieved when they reached the theater. She couldn't believe they were going out to see John Wayne in Poland. The plush red velvet seats reminded Amy more of small love seats than theater chairs.

The film started abruptly, without any advertisements preceding it. During the film, Amy could smell a faded cigarette smell coming from Piotr's sweater, along with the slightest whiff of fish and something else, indefinable. She found herself watching his profile in the flickering lights.

When the film was over, the lights went on before the credits could be shown. Piotr picked up her coat and held it for her. "Could you follow the English all right?" she asked.

"Of course," Piotr said.

"Yes, I'm sorry. Your English is very good. Excellent really."

"If only it were. No, I wish my English were as good as my Russian. I hate Russian."

"But you can speak it?" Amy asked with admiration.

"We all must learn it," he answered, "starting already in the fifth year of primary school. But I will never speak one word. A Russian could stop me and ask directions, and I'd still pretend I didn't know what he was saying. We were forced to learn the language from an occupying force. They can't make me speak it."

His vehemence surprised Amy, but he had come alive before her eyes. The sullen teenager of earlier that evening was gone. In his place stood a tall young man certain of his convictions. This was different from the more docile attitudes she had encountered with other Poles.

"You would like to change a few things around here, wouldn't you?" she asked as they stepped outside again. She looked up at his face just as he looked down, as if to see if she had meant what she said.

Their eyes locked and Amy had to make a conscious effort to remind herself, *Don't. He's sixteen.* Amy looked away first.

"Yes, there are a lot of things I would like to change. And don't tell me I should pray about it," he said again, a bitterness sneaking into his voice.

"I'd be the last one to tell you that," she mumbled.

"Pardon?"

"Oh, nothing."

"No, what did you mean?" he insisted. He reached out and took her by the arm. They had climbed a hill and were now looking down on the harbor and the Baltic beyond it. Amy could see the blinking lights of ships waiting at sea. The sharp wind came straight in off the water and cut through her winter jacket. At the same time, his touch burned her.

She gasped, her physical reaction to Piotr surprising even her. "I . . . I'm not what I seem."

"None of us are," Piotr said darkly.

They stood like that for a few moments longer. He would not take away his hand. Finally, he broke the silence. "I am a pastor's son in a family that has suffered much in the name of Jesus. But I don't believe."

The last words were whispered, as if he feared a lightning strike. *Why should he open up like this to me? Am I so safe?*

Piotr continued in the same hushed tone, "I don't believe in a

God that makes my family suffer because they follow Him. It's just not worth it, the risks we take—" he corrected himself, "the risks *they* take in the name of God."

Amy had never thought she would hear such a thing from a member of a contact's family, and especially not this family. They *had* risked so much and still did so every day. Aad had said these people risked more than most, knew what they believed and why. *Evidently not all of them.*

His frankness encouraged her to risk her own confession. "Me, too. I mean, I've been baptized and everything, but all of this, what Aad does and . . . well, I can't judge your parents, but a lot of what I've heard on this trip—it seems sort of fanatical to me."

Now he was really looking at Amy. "What are you doing here?"

"Good question," she said. "Listen, I don't even know you. Maybe we shouldn't be talking this way. Let's just go back. I'm so cold."

Piotr said nothing. He just looked at her strangely. But when they crossed the busy street just in front of his apartment block, he put his hand against her back protectively. After he took it away, Amy could still feel it there.

That night she spent listening to Aad's gentle snoring on the other side of the room. It was not the first time they had slept in the same room. It was often the only solution when money was short and rooms were at a premium. Here, it would have been more awkward for him to sleep with the family.

Yet it wasn't the snoring that kept Amy awake that night. She lay in the sofa bed, thinking about her trip and Ron and her Jacek . . . and Piotr, beside her, on the other side of the wall.

I have to find a way of staying longer, she kept thinking.

The next morning, she and Aad were already dressed and folding up the bedding when she broached the subject. They could hear the family moving around in the next room and wanted to give them some privacy until the time they had agreed on for breakfast.

"I don't want to leave Poland," she said.

He nodded, as if he had expected as much. "I know. That's how I felt after my first trip. I still feel that way, actually. This place has that effect on some people. Like I told you, you have a heart for Poland, so now you'll be homesick whenever you're not here. I have that for a few favorite places in the world, but it's strongest about Poland. Well, Amy, what can we do about that?"

"Can I stay here? I mean, I have nothing to go back to. Can I do something for the mission? Can I become a student? I . . ." she searched for a reason, "I want to improve my Polish. I can only do that in-country. You said yourself that no one can learn a language with just tapes."

"Yes, well no one but the Piekarz family, as I'm sure you've already noticed. That Piotr is something special, isn't he? You'd never know he hadn't studied English in the U.K."

"You're changing the subject. But while you're on it, yes, he is a very unusual young man. Why did you and Reverend Piekarz exchange that look last night when his wife talked about Piotr's school?"

"Oh, I, um, the last time I was here was two years ago. Piotr was different then, brighter and full of promise. I guess things haven't worked out for him."

"Yes, he seems disappointed about something."

Aad shot her a look like she was closer to the truth than she knew, but he said no more. There was a knock on the door, and Hanna's voice invited them to come use the bathroom and eat breakfast.

When they entered the next room, it showed no signs of three people having slept there. The tantalizing smell of fresh-baked buns floated out of the corner. Piotr was sitting at a table, arguing with his father about something. They stopped as soon as Amy and Aad came in. Piotr stood up and said good morning but did not look at Amy. *So he's been thinking about me, too.*

At the breakfast table, Tadeusz said grace. "Lord, we give thanks as a family for knowing who we are in God's eyes and not the world's. And we pray for the safety of our dear guests. Amen."

Amy opened her eyes early and looked at Piotr as she said, "Amen." His head was bowed and his eyes closed. *He looks like he prays.*

Once they had all helped themselves to the cucumber-and-cheese sandwiches and Hanna had poured cups of steaming tea, Aad asked, "Tell me how Jan is."

Amy was still watching Piotr and trying not to be too obvious about it. A cloud seemed to pass over his face at the mention of his brother.

Tadeusz said, "He's fine. Working hard. We're very proud of him." As he spoke, Tadeusz reached for a pad of paper and pen in his coat pocket and began scribbling. He seemed to have no difficulty whatsoever in saying one thing as he wrote another. When he had finished, he held up the pad so both Aad and Amy could read the words: "There are very few we would admit this to, Aad, but we know you and Barbara take similar risks yourself. Jan is not really in Warszawa. Remember your last trip here two years ago?"

Aad nodded, took the pad, and scribbled, "The Russian Bibles?"

Tadeusz flipped over to a new page and wrote some more. Then Amy read, "Yes. Well, Jan has found a way to get them inside Russia and has even been able to contact a small network of believers there who can distribute the books. They are ten times more desperate for learning materials than we are. Here in Poland we are blessed with a freedom the Russians can only dream of."

"How does he do it?" Amy asked out loud. She saw no harm in the question as such.

Hanna answered, again careful not to mention specifics, "Our Jan does not tell us too many details, of course. But he works very hard. He takes risks. At a time when hardly anyone dares to, when everyone thinks, 'Don't risk too much,' he talks about no risk being too great. Even just two years ago, people were still behaving, still not daring. I think slowly our eyes have been opened to the fact that we won't be killed—" Here now, Hanna wrote the additional words, "for bringing in Bibles. He is even trying to find a way into Albania. Which is why we need your help, Aad."

"Yes, do you think your organization can get Bibles printed in either one of the Albanian dialects for us?" Tadeusz now scribbled.

Aad was beaming. He wrote, "If you can get them into that dark, closed country, the least I can do is get them printed for you." He added out loud, "Of course. And when you see Jan, tell him my prayers are with him."

After the meal Amy said she wanted to take the train into Gdańsk. "I've always wanted to see that city. I've read so much about the architecture."

"Yes, my friend here is an artist at heart," Aad said. "Barbara, you know the Poles copied Holland. Gdańsk has many houses rebuilt in the original Dutch Renaissance style."

"Or did the Dutch copy it from us?" Piotr asked, addressing Aad for the first time.

"Ah, it speaks. Glad to see you're finally awake, my boy. I can remember when all you did was talk my ears off every time I came to visit." Then to Amy, "Of course, do some sightseeing. But remember not to take your camera out in the train station. They might take it away. Now, I'm planning to leave tomorrow morning early, so this is your only chance. Tadeusz and I are meeting with a few people today, so go enjoy yourself. Yourselves."

Piotr shot a shining smile at Aad, then turned its beam on Amy. "I don't suppose you'd like a guide and interpreter today. I'm free."

His quick change in mood surprised Amy. She laughed uneasily and tried to cover up her discomfort with a joke. "You don't cost anything, or you don't have to work today?" When she saw his confused look, she quickly added, "No, I mean, I could use your help actually, Piotr. Thank you."

They left together and walked to the train station. Walking beside him, Amy thought, *What do I have to lose?*

"Piotr, I have to find something out while I'm in Gdańsk. I don't want you to get in trouble for being with me. So maybe you should leave me alone for a few hours, and we could meet back later. If what I'm doing turns out to attract the wrong kind of attention, you stand to lose more than I do. And your family is already taking enough risks."

He stopped her and moved close so that only she could hear him. A shiver went across her shoulders as she bent her head up to look at his face. Clouds raced behind his head in a stormy sky. "Believe me when I say that Jan is not the only one to take risks in this family. Whatever you need to do will have a better chance of success if a Pole does it for you. Although you do not look American, your accent gives you away as soon as you open your mouth."

So while sitting on a dirty train seat made for one and a half people, Amy told Piotr her secret. He drew it out of her, and his eyes never once left her face as she spoke. She told him about her parents, about the last ten years, about death, about her lies to Aad. "He's such a good man and he's doing such good things, and I'm only using him."

What will he think of me now? she wondered. Then, *Why do I care so much?* And all the time she talked, Amy was acutely aware of Piotr's presence, his arm against hers, his shoulder near her cheek, their legs bumping each other as the train took a curve.

He listened quietly, and when she finished, he took both her hands in his and brought them to his lips. "You will never know how much it means to me that you have told me the truth like this. I am grateful. Truth is a rare thing, and I treasure it when I find it, as I have in you."

All she could do was gaze back at him, conscious that some line had been crossed and she was unwilling to step back over it.

———— ✑ ————

Piotr knew exactly which offices to visit. In each of the long string of different places they were sent to, he also knew when to seem casual about his questions. To some he said he was looking for a long-lost uncle who owed some money to his father. To others he said he needed the records for a population project the Young Pioneers Club was working on. He smiled and looked serious with the officious bureaucrats. He winked at the older women and was businesslike with the mustached men. Who was the woman with him? A deaf sister out for a day to the city.

They laughed together over the last joke as they left yet another office. "Are civil servants the same in your country? Here they will believe anything if you say it like 'of course it is true.' They come from all different backgrounds; some are nothing more than peasants."

"And you are a member of the *inteligencja*, I suppose."

"You surprise me, American imperialist. Your Polish is not so bad for someone who is deaf."

This started them laughing again. "Well, I could tell you some stories about the civil servants in Boston. I remember when Ron and I were doing this." She stopped.

"Ron? You didn't mention him on the train."

"Ron was my . . . husband. Well, we weren't married, but he was my husband."

"I understand."

"Do you? Anyway, all I wanted to say was that he and I spent a lot of time doing the same search and visiting a lot of the same offices, but in Boston instead of Gdańsk. And civil servants there are just as—"

Piotr held up his hand, and then his finger to his lips. Amy stopped talking and noticed a middle-aged man watching them. He was overweight and had a thick mustache. She caught her breath and looked at Piotr. He signaled with his eyes: *Just do what I tell you.*

They walked the rest of the way to yet another ministry building in silence. The man stayed behind them. Amy could feel his eyes as they turned to go inside.

Piotr motioned for her to sit on a bench just inside the door, then he disappeared up the wooden stairs and was gone by the time the man entered.

He looked around, seemingly surprised to find Amy sitting right next to the entrance. He nodded at her, then backed out the door.

Amy waited a half hour for Piotr to come downstairs. She was worried, but she had learned enough from Aad to know she should stay put and keep quiet. When Piotr finally returned, he motioned for Amy to follow, so she stood and crossed the foyer to him. On the way she glanced out through the windows in the main exit. The man was still leaning against a pillar, smoking a cigarette.

Piotr led her toward a back exit of the huge building. They ended up in an alley full of cardboard boxes and something that stank. They walked past a few streets, crisscrossing as they went, Amy staying a good distance behind Piotr. When she finally saw his hand motion for her to move forward, they were just outside a tall, narrow church. She caught up to him, and they ducked inside.

Three women wearing scarves sat in a corner waiting for the confessional to open. Otherwise the church was empty. The worship space was quite small, more a chapel than a church. Amy was immediately struck by the beauty of the black marble and amber carvings around her—black and gold. The winter sun shining through stained-glass windows sparkled in every corner. The moment took her breath away, it was so still and full of grace.

Piotr led her to a back pew on the other side of the chapel. When they sat, he took her hand in his. "Are you all right?" he asked in his deep voice.

"Yes, of course. That man was waiting for us."

"I know. I saw him from the upstairs window. We lost him, though."

"You know him?"

"Not really. Listen, we finally went to the right place. I have some news for you."

Amy gasped. It was remarkable enough that she was getting Piotr's help in her search, but that they would actually find something was almost more than she had hoped. "Jacek?"

"Yes, Jacek. It's not much, but I did find his name in the registry. Some facts are missing because of the war. The Russians burned a lot of the files in '45, so what I have is incomplete."

"Tell me," Amy whispered.

"The dates you have are correct. He did emigrate with his parents in 1912. He was born in 1909. And he . . ."

"And what? That's all we knew. You know more?"

"And he was here in 1939 and 1945."

"What? He's alive!" Amy knew it. She had known it. The emotion of the moment forced her to turn away for a moment.

Piotr took her chin in his hand and turned her face back toward him. They stared at each other for a few moments before he said, "I must tell you this. *Was* alive. '45 was the end of the war, twenty-five years ago, and now he would be . . ."

"Sixty-one. Oh, he's alive. I know he is."

"But you cannot know that. So much can happen, Barbara, especially here. And even if he is alive, do you really want to meet him?"

"Of course. He's my . . . blood father."

Piotr was quiet. "I'm afraid I can't help you much more than this," he said after a minute. "It's a dead end. I tried—that's why I was gone so long—but there's no trace of him after 1945. I'm afraid . . . you know that was a crazy time, with people disappearing all the time. If the Germans didn't kill him, the Russians probably did. Most men in Gdańsk had a funny way of ending up dead or in Siberia. And if he was over here as an American for some reason . . ."

Piotr seemed to be thinking out loud. Amy let him follow his train of thought. "Ya, it doesn't make sense. Maybe he left here, then returned because . . . he was looking for someone. Maybe family who were caught here by the war. It doesn't matter. Just being from the U.S. here when the Russians were liberating us would have been suicide. I'm afraid he disappeared that year because that was the year so many vanished and never came back. Do you understand what I mean?"

"Yes. But, Piotr, I know he's still alive. I just know it. *I feel it.* I knew he didn't die in France. I had a feeling about that, and I was right. Now I have the same sort of feeling."

"It could be, but there is no way of finding out. I'm sorry, Barbara. It is strange enough that I could find this much out. Usually everyone must register when they move somewhere, especially to a region where the military is present. This Jacek Skrzypek is registered as being here, as I said, in 1939 and 1945, but there is never a forwarding address. He just arrives and arrives again. He never leaves. And there's something else."

Amy was still trying to assimilate what she had just heard. "What?" she asked.

"I know, it's very, very strange. Very unusual. But 1939 and 1945—those were years when no one was keeping track of anyone. I mean, they were years of chaos. So it's almost as if your Jacek must have done this on purpose, as if he *wanted* to be noted as having been in Gdańsk, as if he were trying to leave a message for someone. Maybe."

Amy was quiet. *What does it mean?* "Well, he's alive. I know it.

And you . . . you have given me this knowledge. I don't have anyone anymore, and just knowing this Jacek is alive somewhere does make a difference. Thank you. Thank you so much."

She was so grateful for what Piotr had found out that she almost threw her arms around him. Then Amy remembered that it was while searching for Jacek's name back in Boston that she had first grown close to Ron. She also remembered how she had felt when they sat close together on the train, and she checked herself. *He may look twenty and act thirty, but he's sixteen. Leave it.*

She simply laid a hand on his arm and murmured a friendly, "Thank you." For the rest of their day together she avoided his eyes and his touch.

When they returned to Gdynia, he wanted to take her to his favorite ice-cream parlor, but she said they should probably be getting back. Just before they reached his home, he stopped her. They stood beneath a few trees in a small park. The moon shone bright, and there were no clouds. As they spoke, they could see their breath.

Piotr said, "You're leaving tomorrow early, so I must say this. I . . . I felt something when we were together today. You felt it, too. I . . . I'm not as young as you think. I know we've only known each other for a day, but from the moment I saw you . . ."

He stopped, to Amy's great relief. "That is a cliché, and I'm sounding ridiculous. Barbara, please, will you promise me one thing?"

Amy was kicking herself for not having kept her own emotions better in check. He had seen too much. "Yes?" she asked, still not meeting his gaze.

"Write me, please."

"But the censors—won't it attract attention? No, I don't think I should. Besides, Piotr, I'll be back."

"Will you? You do not believe in what Aad is doing. You are like me, a black sheep. You don't belong with these Christians. You came here for one thing only, to find out about your father." His voice was growing more indignant, sounding younger. "Now that I have helped you get that information, you don't need me anymore. You will go home, and that will be the end of it. Don't you hear what I am saying? I have never said this before to any woman. Barbara, I love you."

"How can you say that?" She shook her head. "You've known me for one day! I loved for five years and then lost my love. You're sixteen, what do you know about loss? What do you know?"

Now his face was filled with scorn. "I know enough. Who do you think you are, spoiled American? I know that so many Westerners promise us so much when they see the need, but after they go home, we're lucky if we get a Christmas card."

"I'm not like that. Piotr, I will never forget what you have done for me today. You've given me back hope. You gave me that. I will never forget. . . ."

"You'll forget all right. Especially you. Why should you remember? What is there to keep me in your memory? I can't imagine what you are going home to. We are so very different really, aren't we?" This last was hissed in bitter irony.

His indignation was so ferocious, Amy had no idea how to calm it. But he had upset her terribly. Not since the funerals had she felt this raw, this vulnerable. She was afraid that what he said was true. They had been together only one day, but in that day her whole world had somehow shifted.

"I . . . don't want to argue with you. Please. Maybe you're right, we are so different."

And then Piotr put both hands around her waist and pulled her to him. He turned her so her back was against the tree, and he kissed her—hard at first and then more softly.

"You," he whispered. "I've dreamed of you before I even saw you."

"No!" Amy cried. "No, don't do this. You're only sixteen." She tried to pull away, but his grasp tightened.

"And if I were ten years older, or twenty, that would make a difference?"

He still would not let her go, but his voice was calmer. Amy felt herself weakening. He was right. His age was the only thing keeping her from returning his kisses. But he didn't need to know that.

"No," she said again, forcing her voice to be even. "No. This is—I don't know, it's just the day together, sharing secrets. . . ."

Now she looked at him and squinted her eyes. "You don't even know who I am."

"I think we recognize each other more than you will admit. Barbara Skrzypek. So, is that your real name?"

She shook her head. She did not trust her voice.

A long strand of black hair had fallen into her eyes, and Piotr's fingers brushed it over one shoulder. "Tell me. That's the least you can do after using me like this."

"*I* haven't used *you*," she said. "And you already know too much about me. It could hurt you." She had to get away from him.

"Tell me," he insisted.

"Amy. All right? Barbara was my mother's name, Jacek Skrzypek's wife. Now, please. . . ."

"You will write me?" He was letting her go.

"Yes, all right, I will write you."

She pushed him away and ran out of the park, feeling like a fool, like she was the sixteen-year-old, feeling confused.

"Amy, is there something you want to tell me?" Aad asked during their long drive west the next morning. All morning they had been passing through little villages that all looked the same. Now they were stopped to wait for a horse-drawn cart followed by some geese to cross the road. Beside the van stood a small group of children bundled up against the cold. They were waving at the van with its Western plates. Aad waved back.

"Why would there be anything to tell you?" she asked.

"You've been so quiet. Is there something wrong?"

"Yes. We're leaving too early; that's what's wrong. Why didn't we stay longer? It was great to finally be with people who spoke fluent English. I guess I just don't want to leave Poland."

Aad said, "I don't either. But we've given away all our Bibles. We have nothing more to offer, and if we stayed longer, at the Piekarz' for example, we would just be a burden. That's one of the reasons we couldn't stay longer. But we're also needed back home. I want to get started on those Albanian Bibles Tadeusz was talking about. We need to find more funding somewhere."

Amy was glad when Aad fell silent. She had a lot to think over.

14

———— ∽ ————

FALLS

1 Kings 18:38

1970–1971

"Wesołych Świąt! Bożego Narodzenia! Merry Christmas!"

Assistant Minister Jacek Duch heard the shopkeeper calling after a friend as the door tinkled closed. There was no answer, and Jacek found himself responding in his mind, almost automatically, *and a happy New Year....*

But it was more than a new year. In just a few short weeks, 1971 would arrive, closing out the first year of the new decade. Jacek wondered vaguely if the seventies would prove as fruitful and satisfactory as the sixties had.

But even the sixties had begun inauspiciously enough, with Jacek following Izzy's orders to lay low after the defection of Goleniewski. For nearly five years there had been no intelligence packages, no visits to Izzy's "inn." Jacek had simply concentrated on his work for the Polish Communist Party, streamlining the efforts of his particular department and working closely with the SB as Roman had directed.

His efforts had not gone unnoticed by the Party bosses.

In 1964, the big satellite dishes in West Germany and The Netherlands had picked up the radio broadcast in which Jacek was sworn in to his ministerial position, together with several other new members of Poland's government.

It had gone against Jacek's personal credo to be placed in such a conspicuous position, but he could hardly decline the honor— nor could he deny the satisfaction. He had stood on the podium

178

and breathed the sweet scent of power, gazing out over a crowd that stretched to the far ends of the square. The entire ceremony was being broadcast over the radio live from Warszawa. Jacek remembered running a hand along his graying temples and noticing that he was the best-looking man there. *The rest are all twenty kilos too fat from all their vodka and pastries.*

When it was his turn, Jacek had stepped up to the podium, leaned toward the mikes, and said, "Thank you. Thank you to the Party, and thank you, the people of this glorious People's Republic. I swear to serve this proud nation in every capacity, to guard her from imperialist threats. . . ."

And in that moment he had once again felt the familiar clear-headed surge of adrenaline that told him he had not lost his touch. This was the game he had been longing to play again.

For these specific words had been chosen according to a previously agreed-to code. The second sentence had begun with a sequence of words that signaled something very special. On that day Jacek had been announcing to the "folks back home" that he was back in action.

He had been in action ever since, performing his official duties while reporting back to the Company what was developing in Poland.

That first year, 1964, most of Jacek's reports had told of growing resentment among the Polish population, and Krushchev's fall from power in the USSR had only added to the uncertainty. General Mieczysław Moczar, now Minister of the Interior, had ordered a stricter censorship policy, further compounding the sense of frustration and disillusionment.

By 1965, however, a year into his ministry job, Jacek was reporting that First Secretary Gomułka was finally willing to offer certain compromises. The borders had opened a crack, making foreign travel possible as long as immediate family members stayed behind and the passports were surrendered to the government upon return.

In 1966, Jacek's department had been asked to work with the SB in making sure the celebrations of the Polish Millennium did not get out of hand. The State and the Roman Catholic church had differed distinctly on how this thousand-year anniversary should be celebrated. This had been a sticky time for the counterintelligence service. The SB had to keep one eye on the KGB and the other on developments within Poland's own Security Service.

General Moczar had vowed to use his own group, called the Partisans, to cleanse public life of all "alien" elements and "Zionist agents." This had left many Poles frankly baffled, since the only place where a substantial number of Jews could be found in Poland was in the higher echelons of the Party. The purpose of Moczar's anti-Semitic campaign had been to make Gomułka look bad and himself look good as he saved Poland from imaginary enemies—a common enough ploy. Jacek had been acutely aware, however, that the campaign was not only overtly anti-Semitic, but also covertly anti-Soviet.

But Mozcar's campaign had failed, and the result of that failure had been the dismissal of fourteen generals and two hundred colonels from the Polish armed services. In their place, after 1968, had come a new type of officer, reliably pro-Soviet, but factionally neutral and much better educated professionally. Change was in the air, and Jacek had faithfully reported these changes back to his American handlers.

All along, Jacek had been telling his station chief, as well as himself, that conditions in Poland really were improving. The freer discussion, slightly livelier press, and possibilities for foreign travel helped a little, but not enough. Then in March 1968, when Gomułka hiked up the food prices yet again, the first riots had broken out. Students had marched in protest, inflamed by reports of rebellion and reform in Czechoslovakia.

Jacek, unlike some of his fellow agency men in Eastern Europe, was not supposed to aid in any efforts aimed at insurrection. His position was too vulnerable; he was too visible. There had been agents in Czechoslovakia that spring, however, who goaded and assisted the Czech underground to call the Soviet Union's bluff. They had promised Western military support if things got tough. When the tanks roared into Prague that August, however, the only sign of foreign support had been Polish and pro-Soviet—in the form of Polish drivers sitting inside some of those tanks. In Poland at least, people had behaved, more or less doing what they were ordered, and the student protests had been quickly suppressed.

Nonetheless, there had been murmurs, and the unrest had continued, sometimes overtly, sometimes just under the surface, simmering, waiting to break through into another round of violence.

Even now, Jacek was in the border city of Szczecin to see for himself if the riots of December 1970 were nothing but rumors. Polish radio news was blaming the usual revisionist troublemakers. Elsewhere he had heard earlier that week that this latest wave of worker unrest might actually bring down Gomułka. So Jacek had come to the border to find out just how serious the situation was.

He knew it was risky to go there as an assistant minister; someone might recognize him. But Jacek had disguised himself with a beard and wore a hat. As he walked, he kept his head down, but his ears open.

The neighborhood around the Szczecin train station looked normal enough. There were even a few Christmas decorations up. But as Jacek neared the docks, he could see for himself that the reports were anything but exaggerated. He heard the shouting before he saw the crowd.

Jacek turned the corner and ran straight into the marchers. He edged up against the side of a building to let them pass. There were dock workers and factory workers, men and women. *Who are the leaders?* That's what he was there to find out.

Then he felt the ground shake and looked back around the corner, down the street he had just come from. A fleet of armored ZOMO vans screeched to a halt, lining up on the sidewalk. ZOMO squads poured out of them, men dressed in helmets with masks, each carrying riot shields. Jacek sucked in his breath when he saw the Kalashnikovs they carried.

I've got to get out of here. He had nothing but his handgun, tucked just above his ankle. But he was trapped. He couldn't run straight into the ZOMO, because seeing him dressed in civilian clothes would be reason enough for them to hassle him with the rest of the crowd—they wouldn't ask questions until it was too late. But the only way to avoid them was to join the marchers. He ran into the fray just as the milicja turned the corner and caught up with the crowd.

The marchers turned almost as one, and in that instant the demonstration turned into panicked flight. The ZOMO had chosen their point of attack well. There were no side streets off this one.

Jacek worked his way forward along the side of the crowd. And when he could get a little visibility he moaned. In front of them waited more ZOMO, lined up beside half a dozen water cannons.

All around him, Jacek recognized the smell of fear. It came back to him like a wraith from the war, refusing to be put to rest.

———————— ✎ ————————

Despite the pain in his side, Jacek managed to drive himself back to Warszawa. He kept wanting to pull over and fall asleep, "Which means you probably have a concussion, too," he mumbled to himself as he drove through village after sleeping village.

Talking out loud was one way he kept himself conscious. Keeping the window rolled down was the other. The snow blew in and bit against his face until he could no longer tell the difference between the pain and the cold.

When he woke up the next morning, by some miracle, he found himself in his own bed, Wiktor's ugly face looking down on him. "How did I—? How on earth did you find me?" Jacek asked. Had he left instructions for Wiktor to follow?

"I think I had one of your 'feelings,'" Wiktor said. "I knew something was wrong, so I went over to Szczecin, and on the way I saw your car parked on the other side. Your window was rolled down. Were you—"

"Robbed? No. Just trying to stay awake." Jacek shifted his position, and a flame of pain shot up his side. He was suddenly unsure of how much he should tell Wiktor. How on earth had he known where to go to find Jacek?

That's ridiculous, I must have told him. Jacek was confused. "Has anyone seen me like this?"

"Only Gabi. She helped me bandage your ribs. What happened?"

Again Wiktor surprised him. He never asked questions. It was part of their unspoken agreement. "I got caught in a crossfire,"

Jacek said in a tone that let Wiktor know it was none of his business.

———— ⤳ ————

Three weeks later, Jacek sat in the finest hotel Warszawa had to offer, sipping his coffee and reading the newspaper. The headline on the front page was dated January 1971. It applauded the election of Edward Gierek as First Secretary of the Polish Communist Party. Gomułka was out, and Gierek was the new ruler of the Polish People's Republic. The riots that had swept through the country just a few weeks earlier had been responsible for bringing about Gomułka's downfall after all.

Jacek put the paper down and wondered how the changes would affect his own position. He glanced impatiently at his watch. He had assumed that was what Roman wanted to meet with him about, but Roman was late. Jacek would give him another half hour. After all, Roman was the only Party leader of the many Jacek had met who even knew the meaning of the word punctual.

"Duch." Roman's voice. Jacek was annoyed that he had been taken by surprise. As Roman slipped into the seat opposite Jacek, he passed him a small gift-wrapped box. "Don't open it until I leave. Am I late?"

"No. Right on time, as always."

Roman squinted his eyes. "You never could lie."

Jacek almost coughed up his coffee. Instead, he swiveled the newspaper around so Roman could read the headline about the change in command. "You've been busy."

"Yes, there are a few of us who think Gierek will do a decent job. Gomułka screwed up too often. He was good at making promises."

Privately, Jacek wondered how Gierek could do any better.

Roman continued, "I've been told our SB has you under tight scrutiny. They don't have anything to scrutinize you about, do they?"

Easy! Take it slow and easy. It took most of Jacek's self-control to mask the shock he felt. Roman was watching him closely, too closely. A lifetime of practice took over as a voice in his mind told him to calm down. *He's playing with me.* He took a deep breath and spoke slowly, leaning forward. He could see the place below Roman's lower lip where he had missed when shaving.

"If I'm not mistaken, I've been under surveillance for the last ten years," Jacek said in a voice just barely above a whisper. "Ever since you asked me to check out that Goleniewski turncoat. You weren't setting me up on that one, were you?" Jacek saw his answer in Roman's steely gaze. For a moment, a spark lit the eyes turned on him, then died back down to an ember.

"Well, I knew you were observant, or I never would have picked you. All the Party's ministers like you are picked, you know."

"And we can be unpicked."

"My point exactly. You are on top of things here. Perhaps I underestimated you, Duch."

Jacek knew he was supposed to pick up on the hostile tone. He was not altogether sure what was going on. His heart still beat like a drum, but there was a chance that maybe the worst thing he had to expect was a simple demotion.

"I just came here to let you know the same people who were in charge of the country are still in charge." Roman was grinning at him. Then he stood up and motioned at the little box, still in Jacek's hand. "Welcome to the new government."

Only after Roman left did Jacek notice the little flashes of light in the corner of his line of sight that signaled the onslaught of a migraine. He opened the box. On a cushion of cotton lay something small and hard.

If he wasn't mistaken, it was the bullet he had shot the elk with.

15

EXECUTES JUDGMENT

Isaiah 66:16

1968–1971

Jan returned to Warszawa after his birthday visit and spent the next months raising money to pay for Bibles printed in Russian. His personal following—Sister Emma and her circle of war widows—surprised him by giving far above their means. Again and again he was touched by how the poorest in the congregation could give so much. The idea of viewing themselves as givers instead of takers, of helping others rather than being victims, caught hold of the church and would not let it go.

When he finally had the books, Jan applied for and received the passport that allowed him to travel within the East bloc. Thanks to a written invitation from a friend of his father's, he was granted the necessary visa to get into the USSR. Then he simply boarded a train for Moscow and went there. He crossed the border in the middle of the night. The guards happened to be short of men, so they conducted only random checks of all the passengers' luggage. And no one opened either of Jan's boxes.

When Jan arrived in Moscow, he put his boxes in a taxi and gave the driver the address his friend had given him so many years earlier, back at summer camp. In no time, he was knocking on a door.

"Konstantin?" Jan didn't recognize the bearded, boyish face confronting him suspiciously when the door opened.

"Comrade Jan?" The two young men broke out laughing as Jan pointed at his boxes and covered his lips with a finger. They stored the boxes under a bed and were out on the street in five minutes.

"What on earth? Aad told us you might be dropping in." Konstantin hit Jan so hard on the back that he stumbled a few steps.

"Ah, so he spoiled the surprise." Jan felt like he could fly straight to heaven and back. It had all been so easy.

"Yes, well, he may have warned us of what your church is doing, but I don't think you've seen him since then. So maybe he hasn't warned you yet."

"Warned me?" Jan's euphoria suddenly dimmed, and he cast a furtive glance over his shoulder.

"No, my friend, I mean maybe he hasn't warned you about what our church is doing. You know us; anything the Poles can do, the Russians can do better."

Jan shook his head and laughed out loud. "I can't wait to hear this, Pastor Rybnikov."

"All right, it's simple. Now I've been busy setting up a distribution network," Konstantin said.

"You have? That was my next problem."

"Make it my problem, and it's all taken care of. But now I want to try an idea out on you. I say one word. *Albania*."

"What Albania?"

"Albania where people live like animals."

"That Albania. Yes, I know, it's bad."

"It's worse even than here," Konstantin said. "Enver Hoxha has made that country a bastion for communist hardliners. Albania makes the USSR look almost capitalist."

Jan nodded. "Yes, I've heard. They're completely cut off from the outside world."

"Which is why our Moscow church wants to do what your church in Warszawa has been doing, but for Albania. We need your help, though. You can travel."

"Yeah, as long as I leave my brother and parents in Poland for them to arrest if I don't come home," Jan said bitterly.

Konstantin squeezed his arm. "But still, you can travel. And so what if you have to turn your passport back in every time you come home? *You can travel*. We can't. But we can raise money, what little we have. And God will honor that, I'm sure. At least, that's what I tell my congregation. . . ." Konstantin's voice trailed off for a moment. Then he continued, "So can you talk to Aad? He won't be coming back here for a while, he said. If you can help us, we might be able to help the brothers and sisters in Albania."

The ripple effect Jan had envisioned grew wider and wider as the easier traveling laws introduced by Gomułka enabled more Western missionaries to visit Poland more often, and this meant more trips to the USSR. Gradually Jan put together a network that reached into the Ukraine and out to churches in the Baltic republics of the USSR.

But as the year wore on, he had come no closer to helping Konstantin's church in their undertaking. He could not even find out who they should contact in Albania, let alone how they should get Bibles into that country—if they could get Bibles translated into the Albanian Tosk dialect in the first place. The Tosks lived in the south of the country, where he was focusing his efforts because the northern two-thirds of Albania was predominantly Muslim. In the south, he had heard, people were mostly Eastern Orthodox. For all Jan knew, however, they might be supplying churches that did not even exist. His various inquiries had met with nothing but dark silence.

Just before his twenty-fourth birthday, Jan was ordained a minister of the Baptist church. His parents attended the ceremony in Krzysztof's church in Warszawa, where Jan had now been apprenticing for more than a year and a half. Piotr came with them but seemed mainly interested in visiting the student cafés in the city.

As an added bonus, after reapplying in both 1968 and 1969, Jan had finally been admitted to the university in Warszawa. He would begin that autumn with evening classes. It had already become clear that his years of independent study had paid off. The administration had agreed he could sit for exams that would enable him to earn his engineering degree in less time than usual.

Jan threw himself into his studies. Then six months later, in February of 1970, he heard from his father that Aad had managed to match the funding Konstantin's church had been raising. His group could get Bibles printed in the right Albanian dialect to Jan by March of 1971. That gave him only a year to find a way into that country.

Jan's next shipment of teaching materials for the USSR was too large to take on the train. So now he had a problem. "It's a good problem," he told Sister Emma one afternoon when he was reading to her, "but it *is* a problem."

"You need a helper," she said.

"Or another form of transport," Jan rejoined. "We've been blessed so far. But I would be conspicuous making two or three train trips in a short period. The entry stamps in my passport would give me away."

"Why not do it the way the angels do?" she said. Jan looked at her and could have sworn she looked five years younger as she added, "Fly."

So Jan took some of the money out of his next paycheck and bought the cheapest ticket he could find on a LOT Polish Airlines flight to Moscow. He checked the four large suitcases filled with Bibles and climbed the metal stairway. The whole flight, he couldn't take his eyes off the billowy sea of clouds. *The way the angels do*, he thought more than once.

At the Moscow airport, he felt fear at the sight of so many armed Russians in the same building. Some were police, but most looked like soldiers on their way to some sort of military exercise. When he watched them more closely, he noticed that most were carrying duffel bags over their shoulders and looked as lost as he felt.

Jan watched his suitcases being unloaded from the truck that came from his plane and then placed on a table. As he stepped forward to claim them, a customs man put them into a curtained-off area on another table.

"Excuse me; that's mine," Jan said in his best schoolboy Russian. He pointed where the first suitcase had just disappeared.

"One moment, please. We must see what is inside."

Jan's heart froze as the fear seemed to seize his spine. *What do I say?*

"What's in these?" the customs man asked, patting one of the remaining suitcases.

What do I say? Oh, Father, help. . . .

The woman at the other table called the man over, and she pointed to something. Jan couldn't see what until the man walked over to the woman's table and returned with Jan's case wide open, cradled in his arms. As the man set it down with a grunt, he looked at Jan again. He hit the sides of the other cases. "Are there books in here, too?"

"Yes," Jan whispered.

"Well, what kind of books are they?" As the man spoke, he clicked open one of the locks on the suitcase under his hand.

"Bibles."

"Bibles?" The man stopped fiddling with the second lock.

Jan nodded. "Jesus was the first communist."

The man looked at Jan as if he were speaking a foreign language. Jan started to open his mouth and then heard a familiar voice calling, "Uncle Feodor, oh, Uncle Feodor! You found my friend's lost luggage. Oh, I'm so glad."

In no time Konstantin had swept down on Jan, pressed something into the hands of the customs guard that made him look pleased when he opened his palm, slammed shut the open case, grabbed up another, and motioned for Jan to seize the other two suitcases and follow quickly.

To Jan's utter amazement, in less than ten minutes they were out of the hall and had all four suitcases deposited in a waiting *Volga*, mysteriously driven by someone with even more facial hair than Konstantin.

"Can you tell me what that was all about?" Jan asked, surprised himself by the edge in his voice.

"Customs officials who like dollars. You know, dollars, the solid currency. Those grubby old bills produced long ago by the U.S. Mint that now provide a means for exchange throughout Eastern Europe's thriving black market."

"I'm not talking about the dollars," Jan said impatiently.

"Oh. Well, then let's talk about what you said back there. Did I hear that right? Were you entering into a philosophical conversation with that poor son of a peasant? 'Jesus was the first communist'? Jan, you can do better than that!"

Jan finally felt the fear lift and the laughter begin. Only when his ribs began to ache did he realize how close he might have come to disappearing inside an interrogation room. He looked at his watch. "Wait a minute," he gasped through his tears. "Wait a minute." He shook Konstantin. "Where are you taking me?"

"What do you mean?"

"Well, I'm taking the train back home in an hour. You're only supposed to pick up the Bibles, not me!"

Konstantin leaned forward and said a few words to his friend. The car screeched a U-turn and made its way toward the train depot. "Of course, you were counting on my showing up, yes?" Konstantin asked.

"Yes. Of course," Jan answered, mimicking his friend's self-assured tone and upraised shoulders. "But we don't have much time together, and before I go, I have a confession to make. I'm still trying to find a way into Albania, and Aad is helping me, but I just don't know . . . do you think there's even any interest down there?"

Konstantin cut him off just as the car pulled up in front of the station. "There is nothing to know except this. We *know* Bibles are supposed to make it into Albania. Members of my congregation are sure of this. Keep trying, Jan. If anyone can find a way, you can. With the help of Jesus, of course."

With Konstantin's words burning in his heart, Jan returned to Warszawa and his studies, returned to pastoring, returned to prayer for a country he could hardly envision. But he had to pray for Albania since he had to find a way in and get some information about it.

"Why has God given these crazy Russian Baptists a burden for Albania?" he asked Krzysztof.

"Probably for the same reason that He gave you a vision for the crazy Russians, Jan."

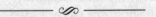

In December of 1970, Poland erupted once again in workers' strikes, many of which were viciously put down by government forces. In Gdańsk and Szczecin, people were even killed by the ZOMO. Jan heard from his father that in Gdynia it had been the Polish Army that fired on its own people.

Rumor in the hotel kitchen had it that Gomułka's days were numbered. And when the change in government did come, it marked more than a new year. The era of Edward Gierek had begun.

Jan would always remember the day the State press heralded the new Party First Secretary. It was the day Jan made more money in one morning than he usually made in a week. It was an answer to prayer when too many of the waiters called in sick after the election results had been announced and the entire country had celebrated. At last Poland could start becoming Poland.

As a result of the national hangover, the hotel manager asked Jan to fill in as a waiter. His first order came from a well-dressed man sitting in the hotel restaurant who ordered a coffee. He was joined by another man, who arrived in a huge Party limousine. Jan heard this later from the head waiter. He would never forget any detail of that day because it had marked beginnings and breakthroughs on more than the political front.

That was also the day when Jan found a way into Albania. The money he earned that day just happened to cover the cost of gas for the car he had borrowed. He had been told that driving was the only way to get anything into that country. The Bibles would have to be well hidden. And he would need a definite drop-off point. But he had someone now who could tell him these things, and that's what mattered. Jan's contact was a friend of Krzysztof's who had heard from someone who had heard from someone that they were trying to find a contact in Albania.

Two months later, in March of 1971, Aad and a Belgian woman brought the long-awaited Albanian Bibles and left them at his parents' house in Gdynia. Jan was ready for them. He had a route, and he had a contact in a village just over the border. He didn't like all the unknowns, but they came with the territory. For some reason, he was still being allowed to have his passport whenever he wanted to leave the country. Others like him who tried to travel less frequently were often denied their papers. Jan had heard from Aad that the American girl who had traveled with him in the winter of 1970 had been waiting more than a year to return to Poland.

Jan drove the bad roads alone, headed for a destination prayed for by people in more than three countries. He had crossed three borders with no problems. From Poland into Czechoslovakia, from there into Hungary, then into Yugoslavia. He was seeing these countries for the first time in his life. As he headed farther south, late spring became full-blown summer. He camped outside in the warm nights. It had become a private pilgrimage.

Jan imagined the angels around his car. There was no way this mission would fail. *In Your hands*, he prayed.

He had chosen a remote border crossing, one only open at certain times of the day. He waited to join the line until just before closing time, when the officers would leave to eat their midday meal. Jan was very aware of the sounds of the birds in the fields around him, the smell of diesel from the truck ahead, the endless blue sky. In the distance smoke curled from the chimney of a farmer's shack. *Someone's home.*

A guard motioned him forward, and Jan surrendered his papers. He fought the temptation to hold his breath. This was the country with hardly any foreign trade and where all foreign investment was banned. Would what he was carrying be construed as trade?

A second man opened the trunk and started removing the top box, which was filled only with children's clothing. Jan got out of the driver's seat just as a little girl came running up to the guard and began tugging at his pants leg. *She's calling him to come home and eat*, Jan realized.

Quickly, Jan stooped to the box, brought out a bright pink dress, and held it up to her. He motioned with his hands that she could keep it, and to Jan's utter amazement, the girl flung her arms around his neck. When he pulled back, her huge brown eyes burned into Jan. Jan looked up at her father, who was grinning with pride. Jan stood and smiled, nodding at her. Since the man was not Russian, Jan spoke in Polish, knowing his words wouldn't be understood, but hoping the meaning might. "Very pretty. It's hers. You're a lucky man."

The guard nodded and grinned some more, swinging his daughter up over his head and onto his shoulders. He said a string of words to Jan and returned the papers, then walked back to the station, calling to his colleague as he went. Jan hurriedly lifted the box of clothing back on top of the boxes of books. He slammed the trunk closed, climbed into the car, and waited as the man lifted the barrier. When he passed through, the little girl waved her new dress at him.

The way the angels do, he thought yet again. A lark began to sing in one of the pastures to his right.

When Jan returned that spring from his trip to Albania, he could not wait to get back to Russia and tell Konstantin about how successful he had been. The friend of a friend had found no fewer than four churches in the southwestern part of Albania that were willing to distribute the clothing, medical supplies, and Bibles Konstantin's church had sponsored.

Jan's own church had put together another shipment of things needed by the Russian church, so that summer he set off for Moscow again. Sitting on the train, staring out into the night, Jan was struck, not for the first time, about how his life in Warszawa all seemed to be fitting in so well with the ministry. In Warszawa, Krzysztof could cover Jan's parochial duties, and there were more than enough young men in the church willing to fill in for his dish-washing job.

Since the first time he had tried the trip, Jan had taken only the night train. Now he was asleep when the border police entered his compartment, empty except for another man around his age. The officer turned on the light and started yelling at them both to take down their luggage.

Jan had not expected this. In a flash, he felt that same fear that had crippled him at the Moscow airport. He reached for the box by his feet, but the guard pointed at the suitcase in the rack above his head.

"That one. Open it up," he barked in Russian.

Let there be a distraction. What do I do? What do I say?

"Hurry up!" As the guard spoke, another entered the compartment and began pulling apart the cushions of the seats, feeling along the edges and testing the seams.

Jan waited for his miracle, his heart beating so hard it hurt his chest.

"Open it," the guard roared.

Jan bent and opened the suitcase. The guard threw aside the clothing and revealed the teaching materials and Bibles. He went through the case, dashing its contents to the floor. Then he reached for the box himself and emptied that out as well. Then he reached in a pocket and pulled out Jan's passport, which Jan had handed over to the conductor at the beginning of the trip. The guard waved this in Jan's face and hissed, "You won't be seeing this for a while. Follow me."

Jan was taken off the train and put in a cubicle at the back of the border post. He sat in darkness as he listened to his train pull away, heading eastward. A few moments later a Soviet police agent entered the room. He turned on the light and read the papers in his hands.

"Who are you traveling with?"

"No one," Jan answered.

"What else did you have with you besides the books?"

"Nothing."

"Who paid for the books?"

"I did."

"Do you have money for me now?"

Jan squinted into the light. He had no money, but even if he did, he wasn't about to give ministry money to this man. He shook his head.

The guard snorted. "Too bad."

Jan knew they could arrest him. They could ship him off to a labor camp elsewhere in the country, far away from the border. He had no rights whatsoever, and no papers or identification. "What will you do with me?" he asked.

The guard had been heading for the door. Now he turned around and said, "You are being denied entry to the USSR. We will send your papers to your local police. You will have to find your own way home."

"I'm free to go?"

"Of course."

Jan was tempted to ask about his Bibles, but he didn't dare. It was better if he just left as quietly and quickly as possible before this man changed his mind.

It was punishment enough to travel the distance on foot, but it was summer, and Jan knew he had been very, very fortunate. Next time they might not be so reasonable. Jan shook his head in wonder as he headed west through the night. He watched the stars swing from one side of the sky to the next and thought, *You protected me back there for a reason*, he prayed. *Show me why.*

At first light he hitched a ride on the back of a farmer's wagon full of milk cans. Then he hitched another ride, and another. It took the full day, but by that evening he was back in the capital.

Jan lost no time trying to get his passport back. After the first denial of his request for permission to travel, he tried again, and again. Each time the authorities refused him.

Finally, Krzysztof intervened and warned Jan to stop applying. "Don't you see? It's attracting too much attention. I believe they will be watching you now, too. Perhaps you should let others in the church try to go and wait until the following year."

"But it's my ministry," he protested. "My routes, my contacts. . . ." As Jan listened to himself, his voice trailed off.

Krzysztof raised a bushy gray eyebrow. "You know better than that."

Jan nodded, chastened. "Of course."

"Wait until next year," Krzysztof said gently. "Isn't Aad bringing more Albanian Bibles next March? You could try again then, and you would probably have more luck." Krzysztof paused a moment, then said, "Jan, this is difficult for me to suggest, especially since I've grown to rely on you so heavily. But perhaps you should think about returning to Gdynia. You're far enough in your studies now to finish up and earn your degree without having to be in Warszawa. Go home until things have cooled down a bit. We have to think of the church here."

"Yes, of course." Inside Jan was fighting for control. He tried to convince himself that, no matter how he felt, something precious had not been taken from him.

Jan returned home in time for Christmas. He was both shocked and glad to be back when he saw how much weaker his parents had grown.

Piotr, too, had changed. His deep disappointment seemed to have coalesced into a surly, brooding anger. Although he had finished his carpentry training that spring, he didn't have steady work. Yet he was rarely home, and he rarely talked when he was at home. No one mentioned his violin, which Hanna and Tadeusz had refused to sell and now stood gathering dust in a corner behind the door. Piotr would still not even listen to any suggestions that he reapply to the music academy or start practicing again. The violin was a closed subject.

"Pray for him," their mother simply said when Jan tried to broach the subject. But none of his prayers could quell the constant irritation Jan felt at the way his brother was acting. Abruptly the irritation turned to fury on the night before Christmas Eve, when Piotr admitted to Jan his year-long involvement in the underground. "You're what?" he asked, incredulous. "How can you be so selfish, so immature? Can't you see what this is doing to Mamusia and Tatuś, what it could do to the ministry? Isn't it enough that we're probably already being watched?"

Piotr glared back at him with smoldering eyes. "What do you think your being arrested at the border with contraband did for us, Jan? We were already on enough lists."

Jan knew it was true. He had brought trouble home with him. "I . . . know. But what you're doing is—"

"Is what?" his brother broke in on him. "Not a worthy cause?"

"I was going to say, is different." Jan took a deep breath. "Piotr, can't you see how foolhardy it all is? I'll only say this one time. You're gone from home for months, and the family is suffering more than ever because of the risks you're taking."

Piotr shoved him away, raising a hand to strike Jan for the first time in their lives. Jan watched as the fist uncurled and fell at Piotr's side. "You . . . you have no right to tell me which risks are worth taking," Piotr gasped. "All right, so I'm leaving again. Does that prove you right? I'll be gone for six weeks this time, and glad of it. Besides, big brother's back now to take care of everything, right?" Piotr pushed past Jan and left the room.

Breathing heavily, Jan stared after him. *Why did I have to lose my temper?* Jan knew Piotr would make sure they could not talk alone again before he left on his next trip. Now there would be no chance to resolve the conflict.

Lord, forgive me. And keep Your hand on my brother. . . .

Even at Christmas Eve dinner, Piotr hardly said two words. Jan could tell his parents were hurt by his behavior and by the obvious tension between the two brothers. Feeling responsible to lighten the mood, he took his mother's hand. "I can't tell you how good it is to be home again."

Tadeusz looked over at him and gave Jan a smile of thanks. "Yes, I've always said home is paradise. I don't think the good Lord can do much better than what we have right here."

"What is home?" Piotr asked abruptly.

They all looked at him for a moment. Then Jan heard himself answering, "Home is where you're not afraid."

16

IS LIKE MY WORD

Jeremiah 23:29

1970–1972

Piotr's first letter arrived a few months after Amy returned from Poland. She was working in the ministry's main office in The Netherlands, out in the countryside. She kept busy doing administrative work for Aad and studying Polish while she waited for her visa to be approved. She had already applied twice and been turned down for no apparent reason.

Amy was surprised when Aad handed her the envelope. She had received no mail since coming to Europe. It was addressed to Barbara Baker, but Aad said nothing about that. Instead he suggested, "Look at the back. That's how you can tell the censor office has had a peek. They can steam an envelope open, then glue it closed and no one can tell. But if you tape the back closed, those tape marks show it's been tampered with."

Amy had just been planning to walk to the nearby village for some supplies when Aad handed her the letter. She took it with her and walked along the nearby polder, a large field with canals on all sides. She climbed up onto the dike and sat down beneath a row of cypresses. Here and there, clumps of wild daffodils dotted the field. She took a deep breath and opened the square envelope. The paper was thin and rough. The handwriting scrawled on the pages was tall and spidery, like an old woman's.

Dear Amy,

You have not written me yet, so I thought I would begin. I know who you are, but you do not know much about me. I realized that too late, after you were gone. Please forgive my impatience and anger. I am always fighting these things in myself. You have never been far from my thoughts these last months. I think of you in every thing of beauty I see.

There are some things I must ask you. Do you believe literature and poetry can express as much of the soul as music can? This is something that interests me very much. I think the answer may be no because, to me at least, music speaks so much deeper than words. But then I think that some writing can indeed touch the one who reads it so deeply that you see and learn about a part of yourself you didn't know was there. Will my letters do that for you?

Also, what do you think of Russian literature? And is Viennese architecture as exceptional as everyone claims?

The letter continued with more questions and chat about the weather, then closed with "Your trusting servant, Piotr."

Amy did not know what to make of it. Her time with Aad's organization had taught her that it was possible to express a message in words that seemed totally unrelated. Was Piotr trying to do that with his ramblings about literature and art? She wasn't sure.

But she was sure of something. She had promised herself that if she heard from Piotr again, she would write him back. It was the least she could do. He had risked his life trying to find information about Jacek for her. And she had been thinking of no one but him since leaving Poland.

Amy wrote Piotr. And Piotr wrote back. And so it began. Sometimes she noticed he referred to things she was supposed to have read in past letters. In this way she knew some of his letters were not making it out of Poland. They repeated subjects to each other as a way of checking which was the last letter to reach its destination.

Amy looked forward to Piotr's letters as she did nothing else in her life. Without the distraction of his physical presence, she had a chance to get to know the person he really was. And because only he knew who she really was, her contact with him was like getting back in touch with her real self.

She was feeling annoyed with having to maintain her masquerade around the other members of the mission. The months had slipped by one by one until a full year had elapsed since her trip to Poland. All that time she had been trying to go back, but she still had not received her visa, although she had been able to go on numerous trips to Czechoslovakia and even Romania. There was no explanation for why she could not get into Poland, although the recent unrest there hadn't helped. After the worker riots late in 1970, the government was more wary than ever of anything having to do with the West, especially the United States.

Aad had secured the Albanian Bibles and was planning to return to Gdynia in March of 1971. Amy wanted desperately to go with him. She was afraid she had fallen in love with Piotr through his letters, and nothing short of seeing him face-to-face would help her out of the confusion she felt concerning him. The more time that went by, the more she knew this to be true.

But yet she still could not procure a visa, and so a Belgian woman accompanied Aad on his trip.

When they returned, they were full of stories about ZOMO armed vehicles roaming the streets and random roadblocks slowing their progress. A border guard had confiscated half the Albanian shipment, and Aad had to bribe the man in order to keep what remained. The guard said he needed something to show his superiors.

"Put the bribe money down as support." Aad smiled. "Here, someone gave this to me for you." He looked concerned as he handed Amy a letter but said nothing.

This letter from Piotr was different from all the previous ones. He knew Aad would be visiting and so had written without fearing the censor's eyes. For the first time, Amy could read Piotr's words for what they were, without having to search for double meanings.

My dearest,

Yes, I write those words because I know now without a doubt that I am in love with you. If you would find a way back here and see beyond our age difference, I know I could convince you of my love. What have you done for me? I will tell you.

I was so angry last winter when you first met me. In another letter I will tell you why that was. Just part of it is my growing up in this family and not being able to embrace what they believe and believe in the worth of their sufferings. There is more.

Now something has happened, and all has changed. You came into my life and washed away the bitterness, the sense of betrayal that has dogged me all my life, it seems.

And in December there were riots, just as there had been in March of 1968. Gomułka raised the food prices yet again, and it was too much. I can write frankly since Aad will take this directly to you, but I will not write much. I have joined the underground. And that, together with my love for you, has changed my life. I am finally doing something I believe in, something that makes a difference, something that will make this country free and give my parents more than their religion ever has.

I must tell you that I have recently made some progress in your search for your father. I could never write you about this before because it was too dangerous. Even this is taking a risk, but I can say I have found a friend of a friend and have managed to follow Jacek's movements during the war up to a place called Katyń. I will tell you more when we see each other.

It means so much to me that you have tried for so long to return. From what you write, we share the same love of this land. It is such an honor finally to be actively fighting for her freedom. It is as we sing in the national anthem: "Poland is not yet lost."

My love, your secrets are safe with me. Sometimes I wonder why you have had to wait this long, if it is not because you feel the same as I, that this is a waiting time for us. And that when it ends and we are finally together, we will both know a new kind of freedom.

Write me, my love, and I will hope to receive your next letter from your own hand.

Your servant always, Piotr.

Amy's hand shook as she set the letter down. She had thought Ron would be her only love, but this connection she had with Piotr was just as real, and one tempered with danger and adventure. Amy was discovering that this was something she liked. She wanted more.

———— ✍ ————

That summer Amy completed the two-year intensive language course she had been following. She had begun it thinking it would ease her desire to return to Poland while she waited for a visa. And whenever the sheer frustration of waiting threatened to get her down, Amy had thrown herself into her studies. She had sworn to herself that she would finish the course and then, if she still hadn't been allowed back into the country, she would leave the mission.

Now that the time had come, Amy knew she had some decisions to make. Surely it was time to leave, but where could she go? She still owned the farm in the States, but that seemed a million lifetimes ago. Poland now seemed impossible. Her life in Holland was based on a lie.

What next? In frustration, Amy searched for an answer.

And as she searched, Amy turned down an unexpected path.

It began when Aad called her into his office one afternoon. When she arrived, he was staring down at an essay she had written in Polish. "I've never seen such devotion," he mumbled. "Your Polish is better than mine. You're the only one I know who ever bothered to learn all the cases." Then he straightened and gave Amy that look which always seemed to cut right through her.

"Amy, the administrative and PR work you've been doing with us has been a great help. But I think we both know it's not where your heart lies. Most of our people don't stay as long as you have. You're waiting for something. I wonder what that is."

Amy felt the panic rising. Had she been found out? For some reason, Aad seemed to be asking her the very questions she had been asking herself.

He continued, "Most of our people are younger than you. They come here for a summer or a short year, meet a nice Christian young man or woman and leave us to get married." He smiled. "It happens, and I've learned not to mind, because God always sends someone to take their place. But you, you've always been different. Will you do me a favor? Will you pray specifically that God show us both what His plan is for you? I hate to see all that Polish going to waste, and yet the door to that country stays firmly closed against you." He paused and sighed.

After a few moments Aad said slowly, "Perhaps . . . Amy, what is your heart's desire?"

The question made Amy look up. She opened her mouth, then closed it.

Aad said, "No, I don't need to hear it. But you need to know the answer. It's absolutely imperative that you do."

That night Amy's walk took her far out among the fields. The half-moon's light could not block out the stars that stretched across the horizon. A soft glow shone in one direction, where the nearest city stood. She heard a sound above her, growing louder. When she looked up, a V-shaped flock of geese was moving between her and the stars. Their call came right over her, then faded away. Cold and fog hung in the air, warning that it would soon be winter again.

My heart's desire, she repeated Aad's words to herself. *What is my heart's desire?*

"Piotr," she answered herself out loud. "I want him. I want us to have a chance to see if it would work, maybe even a life together. I can't go back to a rich suburb in Boston and wonder all my life if this was the man I should have stayed with. And . . . I want to find Jacek. And I want to be in Poland. Oh, I want to go back so badly. And . . ."

Here Amy surprised herself. Was there more? She kept thinking of Aad and how she had grown to admire him during the past two years. His quiet courage and dry sense of humor. His wisdom and insight. . . .

He knows. The thought came to her out of nowhere, but as soon as she formulated it, she knew it was true.

"He knows I've been using him and the mission, but he doesn't know why. He knows I don't believe like he does. He knows." Why then would he ask her to pray that prayer about God's plan? *Why has he let me pretend all this time?*

Amy's thoughts flung themselves back and forth as she walked on, following the line of the dike. She moved alone in the dark, her thoughts on the other side of Europe. *What if I never get a visa? What can I do? What has it all been for?* She felt the frustration welling up inside. *Why haven't I been able to go back? I have to go back to Poland. I have to.*

She thought again of Aad, of driving with him past empty

fields, down crooked streets between shabby, lovely buildings. And then she knew.

Poland was her heart's desire; it was what she ached for and dreamed about. Something in her had bonded with the land, had risen and recognized it as her own. Her search for Jacek, even her budding love for Piotr—they were almost peripheral to this overwhelming need to be in that country and explore the part of herself that could learn the language as she had, with all her heart.

"I have to go back there, please. Oh, please." The tears stung her cheeks, but they would not stop.

A part of her was saying, you don't believe. Another part was remembering Aad's challenge.

I can't pray like they do, she thought.

Pray like you do, then, came the answer.

I don't believe like them, she protested. *I don't. I can't. They're all just too extreme.*

She didn't believe, and yet . . . *If You're as real as they say, then help me get back into Poland. Just one more time, please. I have to find out if Piotr—if I am who I think I am. Please.*

She stopped, stood still, looked around her at the starlit fields. Everything seemed quiet, unchanged.

The thought occurred to her that if all Aad stood for was real, she couldn't afford *not* to know that. He always liked to say during the staff meetings, "God can handle your doubts and fears. Dare Him to help you."

"Well," she told herself with a bemused smile through her tears, "I guess I've done that, huh?"

She returned to the mission house and got ready for bed. Just before turning out the light, she idly turned to the Dutch Bible that had been furnished along with the room.

I've lived here two years, she mused, *but my Dutch isn't nearly as good as my Polish.*

Without thinking, she began thumbing through the pages. She had hardly bothered to pick it up before.

It was the word *wacht* that caught her eye. *"Wait." Well, I know enough about that.*

Her eyes were running up the column, looking for the context, and then she saw the other words. *Delight in the Lord*, she translated to herself, *and He will give you . . . heart's . . . desires.*

Amy dropped the book as if she'd been stung. This was too strange, and she was too tired to think about it anymore. She turned to switch off the light and lay down in the dark, feeling drained.

--------- ◦∕∕◦ ---------

The next morning at the prayer time, Aad greeted them with the words, "Today God will change your life."

He looked at Amy. And then to her utter amazement, the tears began again.

For most of the next few hours, Amy cried. She wept for Ruth and John, and for Barbara. She shed bitter tears for her lost love with Ron, so young and so strong with promise, so bitter and distant when they last saw each other. All gone. She sobbed, overwhelmed by her confusion and guilt. And the tears still flowed as she asked forgiveness and said yes and felt the burden of her secrets lift.

The other workers at the mission prayed with her and for her, coming over from time to time to the corner where she sat weeping. They touched her gently and murmured words of comfort she barely heard. Then, one by one, they left the room until Aad was the only one. He sat beside her quietly until Amy finally opened her eyes, feeling as if she had just emerged from a cocoon without ever having realized she was in one.

She looked at his face and saw that it was wet as well. "You knew," she said.

He nodded. "From the very first moment you walked up to me in that church."

"Why didn't you—?"

"I've never been one to walk away from a woman who gives me hundred-dollar bills." He chuckled, and Amy smiled wearily. "I just had a feeling. I could see it in your eyes, dear Amy. You were so desperate, and you were searching so hard. Amy, God honors those who look for Him. You've found Him, now keep on searching, but this time with Him at your side."

--------- ◦∕∕◦ ---------

In the next months Amy felt as though she was waiting again, but was not quite sure for what. This time, though, she felt that she was in the right place, as if she belonged to something. She experienced in a new light the witness of Aad and the other Christians around her. Christmas came and went. She still waited, this time more patiently.

Then in March it happened. The visa that finally arrived would allow her to stay in Poland for a year, as a student. She still had no explanation for why it had taken so long or why she would now be granted such an extended stay.

She would be required to pay a per diem up front for each day she would be in Poland. She wired her banker back home for money without a second thought. More than anything else, she wanted to stay and study, and she hadn't even realized it could actually happen until the visa arrived.

Two days before she was due to leave, Aad's friend Corrie stopped by. She had just been to Poland and bore a message from Tadeusz, a request for more of the Albanian Bibles. Aad had already anticipated the need and had the boxes loaded into the van. Corrie also carried a letter from Piotr for Amy. "Tadeusz said to tell you his son gave him the letter last month. He hasn't seen him since."

Amy thanked her, pretending not to notice the look Corrie and Aad exchanged. She went to her room and opened the envelope. The many pages tumbled onto her lap and fell over her feet. The letter began, *I was born nineteen years ago when my father was in prison. . . .*

She sat there a long time as the words washed over her, carrying Piotr's love even deeper into her heart. She read his entire story and grew to know all that drove him, all that haunted him. As she did so, Amy could feel herself able to fully love again, love as she had once loved Ron. She knew now that God had given her Piotr, had used even him to give her that gift.

Carefully she folded the letter and replaced it in its envelope. Then she stood and began packing. The time had come for her to stop watching the world go by.

17

TESTS

1 Peter 1:7

1973

I was a bitter young man until I began loving you.

I often torture myself and ask, What if? *What if I had listened to you that day when you came to me? What if I had never lost you?*

Three things have given me purpose in life: the violin, my love for you and now, the underground.

You cannot know the effect you had on our home during your first visit to us. That night when I came home and found you sitting at the table, I could not stop staring. You are so beautiful, in the real meaning of the word, so deeply beautiful. I know you think I was just some tongue-tied adolescent back then, but I certainly felt the attraction from the very first moment I saw you. You would laugh, and I could see you were unsure. You didn't belong; you were like me.

I could sense that even before you told me, before that night when we looked out at the ships and you told me why you were really in Poland. I was annoyed with you for bringing up our age difference. All my life people have been assuming I was older. Since I was thirteen I already felt like a man, but when others discover how young I always am, they treat me like a child.

You went on and on about it, but then you started talking about yourself and I was amazed. Another deceiver, *I thought.*

The next morning my parents were praising Jan as usual, even as they sat there passing notes to you and Aad. I had to admit to myself, *Jan* is risking his life for something he believes in. Even if I don't believe the same, it is still admirable that he does these things. Me,

I'm learning to hammer wood. Where is the difference?

But you gave me the chance to make a difference, a difference in your life. For the first time ever, someone opened up herself and needed me.

I fell in love with you on the train to Gdańsk. It really did happen that quickly, from one moment to the next. You were brimming over with the truth. You could not have disguised it if you had tried. The words kept tumbling out of you, stories I could not even imagine, places and experiences I would never know. But as you told me your life story that morning, I thought to myself, I will never find another woman like this. Never in my life.

I had never seen anyone tell the truth like that before. Truth had a hold on you and would not let you go. Each word was a precious gem as you gave it to me. And I felt I had so little to give in return. The least I could do was help you in your search.

I must admit I thought it was a futile search. You cannot know what it is like to grow up in a country where every single person has been touched by the deaths from the war. You talked about the missing-in-action from your Vietnam war. You have a list of these men. Well, thirty years later, we still do not know even who *is missing, so we cannot make such a list, and we can only guess at who is dead. If there was no one who knew you who survived the war, how can you be remembered?*

You have remembered your father Jacek. So we are looking for him. If no one had remembered a Jacek Skrzypek, no one would have known he was missing. I have always wondered why you pushed me away after we looked for him together that first time, and I gave you the news that he had been in Gdańsk twice. I, too, felt the emotion of that moment, a man remembered, a man resurrected because his daughter had been looking for him for ten years. Who knew how long it had been since anyone had let the sounds of Jacek Skrzypek's name pass between their lips? But you have brought him back to life just by believing, just by feeling, as you say it, that he lives.

And when I could finally give you something in return for your honesty earlier that morning, you turned away from me. I have not written you about this earlier because I did not want to think of you turning away ever again.

Now I have done the same.

My love, I tried so hard to believe in us. During the two years we were kept apart, I set your search as my way of proving a love so strong

*that time and separation could not tarnish it—a love like my parents'
love, that carried them through a war and brought them together again.
I told myself that if I could carry on your search, I was still connected
with you. I made the goal of finding out about your father a test I must
undergo before I was worthy. Perhaps, as you may have thought, I began
this game as a boy, but I have ended it as a man.*

*I continued the search, thinking that if this Jacek left signs in Gdańsk,
maybe he's left similar tracks in other major cities. Then, in Warszawa
and Brześć, or Brest as they call it now that it's part of the Ukraine, I
found him again—the registration of an arrival date, but never any departure. The key to the search was his last name, Skrzypek. If you don't
know that, you don't know what to look for.*

*After Warszawa the trail dried up again. But by the end of 1970 I
had made the move into the underground. A world opened up to me,
together with a brand-new network of knowledge, and of people who are
willing to risk something for truth. I told my cell leader about how I was
trying to find out what happened to a man called Jacek Skrzypek. He
never asked why. I told him what I had already found out, and my suspicions that this signature was a way of leaving a message for someone.*

*As I wrote in that letter I gave to Aad in March 1971, he found
someone who knew someone from the Polish Home Army, I think. He
found the name in the form of an officer in the Polish forces, a man from
Warszawa who had fought at the beginning of the war just after the
Soviets invaded Poland. He fought somewhere near the Bug River
against both the Germans and Russians and was caught. Everyone in
that regiment was either killed or sent to Katyń.*

*I could not wait to tell you that we had managed to follow your father's
movements up to Katyń. Of course, it was either that, or he was dead.
That first night you were finally back in Poland I told you all. I remember
how your eyes shone. We had been apart so long. I told you and for some
reason, I felt you pull away. I wonder now why it is that whenever I offer
you more knowledge of your blood father, I lose you.*

*Through my interest in the search for your father, through you
actually, I became involved in a specific group in the underground who
were trying to uncover evidence that it was the Russians and not the
Germans who killed all fifteen thousand Polish officers in Katyń. This is
a research project of national importance. There are many who still believe
the Soviet lie. If it can be proven without a doubt that the Soviets killed*

those men, we will have Poland on our side, and the fight can come out into the open.

I have even met an old man who was a soldier working in a camp near there. He was a brave man to speak with me. We walked together outside because he feared the secret police had put microphones in his apartment. He told me he saw the Russians digging the pit in the woods. He had been arrested and put into a truck with other officers. It was September, he said. During the transport, they stopped. He jumped over a fence and took some apples from an orchard. A lady came out of the house nearby and shook her fist at them. "You are bad boys taking apples," he said she called after them.

This old man said, "We were soldiers, so we laughed at her." I liked that and wrote it in the report. Then the old man tipped his black beret off his forehead and scratched his head. He said that as he rode away, he had this sudden desire not to be rude. It was an extraordinary thing to do under the circumstances, I mean, these men were on their way to a prison camp. But he started collecting coins from the other officers, then jumped out of the truck and ran back to the woman and shoved the coins into her upraised fist. Then he hurried to catch up with the convoy. He managed to catch a truck, but not from his unit. These were not officers, and they were sent to a different place. Later he heard that the officers had been sent to Katyń. And when he escaped from his camp, he saw the soldiers digging the large hole for the officers' bodies.

In my work, this one old man with a cane was not the only one who wanted to talk, but he was one of the few not too afraid to talk. I have tried to travel to the site itself, because I understand the people who live nearby have also seen and heard things. But of course, it is impossible to get permission to travel to that area.

Except for the connection with your father, this does not have much to do with you, but it has touched me. This is my work with the underground that I've written about so often. The more I have asked and searched, starting with your own questions, the more I have become convinced that this has to happen so that "Żeby Polska była Polską?"—so that "Poland may be Poland."

All of this is why I told you the sad news, when you returned to Poland, that your father must be dead. Even when I said that there is proof of only one man being sent out of Katyń alive, you would not accept the inevitable.

Now I have reason to suspect that your feeling was right. Perhaps the only one survivor to leave Katyń was your father. We know that someone was sent out of that camp for questioning elsewhere in the Soviet Union. We don't know where. I hesitate to tell you this and the rest of what I have discovered and get your hopes up again. The chances that this one man is the one we seek . . . it would take a miracle.

You fell in love with me through our letters. When I realized that, for the first time in my life I came to believe in miracles. A miracle was each time I held one of your envelopes with a Dutch stamp in my hands. After I had kissed you, after our day together looking for your father, I thought I had pushed too hard. You were so right. Who was I? What did I know about love?

But you taught me. I thought at first that you had used me, but I really did love you. When I found the courage to write you a month later, I tried to behave better in my words. I never told you, but the letter you call my first was really my fourth. The censor office is enjoying the other three and many others, I fear.

You wrote me back with the same honesty that is so much a part of you. You opened up yourself to me, regardless of the censors. I could not be so free; the thought that some Polish communist would read such thoughts of mine inhibited me. But you let me really learn who you are.

It was not until Aad visited us in 1971 that I could put my true feelings onto paper and know no one but you would read them. I could tell you of what I had discovered about your father having been in Katyń, but I could tell you no more. In the letter you wrote in answer to that one, you used the word love *for the first time. Then you were my miracle.*

I thank his God that Aad shared your vision of staying in Poland, maybe as a student in Gdańsk. The thought of your paying so much per diem worried me, but you had promised you would come back. I did not believe it until the night you called from Słupsk and said you had car trouble.

I had waited two years to see you. Neither Tatuś nor Mamusia knew of our love; they know so little of me these days. In fact, I had told no one. Who would believe me? A Pole with an American girlfriend? More than a month earlier I had poured my heart out in a long letter I gave to my father for the next time someone from the mission came to visit. How was I to know you would receive it just days before our reunion? When I wrote it (I can't believe that was almost exactly a year ago), I didn't think

I could bear being apart from you for one more day. And then there you were. That night you called was the first time I had been home in six weeks. Tatuś took the call and told Jan and me to borrow Uncle Marek's car and go help you.

Jan and I had not spent any real time alone together for years. He and I sat in that white Polski Syrenka that always seems to be breaking down, our knees practically under our chins, and Jan cracked a joke like he can so well, making all the tension go away. It was like we were boys again, going on a made-up adventure together.

Tatuś had told Jan we were going to help a friend of Aad's whose car had broken down; this was because you had mentioned Aad's name on the phone. Our phone is bugged now, but you didn't know this. Tatuś believes the apartment also has microphones, so he didn't say much more. But I know he hasn't told Jan about my writing you, since Jan's joke was about how soon the American woman we were rescuing would have to fix our Syrenka if she wanted a lift.

We got to the part of the woods outside of town where you were supposed to be, and I saw you waving at us in the headlights. Seeing you like that, surrounded by light, the trees outlined behind you, touched me so that I could say nothing to Jan for a few moments. You could have been a village woman trying to get a lift. I only pointed. You are so very sure of yourself. I think only women from America must be that way. That is something else I wanted to ask you. There is so much I still want to say.

I remember Jan stopping the car so the headlights shone on your car. You put a hand out to block the glare. Jan jumped out first. "Piotr?" you called. I think then you were a little scared when you saw a strange man coming toward you.

Watching you for those few moments from the car, I was mesmerized by your hands, your hair, your every movement. It was like watching a black-and-white movie, one where they use strong lights and shadows and filters to soften the faces.

I heard Jan say, "No, no, it's all right. I am Jan, Piotr's brother. Of course, you two have met. Everything is all right. My father told us to come help you."

You hesitated, then stepped out of the light and extended your hand. As he brought it to his lips, I suddenly saw my brother in an all-too familiar light, taking what was mine. I told myself at the time, Don't be crazy. You can't be jealous of Jan. Not that way. *You see, I had never* thought of Jan as someone women would be interested in. I thought he was too stooped, too thin, and he always gave off this air of being unsure of himself.

But I see now I have always been jealous of Jan. Jan could exceed my parents' expectations, while I was never good enough. Even that night in the car, we had both been careful not to continue the discussion that had been going on when you phoned. Tatuś and Jan and I had just come in from a walk when they had been trying to find out what I was doing for the underground, as if I would tell them. And they were implying I could put their own mission work at risk. But I never chose that work; they choose that themselves. He probably never meant to, but Jan has stolen all I've ever wanted. And most of the time, he did it in the name of God.

The jealousy was like a flash of lightning, searing and sudden, illuminating all that was hidden. I swallowed hard and got out of the car. "Barbara, it's been so long." It was my way of warning you that Jan knew nothing about us, and that I didn't want him to. You understood.

I could read the relief on your face when you saw me. You said, "Believe me, it is so good to see you again. Hello, Piotr." Your love for me was in the way you spoke my name. I was thankful Jan was already looking at the motor of the van, for you gave me this gift in plain sight for all to see. I so wanted to take you into my arms right there. To kiss you, to welcome you back to our beloved Poland. Why was I so afraid of what Jan would think? Now I don't know anymore.

The words we said after that seemed as if they had been written for a bad play. "Did you have any problems getting through customs?"

"No."

Only then did I wonder why you were alone. "But where is Aad?"

Jan poked his head out from behind the hood and said, "Yes. Where is Aad?"

You laughed. "Your expressions . . . you look like you think I left him behind at the border. No, I'm afraid Aad had a death in the family the day before we were due to leave, so he stayed home."

"He let you drive sixteen hundred kilometers alone?" Jan asked as he wiped his hands and walked around to look inside the van through the back window.

"Aad knew better than to try and stop me. I know what you're looking for. And yes, Aad gave me the last of the Bibles." I could see that you almost said, "For your work in Albania, Jan." But you didn't. You stopped yourself in time. "And they're all still there. I didn't lose even one book at the border." Then you batted your eyelashes and said in Polish, "Sometimes being a helpless female has its advantages."

Well that caught Jan's attention if nothing else had. He looked at me, and I shrugged my shoulders. What else could I do? Jan said, "Your Polish is very good, especially for an American."

You said while looking at me, "Your English is very good, especially for a Pole." And we all laughed, even as I still felt we were just going through the motions.

Jan and I managed to repair the van. The gas line was broken and we could hook up a new one running along the outside of the van. It just had to get us to Gdynia.

I was already thinking about how I wanted to drive back with you in the van. Luckily, I didn't have to suggest it, as Jan said he would follow us to make sure nothing more went wrong.

And then we were alone, you next to me. And I could say the words that had been burning on my heart for years. You are my first love. I dream of your face, your hair, your scent, as you sat in the moonlight that cold March night.

In the van that night, a little less than a year ago now, I said to you, "You shouldn't have come alone. If I'd known you were alone, I would have met you at the border."

I'll never forget your reply.

"I couldn't wait another day. I had to see you. I was so anxious to go." I took your left hand in my right one and squeezed it. Flames ran up my arm. You have always had that effect on me. All of me always wants you.

I didn't know where to start. So much had been covered by the letters, so I started where we had left off, with what had brought us together in the first place, with your father. I picked up where I had stopped in the letter, about how he probably had been sent to Katyń if he didn't die earlier. Then I told you what Katyń was. You wouldn't believe me when I said he was dead. You kept wanting to hear more about that one survivor. But all I wanted was to get back the magic we shared the first time we searched together.

How was I to know that God would play this cruel trick on me?

You said my name and then, "I've learned it's not luck at all that runs my life. In fact, I'm not really very lucky. But I'm not blind, either. What I feel for you goes beyond the favor you did when you found my father. Don't you remember the letters? They said it all. Listen. Hear the words for the first time and believe them." You paused and said in Polish, Piotr, I love you.

I may write this for you, but it will never be sent as the rest were never sent. I keep all your letters stored in a special wooden box. I had to write all this down for you, for me. Written down it looks more like it really did happen, more concrete. On paper like this, it seems more likely to be comparable. I want to be able to say I made my mistake on this page and that I corrected it on that one. I want to break our story down into segments, analyze them, discard the bits I don't like and memorize the ones I do. For if that's not possible, if I can't do that, then I feel terror in the real sense of the word.

Terror. Perhaps that's the real State secret. They manipulate and terrorize and control until no one wants to fight anymore. It is exactly this inertia that we are working so hard to erase. If people could just find it in themselves to become angry again, we would win. Instead, we have become a country of complainers and acceptors of what we are told. The average Pole believes every rumor and curses the Russians for all problems. But that's as far as it goes. If only we could come up with a cause that could unite both the workers and the intelligentsia.

Inteligencja—every time I hear that word, I think of when you first accused me of belonging to that group. In truth I belong nowhere. I am being taught at the moment by one of the best in their ranks, but I wear the clothing of the workers in our movement. So you see, you are not the only one who can change.

To this day, that remains the source of my terror. Your change.

We arrived home and you slept in my old room, this time alone. The next day, finally, we could go for a walk in the same woods behind Gdynia where Tatuś used to take me. Finally I could kiss you, I could hold you. This meant everything to me. Just a month earlier I had poured my life's story onto paper and sent it to you. Now there you were accepting me, loving me even in spite of it. Perhaps because of it.

We walked past fields hand in hand. I was again spending too much time looking for the right thing to say. Never in my wildest dreams had I thought a woman like you would love me. I saw no hope for such a thing *after my life fell apart and I was reduced to studying carpentry instead of playing the violin.*

Once I joined the underground, I felt passion again. But being with you brought out a different degree of passion. You made me live again.

Your smile, your eyes, I couldn't get enough of your voice. I thought your Polish was charming—lovely, proper Polish like very few speak anymore. I teased you, teaching you the slang that they use down by the docks.

But I still felt so unsure of myself. And then you brought up the age difference again. I hated that. But you were right. "Piotr, it's something we need to at least acknowledge. Fourteen years is a big gap. And because you're so young, people will say things. I don't care. I've waited two years to be at your side, and for at least one year of that time I've known I loved you. Nothing anyone says will change that."

"The same is true for me," I said. There had been something I had been thinking about. I still wanted to keep us a secret from my family, and now I saw a way to do so without explaining it to you. How could I when I could hardly explain it to myself? "Shall we not tell anyone for a little while?"

"Oh, I think that might be taking it too far," you started to say. Then you looked up at me. "If that's what you think is best, all right."

Yes, this is how it would be with us. From the beginning, you let me be the leader, the initiator.

The one to grope blindly in the dark and not see what was right in front of me.

18

Separates

Acts 2:3

1972

Amy and Piotr had a week together before he had to go on his next trip for the underground. Because Jan had left immediately with the Bibles Amy had brought, they were able to find many moments of privacy. Piotr helped Amy find a room to rent in Gdańsk and a roommate to share the rent with her. Then he helped her sign up for classes and showed her Tadeusz's office in case she ever needed to find him on campus.

Then he left. He did not tell her where he was going. She knew he couldn't.

Strangely, it was only when he was gone that she felt she had finally arrived in Poland.

He was gone for nearly a month. Amy had no idea when to expect him back. She spent the weeks attending classes, trying to explain her presence to everyone who heard her accent, and visiting Tadeusz and Hanna. She could see it was hard for them when both sons were gone.

She was just returning from a trip to Gdynia when she walked around the corner and caught sight of Piotr standing in front of her apartment building as if he'd never even left. He had just finished smoking a cigarette and was grinding it dead with his foot, looking down. He looked so serious.

Amy stood still for just a moment, drinking in his nearness,

217

then she could not wait any longer. "Piotr," she called out as she started walking toward him.

He looked up as she reached his side and swung her around until they both were laughing. "Come, we must talk." Amy could sense more than his usual intensity.

"What is it?" she asked.

He put a finger to his lips. "Wait." So she slipped an arm through his elbow, and they walked down the street to the little park and found a bench in an isolated corner.

He was nervous. He leaned forward, elbows on knees, blew out a breath, leaned back again. She had to hold herself back to keep from brushing a stray curl from his forehead, touching his face. She waited.

"I've been finding out about Katyń," he finally blurted out.

"In the Soviet Union?" She was startled. After two years of trying to get a visa into Poland, she knew well that getting permission to visit a controversial war site would be nearly impossible.

He nodded. "I've discovered that the mass grave is covered with grass and bushes, but everyone knows it's there, though no one living nearby will even talk about it."

Amy opened her eyes wider in surprise. "Then how did you find out about it?"

"I met an old man who has seen the graves, who used to live near the forest during the war. When I started asking questions, he wanted to know if I meant the Polish officers from the war. I said yes, all the time looking for the police, suspecting a trap. But he was just one of the many people you can find who used to live in what once was Poland but now has become the Ukraine and part of the USSR. At the end of the war, when the borders shifted westward, he shifted westward, too."

She couldn't take her eyes off his stricken face. "What do you think—what did happen, then?"

"I think the evidence of fifteen thousand corpses is still there for all the world to witness, even after thirty years. Thirty years, and still no justice."

She looked down to see that his fists were clenched and white. But his voice now was controlled and steady.

"Of course, the Soviets have never denied the existence of

Katyń. So all I have to do is prove that they, not the Germans, were the ones who committed this atrocity."

He turned to her, and his eyes were burning. "This is the key, you see. The way to mobilize my people against the Russians."

Then he saw the questions on her face and misunderstood.

"But you're wondering if I found out anything about Jacek." He lifted her hands to his lips. "I'm so sorry, my darling. I'm afraid I could find out no more information about him."

She shook her head. She was scared. "No. That's not it. Piotr, why are you telling me these things again? You don't have to jeopardize yourself, you know."

To her surprise he seemed pleased with her warning. "That's just it, don't you see?" he said excitedly. He stood up and started pacing back and forth in front of her. "My mentor thinks I can recruit you to our cause. It would be very good if we could claim an American among our ranks. He says that the fact that you're a woman will just mean you can get into places others can't."

Amy wasn't ready for this, not yet. She'd only just gotten settled. He almost sounded like he was trying to sell her something. Or worse, that he had sold *her*.

Amy could see the confusion in Piotr's eyes as he persisted. "You share this with me, I know you do, this deep desire to free Poland. Some want to take the terrorist route, but I promise you that won't be our way. Tatuś preaches that where the fire burns, that is the only place where change can happen. That's where I want to be—in the thick of it. I feel so passionate about this.

"Amy, listen, I really believe Katyń is the issue that will anger Poles enough to wake them from the sleeping spell cast on them by the Soviets. I feel like my life has taken on new meaning. Don't you see? This is my heart's desire. . . ."

They had been talking in Polish. When Piotr said this, Amy put up her hand to stop him and repeated in English, "Heart's desire?"

"Yes, I suppose you could translate it like that. Why?"

She stood up and saw she was shaking. She had been dreading this moment. All month she had rehearsed her next words, and never once had they sounded right.

"Because that's my cue, that's why." She sighed to cover her fear. *What if I lose him?*

"I didn't know when to bring this up," she said carefully. "Last time you were home, it was just so good to be with you again and rediscover our love. But now I have to tell you something."

"What? Anything. Oh, I know I've been full of myself. But if you decide it's too soon to join the underground, I'll understand. Anything you decide to do is fine. It's just that . . . if we could take on this fight together, nothing could stop me. The way I feel now, I could take on the Almighty himself."

Amy covered her mouth to stifle a small gasp.

"What is it?"

"Don't say that." Her tone was sharper than she meant it to be.

"Why? What's wrong?"

She saw the fear pass over his face like a shadow. Did he have a premonition of what she would say? He drew close, kissed her, pulling her to him as though he feared losing her. She kissed him back, reaching up to touch his warm cheek with a hand that felt cold as ice.

"My Piotr," she whispered. "You said the words that changed my life. *Heart's desire.* I found that here with you. But there is something you need to know. I've changed."

"We both have, but for the better."

"Yes." She hesitated, knowing her words would cut him, needing to speak them anyway.

"Piotr, during the two years away from you, my heart was finally touched by the message and the risks of the people I've been working with, especially Aad, well, and people like your parents, too. Listen, I don't know how to tell you. . . ."

"What happened?" The words were calm, but they sounded strangled, as if he could barely choke them out.

"I'm not saying this right, I know. 'What happened?'" She searched for the words, could find none of her own to explain. "Aad says my heart was touched and my mind opened to the gift of forgiveness offered by Jesus."

He looked at her blankly. Then he stepped back, stared at her at first uncomprehending, then furious. The anger singed his voice. "Don't tell me that. Don't talk to me about touched hearts and opened minds."

Amy winced at his tone.

"I've fought this enemy all my life, and I've always lost. Why would now be any different?"

She tried to draw close. "But I *was* different, Piotr. I *am* different. This isn't something I did to hurt you. Don't you see, I love you."

But he had already shut her out. It was as if he could no longer see her face. "So what do we do now?" she asked timidly.

"We," he spoke the word with hard irony, "we go on about our business. You keep on with your studies and your search for Jacek, which is why you came to Poland in the first place. You spend time with my family, who will be overjoyed to discover that now you really are what you claimed to be." The words cut into Amy, but he hesitated only a minute, then went on. "And I will go back to my work, which is what I, too, would be doing anyway."

"I mean 'we' as in 'us.' What do *we* do now?" she asked meekly.

He rose from the bench, his controlled smile hard with anger. "Amy, there is no 'us.' There probably never was."

I left on my mission and was gone for weeks at a time. Even when I was back in Gdynia, I often did not let you know. I think I was punishing you, for I knew you did love me and I knew this would hurt you. Maybe I was testing you.

I traveled to other cells and spoke about my findings concerning Katyń. I had gotten hold of some photos from the area and was organizing a huge propaganda effort around the entire Katyń issue. News had to get out that the Soviets had lied all these years. Add this lie to all the others and maybe, just maybe, we could get the country behind us.

Early that July I came home and found you in the living room laughing with my family. After dinner, when you suggested we go for a walk together, I was surprised. You asked about my speaking engagements. Were they always about Katyń? So I offered to rehearse the talk I had just given. I was becoming quite a speaker for the movement.

What I really did was give you another sermon, the very thing I so hated in the church meetings I grew up hearing. I could not stop myself, though. I had been speaking so much to others about the cause, I would not listen to you. I could listen only to myself.

"What kind of country is this where the only way to provide a decent living for your wife and children is to forget all you've been taught about soul and conscience? What has our country come to? It has been torn apart for no good reason, our hopes repeatedly dashed. Our leaders are corrupt. Despite our wealth of human and material resources, we live in worsening poverty.

"After three decades of all-sacrificing reconstruction, the country is bankrupt. The Germans make fun of our polnische Wirtschaft, or chaotic Polish economy. Humiliation is the name of this game.

"Why is it that any mention of Katyń in public can lead to instant arrest? Foreign visitors to Poland are taken to the Warszawa Ghetto or to Oświęcim, but not told the whole truth about the Warszawa Rising, when the Soviets stood by and watched as the Home Army fought alone against the Germans at the end of the war. Historical museums make reference only to the achievements of the communist underground and the People's Army. Monuments were raised only to the 'victims of Nazi aggression.' Every town has its war memorial to heroes of the Soviet Army of 1944 and 1945, few to the Polish men and boys who died for Poland from 1939 on.

"We Poles are condemned to bear the deaths of our 'lost generation' in silence, but must also sever ties with anyone abroad. We must pay constant tribute to the Soviet liberators, blame our problems on ourselves, and pretend that our tragedy is actually a victory."

I stopped. You were listening, but you did not tell me to go on. This was a good speech; it had brought many groups around the country to their feet. We had met in secret in barns and coal mines at night. I considered it an honor to talk this way for Poland.

But at that moment I could only stare at your dark beauty, so distant from me, somehow no longer mine.

19

FLASHES

Song of Solomon 8:6

1972

It began that summer, on a trip to Moscow.

Jan told Amy he was looking for someone to help him deliver a shipment of Bibles and medicine. He promised to get her back to Gdańsk before her classes started again.

Amy said she'd be happy to join him. "It will give me a chance to see more of Poland and see Russia for the first time. Will my visa be a problem?"

"I don't think so. Ever hear of *détente*? They're desperate for Western currency now, tourist dollars. It should only take a few weeks to make the arrangements. If you come, we can take Aad's van and I won't have to go by train."

"Aad's van?" Amy laughed. "You're crazy if you want to take that all the way to Moscow! It will never make it. Aad told me to keep the hunk of junk when it broke down *again* in Słupsk. I think it was running on prayers anyway."

"Then it will run on prayers again." Jan smiled back at Amy, and she shook her head at him. "And we can fit more into the van," he went on. "Besides, with you at my side I have a much better chance of getting past the customs people. You can be my rich American cousin, and I'll be your poor Polish guide who speaks fluent Russian. And didn't you once tell me that being a helpless female sometimes has its advantages?"

Amy grinned. "Ah, it's good to be with someone so simple."

"So, you think I'm not so bright?" Jan asked with mock astonishment.

"No, simple as in not complicated. I guess I've just been around too many university intellectual types. Let's drop it, all right?"

Jan was surprised that she suddenly seemed so sensitive, but pleased that she had agreed to accompany him. "You know, this will be my third attempt in almost a year to get some more help to the Russian Baptists I have contact with. I was beginning to get desperate. The first time, border guards confiscated all the books." He chuckled. "At least if they read them, it might be worth it," he said wryly.

"How can you joke about it?" she said. "So much could have happened to you!"

"Well, I don't know. But you know how expensive these Bibles are. My father's congregation, together with Marek's and two others in the area have donated the money to a group like Aad's. They got the Bibles printed in the different languages of the Soviet Union, then smuggled them into Poland. Knowing how little money these people have to spare only makes the Bibles that much more precious." He paused.

"What is it, Jan?"

"It's just—I *have* to succeed this time."

Amy looked at him a few seconds. Then she asked quietly, "What are we up against?"

Jan thought Aad had trained her well. "Our own people are our worst enemy," he said. "Once, I was meeting a new contact in the Ukraine. I got off the train at *L'vov* with all my heavy suitcases. I had a lot of luggage, you understand, and the poor soul who had come to meet me was so anxious to hold his first Bible that he opened one of suitcases and spilled the contents right onto the platform. He wanted to unpack everything right there. He was so excited that it never occurred to him to be more careful. Well, someone saw us, and in no time there were four police or milicja, or I don't know what they were, but they took away the books and my contact. We haven't heard from him since."

"That one bothers you a lot; I can tell."

He nodded. "Yes. I should have been able to prevent it somehow. I blame myself, and I pray for him often. I don't know what else to do." He looked up and was surprised to recognize his own sadness in Amy's eyes. He remembered the stories Aad had told him; she had known much sorrow in her life as well. So much loss. Suddenly he found himself wanting to ease some of the pain his story seemed to have brought to the surface. He knew of only one way. "Now I have a question for you. What's a 'hunk of junk'?"

"You'll find out." And she was laughing again.

So they became, first and foremost, friends. Friends who could share sadness and laughter. And on that long cross-country trip, they grew into friends who could listen well to each other.

During the drive out of Poland Amy often commented on the rustic beauty of the countryside. "You see it with an artist's eye," Jan said.

"Not really," she said. "I just feel so at home looking at all these little houses with the dahlias blooming out front, the old ladies with scarves around their heads, sitting like those over there, gossiping in the sun."

"You feel at home? Is it this way where you come from?"

Amy looked at him for a moment, then shook her head no.

A little while later, Amy asked Jan to help her learn how to pronounce all the names of the tiny villages they were passing through. They made a game out of trying to find English equivalents. "How can anyone name a village 'Small Pig'?" Amy asked.

"Who knows. These are old, old names that go back before the Prussians and the Russians and the Hapsburgs and the Swedes and before half of the rest of Europe occupied Poland. Who knows where this little pig came from?"

Jan had been thinking Amy seemed preoccupied with something. Several times he cracked jokes about it, offering a *złoty* for her thoughts, a single worthless *grosz* maybe, but he could not discover what was bothering her. Finally, he simply asked.

"It's sweet of you to notice, Jan. I . . . yes, I do have a problem. A few weeks ago . . . there's someone I've hurt badly, and I don't know what to do about that. He won't listen when I try to explain—oh, what's the use?" She sighed.

Jan didn't say anything for a while, and Amy continued, "You see, Jan, you don't know me that well. I'm not what I seem."

"Who is?" he said quietly.

"Well, maybe so, but I was not really a Christian when I joined Aad's group. I just wanted very, very much to come to Poland, and the mission was my ticket in. I didn't become a Christian until last November."

Jan didn't ask any questions. He liked her frankness and knew enough not to ask for more than was given. Besides, they were approaching the border, and it was time to start concentrating on what they were doing. "Are you all right about this?" he asked, nodding toward the border post.

"Yes. I have all my papers right here. And I'm praying with you. It'll work this time, Jan. I know it will."

He nodded. *It has to. Just blind them, please,* he prayed.

They turned the motor off and waited for the line of cars and trucks ahead of them to crawl forward. Every ten minutes they did the same, until they were almost by the first booth. Amy rolled down her window and handed their passports to the guard. He grunted and stamped them, then waved them on.

"Right," Amy said out loud. "That was Poland. Now . . ."

"For the Soviet Union," Jan finished in a whisper.

Amy surprised him and took his hand. "It'll work. Aad says I'm his good-luck charm. If that was true all the times I was pretending to be a Christian, just think what it could mean now."

He smiled despite the tension.

There were three cars between them and the Soviet border post. The first car was through. The second car stopped. Then the guard speaking to the driver stepped back and waved that car to the side. The people inside had to get out, and two other guards came to nose through the items they took out of the trunk. The car had West German plates.

Only one car to go, thought Jan. That car went through without incident, then it was their turn. Amy was perfect. She said hello in Russian as he had taught her. As she handed the documents over, the guard peered inside at Jan, then glanced behind them at the back of the van. "Open it up," he said in Russian to Jan. Amy said nothing as Jan got out of the van. The guard handed their papers to a man inside the booth.

Jan slid back the door. The boxes of books, vitamins, and medicine were covered with piles of secondhand children's clothing and shoes. "Are you carrying any electrical appliances?"

"No," Jan said.

The man snuffled around in the clothes, then asked. "You are Polish. Do you have some vodka for me?"

"No, I'm sorry." Jan held his breath. Now the guard would either go looking himself, or he would let them go.

The other guard emerged from the booth carrying their papers. He handed them to the man standing with Jan and whispered something to him. Jan heard the word, *Amierikanskij.*

Then both men walked away from Jan and back to Amy. He closed the van and locked it without being asked. As he climbed up on the seat next to Amy, he heard one of the guards ask in English, "Dollars?" He held out his hand. His comrade laughed uneasily and looked anxiously around. The first man shoved an upturned palm in front of Amy's face.

Jan knew what they wanted, and it was obvious they didn't want anyone to see the transaction. Before he could say anything, Amy was reaching into her pocket. "Don't!" he whispered, but it was too late. She had already shoved two twenty-dollar bills into the dirt-creased hand. In a second the man's other hand was hitting the roof of the car, a sign that they should move on.

Amy turned the key, shifted, let out the clutch. As they rolled past the car from Bonn, its occupants stared after them. All their belongings lay spread out on the sidewalk next to their car.

"You shouldn't have done that," he blurted out before he had time to think. "I don't bribe. Maybe Aad does, but I don't believe in it. We would have made it through without you throwing that money away. I don't believe in it. God is big enough to get us through without a bribe."

Amy looked at him in surprise, almost as if she recognized his outburst. "I'm sorry, Jan. No, Aad doesn't bribe as a rule. But I had a feeling beforehand and had put that money there just in case. It's worth it, isn't it? Now the Bibles will reach the people who need them most. I'm sorry, I should have checked with you first, but there wasn't time. They didn't want anyone to see they were asking for money—they probably would have had to share it then." She laughed. "Besides, the important thing is, we did it!"

Jan had to agree with her. He was a little surprised at himself for lashing out at her. "You're right, of course," he said finally. Then they both breathed a long sigh of relief, and both laughed that they had done it at exactly the same moment.

The rest of the drive was uneventful, as miles and miles of countryside passed by their windows. They spent two days driving on bad roads through fields and small villages. In the evenings they camped by the side of the road. It was warm at night, so Jan slept outside, while Amy slept between the cartons on top of the old clothing inside the van.

As they drove through towns crammed with high-rise apartment buildings even uglier and grayer than those in Poland, there were more bad roads and then, finally, the suburbs of Moscow. The only feature that made them suburbs was the presence of even more ugly apartment blocks. There were none of the little fruit and flower stands that dotted the street corners in similar residential areas of Polish cities.

The drop point was a playground behind one cluster of the huge, faceless buildings. Even the laundry fluttering from the minuscule balconies in the late-afternoon sun did nothing to color the drab appearance of these endless rows of high-rises.

Amy parked the van and they waited. Jan had said it might be a few hours, so they took turns sleeping to the sound of the children playing and smells of cooking drifting down from the homes above them. Even though it was summer, the air stank of brown coal.

Jan woke to Amy's cool touch on his arm. "Is that her?" she asked.

He straightened up in the seat and saw a bent and twisted little old lady making her way toward them in the deepening twilight. He chuckled. "No, but the thugs behind her are." He pointed at a group of what looked like long-haired teenaged boys pushing one another around on the other side of the playground. They were slowly ambling in the direction of the van. One carried a transistor radio on his shoulder and was swinging to the rhythm of a Beatles song.

Amy laughed. "Now *this* is like being back home. You know these guys?"

"Well, I only know Konstantin, the one with the beard. We met at a summer youth camp when we were teenagers. He's not as young as he looks." Jan laughed. Then he climbed down from the van and slapped the biggest of the four on the back. Konstantin threw a punch at Jan, and Jan ducked. "Who's your girlfriend, Jan?" the young man asked.

"Just a friend helping out," Jan answered in Russian. "Barbara, meet Konstantin." He didn't introduce the other three men. They were strangers, and Jan knew Konstantin would not introduce them. The fewer names exchanged the better.

At that moment two of the other men went over and unlocked a truck that had been parked near the van. They started the engine and backed the truck in Jan's direction. Jan took his cue and slid open the door of the van. He noticed that one of the men was acting as a lookout while Konstantin and the fourth man started loading the contents of the van into the truck. With Amy's help, they were finished in seven minutes flat. Jan glanced around. No one seemed to be watching them.

They hurriedly said their good-byes, then Jan gave Konstantin a hug as the others climbed into the back of the truck and shut the door. Then the truck was gone. Jan sighed. "Now *those* were professionals. All we had to do was get the Bibles here. They'll be distributing them, as well as the clothes and medicine, to churches all around Moscow."

Amy had climbed back behind the wheel and was carefully backing out of the parking lot. "What was it everyone was saying in Russian?" she asked. "You kept repeating the same phrase."

Jan had to think for a moment. "Oh, we were blessing each other in the name of God."

Amy shook her head. "In my country we call them Jesus Freaks."

"Freaks?" Jan asked absentmindedly. His thoughts were still with Konstantin.

"Hippies who believe."

"Well then, if long hair is all that makes a hippie, then we are not far from being Jesus Freaks ourselves, are we? Especially some of us," he reached over and tweaked her black braid. He was surprised at how soft it felt.

"No, I suppose not," Amy said. She looked at Jan curiously, but he was too drained to think much about it. At the same time, however, he also felt charged, energized. He let out a deep sigh.

"I can't tell you how much this meant, both to the people at home and the ones here. After the last foiled attempt, I got word to Konstantin that we had to do this differently. I've worked with him several times before and knew I could count on him. He really came through for me."

"Who is he?" Amy asked.

"The son of a pastor and one himself, just like me."

"And the others?"

"I don't know. Hey, listen, shall we get out of the city and back into the countryside before we pull over for the night? You've been driving all day. I could take over if you like?"

She shook her head. "I'm wide awake. It's all so new to me."

Jan put his head back and relaxed, then mumbled, "There are advantages to having a chauffeur." His reward was a punch in the shoulder.

They spent the night parked on a country road with an oak grove to one side of them and a carpet of stars glittering above them. The only other lights were from a farmhouse far to the east.

Despite his fatigue, Jan was restless. He tossed and turned in his sleeping bag outside. The crickets and other night sounds were too loud to fall asleep. He felt so much safer out here than in the city, where too many curtained windows could hide the fact that you were being watched, but he still remained wary. Russia was not exactly one of his favorite places to visit.

After a while he crawled out of the bag, pulled on his shoes, and paced up and down, trying not to wake Amy. He could hear her gentle breathing from the open door of the van.

This was not the first sleepless night Jan had experienced in recent months. He wondered what it was that stirred his soul so much these days. Why the restless uneasiness, this sense that something was just not right?

He looked up at the stars and sighed. At least these dark hours gave him plenty of time to pray. He gave thanks for what had happened that day, for Konstantin, the others, their families. He prayed for his mother, for her healing, for his father and his work, for the soul of his brother, that he would believe. For Amy, so near to him he could hear the sound of her breathing, that the pain he had seen in her eyes earlier would soften.

Jan paced and prayed as the huge summer moon worked its way across the sky. He prayed as his heart led him, touching on each person he loved, ending with himself. *I don't know what troubles me, but I pray You would show me what You want me to do.*

He knew part of what the problem was. He had only recently admitted it to himself. Jan would be turning twenty-seven that month. He had finally completed the requirements for his engineering degree a few months ago. Yet despite the deep sense of satisfaction that had given him, despite his work, his daily contact with people, his faith, Jan knew that he was lonely.

He felt impatient with himself for feeling this way. God should be more than enough. What was wrong with him that he always wanted more, that he never was satisfied?

Jan had even gone to Marek about the problem, telling him how inadequate it made him feel in his relationship with God. Marek had simply told him he didn't recommend the single life.

Father, you know me better than I do. Don't let me be blinded to Your will by my own desires. Show me how to be content.

After he had prayed, Jan just stopped and listened. It was something his mother had taught him to do as a small boy, to be still at the end of a prayer. When he finally felt at peace, he heard Amy mumbling in her sleep and went to check on her.

The light of the full moon had fallen on her face; that was probably what caused her to stir. In the half-dark she looked like a young girl, her face smooth and relaxed, incredibly peaceful, Jan thought. He watched her enviously. Sleep never came to him like that. When he slept, he rarely dreamed, and if he did, he was often troubled with nightmares.

He listened and watched as her breathing became more regular. He noticed things about her he had never noticed—the smooth arch of her eyebrows, her strongly angled chin. The way she slept with one hand under her cheek, like a child.

And he was struck by an overwhelming need to protect this woman from harm. She lay there so trusting, so vulnerable. He knew she had suffered, but what he felt at that moment was unrelated to her past. As he stood with the moon at his back so he could block the light from bothering her again, Jan wanted only to keep Amy from ever hurting again, from ever feeling as he did at that moment.

It struck him again how selfish his unexplained pain was, when there were so many others around him who were suffering in the real sense—like his parents, like Amy in her grief perhaps.

The sudden stirring of a warm breeze brought Jan back to himself. He shook his head and looked around at the lightening eastern sky, the open pastures, the smell of grass, birds beginning to call to one another in the distance. He heard air moving above him and looked up. Two storks flew beside each other, necks outstretched, black-striped wings moving in tandem. Somewhere in the back of his mind a memory stirred but wouldn't come forward; still, he felt better somehow.

A new day, he thought and gave thanks. Then he crawled back into his sleeping bag and found he could finally close his eyes and sleep.

20

IS A WORLD OF EVIL

James 3:6

1972–1973

Jacek read the ministry memo and actually thought he felt his world shift a little in the direction of normalcy.

Someone, somewhere had decided it was time for the communist version of history to take a more lenient view of those who had served in the Polish Home Army. And with that one little piece of paper, one of Jacek's greatest fears melted away.

Now, if anyone did manage to link Jacek with the Home Army leadership, the penalty would no longer be expulsion from the Party and a possible death sentence.

It seemed that after thirty years, the Party had made a major policy shift. The memo announced the intention to actually award medals of honor to those who had formerly been denounced as traitors. The same people who had survived the Soviet camps or avoided the Soviet firing squads, who had trembled in silence, not even daring to tell their children the truth about fighting in the Polish Resistance—these same people had become heroes overnight. Those who had been sent away to Siberia in the forties and came home in the fifties had finally been declared fully "rehabilitated."

Jacek nodded to himself. It was one of the few times the Party had done something right.

But this brought up another question. *Should I come forward, too?* That would require some thought, some reassessing.

If the SB somehow knew of his Home Army connections, he

could perhaps deflect problems by taking advantage of the new openness and claiming to be a hero. But if they didn't know, admitting to a secret past might simply open Jacek up to more scrutiny, and then what else would come to light?

He sighed, suddenly weary with the need to keep devising strategies. He looked around him at the well-appointed office, the heavy desk and important-looking files, the well-tailored coat hanging on the rack. He did appreciate the comforts of being on the right side of the so-called prosperity.

On the surface, things had been going well ever since Gierek had taken over. It appeared that the new First Secretary was saving Poland from a Soviet invasion. When Gierek had first assumed power, the newspapers and TV had run endless shots of Gierek visiting the bereaved families in Gdańsk and the textile factories in Łódź, where women had led the strikes and ensuing riots. Gierek was the national hero and, as a member of Gierek's government, Jacek was riding the coattails of his success.

Never mind the fact that the collapsing economy was forcing Gierek to take out ever larger loans at ever higher interest rates. For the time being, Poland enjoyed a false prosperity based entirely on enormous subsidies provided by the State. For several years now, prices had remained frozen as salaries continued to climb.

It couldn't last. Jacek, more than most people, could see that.

What he couldn't see was that revealing more about his past would protect him from the future.

And how much would he reveal anyway? How could he keep his stories straight? If he let them, the scenes would run through his mind like a film at high speed, and it was hard to know which clips to show. For the Home Army officer was also the Soviet prisoner, also the underground assassin, also Rokossovski's spy, also . . . Once he let the films start to roll, where would they end?

Almost imperceptibly Jacek shook his head. The ghosts were behind him now. His ministry position was as secure as it could ever be, and Roman had assured him that the Party was pleased with his work. He knew the SB was watching him, but he was used to being watched; he knew how to function under surveillance. And he was doing his job well, feeding information regularly to Izzy and her colleagues. There was no need to take chances by splicing in new film.

With routine efficiency, he filed away the memo and picked up the next piece of paper demanding his attention.

And that was Jacek's first mistake.

———————— ✍ ————————

The Polish secret police had always found Jacek's case an interesting one—not because of what they knew, but because of what they didn't know. The first entry they had in their file on him stated he had simply walked into Rokossovski's forest camp during the last winter of the war, seemingly out of nowhere.

He had first risen to power as part of Rokossovski's machine, but he did not have a military background. What was his background? The lack of a past is as suspicious as a shady past. And so they watched him, and they dug a little deeper, and then it was not hard to find that Jacek was not the man he claimed to be.

When Jacek initially reported to Rokossovski, they discovered, he had known a contact of the Soviet secret police stationed in Kraków, code-named Paul. So he had been in Kraków during the war. At that point the trail turned cold until the early seventies, when members of the Home Army became heroes overnight. Then finally, the SB learned more.

Just before the end of the war, a man named Felek had been picked up by the Soviet security forces on the outskirts of Kraków and arrested. The partisan patch he wore had told them he was a high-ranking officer in the Home Army. But all the time Felek had been back from the *gulags* of the Soviet Union, he never once had let slip a name from the Kraków cell of partisans. He had said nothing to his interrogators in all those years.

Felek had returned to a Poland recovered from the war, but not from its aftermath. And so it was after Felek was decorated for serving in the Home Army that he lowered his guard. And only then did the Polish SB and the security services in the Soviet Union manage to get the information they had been trying to find out by tailing him off and on for two decades.

Felek had been drinking with an old family friend after the medal ceremony when he began to talk about an assassination attempt he had helped coordinate back in Kraków. The target had been none other than Hans Frank, the Nazi king of Poland during the war. "After Ina was arrested," he slurred, "there was only one man capable of pulling it off. We gave him Ina's commission when the Nazis took her. Jacek, his name was—the dark man with no past. Said he was a mathematics professor, but he never fought like any professor I ever saw."

The friend, bored by the endless recitation of war stories, had merely nodded and taken another drink.

The SB agent sitting at the next table sat quietly for another ten minutes, then rose to make a phone call.

So Jacek had fought with the Home Army, had been a hero, even. And that raised more tantalizing questions for the SB.

These days, Home Army partisans were coming out of the woodwork, eager to claim their medals and their belated glory. But Jacek said nothing, just had gone on with his official routine. He made no attempt to contact old colleagues, told no one of his Home Army past.

The SB wanted to know why. He worked alongside them, but as a Party man, a Party spy. They knew that and only gave him "safe" assignments. But if there was more to Jacek Duch than what he claimed, then that made him an even greater threat, a reason for the SB to target the man in their midst with deadly accuracy.

What was it, they wondered, that Jacek Duch had to hide?

———— ❧ ————

As more and more stories surfaced about the war, a word started to be whispered that seemed to incarnate the fear and betrayal of that time; Katyń. The Katyń Forest was near Smolensk in western Russia, near the border of the Byelorussian Republic. Other place names were mentioned—*Charków* and *Miednoje*, where countless skulls had been found, scattered in mass graves.

The question was, had the Germans committed the atrocities . . . or had the Soviets? When the corpses of officers, professionals and reservists, educated men, doctors, civil servants, and teachers were found in the Katyń Forest, each one had his hands tied behind his back and a German bullet in the base of his skull.

In the seventies, as people dared to share personal accounts of what they had witnessed during the war, they told in hushed tones their own versions of what they thought had happened in Katyń.

Jacek had been reading reports on some of these people and on others who were investigating the case. It was the topic of the day. At home one night he was musing on how close he might have been to ending up in Katyń when he happened to hear Wiktor say he had lost a father there, taken into custody just because before the war he had been the local police chief in Wiktor's village.

At this point, Jacek made the second mistake.

"Interesting all this talk about Katyń you hear now," he said. "The Soviets say it was the Germans, and the Germans say it was the Soviets. The bodies they've dug up there were wearing summer uniforms, so the Germans couldn't have done it in the winter of '41 after they invaded the USSR, like the Soviets claim. It had to have happened in the spring of '40. I was there then. . . ."

He stopped. Was it old age, or was he losing his mind, talking like that about his past?

Jacek looked around the room. Wiktor was watching television and seemed not even to have heard Jacek. *It's just as well*, he thought.

———— ✑ ————

The wheels of the SB interlocked with those of the KGB, and soon the name "Jacek" surfaced in the form of a prisoner who had indeed been imprisoned at Katyń but had been transferred for further questioning before the other inmates were executed.

Two men in impeccable suits and Italian shoes climbed the eight flights of stairs in an apartment high-rise just outside of Moscow. When they knocked on the door, there was the sound of several bolts being pulled back. The door opened to reveal a bent old man. "Please come in," he rasped. And after the men did so, he stuck his head out to look up and down the hall to make sure none of his neighbors had seen the visitors.

"We are, er, adjusting our records," one of the men said, even though everyone in the room knew he had no need to explain himself.

The other man drew out a photo of a man with steel-gray hair. "Imagine him with black hair and about thirty-five years younger. We are looking for an ex-prisoner of yours during the Smolensk days. Can you remember him?"

"Just a moment, please." The relief in the old man's voice was plain. He reached over and picked up a pair of glasses from the table. Then he took the photo from the man and scrutinized it. After a moment he said, "Yes, I remember him."

"How can you be sure?" the first man asked him.

"I will never forget him. He was the only one I could not break. I had to send him on to another camp for further questioning. If you don't believe me, check the records. They were written in my own hand."

"We have checked the records," the second man said.

The old man looked wary for a moment. Then the first man stood. "You did an exemplary job at the time," he told the old man. "Your service then and today has been duly noted."

As the two men filed out of the crowded apartment, the old man stood and saluted. He was smiling like a child whose mother has finally remembered to reward him.

21

GIVES THEM LIGHT

Exodus 13:21

1972

Amy visited the Piekarz household more and more often in the weeks following her trip with Jan to Moscow. She busied herself helping Hanna in every way possible—with the cleaning, the wash, the cooking and, most tiresome of all, with the shopping.

Vegetables, toilet paper, meat, fish, each item had its own line at its own shop. Amy had told them how in America you could buy almost everything you needed at one store, a supermarket, and then only stand in line once, sometimes just for a few moments. Jan and his mother had marveled at the efficiency; the small Polish *Supersam* department stores hardly compared with Amy's description.

But Amy seemed not to mind. Maybe it was because it was such a novelty. She said she practiced her Polish with all the old ladies around her, making small talk and learning the local dialect. Jan thought it was just her inherent nature of seeing a need and meeting it.

He noticed Amy did something else for their home, too. She brought out many of the old stories he hadn't heard in years. She would ask the most unrelated questions, and Mamusia or Tatuś would bring up subjects Jan had always been too afraid to ask more about because he feared it would just open up old scars. Amy's being around did just the opposite. It seemed to clean out old wounds.

For instance, one afternoon he came home for supper and

found Mamusia talking about her illness. It was something they all lived with and helped Mamusia with in as many ways as possible, but it was not something they readily talked about. Tadeusz was out of town, so it was only Jan who joined the two women and poured himself a cup of tea, settling back in a chair and comparing what he heard with what he remembered.

Mamusia must have been baking that morning because the apartment smelled sweet and her face was flushed from the heat. Tight curls framed her face, too often lined with pain lately. Jan wondered how Amy had gotten Mamusia to open up about this particular memory, one so painful that she had kept it to herself for years. *You are a source of healing in my family,* he thought as he watched Amy encourage Mamusia's story in English.

"In 1964," Mamusia was saying, "I died and recovered. It sounds more dramatic than it was. I remember very little, except waking up to my dear Tadeusz's concerned face over me. He told me later I had been calling out for him. They say I was dead, dead as in not breathing, no heartbeat.

"You see, I used to be a very active sportswoman. I swam and I skied and I liked to work and knew how to work hard. And yet, after the birth of our second child, strange things started happening to me. Doctors could not diagnose the illness. I received hundreds of wrong injections, and an overdose of this kind led to terrible pain and, finally, clinical death.

"I *do* remember I had already traveled far from life and was in a wonderful light. Tadeusz tells me the nurse who had given me the wrong injection phoned our doctor, who came immediately and rescued me. For half a year afterward I was very ill, and we later learned that one person in a thousand survives such poisoning.

"After that, finally my sickness was diagnosed as MS. Dear Jan used to come with me all those times to the hospital, all those years when no one knew what was wrong with me. After we knew, it was not much better, because no one really knew how to treat the disease. All the doctors could say was that it was incurable and progressive—that I might go blind, I might eventually be paralyzed. But maybe not for a long time.

"I had my first bad attack when I left Poland for the first time earlier in 1964 to visit my cousin in West Germany."

Jan noticed Amy lean forward, almost as if she anticipated what his mother was going to say.

"That trip was not so good. I learned I should pray for Christians in the West, that they find the strength to resist the temptation of materialism. My family was of German extraction, so I did not feel foreign. But just because I came from Poland, I was treated as a second-class citizen by my family and by everyone I met on that trip who learned where I lived.

"On the way home a suitcase fell on my back in the train. Although I seemed to recover, a few days later when it was very warm, like now, I was suddenly paralyzed on one side. I went to the clinic, and that's when I started getting the wrong treatment.

"Since then Jan here and my dear Tadeusz and sometimes Piotr, when he was still at home, would go with me to the different treatments. We've tried many different approaches and cures, including massage and special exercises. This has taught me about acceptance again."

"Again?" Amy prompted.

Jan saw his mother seem to draw a curtain over the years and come back to the present. "I think that's enough for one afternoon. Now come, I must go. I promised Iwona I'd come visit this afternoon. Poor thing can hardly get out of bed."

After his mother had left, Jan and Amy were doing the dishes when she said, "I had no idea your mother had received such terrible treatment. Can't you take her to a better clinic?"

Jan shook his head. She was very naïve. "Our medical expenses are paid for by the State, but the care varies widely, depending on where you go. Some clinics and hospitals are better than others. Here, if you're willing to pay extra, you can go to a private clinic. But medical care is very out of date and is very poor in all communist countries. That's what Aad tells me anyway— and that's why you're always bringing medicine over here. I would not mind the poor care so much except when I think of people who could be helped in the West but aren't helped here. Our neighbor Iwona has a daughter a little younger than me. She went into the hospital as a child for a minor operation and came out blind in one eye."

"Is there no system of compensation?"

"What, like your suing? There's not even any referrals for therapy or other aids to help her cope with her handicap. Any treatments we try, we have to research on our own. We investigate the possibilities ourselves, then have to find someone who can do the therapy. Here, if you are in a wheelchair, you stay inside all the time. There are stairs everywhere, and the elevators hardly ever work."

Amy shook her head and said to herself, "I was wondering why I saw no disabled people around. They're all shut-ins."

"You call them 'shut-ins'?" Jan said. "Yes, that's a good word." It was too tempting to wonder what kind of life his mother might have had if her illness had been caught sooner and treated correctly. Jan could still remember hearing her tell them about MS for the first time. He had been nineteen when she came home from the hospital that time, paralyzed on one side.

Jan didn't like to remember, but Amy's conversation had brought it all back. It was the only time in his life that he saw both his parents cry. Mamusia had called him and Piotr, then put her good arm around them both. The room had been full of noise, the radio with some sort of swearing-in ceremony for the new government.

Mamusia had told them, "It's all right. Lord knows, we are survivors. Now we're going to fight this and keep on doing all we've been doing. We'll keep on going to school, we'll keep on singing in church, we'll keep on swimming in the summers. We'll keep on trusting in Him, do you understand?"

Tatuś had taken his wife's face in his hands. "If only it could be me instead. If only it were to be my nerves, my muscles, not yours." Jan had wondered if he would ever love anyone deeply enough to say such a thing.

Now, thinking back to that day, it occurred to Jan that perhaps Mamusia's coming home from the hospital had been the beginning of Piotr's anger that had so marked him since.

Jan looked at Amy. Ever since they returned from Russia, he had noticed a change in her. She seemed quieter. He had often wondered if he was imagining it, but each time he was alone with her again, it seemed as if she were waiting for something. She certainly gravitated to his parents; she was in their apartment more often than her room in Gdańsk. Well, he thought, her room was very small and filled to bursting with the two beds, two desks, and little one-burner stove Amy and her roommate used. Besides, maybe it made sense that she wanted to spend time with his parents, considering the deaths of her own parents.

She surprised him by speaking out loud some of what had been on his mind. "Do you think there's reason to worry about Piotr?"

"You do have a way of starting new subjects. What brought that on?" He was half-afraid she could read his thoughts.

"Well, I know your mother worries. Is she overreacting?"

Jan looked at her carefully. He could not believe that Mamusia had told her about Piotr's work with the underground, so Piotr must have told her himself. Jan couldn't be sure, though, and he didn't want them discussing it in the apartment. He might not agree with what Piotr did, but Jan would do nothing to further jeopardize his brother's life. "Well, you know how mothers are."

Amy cocked her head, and he immediately pointed at the walls. She understood. It was the signal to save the subject for when they were outside. So when the dishes were dried and put away, Jan and Amy went for a walk. As they passed other groups doing the same along streets lined with old, square buildings, Jan finally answered her question.

"Yes, I am worried. We hardly hear from Piotr at all anymore. The last time he was home was over a month ago, in July. The reason I wanted us to leave the apartment is that he had an argument with Tatuś and me the night you arrived in Poland. We were discussing something concerning him that shouldn't be talked about with others listening in." He waited and was not disappointed. She had known what he was after.

"It's all right, Jan, I know. He told me himself. And actually, I think I know more than you do about why he's staying away from home. You see . . . oh, this is very hard. I've been waiting for the right moment to tell you this, and it never seems to happen." She sighed. "You really have absolutely no idea what I'm talking about, do you? Oh!"

Jan looked at Amy dumbfounded. He felt confused and somehow to blame for her discomfort. Was this what she had been waiting for?

Amy took a deep breath and started talking. "Your brother and I had a romance. On paper, mostly. He helped me to do something, look for someone, actually, here in Poland. He helped me, and we got to know each other through letters, and I thought we had fallen in love. But actually it was just an infatuation, because once I got over here, we argued almost right away, and then he broke off whatever it was we had. I think he's channeling all that energy from being angry at me into the underground movement."

Jan stood still, staring at her. "Amy, you never cease to amaze me. I had no . . . I mean, but I never dreamed. . . . You've taken me completely by surprise. I don't know what to say."

They walked a ways in silence until Jan finally said, "Piotr is quite brilliant, you know. He doesn't have to be a carpenter; he could have been pursuing a career as a concert violinist. But he got a bad break when they gave his place away at the music academy. Then he only made it worse when he chose not to reapply, to stop playing the violin altogether.

"I'm not surprised you were attracted to him. He has always been extremely mature for his age. Even when he was a boy, Piotr was more daring—I think because he didn't grow up with that fear from the fifties. You see, he could economize his brilliance for later. He can learn tremendous amounts in spurts. He taught himself an entire term's worth of Russian in a week." Jan wasn't too sure why he was saying this to Amy, partly to cover up his surprise at what she had just told him.

Then Amy voiced yet another thought he'd had earlier. "This anger Piotr carries around in him; he's had it for a long time, hasn't he?"

"Yes," Jan said, wondering at her perceptiveness.

"You see," she said, "since we quarreled last spring, I've tried several times to reason with him, but he won't. He just wouldn't listen."

"What did you quarrel about?"

"My new faith. He hated me for it."

"Ah, I see." Jan hardly wondered why he felt relieved that Piotr had been the one to break it off. He had not even known his brother was serious about Amy, although he had noticed they liked to spend time together. And Mamusia had mentioned that Amy's letters had arrived regularly at the Piekarz home after her first visit there.

He recognized now the sadness he had sensed in her when they first started spending time together. That feeling of wanting to protect her from harm rose in him again, and Jan felt himself start to sweat as he heard himself suddenly saying, "I . . . I would love you for it."

Amy looked at him incredulously. Jan couldn't believe he had just said that. He felt sure she would laugh at him. A poor, skinny Pole, who was he to this woman? Perhaps she herself was simply infatuated with the romance of Poland. It was an attractive enough country if you knew you didn't have to stay here.

She did turn away from him, and he heard her say, "Oh, I'm so confused by all this. I don't know what to say or do."

"I'm sorry," he rushed to say. "I shouldn't have said such a thing." Shame flooded him as he realized he had just betrayed the friendship he only now had realized was so precious.

———— ✑ ————

Two weeks later, Amy was invited to go camping in the mountains with friends from the university. During her absence, Jan kept busy, but he also caught himself missing Amy and wanting to see her again, to ask her something, but forgetting what, and he didn't want to admit why. He missed her quiet presence in their home, missed talking with her, missed seeing her. Especially after what he had learned about Piotr, what he was feeling seemed all the more impossible. So he simply refused to acknowledge the changes going on inside him.

Then one day late in September, Jan was sitting on a bench next to his mother in an empty hospital waiting room. Her paralysis was getting worse, although she wouldn't admit anything. He knew for certain that she suffered sometimes from numbness, sometimes from intense muscle pain. They had been waiting an hour to meet with Hanna's specialist, and a nurse had just come out to tell them it would be another hour.

Jan thought his mother was dozing, but then, with her eyes

still closed, she asked him, "Tell me what you know about Piotr and Amy."

"Mamusiu, that's their business, not mine."

"It doesn't matter," Hanna said. "*I* know already. I just wondered if you knew."

Jan sighed.

Hanna said, "I'm only asking because I had a certain conversation with Amy before she left. She told me about her conversion, about the lies she told poor Aad. And she told me why she did it."

Jan caught his mother looking at him out of the corner of her eye. *So she knows more than I do*, he thought. "Oh, and what else did our mysterious Amy tell you?"

"*Your* mysterious Amy, my son. Don't you see? Men are so blind sometimes—and I've had to live with three of them. She loves *you*, Jasiu."

Jan did not answer. He could not breathe for a moment.

"I've been watching you lately. Have you been running away from it maybe?"

"No, Mamusiu, I haven't. There's nothing to run away from. We're good friends, that's all. Something like that would never work. We're too different." He wished he sounded more convincing.

"Not as different as a German and a Pole during wartime, believe me—and look at the life your father and I have shared. No, Jasiu, I'm not saying this has to be or even that it was meant to be, I'm just reminding you of something you still don't seem to have realized. God sometimes has better ideas than you do."

———— ✎ ————

His mother's words had broken something open in Jan, and he prayed as he never had before. By the time he saw Amy again, he was ready to tell her that he had been thinking of her ever since she left. "Mamusia told me about your talk," he admitted. "I'm very confused by all this."

"Well that's reassuring," she said. "I don't know what's going on, either. Your mother may have made too much out of my ravings."

"All I know," he said carefully, "is that I think of you all the time. I play games with myself, imagining you will be home each time I climb all those stairs. I love to be around you. You make me feel less . . . restless." Yes, that was it, he only then realized. Amy was meeting that need.

Jan tormented himself with questions. How could he fall in love with her in two months' time? Then Amy would ask him the same question, almost word for word, proving again and again that she was thinking along the same lines.

They prayed together, they prayed apart, and the attraction grew. Amy seemed to lean on him as more weeks went by, and they spent even more time together. Jan thrilled to the feeling of being there for her. She said things like, "You are my rock. You are my compass." When she was with him, she said, she knew she was going in the right direction.

As the autumn progressed, the romance moved faster than either Amy or Jan could have anticipated. Jan felt strangely off balance, less in control than he liked to be. But he noticed he was sleeping again for the first time in years. And he was happy—no, it was deeper than that. It was joy. For the first time since Jan had started school, he felt joy. God had returned that gift to him, through Amy. He prayed every day, every night, for clear guidance.

My heart is in Your hands.

22

FLAMES WITHIN

Exodus 3:2

1972–1973

Amy couldn't believe she had landed in such a mess. *Am I out of my mind?* she asked herself repeatedly. How could she fall in love with two brothers?

Or was that even what was happening? Amy's feelings went back and forth; nothing seemed right. She didn't even know what it was that she did feel.

At night she tossed and turned so much that her roommate asked what the matter was. "I have a problem," she said. *That's an understatement.*

But she could not make light of the situation. This time she had truly sailed into uncharted seas.

She could not believe that a man as good as Jan would love her. But more and more clearly, she saw that he did. And she liked it that he loved her. She wanted him to. She ached for him to.

And something about his love felt right to her. She wanted to accept it, make it her own, return it made over by her, for him. When he was near she felt steady, strong, somehow safe. And he made her laugh; his wit was gentle but quick. And she thought he was handsome, too, in his way, with clean-chiseled features and gentle brown eyes that held just a touch of sadness. When he entered a room, she felt a sudden sense that colors deepened, that everything shifted just a little closer. Life touched her when Jan was around, and she could not turn away.

And yet, she knew there was a part of her that longed for Piotr.

She loved his dark mystery, his passion and genius, the strangeness that echoed her own. Yet she loved the quiet strength, the intensity and wisdom in Jan. She didn't want to compare them. She didn't want to choose. She didn't want to be caught in the dark, storm-tossed waves her emotions had flung her headlong into. *What's wrong with me?*

She told herself, *I'm too old for this. I've made too many mistakes in the past. I've never belonged anywhere.*

Then a small voice would whisper, *But maybe in Poland.*

And she would answer back, *Yes, that feels right. Yes. Poland. But how . . . and who?*

It infuriated Amy that Jan was so sure of his love for her. He might show some uncertainty about the speed and final destination of it all, but since she had returned from her camping trip, she had known Jan did not doubt his feelings for her.

She herself did nothing but doubt. And most of all, she feared hurting either Piotr or Jan. Who was she to waltz into their worlds and cut them open like this? Then she would snort, *You flatter yourself.*

Finally she went to Jan with just part of what was troubling her. "Jan, what you and your family have gone through in God's name is so noble. You're too good a person to love someone like me."

"No," he said. "Don't ever say that. I think you've gotten too caught up in my talk of persecution. It's impressed you the wrong way. I'm not as brave as I sound. I'm the worst of men," he added softly, "to want you as much as I do."

And that, of course, just made it worse.

———— ✧ ————

"Have you thought about what you're going to do when your visa is up?" Jan finally asked her one day. They were out in the woods, looking for the last mushrooms of the season. It was probably one of the final sunny days of autumn before the winter storms would blow in from off the Baltic. He had taken her to a special hazel grove near a little village, a place his parents knew of.

"No," she answered. "Well, yes, I mean, I have to find a way to stay. It's as simple as that—oh, is that one?" Amy had spotted a little brown-capped mushroom in the carpet of leaves.

Jan smiled and shook his head, but he didn't answer. He had seemed that way ever since they left his apartment. Happy, even lighthearted, but preoccupied.

"I've been filing for reapplication," she answered him, "but it's been turned down twice already. Last time it took me two years. I don't want to go through that again."

"You may not have to." Jan grinned. Then he started to say something, but instead started coughing. Amy wondered what was wrong with him. Usually Jan was relaxed and easygoing with her, but today he seemed almost childish in his anxiety.

He took her by the hand and brought her to a stump that overlooked an open field. "Amy, we need to talk."

"Good talk or bad talk?" She suddenly felt intensely nervous. Her hands would not hold still. As Jan switched into English, Amy had a sudden premonition and started to shake her head no. He placed a finger on her lips.

"Amy, I love you."

She turned away from him, afraid of what he would say, surprised by the intensity of her reaction.

"No, please look at me. Let me finish." He looked into her eyes and started again. "Four months may seem a short time, but I've been learning that, well, that God sometimes has better ideas than we do . . . than I do," he corrected himself.

Amy could not tear her eyes from his face. She knew the features by heart, remembered them at night in bed, woke up to the image of them as they looked at her now.

His voice continued, "Now, I don't want you to think I'm doing this because of the visa. . . ."

She felt like a deer transfixed by headlights, watching disaster loom, unable to stop it, unable to comprehend why she felt so unsettled by something she had known was coming. But she had been clinging to denial, stubbornly refusing during the past months to see where their love might lead them. But now, in the split second before all would irrefutably change, Amy wanted to run away, propelled by the sudden certainty that she would bring nothing but disaster on this family she had come to love.

Everyone I love . . . dies. The thought, when formed, shocked Amy. She backed away from it warily. Jan must not be allowed to continue, the ensuing events to unfold.

But Jan would not stop. "No, that was wrong," he was saying. "I mean, there is only one way to be guaranteed a visa, and that's to obtain a resident's visa, and there's only one way to get that and that's to marry a Pole. You know you want to stay here; you said you do want to make this your new home."

Amy's thoughts raced. These were words she had denied herself and feared, but at the same time she had waited half a lifetime for them. Amy yearned for their sounds.

Jan said, "If we already know we're going to marry, why wait? To be more sure? We are sure." He paused.

And now it's too late.

"Oh no," he said, "I've said it all wrong, in the wrong order. Let me do this over." Amy's eyes widened as he knelt in the dried leaves at her feet, gold, red, russet.

He held both her hands in his. "Amy Baker, you came into my life and took me completely by surprise with your beauty, your soft spirit. It was as if God gave you to me from heaven itself. I've been spending most of my time telling Him you were too good to be true, too good to be for me. But I am so in love with you, I can't pretend anymore. I love you. I want to share the rest of my life with you. With God's blessing I could bring you half the joy you've given me already. It's only been a few months maybe, according to the world, but in heaven it was just the initial stage of what I pray will become an eternity spent loving you."

He stopped and took a deep breath. "Amy, will you marry me?"

Amy fought back the tears. She could not, would not turn her back on Jan, the vulnerability etched in his face. She knew she loved him. But how could she say yes?

The words were out. She knew Jan was waiting. On his face she saw his dawning realization that she was not going to say yes. *Oh, what have I done?*

"Oh, Jan," she began softly. "You deserve so much better." She knew this wasn't what he had wanted to hear, but she had no choice. "I have so many doubts, so much I don't understand."

"*I* believe," he said. "Let me carry your doubt. I have enough faith for both of us."

"You don't know what you're saying," she told him sadly.

"Amy, please. Don't make me beg. I've never in my life felt that something was as right as this is. I'm so sure of our love. Please, give it a chance. We don't have to marry now; we can keep on growing together. That's better, maybe. We can give it time. But I *know* we belong together."

"Sweet Jan." She brought her hand to his cheek, and he grabbed it and held it there. "I was in love with Ron. We were like husband and wife."

"I know all that. You told me, and it's all right. It doesn't matter. Nothing matters but what we choose for the future—that we choose together."

She continued, "And then there was Piotr. I hurt him incredibly by letting my feelings get in the way of common sense."

"But he ended it. You owe my brother nothing."

"I know that. You shouldn't have to convince me like this. Don't you see—you deserve some nice Polish Baptist girl who loves you as unwaveringly as you love me."

"I will take your love in whatever form you can give it," he said, hanging his head. She lay a hand on the side of his face and thought her heart would break at the sadness she saw there.

"Jan?" she said gently.

"Yes?" His voice sounded drained.

"Don't give up on us yet. I'm the problem here, not you," Amy said. She waited a long minute, wondering desperately what to do, and then it came to her.

"Jan, listen." She swallowed hard. "Jan," she asked, "could you let me go back to the States?"

As he started to shake his head, she quickly added, relieved by the idea, "It would only be for a short while. As long as my visa is still valid, I can get back into Poland. We have until the end of February. I need to take care of some business there, anyway, and it will give us both a chance to think about all this. I just won't make the same mistake twice," she told him. "Please, Jan, I beg you. Give me a little time."

He looked up. The energy that shone from his brown eyes a

few moments earlier had seeped away. In its place Amy detected an all-too-familiar expression of joy having been stolen. Piotr's face had carried exactly the same countenance. *Have I done this? Already I cause him pain.* How swiftly she had transformed his look of love into one of disappointment.

Jan said, "Always my love," as he brought her hand to his lips.

———— ✑ ————

Amy flew out of Warzsawa at the end of the next week. And the first thing she did on her arrival in America was to find Aad. The Vienna office had told her before she left that he would be on the East Coast doing fundraising. She had his itinerary, and one evening she showed up during one of his talks.

The meeting was being held in a church hall that also served as a day-care center. Children's cots were piled in one corner, together with boxes of toys. As Amy slipped through the door and took a seat at the back, she smiled to see that the room was so crowded. At least a hundred people of all ages, but mostly students, sat in the folding chairs around her.

Aad was just winding up his presentation, his animated gestures dear and familiar. "Are there any questions?"

Several hands shot up. Amy paid no attention to what was asked. She could feel herself letting go and relaxing for the first time since she had said good-bye to Jan at the train station. She had been thinking in circles ever since, going over and over all that she had said and Jan had said, thinking and rethinking the decision hanging over them. Now though, in the same room as someone she hoped could steer her, Amy felt like maybe, just maybe she might find her way out of this endless maze.

The sound of her name brought her back to the present. "Amy Baker." Amy looked up and saw that the people in front of her had all turned around and were staring at her, smiling. Then she heard Aad laugh. "Welcome back, Amy. I was just saying, maybe you can say a few words about what it was like for you in Poland. Amy is one of the few people I've worked with who has learned to speak Polish during her time with the mission."

She glared at Aad and shook her head. She should have known he'd do something like this. He was always saying it was good not to feel too comfortable. *All these people looking at me.*

But there was no helping it. Aad wouldn't let her get out of this. She would have to say something. She scraped her chair back and stood. "Yes, thank you, Aad." She squinted her eyes at him, and he chuckled. "I just got back to the States yesterday after being gone for three years. I haven't caught up with myself yet, so you'll pardon me if I fumble around a little here. Only one year of that time was spent in Poland. But . . . that country has certainly changed the way I look at everything. I have a feeling it will change the way I look at my future, too." She swallowed and cast a desperate glance at Aad.

"Go on," he said softly.

"Maybe it sounds like this Bible-smuggling is glamorous—the danger and the adventure and all. But then you've missed the point. The Christians in Poland are normal, hardworking people like all of you. Some students, some parents with kids. They are proud, like you. They don't want hand-outs. The difference between them and you is that just because they're not members of the Communist Party, they have little hope of promotion or advancing their careers. Although they can attend university, their children are often passed over in favor of those from so-called 'nonprivileged' backgrounds. But most of these people do not feel persecuted. They don't see it that way. They don't think about the things they don't have but enjoy what they have, simple pleasures like going camping or sailing on the lakes, skiing, or going on vacations in Bulgaria or Hungary.

"Still, things are not what they seem. They have made the choice to be different, and being different carries its risks. The secret police can make their daily lives hell.

"So put yourselves in their place. You get arrested for no reason. Your phone is bugged. You're stopped on the street and asked for identification. Armored cars slow down outside your house, and your neighbor is reporting everything she hears and sees to people who pay her for the information. You believe, you love Jesus, but you pay a price."

Amy stopped, her last words echoing in her mind. No one made a sound. She felt hot and flushed and she was trembling. "One more thing. The Polish Christians I know are praying for you, for us, for Christians in the West. Do you know what they pray? For our discernment, that we can recognize the enemy and resist the temptations of materialism. That's something to consider maybe. Don't think you're doing an act of charity if you give your money to this cause. All you're doing is sharing with a brother and sister. Maybe next time you'll be the one in need."

Then Amy sat down. Not all the faces turned her way looked happy with what she had said.

Aad closed the meeting with prayer. As everyone filed out, Amy stayed in her seat. It seemed the safest place. Only one woman smiled at her on the way out.

When the room was empty, Aad came and sat beside her. "Sorry about that," he said.

"No you're not." Amy shook her head. "You knew exactly what you were doing."

"Well, I should bring you along more often."

"Right. Did you see how hostile they all were at the end?"

"Oh, that's okay. The best sermons are the ones that make people uncomfortable. It gets them thinking. Now, what can I do for you, Amy Baker?"

"Do we have to go somewhere?"

"No. We're staying right here. Tell my why you're back in the States when that visa you waited for so long hasn't even run out yet?"

"Oh, Aad, I've really done it this time." The relief of finally being able to talk with someone about her dilemma overwhelmed her. Aad said nothing as Amy told him everything about the last months.

Finally there was nothing left to say except, "So I came back, and I don't know what to do."

Aad reached out his arms and held Amy close for a few moments. Then Amy heard him ask, "Do you really not know what to do?"

"No. I won't drag Jan down. He's too good a man for that. Look what he does. He's like some saint—he's suffered, and he knows what he believes and why, and he's so caring and sensitive. I would destroy someone like that. I'm not good, you know that. . . ."

"What? You mean. . . ?"

"Because I'm a liar?" she finished for him. "Well that, but there's also . . ." Amy suddenly could not say the words. It was such a deep-seated fear, words gave it too much power. And yet, she hoped, maybe it was time to bring the things out of the dark. "Aad, I really don't know how to say this, but look at what's happened to anyone I loved," she ended in a whisper. *There*.

"Amy, you know better." The way he said her name told her that these things had lost shape in Aad's light of day. "Besides, that wasn't my question, Amy." Aad sounded stern. "Think like an adult, not a child. This is called switching from milk to meat, in biblical terms. Now, do you really not know what to do? What is your—"

"Heart's desire." She sighed. She knew, she had known deep down, that he would come back to that. "God's plan for my life. It can't include someone like Jan."

"Why not?"

"Because he deserves so much better."

"What does Jan say about that?" Aad asked softly.

"He says he *knows* we belong together."

Aad was quiet for a few moments, then, "Let's pray." He bowed his head and took Amy's hands in his. "Lord, we know You have a plan for both Amy and Jan. Guide them clearly every step of the way."

Amy wanted to say something but couldn't. Aad waited a few minutes, then he said, "Amen," and stood. "You don't have to decide this moment. Don't forget to reach out your hand and expect His help."

―――――― ∽ ――――――

Amy spent the next few days shopping. She caught herself buying gifts for everyone she knew back in Poland—coffee, chocolate, nuts, bananas. *I guess this means I'm going back.*

Then Amy visited her parents' farm. Her farm. It was strange to think of it that way, since she hadn't lived there since her mother died.

The place had been rented out during her absence, but she didn't need to go inside the house. She spent an entire afternoon walking in her father's woods. She wanted to remember what it was like to go fishing with him at the pond, but instead she could only think of Jan, his gentle voice, his kindness, his surprising strength.

She sat on a stump and listened to the waves lapping the shore in the wind. The trees sighed above her. In her mind, Amy went over Jan's proposal again and again. She had no more words to pray. Poland seemed like another planet, like a dream.

And it was in that quiet moment that Amy suddenly knew. It was all right to dream. It was all right to dare a dream to come true. It was all right to take a chance, to risk everything. Even love.

———— ⌗ ————

That night Amy dreamed and woke up still smelling Poland, sure she had just been back. In her dreams, she had heard the love in Jan's voice. She remembered the love, but not his words.

And then Amy realized what attracted her most to Jan. His courage. As a single man he risked his own freedom for the sake of what he believed. Jan took on whole nations for the sake of his vision. His courage drew Amy like a moth to light, coaxing her to step away from the fear and doubt and shame and guilt . . . these things Amy had wrapped around herself, had become so familiar with. And then that morning she could wait no longer to see him.

She had thought she must distance herself from him to make a decision. But in truth, there was never a choice. Her heart had already opened and taken him in. And now she found herself hungry for his touch, his voice, his scent. For the feel of his arms around her, holding her safe at his side.

When Jan held her, she knew nothing else than his true love. And in this, she finally knew—in this she trusted.

23

WILL SALT EVERYONE

Mark 9:49

1972–1973

Jan had taken Amy to the train station with a sinking feeling that he would never see her again. Before she left, Amy had told him the "business" she had was the small matter of her parents' inheritance and farm. When she mentioned the amount, he gasped. It was a fortune in Western currency. Who would have guessed that Amy had that kind of money? Nearly thirty thousand dollars was more than he could hope to earn in a lifetime.

Jan had spent all his life believing in the "pressed down and overflowing measures" of God's rewards, but he had never guessed what that could mean. For one dreary, dark morning as he saw Amy off, he understood.

Jan had already spoken to his parents about what he hoped to do. Before he could even ask about inviting a wife to move into the apartment, Mamusia had answered his question. "Whenever you want to bring Amy home, she is welcome. In a home where there is love, walls can stretch."

They could have Jan and Piotr's old room. It was more than many young couples had.

While Amy was gone, Jan used the time to pray and to get the room in shape for the day when he could bring her there as his wife. He did it as an act of faith, not assuming or daring God to answer his prayer, but hoping, hoping with all his heart.

And then, when Amy had barely been gone a week, Jan received a telegram from the U.S. His hand shook as he opened it and read that she was coming back, arriving the next evening at *Okęcie*, the Warszawa airport.

Jan took the early-morning train to meet her. He could hardly sit still during the eight-hour trip. He paced up and down the passageway, his stomach tied up in knots, his head pounding. *What if she's just come back to say no? What if she's not on the plane?* A thousand scenarios ran through his mind, each worse than the other.

Once at the airport, Jan felt no better. He kept looking at the clock, and when he had waited long past the time of arrival, he finally approached a woman behind the desk.

"Excuse me, about the flight from New York. *Jakie jest opóźnienie?* How long will the flight be delayed?"

"Are you family?" she asked.

Jan did not even hesitate. "Yes."

Then she leaned forward over the counter and told him in quiet tones, "You must not repeat this to anyone. But the plane has arrived. Unfortunately, it is now circling over Warszawa, unable to lower its landing gear." She pointed out one of the far windows. "We will just have to wait and hope they can correct the mechanical difficulty."

Jan felt the tension he had carried with him all week suddenly snap. That had been imaginary; this was real. He ran to the window and saw fire trucks approaching the landing area. *They're getting ready for it to crash.* He looked up and could see the plane's lights blinking in the dusk as it circled, lower and lower, then higher. Still no wheels in sight.

Jan closed his eyes. This was his bride. She was up there now, and in the next few moments he might have to watch her die. *Abraham felt this while Isaac lay under the knife.*

He waited, the ache so great he could not put his prayer into words. Then Jan listened.

A few moments later he heard a murmur go up among the people standing near him. He opened his eyes and saw the plane glide onto the landing strip, its wheels down, the fire trucks swarming to its side as it slowed to a stop.

Agonizing minutes later, Jan caught sight of Amy walking from the plane to the customs hall. Jan knew he still had a long time to wait. Amy would have to collect her luggage, then she would have to answer all the questions at the *kontrola paszportowa* and *kontrola celna* booths. She would probably have to endure a full-scale search of all her belongings.

A full hour passed until Amy finally came through the gate. Jan saw her before she saw him. She wore new clothes and had three suitcases with her.

"Looks like she's planning to stay awhile." Jan heard the voice directed at him. He looked around and saw a middle-aged man, smoking a pipe, standing to his left.

Jan grinned in reply. "I hope so."

Then Amy was in his arms, and Jan's heart filled with relief and love and concern for this woman, his love, his own gift from God. He turned to say something to the man who had just spoken, but he had disappeared.

"Who are you looking for?" Amy asked.

"No one," Jan said. He looked down at her. "You." She smiled. "Do I even dare ask what you have in all these bags?"

"Well . . ." She looked at him slyly. "One of them contains a wedding dress." Tears filled her eyes and she flung her arms around Jan a second time.

"These Americans, so demonstrative," he mumbled, but it was more to cover up his own overwhelming emotions. He looked around again. Their end of the hall had emptied; everyone was gone. "Does this mean you're getting married?" he asked.

"*We're* getting married," she said, "if you'll still have me."

"Yes."

"Yes."

They looked into each other's eyes. Jan felt whole, he felt solid, he felt strong. He wondered that he could be so confident. He felt no shame. This was Amy's gift to him.

———— ✐ ————

During the remaining weeks of November and most of December Jan was often at Amy's room in Gdańsk, helping her pack and study and just making plans for the wedding and their future. He met her friends from the camping trip, and they all went out together a few times to the students' club ŻAK, and to the

Wybrzeze Teatr in Gdańsk. Sometimes on Saturday nights they went dancing at parties with these friends or visited cafés.

They had been trying for some time to get word to Piotr about the pending wedding. It would be a small event, but both Hanna and Tadeusz said it was important they have a party afterward. Married in secret during the war, they had never been able to really celebrate with friends and family. They wanted their son's wedding to be a day to remember. "It should be a day you will look back on in joy for the rest of your lives," Tadeusz had told them. So they wanted Piotr to be there.

Jan had been thinking about his previous talks with Amy about Piotr, and the more he did so, the more convinced he became that there was a question he still should ask of her. A part of him warned to leave well enough alone, but he had to ask it. He had to clear the air of it now.

"Do you still love him?" he asked one evening when they were alone in Amy's room.

She stared at him incredulous, as she had the first time he had said he could love her. "Why do you say such a thing?" she said. "And why now? No, I don't love him. I mean, I do love him, but not the way you mean. That is over. He broke it off, and he was right. Why do you even bring it up?"

"I'm sorry, I just think we need to start off clean, with everything in the open."

Amy took a deep breath. "Listen. My dream for years now has been to live in Poland. My dream for many more years than that has been to have someone to love, a family to be part of. And now both those dreams are coming true. Can't you believe that?"

And you thought you'd be loving my brother. The words crept into Jan's mind unbidden, but he pushed them aside. "I'm sorry," he told her. "Come here. I didn't mean to sound like I didn't believe you."

———— ✐ ————

They held the wedding on a bright sunny day in February 1973. Piotr was unable to make it. He phoned, though, from somewhere in *Śląsk*, to wish them both happiness and health in the future. He said he had sent a gift to Uncle Marek, who would give it to them whenever it was delivered.

For weeks, Hanna had been cooking constantly and directing the culinary endeavors of several friends who had offered the use of their small kitchens. Their coordinated efforts had yielded a massive amount of food for the reception following the ceremony.

All the friends and neighbors and the entire congregation had been invited. The small church was packed, with the children of their friends standing and sitting in the aisles along the walls. Krzysztof and his family visited, as well as several of Jan's special circle of elderly friends from Warszawa. Aad was there, sitting next to Sister Emma.

Jan did not see Amy's imported dress until she walked through the double doors Paweł had designed when he and Tadeusz had planned the church building. Her beauty staggered him, her black hair twisted and up, with wisps framing her face, contrasted sharply with the ivory-colored fabric. The dress itself draped her body in simple lines, the bodice crocheted with roses. Jan could not tear his eyes from her face, thinly veiled behind what he knew had been Ruth's own headpiece and veil.

During the blessing ceremony conducted by his father, Jan listened to Amy say yes, she was willing to serve, willing to follow Jan wherever God led him in the years to come. Jan's heart soared at the words. Yes, God could use them together, as a team. He had finally found his partner, handpicked by the angels, a present from God's own hand.

When I was young, Jan always told me, "Piotrek, you will grow up to be a brave boy."

Tatuś taught me, "When you are with a girl, be courteous. If you are walking with her, always do so with the girl on the right side. When you marry, this is also how you should sleep. It's a sign of respect to your wife.

"If you meet a boy with a girl, you bow first. When you walk together, always let the girl go first, except when you're walking in the snow or climbing a ladder." He taught me that girls should be treated like precious dolls, never discarded or thrown away.

You pursued your studies in Gdańsk, your accent improved in-

credibly over the months. You came often to Gdynia. On the rare occasions I did come home, you were usually sitting with Mamusia, helping her in some task she was unable to perform, while you spoke Polish and she practiced her English.

When I came home for Christmas, I had finally tired of the game I was playing with myself. You were right, your conversion should have no effect on our love. You could still love me, and I could still love you. I was a fool, a wicked fool to laugh at you like I had so many months earlier. In the time since, I had only grown to need you more. When I saw dark-haired women walking down the streets of Szczecin, Bydgoszcz, and Katowice, I wanted to stop them and make them turn so I could see their faces, hoping for a glimpse of you. When I realized you might be leaving in three months, it made me mad with regret. How could I have wasted our year together this way?

So two months ago I returned home after an especially long absence. I went to your room in Gdańsk. I had tickets to a violin concert that Saturday and wanted to share such moments only with you. I waited impatiently until you came home from your classes on the last day before the Christmas holidays.

Eight months too late, a heartbeat away from each other, I tried to apologize. I could not even wait until we were inside. As soon as I saw you coming up the stairs, I ran to meet you. "Amy!" I blurted out as I took your books and led you back to the door. You were reaching for your key and would not look at me. "Amy, I need you so much. Please. I'm so sorry, so deeply sorry. Can we? . . . Can we?" I wanted to ask, can we start over, can we try again, can we pretend I hadn't rejected you?

The door across the hall opened and that old woman came out, staring at us. It startled me. She greeted you by name, well she's your neighbor, I thought, so of course she knows you. But then she stood there, looking me up and down, waiting for you to introduce us, I suppose.

Then you did. And she answered, "Ah, this is the brother."

This letter begins with the words, "I was a bitter young man until I began loving you." As I have written it, I've turned twenty, but I feel like an old man, tired and disillusioned.

Jan and I are very different, so maybe you wouldn't have been so happy with me, after all.

I often torture myself and ask, What if? *What if I had listened to you that day when you came to me? What if I had not turned against you? Would tomorrow have been our wedding day instead?*

And now, you have taught me about loss.

24

=✼=

In His Hand

Genesis 22:6

1973

Amy soon found that the stories of the Piekarz family were like a tropical sea, deep and dark, sometimes unfathomable. They varied like the ocean currents, different with every season. And yet, as Amy let herself be swept along by the rhythms of her new life, she found she curiously liked being brought back again and again to the place these stories defined, to the shore of the home she could now call her own.

After the wedding, Amy soon settled into the routine of helping Hanna keep the household running smoothly. It happened naturally, as if there had always been a place for Amy next to Hanna. As she started to hear them, Amy sensed that, as Piotr had once written her, the family's stories were something precious, something to be studied and cherished, something of power.

"You must realize," Hanna explained to her, "that it is very different here. I mean, things are sometimes not what they seem."

"I know that," Amy said softly. The two women had been swimming slowly from one end of the public pool to the other. It was part of their weekly routine that winter to go swimming three times a week. The doctor had said it was good for Hanna's muscles, and Amy was glad for the exercise after being cooped up in the apartment so much. Curiously, she never seemed to tire of Hanna's company, even though they spent all day, every day, together. The older woman challenged Amy, and Amy sensed Hanna's need to tell her certain things.

Now, as they rested their elbows on the tiled edge, they spoke in hushed tones to each other. "Yes," Hanna said. "But what I mean is that for the last thirty years, the only means we have had of preserving history, telling the truth, is by verbally telling it to others."

"The Indians in America did that, too—storytelling," Amy commented.

"I don't think ours is nearly as rich a tradition. It was just born of necessity, I'm afraid," Hanna said. "It wasn't a cultural question, just one purely of survival. And it's more reporting than storytelling. It has to be accurate. The communists would like nothing better than for everyone to forget what really happened. You'd be surprised what some of the history books say, even that the Nazis came only from West Germany. Some people actually believe the history books."

They swam on in silence for a while until a group of school children arrived and shattered the quiet echoes of the hall. "I'm tired already," Hanna said. "I'm getting out, but you stay if you want."

Amy smiled and nodded. The warm water had relaxed her. She felt as if she could go on forever, stroke after stroke, breathing to the beat of her arms and legs, scissoring back and forth, up and down, right and left.

Amy submerged herself in the waves of events spilled out by Hanna and Tadeusz. It was a sign of their trust in her. It helped her know more about what made her husband so unusual, so special, so brave. It told her where her place was in this remarkable family. The stories were beacons on the voyage she had embarked on when she chose to become a Piekarz.

Hanna gave her stories as gifts. And Amy accepted each one individually, listening and admiring, adding it to her growing trove of undersea treasure, becoming more inspired and touched with each telling.

Just that morning Hanna had taken her arm as they entered the ladies' changing room at the pool and closed the door behind them. "It's a public place. No one will hear us. We're alone here. Come," she had said, leading Amy to the corner. And Hanna had begun to talk in soft tones, like the sea in spring, whispering of warmer days.

———————— ✺ ————————

"As you know, after the war," she said, "even the shape of Poland changed. The Allied leaders in Yalta redrew the borders. A huge part of eastern Poland became part of the Soviet Union, while a large eastern chunk of prewar Germany became a part of Poland.

"What a confused time that was! There were people returning to wherever home might be from the concentration camps in Poland, from labor camps in the Soviet Union, and from hiding places in the southern reaches of Yugoslavia and Czechoslovakia. That's where my mother and I were, where she died. We had almost gone to Dresden right before it was bombed, but we went south to the mountains instead and escaped that fate at least. Poles from the east were hurrying westward because they didn't want to be Russian citizens, and Germans were running even farther west, deeper into Germany, escaping persecution as a losing wartime aggressor.

"There were no embassies, no visas, no options of leaving Poland unless you could prove a German background—in which case you could apply for permission to be driven out of the country. The only form of travel was hitchhiking or by freight train, often on the roof. That is what Tadeusz and I did when we went to Gdańsk from Kraków. Well, we didn't have to ride on the roof, but there were no tickets and of course no money. All the roads, railway lines, and stations were heavily damaged. Jan was just a tiny baby then."

"And that was in 1945?" Amy asked.

Hanna nodded.

"Our first home was in Gdańsk, or actually in *Oliwa*. We had problems there, starting on the very first day we arrived. Oh, at first we were thrilled. You see, it was in a lovely neighborhood, one of the few that hadn't been burned by the Soviets. There was a yard and a park across the street. A friend in Kraków had arranged for us to live there. It belonged to her niece, who wanted someone to take care of it.

"The niece—her name was Renata—was very glad to see us. She wanted to leave Gdańsk as soon as possible, and she wanted someone she could trust to live in her family home. But we would not be living there alone. Because so many houses had been destroyed when the Russians came and so many people were coming to Gdańsk, the city government was requisitioning any space where people could live. We would have three rooms on the ground floor, she said. On the second floor lived an old man, a friend of Renata's family, and his daughter. And just that morning Renata had been ordered to give her attic to a new boarder, a low-ranking Russian officer who had been stationed in Oliwa.

"Renata seemed very nervous about this arrangement. Then, as she was telling us about it, we suddenly heard yelling from the floors above us."

Hanna's eyes widened, almost as if she were hearing it all over again. "Over and over again he said the same words, and his voice grew shriller each time. Renata said the yelling was coming from Mr. Sadowski's room, but she wouldn't go up there. She was afraid.

"Well, Tadeusz understood enough Russian from his camp days to know what was going on. He lunged for the stairs, and I followed him. Tadeusz said, 'He's going to kill someone if we don't hurry.'"

Hanna paused a long minute, staring into space. Amy prompted, "Was it the Russian?"

Hanna nodded solemnly. "He was standing there with a rifle in one hand and an empty potato sack in the other. An old man was kneeling at his feet with his head bowed, and the tip of the soldier's rifle was right up against the old man's temple. The soldier looked up as we came in the room, but did not move the rifle. Tadeusz called out something to him in Russian. And then the old man cried, 'God help me, I don't even know what he wants!' And the soldier shot him. He said two words and then pulled the trigger. The old man's blood sprayed out and hit us."

"Oh, Hanna! What did you do then?" Amy reached out and rested a hand on the older woman's arm.

"What could we do? Tadeusz shouted at the soldier and asked him why. The Russian waved the rifle and then started to speak.

Tadeusz could understand a few words. He was saying something like, 'Thieving Pole. Stole potatoes. My potatoes!'

"Well, we were confused, but the soldier seemed even more confused. Tadeusz took a few steps closer, pointing at the sack. The soldier calmed down a bit. Then he motioned for us to follow him to the bathroom, where he pointed at the toilet and started talking again. I had no idea what he was talking about.

"Finally, the soldier shouted at us one more time and strode out of the room. He kicked the old man's body as he went out—I remember that clearly.

"Tadeusz said, 'I think he's just never seen a toilet before. The poor fool thought it was for washing potatoes, and when he flushed the toilet the potatoes went down with the water. He thought the old man downstairs had stolen his food.'"

"That's incredible," Amy breathed.

Hanna nodded. "We couldn't believe it either, except there were so many things happening in those days we couldn't believe. . . . That was the last straw for Renata. She said, 'I can't stand it any longer. These aren't even people. I can't stay here. Everything in this house, everything here—it's full of terrible memories.' She said, 'You have no idea what those Russians did when they arrived.' And of course, then we did know. . . ."

Amy didn't. She just raised her eyebrows, waiting for Hanna to tell her.

"They raped her," Hanna whispered. "She couldn't say it, though, not until I brought it up. Then she told me—it had happened fifteen times in one week."

Amy gasped. "Hanna, I . . . I had no idea."

"Well, that's why I'm telling you. It's not something you'll find in any of the official versions of the Russian liberation, but it's true. It happened everywhere they went. And it's one of the reasons why it's so hard for us not to hate them."

Amy crossed her arms across her chest to cover the goosebumps, hugging the towel to her more closely. She was almost afraid to say anything, but she felt she had to. "How terrible."

Hanna said, "I know, but many, many women went through it. You moved on because you had to." Hanna paused, then sighed. "Renata was like that. She had to move on."

Amy asked hesitantly, "What happened next?"

"Renata ran to her room and came out with a small bag, her hat, and a coat. She said she was going to her aunt's in Kraków— the woman who had helped us when Jan was born.

"But we were still trying to ask her questions, to calm her down. We didn't want her leaving the house that upset. So Tadeusz said, 'You'll need travel papers.' And do you know what she said then?"

Amy shook her head.

"She said, 'Most of the Russians can't even read. All I need is a red stamp on my identification papers. That's all they look for is the red ink.' She started to laugh hysterically. 'I heard about some Russians who stole the faucets off of walls. They thought if they brought them back to Russia, they could have running water at home. This man with his potatoes in the toilet is nothing. Most of them use it to wash their hair in.'

"And then she started running away from the house, motioning with her free hand that she didn't want us to follow her. So we didn't."

Hanna looked at Amy, then closed her eyes and sighed. "It was the first in a long line of bad signs. After three years of trouble in that house, we finally had no choice but to leave. The authorities forced us out. I can remember how angry I was. I told Tadeusz, 'Surely we have a right to . . .'

" 'To what?' That's what he asked, but he was smiling at me. 'To shelter, food, peace?'

" 'No.' I hesitated. 'To hope?'

"And, Amy, this is what he said to me, and he said it so carefully: 'I think that no one has a *right* to hope. I think that hope is a gift.'

"Store this in your heart, Amy. I saw something then. My Tadeusz had changed. He used to have so much hatred in him, from when the Germans killed his parents. And I had been raised by godly parents who taught me so much about the Lord. But my rebel Tadeusz, right when it seemed that everything had been taken away from us . . . again, he was the one who had realized this thing. There I was, tripping over my dreams, trying to re- member what my parents had taught me, while Tadeusz had grown into a healed man of God.

"I thought of all this as he held me in his arms," Hanna said as she stood up and started taking her swimsuit out of the bag. "I'm ashamed to say I was sobbing like a little girl. All I really wanted was a place we could call our own."

———————— ✑ ————————

The children's voices sounded shrill, echoing on the high ceiling and bouncing off the water. Amy pushed off the far end of the pool and began another lap, still submerged in her thoughts, in the stories. Everything that happened to the Piekarz family, everything they thought and said, seemed to be affected by what had gone before. There were things they talked about, things they didn't talk about, and it all had to do with the stories. Amy felt that in hearing them, she somehow became a part of them.

Tadeusz had told another story the night before while Hanna was out visiting a neighbor. It had started when Amy and Jan had begun talking about money. She had grown to hate these discussions; they just seemed to talk in circles. He was so sensitive about Amy's money. She didn't think of it as so much. Her trust fund was used up and now she had only the inheritance money. To Jan, though, she was richer than he could ever dream of, and that bothered him. There was nothing she could do, it seemed, to make him see that all she wanted to do with the money was to help make all their lives better.

"We won't touch your inheritance," he had whispered harshly last night. Neither of them had wanted Tadeusz to overhear the argument as he sat in his chair on the other side of the room, reading.

"But you couldn't have known your workload would become so much heavier," she protested. "We never thought you'd be taking over so much of both your father and Marek's ministries."

"It's what we've chosen to do."

"I know that, Jan. I'm just saying it doesn't leave you any time for earning extra money as a tutor."

For some time Jan had been supplementing the family income by teaching students from the university whom his father had referred to him. Now he was finding it harder and harder to fit the tutoring in around his pastoral visits. And every week he had his sermons to write as well.

"Please, Jan," she urged, "let me help."

"I . . . can't. Amy, that money—we don't know what's ahead. I'm not afraid of using it, but I think we should save it for emergencies. You never know." Amy thought how strange it was that the very amount seemed to fill him with fear. Jan continued, "Wealth like that could attract a legion of trouble, the wrong kind of attention from the wrong people, not to mention too much temptation. This money brings with it a heavy responsibility of sharing."

"Then we already bear that responsibility," Amy said. "Because we do have the money."

"Why do I feel like it's more of a curse?" Jan mumbled.

"All right," Amy said. "What about this? What if we give part of the money to Aad and ask him to use it as he sees fit."

This was obviously a new thought. Jan thought it over, "Yes." He liked the idea. Aad's was a cause close to both their hearts.

Amy continued, "The rest we'll leave for now. But, Jan, you still have to let me help. I've been thinking of one way I could earn money. What about if I gave English lessons?"

Jan looked at her with amazement on his face. He smiled suddenly, the tension diffused. "Why didn't I think of that? Of course, of course that would be all right. We'd have to be careful not to attract too much attention, not advertise your being American, but we will have no difficulty finding people who would want to learn English from a native speaker. I think it would work. You could tutor like I did, working out of our home."

"Between the two of us, maybe we can start our own tutoring company. Go into business and get rich." She cracked the joke, relieved that the argument had passed.

But Jan stiffened, and Amy felt the tension stretch between them once more. She sighed. She had said something wrong again, stubbed her toe against another of the family's many taboo subjects. Jan started to say something, but then his father got up and joined them.

He placed a hand on Jan's arm. "Jan, it's all right. I couldn't help but listen in a bit. Maybe it's time for Amy to hear a little about our family business."

Amy was looking from one to the other. "I'm so sorry. I can be so insensitive. It's just—your home, it's so safe and I can't imagine. That's the problem. I *can't* imagine what you all have been through. I'm sorry. I had no right." She wadded the dish towel into a knot.

"Amy, it *is* all right," Tadeusz said. He motioned for the three of them to sit around the table together. As Jan spooned coffee into the glasses, his father began the story. Jan told her later that he had heard it only once before.

"It's impossible for you to know what it was like. Of course, if two people do something well, you should be able to think you can make a business together. You call it the American dream—this idea that if you work hard enough, you can build up something for yourself and your family. Is this right? Well, you have to understand something. That was a rule we once thought applied to us. But it doesn't—not anymore. We had to learn that the hard way.

"After the war, you see, no one had any idea what it could mean to live under socialism or communism. We just assumed life would return to what it had been before. Everyone measured their hopes according to prewar standards. We knew, of course, that we would have the small problem of cleaning up after the war." Here he laughed.

"But everyone just generally assumed that in a few years Poland would be back on its feet, both economically and socially. Poles have always been good at trading and markets and languages and working hard. There was no reason why we couldn't recover.

"There was a tremendous feeling of hope at that time. Gdańsk was finally an all-Polish city. After six years, we could finally put the war behind us and move on. But things *were* different, and the changes started to show up in little things, then more important things.

"The government said these so-called changes were necessary in order to level out the society, but the message was clear. A war had been declared on intellectuals and their families, and this included property owners and entrepreneurs.

"In 1947, when Hanna and I were still living in Gdańsk, we decided I should start up an engineering consulting firm like her father had owned in Kraków. There was a lot of rebuilding to be done, so it looked like a sure success. Then in 1949 a government enterprise, the *Miejski Handel Detaliczny* (City Retail Trade Commission) was set up to block private enterprise and undermine any existing businesses. Its goal was a central, government-controlled economy.

"The results were almost immediate. No one said anything overtly; nothing was put down on paper. But the message circulating from office to office was, 'Don't pay private companies.' Banks were instructed to pull in any credit. Since the government wasn't paying the bills, private businesses like mine, with government contracts, had no choice but to fold.

"As it turned out, we were fortunate. For shortly after that, the arrests started. Wherever the government measures had not already managed to break the back of private enterprise, the arrests did. For the crime of being an entrepreneur, any heads of any companies who had managed to struggle on were corrected, reeducated, and given a chance to mend their ways in nothing less than postwar concentration camps.

"By then Poland was almost completely cut off from Western Europe. And news from the East was that the arrests in Russia were even more horrible. Stalin had whole villages shot and buried into mass graves. So the thought uppermost in everyone's mind was, if the Russians were capable of doing this to themselves, cutting down their own, what could they do to us, a nation they had been swearing to annihilate for generations?

"Like the rest, I had no choice. By this time—actually even before my business folded, we had made the move from Gdańsk to Gdynia. It was a huge step of faith, and looking back, it was when many of those changes I was talking about started looking like they were dangerously part of the same pattern. . . .

"We actually walked to Gdynia—there was no chance of catching a train. Hanna and I were carrying our suitcase with everything we owned, and, Jan, you were carrying your little basket with your toys—I had carved them out of stale bread."

Jan smiled. "I remember the bread toys. But I don't remember going to Gdynia."

"It's no wonder. You couldn't have been more than three. But you walked all day with us, very brave. You kept wanting to know if we were going to have a big house. And then, when I told you we would only have a room, you were delighted. You thought that sleeping in the room with us was a wonderful idea." Tadeusz chuckled. "Actually we were thankful that we had any place at all. By then, Hanna's German background was officially known, and there were plenty who would argue we had no right to housing. But we had been given a room in one of the new apartment buildings in Gdynia.

"It was evening by the time we arrived there. I was glad to see there was a lot of construction going on. I thought that this would mean more business for my little engineering firm—I didn't know then I would not be allowed to succeed. Anyway, we found our apartment building between two others that were not quite finished. We all stood looking up at it. It was a new beginning.

"And you, Jan—you bent over backward with one of your little hands shading your eyes and you said. 'Oh, it's *so* tall. Look, look how tall! Are we going to live way up there? It's right next to heaven!' "

Tadeusz had put his own hand up and bent back in imitation of little Jasiu, and Amy laughed. She was always charmed by these stories of her husband as a little boy. "So then you climbed up to the top and found this apartment next to heaven?"

Tadeusz smiled wryly. "Not quite. We climbed all right, but when we got to the door, we found a card posted on the outside that listed seventeen names. But what could we do? We knocked, and the man who answered the door said, 'Let me see your papers.' I handed them over. They were stamped in red ink with the Polish eagle but still printed on the old Nazi stationary with a swastika on the back. Even three years after the end of the war, paper was still scarce.

"Our papers were in order. They had to let us into the apartment. But when we walked in we could not believe our eyes. So many clothes and odd bits of junk littered the floor that we had to pick our way between them. The place stank of sweat and mold.

There were at least seven people sitting on the floor, all staring at us—not until later did we realize they were all part of the same family. It looked like they slept on the floor. The only furniture we could see was a wooden table standing in the very middle of the room.

"And you had to share the place with all those people?" Amy asked.

"We thought so at first," Tadeusz said. "But then the man pointed to another door—it was that door, the one that leads into your bedroom. Apparently that was to be our living quarters. And then the man, his name was Henryk, said, 'There's another family in there. But there's only four, and your boy is small.'

"You see, we had assumed—stupidly enough, we later realized—that the room we were assigned to would be empty. Now we knew better. So we picked our way across the filthy floor and opened the door to our new home.

"An old man was sitting in the corner, taking a nap. Next to him, in a small nest of old clothes, lay a little baby. She was awake, playing with her toes. And actually, the room didn't look too bad. At least it was tidy and clean, although the only furniture was the single chair. All the clothing was folded up in little piles, and the pots and utensils were washed and stacked along the wall.

"Jan, you were fascinated by the baby. You ran over and held out your finger for her to grab. The old man woke up then."

Tadeusz shook his head, remembering. "I had thought it might be better to anticipate trouble, so I had the papers ready to prove we had a right to be there. I had made up my mind that I wouldn't let us be pushed out of there. After all, I had a wife and child to think of and there simply was nowhere else to go. But at that moment I thought it might be better to start off as politely as possible. I said, 'Excuse us, but I think you might have been expecting us. We are the other family who will share this room.'

"The old man said, 'Yes. Well, this is it. I am Mr. Sojka.' He just waved his hand sadly and closed his eyes again.

"And then," Tadeusz had said, sweeping his arm to take in the apartment around them, "then we were finally home."

———— ✌ ————

Home, Amy thought as she pulled herself out of the water and walked over to where she had left her towel. *That is what the stories do; they make me a part of this home.* And often it seemed to Amy that the stories her husband and parents-in-law told were more real than what actually happened around them.

And Amy now knew she lived for the stories. She breathed them like a fish, passing them through her thoughts, taking them into her heart. They were what allowed her, gradually, to become a part of this family. And she swore to remember them, to never forget.

25

IS OF HELL

Matthew 5:22

1974

The SB had invited Jacek to their head office so they could brief him on a pending project. "We want you to go to the site in person, sir," the head of the division explained.

Inwardly Jacek groaned. He and a colleague had planned a weekend fishing trip in the Mazurian Lake district, *Pojezierze Mazurskie*. It had been Jacek's private way of celebrating his sixty-fifth birthday. No one knew that, of course. He looked fifty, still tall and lean and hard. But his hair gave him away; it was now a dark iron-gray. And his skin. The skin on his face was cut and carved with wrinkles and creases. It told the story of his decades-long deception. His face showed the price he had paid emotionally for having lived other men's lives instead of his own. The tucked and fallen skin around his eyes and mouth told a story in a language no one but Jacek could understand.

"Why can't an aide be sent?" he asked.

The man stood and walked around to Jacek's side of the desk, then leaned on the corner closest to Jacek. He reached into a cigar box on the desk and made an elaborate show of lighting it. "It's sensitive, sir. I'm sure you understand."

That night as Jacek flew to Brest with Wiktor at his side, he thought, *Sure I understand*. Not so long ago, he wouldn't have minded a trip like this. But lately he had fallen into a very comfortable routine, beneficial to all concerned. This last year had seen him moving vast amounts of sensitive information through Izzy's conduit.

Now he leaned back in the small jet and allowed himself the luxury of closing his eyes. The last thing he heard was the sound of Wiktor's voice telling the stewardess not to bother them anymore.

"That's no easy thing when there are four of them for just the two of us," Jacek mumbled.

To his surprise, Wiktor chuckled. "No"—he was still speaking to the stewardess—"we do not want any more caviar or champagne."

———— ✐ ————

Jacek was wondering why he had even been sent to Brest in the first place. As it turned out, the job could easily have been done by someone else. Jacek finished his business in a few hours and decided to enjoy the spring evening and go for a walk. He told Wiktor he would only be out for a half hour. *Besides*, he convinced himself before leaving behind his bodyguard, *this is hardly Warszawa.*

Emerging from the hotel, Jacek turned the corner and headed toward the city center, stopping across from the post office. Jacek looked around, surprised at how little the city had changed since when he was there during the war.

But something was not quite right. A familiar tingling sensation he had felt before. The sense that he was being watched.

Am I being tailed? Here? And why? Well, there was one sure way to find out. He bought a newspaper and sat down. His old rule of thumb had never failed yet. The best way to find out if you were being watched was to watch those doing the watching.

Jacek had become so wary over the years, his instincts had become second nature. Now, when a strange feeling came over him, he recognized it as one he had had before, also here in Brest. But then it had been part of Poland, not the Ukraine, not part of the Soviet Union. Then he had been in Brześć.

That last time had been when he had returned here after his internment in Russia. He had opened his post office box where orders from the U.S. military intelligence should have been waiting for him after the first of every year. And he had had that same tingling sensation of being watched when he opened box number 77.

Jacek eyed the people moving across the square. Young mothers with babies, old women carrying cloth shopping bags. A group of men sitting on a bench, smoking. No, he was looking for someone on his own.

The post office stared at Jacek, daring him to enter. *They would like it if I led them back to the same box*, he thought. No, if he was the object of yet another mole hunt within the SB, he would not be the one to give himself away.

Jacek turned a page of his newspaper. He tried to remember exactly what it had been like the last time he was here. What had he been so afraid of?

This was difficult, for he had tried to block out most of the events surrounding his internment. The inhuman cruelty he had suffered during those years would have rendered him incapable of carrying on a normal life afterward, let alone a double life, if he had ever relaxed the strict hold he kept on himself to prevent the majority of those memories from resurfacing. Now especially he was reluctant to open that floodgate.

But the days in Brześć—there was something from those days that he *should* remember. His second nature told him that. What was it now?

Then he knew. The note.

He had returned from Russia expecting to find a note in his box from his contact, and the note should have been dated 1942. Instead he had found instructions dated January 1940. So something had happened to his contact.

He had always wondered about that. When, after the war, he had filed a follow-up request with his new contact about the incident, he was told that the man had disappeared during the war, probably been killed while Jacek was in the camps.

But Jacek did not like "probablys." That missing contact was a forgotten loose thread that might return to trip him up again. Because of who he was, Jacek already had to operate in the dark. Whenever possible, he tried to reduce the uncertainty. The fewer unknowns the better.

The note had been there waiting for him, welcoming him back. *So they knew I was picked up and sent to a prison camp*, he thought. The note had said he should proceed to Kraków and follow the original plan.

Now he remembered. It was that tingling sensation. He had suspected someone was watching him in the post office then, too.

What if? he asked himself. *What if my original contact in Brześć was taken prisoner after he left the last note in January 1940? What if he told all? What if the SB has coordinated with the KGB and . . .*

He waited. There was something there in the back of his mind—there was a link that could give him away, but he would have to slide back the gate to the very beginning of his camp years.

Of course. And what if they found my interrogator, the commandant at the first camp. It's a lot of what-ifs . . . but if they could get that far, if the Russians broke down my Brześć contact, then they may know . . . they may know who I really am. . . .

Suppressing panic, Jacek looked around the square. The skin on the back of his neck crawled. On the other side of the market-place, he saw a stooped figure who reminded him of someone—who was it? The man had done something with his arm and hand that made Jacek think of an old mentor in Kraków—what was his name? *Felek.* But he wouldn't be here. . . .

Jacek stood and moved across the square, drawn involuntarily, folding his paper as he walked. He kept his eyes riveted on the old man. With every step Jacek took, he felt a growing dread in his gut, but he kept walking. One step, two, he was running away from the Russians again.

Just as he reached the man, the man looked up. Jacek searched the scarred face for some recognition. The eyes would not meet Jacek's. The old man mumbled, "Do you have a few rubles?"

When Jacek gave him one, the old man shuffled away. Just as Jacek was thinking, *My paranoia is getting the best of me*, he smelled Cuban cigar smoke. He turned as a well-manicured hand appeared on his shoulder.

"Jacek Duch."

It was not a question, for Roman knew full well who he was. "You should have seen yourself taking the bait."

"You're SB. You work for the Russians."

"Looks that way. But who are you?" He turned away, and another man took his place. "You're to come with us for questioning."

Jacek thought, *The net has closed*. And then, *I wonder how many mistakes I made*. And only then did he remember that Wiktor's father could not have been one of those killed at Katyń.

Wiktor was Russian.

———— ✧ ————

The KGB agent was standing in a corner smoking a cigarette when Jacek was brought into the bare room for questioning. Once Jacek was sitting, his hands tied behind the chair, the agent grunted two words. In Russian.

"I'm Bartek."

Jacek fought the panic. He hadn't felt this way since the last time they had had him, back in the camps during the war. The key was, and always had been, for Jacek to keep them from discovering the shape, the nature of the puzzle they might be trying to piece together. But he wasn't sure he was up to the task. The part of him he had sold to the Soviets so many years ago was still raw. He was an old man now, and much more vulnerable physically. He swallowed hard.

"Bartek. Who is he?"

Bartek. Jacek reached into the dark places of his memory. Bartek. He felt himself slipping into the subservient stance that had helped him survive the camp days. "Bartek was my brother," he answered in monotone Russian.

"When was the last time you tried to contact him?"

Jacek knew where they were leading him. He had to follow, but as he did so, he fought to find comfort in the information he was learning each time a question was asked. "When I was allowed to write him from the first camp." *How much do they know?*

Then they confronted Jacek about when his contact came to check the Brześć post box. They had arrested the man in January 1941. This was all they told Jacek. But it told him almost enough. *Did he turn?*

There was a chance they had picked up the man when he came to put another note in box number 77. Maybe, just maybe, the Russians had killed him before they could identify the post office box, maybe even before the inefficient wartime postal system had brought Jacek's camp letter to Brześć. Maybe the Russians never discovered the letter that had been waiting in the box already.

Jacek wondered if they would torture him. The irony was that if they didn't know enough, they wouldn't. He knew they couldn't afford to because there was always the chance he would go back to his government position and make life difficult for the SB among the Party leaders. He had enough power for that.

The KGB agent reached into his pocket and threw something onto the table. The sweat streamed down Jacek's spine. He took a deep breath and told himself to memorize the photo one last time before he lost it forever.

"Who is this?" the KGB agent demanded.

"My daughter." The truth.

"Where is she? Why do you carry a photo of her like this?"

"She died many years ago, during the war, together with her mother. In a car accident. Sometimes I wonder what she might have become. That's all. Just an old man's sentiment."

Jacek hoped he looked indignant enough.

This might mean he would survive the torture.

26

***

BLAZES

Revelation 1:14

1973

"Aaaa-choo!" Jan's sneezes had a sharp edge to them that hurt Amy's ears. He must have inherited that characteristic from his father, who was sneezing, too. "Aaa-choo." It seemed that Jan and Tadeusz could do nothing but sneeze, over and over again, until finally Hanna announced, "You're both coming down with spring colds. You know what that means. We will not let these colds get the best of us. It's time for the Müller Family Cure." She turned to Amy and added, "This was handed down to my mother from her mother from her mother."

"Oh no!" Tadeusz and Jan both groaned.

Amy looked from one to the other. "I don't understand."

"You will once Mamusia gets through with us," Jan laughed.

"Amy, come here. I never had the daughters I prayed for, so now you need to learn this." Hanna had pulled out the tub of lard she used for frying. She gave Amy a handful of garlic cloves and told her, "Start peeling. We can't have too much."

"No, heaven forbid that we had too much," Tadeusz said, rolling his eyes.

Hanna waved a finger at her husband. "You stop that, Mr. Piekarz."

Jan said, "Amy, do your husband a favor and don't let her teach you how to do this. Future Piekarz generations will thank you." Jan winked at Tadeusz.

Hanna ignored the men's laughter and started explaining.

"First, you crush all the garlic like this." The smell rose up and cloaked the room. The windows all stood wide open as part of Hanna's annual spring cleaning, but the garlic smell still lingered indoors.

"Then you mix it into the lard, and then—"

"No! No, please, we beg for mercy." Jan and Tadeusz had climbed onto the chairs and were covering their feet with their hands.

"The two of you look like women scared of mice. Now, take off your socks, both of you." Hanna approached with the pan on her hip, wielding a wooden spoon as if she were about to strike them. As she waited for them to obey, Hanna turned to Amy and continued her lecture. "Sage is also medicinal. But as a form of prevention, you should always put three garlic cloves in whatever soup you're making. Are you two finally ready?"

Amy grinned at the sight of both men sitting in the chairs now, stretching their legs in front of them, bare toes wiggling. They wore expressions of mock terror. "You see now, Amy," Tadeusz said, "who the boss of this house is."

"Just for that, you go last," Hanna said. "Amy come here. I will need your help with Jan. He has never been good at taking his medicine."

Amy could not contain her laughter any longer as Jan started shaking his head back and forth vigorously. "There's a reason why, Mamusiu. Believe me, I don't think this is necess—"

Hanna broke him off. "Quiet, you. Amy hold on to him. This boy's been known to go wild."

Amy still did not know what to expect. She came up behind Jan and put her hands on his shoulders. He leaned back and said, "Don't let her do this. If you love me, you'll stop her." Even as he spoke, Hanna took hold of one bare foot and started pasting the lard onto it.

Jan shrieked. Amy held on to him and said to Hanna, "So has he always been this ticklish?"

"Oh, my dear, I could tell you such stories." She winked at Amy, which only added to the laughter. Hanna continued with the other foot, painting the stinking grease in between each toe and all around the foot, up to the ankle. "There, now you're done. You can put your socks on."

Amy was laughing so hard her side hurt. Jan panted from the effort. Tadeusz was mumbling, "My darling wife. My beautiful Hanna. My sweetest and most beautiful wife in the world. . . ."

"I'm your only wife."

"I beg you. My cold is not so bad now. Look, I'm already feeling better." Amy marveled at the change in both Hanna and Tadeusz. Normally so serious and old-fashioned, now they both giggled like teenagers. As Tadeusz begged, Hanna smeared the rest of the strong-smelling lard onto his feet. Exhausted by his convulsions of laughter, Tadeusz could hardly put on his socks afterward.

As Hanna cleaned out the pot and got ready for bed, she said, "Right. And, Amy, your job is to make sure Jan keeps those socks on all night. Don't let him wash his feet."

"I wouldn't dream of it." Amy chuckled as she grabbed Jan's hand and pulled him into their room.

———— ✑ ————

Amy tried to help as much as she could in the family's ministry. The prayer meetings still met in the Piekarz home with as many people as it could hold. Every Monday night and all day Tuesday Amy and Hanna cleaned and polished and baked and made sandwiches, so that everything was ready for Tuesday nights. Mamusia continued to entertain with the softest of smiles, Amy noticed. Hospitality was indeed a gift.

Tadeusz told them he was pleased with how the ministry seemed to be progressing. *It may not be as dangerous as it once was, but it's important work. And I'm a part of it. I never would have dreamed . . .*

Their little church was visited by several Western missionaries, but when Aad showed up, he was the only one who knew just when to visit and how long to stay. He never even gave Hanna the chance to invite him to spend the night. Now that Jan and Amy were married, he "happened" to have been invited to spend the night at Marek's.

During his visit, Amy accidentally overheard Jan and Aad

talking softly about her trip to America.

"I don't know what you told her," Jan said, "but I will always be grateful."

"I told her nothing she didn't already know."

"Whatever it was, she came back cleansed of her doubts and loving me more than ever."

"Just make sure you don't lose sight of that," Aad said.

She didn't hear Jan's answer to that.

Aad was one of the few from the West who made sure not to draw further attention to the family. Since more and more foreigners had been visiting Poland since the late sixties, it was becoming less dangerous to talk and meet with strangers—unless you were in the army, since anything having to do with the military was more closely scrutinized.

Aad made jokes about that, wondering if "God's Army" counted. He had also brought Mamusia Christian music and sermon tapes and had the rare gift of knowing how to talk with her about her sickness. Amy heard him say, "The doctor says multiple sclerosis is a sickness for survivors."

Some of the other Western missionaries were not so sensitive to the needs of their Polish hosts. Amy saw these churches through Polish eyes now and marveled sometimes that Western Christian organizations that had been blessed with so much could argue about so many things. They even argued among themselves, sometimes wasting huge amounts of money on repeating each other's efforts instead of cooperating or simply asking the local pastors and church leaders what it was they needed most.

There were exceptions, though. Just a month earlier, they had been given a printing press that Jan had been helping Marek set up in his garage. Amy learned that this was a wonderful breakthrough. She and Jan worked late into the night with Marek setting up the heavy iron press and learning how to use it. Now they could make their own tracts and print their own translations.

Amy loved the sense of making a contribution, of working with her husband side by side. The millions of irritations and annoyances that came from living in close quarters, from living in a closed society, faded when she was gathered with her family around the table, hands linked, saying grace, or when Jan gathered her into his arms behind their closed door.

Never in her life had Amy felt so useful, so purposeful, so loved.

Never had she felt such a certainty that here was where she belonged.

———————— ✐ ————————

Amy knew that Jan worried about her. She could hear it in his voice now as the two of them worked the family vegetable plot next to the railroad tracks. In the six months since their wedding, he had brought up this same subject at least twenty times.

Jan said, "I know things must be very different for you, Amy. You grew up on a farm, surrounded by lovely things. And now you've been reduced to weeding between the lettuce heads as the trains rattle by us."

"Jan, stop it. You know it doesn't matter. Besides, isn't it nice being outside together like this in the sunshine? I thought the winter would never end." Amy glanced over at Jan, hoping he wouldn't think this was another one of what he called "her complaints." She noticed he was pulling the weeds up with a vengeance. "Hey, take it easy over there." When he didn't respond, she tried again. "Jan, what is it? What's bothering you?"

He looked up, his expression at first annoyed, but Amy noticed this softened some as he saw she had stopped to watch him. "I just keep realizing how much you gave up when you married me. According to your world, we live in poverty."

"Jan, we've been over this *so* often. That's not it, and you know it. Now I'm not leaving this place until you tell me what's really been bothering you. Jan, talk to me. What is it?"

He leaned back on his heels and sighed. "All right. It's Tatuś. This morning he spoke to me about your tutoring. I know you're used to doing things your way. . . ."

"Don't talk anymore about what I'm used to, please," she said softly. "What did Tatuś say?"

"He said we would have to put a halt to your English lessons. Amy, look, Tatuś is right. The mission work comes first. The secret police still thinks we have links with the underground, so we have to limit any activities we can that might attract their attention. We can't afford to jeopardize the church."

What he didn't say, she thought, *was that bringing an American daughter-in-law into their home might have already jeopardized their position.*

She rubbed her temples. "Jan, I'm trying to understand this. First you say it's okay for me to help out this way. We get plenty of people who show an interest. I start making money for us, and now suddenly I have to cancel the whole thing."

He nodded.

Amy told herself that this was just one of those times when they had a hard time communicating because of language and cultural differences. Lately they seemed to be arguing too often.

He tried again. "Don't misunderstand me, Amy. We all appreciate what you've been doing."

"Don't," Amy said. "Don't try to be American."

He grimaced. "All right, then. I don't know what else to say. Maybe we can get a few people from the church to learn English, people we can trust."

"Think, Jan. We can't ask those people to pay the prices I've been charging. And if I'm not making money, what's the point?"

"Amy, I support you. I love you. Why can't you do the same for me?"

The look in his eyes broke Amy's heart. She came over and sat in the dirt beside him. "No, Jan, I wish I could make you understand. I was just trying to help, in my way. I . . . I sometimes don't know how to help." Amy rested her head against his shoulder as the sun warmed their backs. "I know I'm new at this—living in Poland, being Christian. I guess I'm having a hard time with what your father would call 'the acceptance of godly riches as a replacement to worldly riches.' Jan, I'm not even sure all that it implies. I'm afraid you think I'm weak."

"No." He turned so he could look at her, putting his arm around her waist. "No, you're anything but that."

"Well, are you not sure of me, then? Are you afraid I might leave?" This last was said in a whisper.

He shook his head in alarm. "No, Amy. But I know you still idealize what the family does."

"Yes, I am impressed. And I'm also devoted to you—don't you

know that?—and to the family." Not for the first time, Amy thought about the quiet bravery she witnessed every day. These last months she had grown more sure than ever why this was a country worth being proud of, worth not escaping from. She thrilled at how people were willing to take a stand, not to compromise, and to suffer because of it.

At the same time, when she herself had to smash her nose into the way things were, she found it hard to accept.

"It really is all right, Jan. I . . . can see that the ministry has to come first. I'll stop tutoring, and then we'll find another way to make some money."

The words sounded more convincing than she felt. She swallowed and hurried to change the subject. "Now, let me tell you of a decision I made. I've decided to stop searching for my father."

"What? No, you can't."

Amy put up a hand to stop him. "There are simply no more clues. With what we have now, it looks like there was some sort of government cover-up, but there's no way any of us can go near something like that. Even I can see that more of that sort of questioning would just focus further attention on the family. I think we both know I can't do that. Maybe there is nothing more to find out."

"Again, I am asking you to give something up," Jan mumbled.

"No, Jan." When would he believe her? she asked herself. Why was it always so complicated? *Don't you know how happy I am with you?*

27

On the Altar

Leviticus 6:12

1973–1974

Not for the first time, Jan liked the feeling of having a partner. He loved the way almost everything Amy had to say came from a perspective he had not considered before. God had made them to complement each other—that was very clear to him.

His parents had welcomed Amy with open arms, even though, technically, she was an American Catholic in their Protestant home. But Tadeusz had never forgotten his own Catholic upbringing. No one commented on her attendance of the family's church meetings rather than the local Mass on Sundays. To Jan, even Amy's Catholic background was a gift, since it brought him a unique perspective and a deeper love for the Catholics who came to them, earnestly interested in finding out more about what the Bible teaches.

Jan thought it was the best feeling in the world not to be alone. He and Amy could talk for hours, just the two of them, and he never ceased to wonder at how many-faceted his wife was. Her life experiences were very different than his own.

Sometimes he thought this must be what it meant to grow in love for each other. And he was thankful. But there were other times when the same realizations filled him with foreboding. It was similar to the sense he had felt when he was twenty and nothing had gone wrong for a while. In love and happy, at the same time, Jan began to fear it could not last.

He knew he asked Amy too often, but lately he couldn't help

wondering, again and again, how could she not miss all the *things* she was used to—things like medicine and electrical appliances that worked and a car and room to breathe. She said no each time, but Jan was not sure she wasn't just pretending and hoping someday she would have it all again. He kept thinking about all he had asked her to give up in becoming his wife, and these worries would not let him go. He often complained to her about how crowded the apartment was, not because he minded, but because he wanted to make sure she didn't.

Then, one morning Amy was making the tea for him from their own one-burner stove while his parents still slept in the other room. It was dark outside and cold. Jan looked around at all the clutter and sighed. "Maybe it's just as well that Piotr doesn't live here anymore. We could never fit another person in this place."

"You're going to have to."

"What, have you heard from him?" The words were out before Jan could stop them. "I mean, it's been almost a year."

Amy looked at him strangely and shook her head. "No. I was talking about something else. Here, scoot over."

He shifted his position on the couch, and she came to sit on his lap. "I was talking about our first child," she whispered into his ear.

Each word fell like a diamond in a pond, reflecting light, reflecting love back to the source.

For the rest of that autumn and winter Hanna and Amy knitted. Endless rolls of yarn bounced their way across the floor and onto the women's laps, being transformed into booties and sweaters and tiny tights on the way.

The quiet household routine became chaotic and confused as Tadeusz and Jan turned their sheet-drying room in the attic of the apartment building into a workshop, much to the annoyance of the neighbors, whose laundry came back dry but spotted with sawdust.

To Jan, this was a special joy, working side by side with his father as Jesus had worked with Joseph. When he was growing up, there had not been much time for him to learn these skills from

Tadeusz. Now, as they hammered and sawed together, Jan felt himself becoming more complete, more competent. Proudly he carried piece after piece of baby furniture into the apartment and deposited them at Amy's feet.

"Where will we put it all?" Amy asked after Jan had brought her his cradle and changing table and set of shelves. Tadeusz stood beside him, looking even prouder than Jan.

Hanna shrugged her shoulders. "We'll find a way. We always do."

Jan looked at his mother and felt his happiness dim just a little. She looked so old and tired—both of them did. He worried that a baby would only wear them out more; even the preparations were becoming an exhausting process. Tadeusz seemed to be needing more and more bed rest, so Jan was taking on more and more of his father's ministry. And although Amy had been helping Hanna, once she had told them about her pregnancy, the roles had reversed.

Hanna now insisted that Amy go to bed in the middle of the day. She gave Amy endless tips on child rearing and getting through a pregnancy, fed her a constant diet of all the things she kept saying she never had when she was carrying Piotr or Jan. Every day, Amy had to drink a liter of goat's milk. Hanna had arranged with a farmer living outside of Gdynia for the milk to be delivered once a week.

Now Hanna motioned at the overfull room. "We didn't have the luxury of having too much baby furniture when Jasiu and Piotrek were born. Please indulge us as we prepare to spoil our first grandchild. I'm afraid we can't help ourselves." Hanna motioned for Tadeusz to come sit beside her on the couch. She sighed. "Those were years I wish on no one. Amy, I could tell you stories of that time that you simply wouldn't believe.

"When we first arrived in Gdańsk in 1945, just after Jasiu was born, it seemed like there were no shops at all, but there were roadside stands. Little markets popped up wherever a few farmers from outside the city gathered to sell vegetables or berries.

"There was no printed money; everything was barter. I saw one woman give away her wedding ring for nothing but a scrawny rabbit in return. There were no eggs or milk to be found anywhere. And there was no flour since there were no mills. But that didn't matter as much as the fact that the farmers had had no wheat or rye harvest that autumn. They had spent that spring getting caught between the German and Russian armies. The United Nations sent tractors, but that didn't bring back the missing harvest. So, whenever I could find corn, we ground that by hand and ate cornflour bread.

"But the lifeline for the entire city continued to be the food sent to us in aid packages by the UNRRA. I can't tell you how precious these United Nations parcels were. They were mostly brought into Gdynia by ship—corn, instant coffee, tea, sugar, or even cigarettes. This last was the most valuable, since we could use it to trade with the Russians or for fresh produce with farmers.

"We had no electricity. Candles could be found—for a price of course. And then, one magic night after New Year's, we woke up and found everything bright and newly lit. The lights had been turned on. It was only a test, and soon there was no electricity again, but it was a sign that the city was slowly coming to life again. For weeks afterward, people talked about the amazing feeling of that night."

Jan listened to his mother's voice, unconsciously rocking the empty cradle back and forth with his foot. He had been thinking back to when he used to ask his parents for stories of his infancy.

Back and forth. The motion seemed to mesmerize him, even as now, as then, Jan prompted his mother. "Tell the stories, Mamusiu. Tell Amy what it was like."

Amy added for him, "Because she needs to know." She looked up, a little alarmed, and started to say, "I don't want to be responsible for dredging up more bad memories. No, I mean, only if you want . . ."

Hanna smiled. "It's all right, dear. Yes, it was a strange time, wasn't it?"

The room was quiet as Jan stopped pushing the cradle. He had to say it. The words seemed driven from within, destined for this place, this moment, even after all the years of not daring. "And when Piotr was born? Mamusiu, you've never spoken to me about that time. Can you . . . can you tell us now?"

He paused and could feel the heat rising in his face. He said in a rush, "All I know is how you went into labor and had to un-lock the door to call for help, how the lady who lived in the other room at the time, Henryk's wife—Dorota? How she came in and helped with the birth, and how I came home to a baby brother. And then so many things changed. And after that, waiting for Tatuś got a little easier. . . ." He gazed at his mother, his eyes asking if he had gotten it right.

Hanna nodded, then said softly, "It was, as the preacher wrote, a time to search, and a time to give up as lost. . . .

"You see, in all that time since they had taken your father away, I had no word, no word at all. I had gone to the police station in Gdańsk, but even there they looked me straight in the face and said they had no record of an arrest of anyone named Tadeusz Piekarz. It was as if he had disappeared off the face of the earth. Everywhere I went, I caught myself listening for Tadeusz, for his voice, for his heartbeat, for the assurance that he lived on some-where without me."

"How long had it been since his arrest?" Amy asked.

"At that point, a half year," Hanna said.

Amy sucked in her breath, imagining it, and Jan reached out to place a protective hand on her shoulder. But Hanna was still speaking to Jan, meeting his eyes, pouring the story into him.

"I . . . at some point I was having an especially hard time. I was so pregnant, and still no word. I ached for some sign that Tadeusz was still waiting for us. And I was so ashamed to pray as Gideon had, begging for a sign."

Something soared in Jan as he listened to his mother. "I was doubting, too. I . . ."—he had to say it—"I blamed myself for his arrest. You knew that, didn't you?"

"Oh, I knew it. Of course I knew it. You, you wouldn't let me in, Jan. You had wrapped yourself in so much blame, I couldn't reach you, even at such a young age. I saw and felt what you were going through, the nightmares, the headaches and stomachaches, do you remember?"

Jan nodded. "All these years, when we didn't talk about it, I thought. . . ." It was so hard. His shame had shaped his childhood.

"You know now, don't you?" Tadeusz's voice broke through

the familiar fog Jan saw his little-boy self surrounded by. "You know it wasn't your fault."

"Yes, I know," Jan answered quietly, and only as he said it did he know it was true. It was the first time he had admitted it out loud—that over the years, God had healed him. Only now could he acknowledge that it had happened.

There was a silence for a few moments, then Hanna said, "I wanted for you, and for me . . . I was numb to everything but the desire to perceive Tadeusz. *I needed a sign.* I didn't think I could save you without one."

"The doubt," Jan said.

"The doubt and the fear," Hanna added. "And then, just as with Gideon, God honored my weakness. That is when I felt the first contraction, and that afternoon Piotrek was born.

"Amy, you'll know what I mean. The movements of your baby—even the pains of childbirth—are such signs of life. And that's what Piotrek's coming was to me. It was as if—no, it really was Tadeusz's own child signaling his father's safety."

———————— ⟨ᗆ⟩ ————————

Jan kept asking Amy if she didn't want to go back to Vienna to have the child. The hospitals in the West were so much better. But Amy stayed. She waited for hours in waiting rooms with other pregnant women for her checkups.

When it came time for her to give birth, Jan was not allowed anywhere near her as she disappeared into a large ward. The hospital was very close to their apartment and run by nuns. Amy told him later that she had given birth in the same room as three other women, with only curtains to separate them. The woman next to her had not had an easy time of it.

His Amy, on the other hand, had delivered a healthy baby boy, a beautiful boy, Tomasz Piekarz. Jan could not have been prouder of this red-faced little person with his thatch of black hair and his wise-looking dark eyes. Jan's world, he thought, was complete.

Little Tomek was a source of endless delight to both the other generations in his new home. No one seemed to mind the socks and cloth diapers and buckets and little tights and caps and outfits hanging all around the apartment. Bathing and dressing the baby became a morning ritual that everyone enjoyed, including Tomek, who thrived on all the attention.

Best of all, perhaps, was the laughter little Tomek gave to Hanna and Tadeusz. Jan never tired of seeing his mother smile as she played with the baby. Jan had worried that the pressures of having a baby around would be too much for her, but now she was blooming in a way he hadn't seen since she had become so ill.

It was amazing, the way this new person in the family could make Mamusia young again. Amazing the promise that comes with a new life.

One night when Amy lay in bed nursing Tomek, Jan and his parents sat perched around the edge of the bed, fascinated by the tiny magic prince who had appeared in their midst and stolen all their hearts.

As Jan watched in wonder, the name came to him. "Ewa."

"What's that?" his father asked.

"Ewa. I remember the name of the baby who used to sleep in here with us when we shared the room with the old man. Her name was Ewa."

"What do you mean?" Amy asked.

"You remember that?" Hanna's face looked pained. "You were so small then—only three, I think."

"I know what he means," Jan heard his father say. "It was just after we came to Gdynia in 1948. Remember, Mr. Sojka's sons had been arguing, and little Ewa woke up and started crying. She was always crying, and it was the kind of cry that gave you no rest. It wasn't even a real cry like little Tomek here makes. It was more a moan or a howl. The family next door started pounding on the adjoining wall. Mr. Sojka joined in the argument. And we were just lying there trying to sleep. Well, Hanna and I were pretending to sleep. Jan, you could always sleep through anything."

Jan stifled a yawn. "This is a skill I wish my son would learn very soon."

"Give it time," chuckled Hanna. "He's still very young." But she was still remembering: "But little Ewa did stop crying that night. The crying stopped very suddenly, and I don't know why, but I just knew something was wrong. And those men just kept on talking. I couldn't stand it anymore. I had to get up. I started to get dressed. And then Jasiu woke up, too." She looked at Jan and was obviously seeing him at three. "You were so solemn. You sat up on your little mattress and said that you didn't hear Ewa. So I just went over to where we had a sheet hanging like a curtain between us, and I said I didn't like to interfere, but I thought something might be wrong with the baby."

Tadeusz picked up the story now. "It was obvious that Ewa's father had been drinking again. Both of Mr. Sojka's sons had been worn down by any number of demons—the war, the poverty, the loneliness. And Ewa's father had just lost his wife a few weeks earlier. They had been on the road, heading west toward Gdańsk, and she had become sick and died. It had only been a few months after Ewa's birth, and she had lost a lot of blood then."

Tadeusz shivered involuntarily, remembering, and Jan realized that the same thing could have happened to his mother after he was born. She had nearly bled to death then, and there had been no doctors. Many times, Mamusia and Tatuś had told him he was their miracle. For the first time in his life, looking at Amy and his own son, Jan felt that he really understood.

"At any rate," said Tadeusz, "they sobered up quickly when Hanna said there might be something wrong. Old Mr. Sojka whispered the baby's name as if he were seeing a ghost. Her father gasped and they both hurried over toward where she lay in the corner, but Hanna was already there. I just stood there—what could I do?—and then I felt this small hand in mine."

Amy said, "That was Jan."

Tadeusz nodded. "He was still half asleep. But he looked up at me and said, 'Ewa is in heaven, Tatusiu.'

"I knelt down and looked into his eyes. I asked, 'Jasiu, how do you know?' And he said, 'I saw her there, with her mamusia. In my dream.' And then he went back to his corner and curled up under the blankets like a little mouse in his nest."

Jan looked up from his son's face. Had Ewa never left them? He had forgotten the comfort that dream had brought. But he was grateful now for the memory and for his new, living child.

Tenderly he lowered himself down behind his wife and little Tomek and thought that life had never seemed so precious.

28

LICKS UP STRAW

Isaiah 5:24

1974–1975

When Jacek was able to walk again, he felt an intense gratitude for the strangest things. The motion of the curtains in the mornings after Gabi opened the windows. The sounds outside on the street below. The hot water in his bathtub. Gabi herself, with her quiet and efficient ways.

Gabi was the one who nursed him back to health after his interrogation, bathing and feeding him until both kneecaps healed enough for him to start putting weight on them. Gabi's cool touch, the slight smell of sweat, the delicious soup she brought up to his room—Jacek was thankful for it all.

He felt this despite the sure knowledge that Gabi worked in his home as a spy for the SB. Izzy had told him this years before when he returned from Gdańsk. It didn't matter as long as he knew. And he didn't feel betrayed by her. Gabi's only crime had been watching him. Wiktor had been the one he had chosen and trusted—Wiktor and even Roman to some extent. These two men had betrayed Jacek. And he had no desire to see either of them ever again.

Jacek guessed he was not the only one Roman had fooled. The Party had claimed him as one of their own, and Roman had in turn recruited Jacek. But an SB spy within the Party structure would not be tolerated. Jacek thought grimly that Roman was smart enough to know he had better disappear far behind SB lines. If he valued his life at all, he should retire somewhere on the beaches of Cuba. Jacek personally would not trust the ability of the SB to protect one of their men against the power of the Party within Poland.

Jacek's situation was exactly the opposite. His home, the visits by the physiotherapist and masseuse, even Gabi's nursing skills were all evidence that he had not fallen out of favor with the Party. They were taking care of one of their own, and he understood that somehow his having encountered the SB and lived to tell it would only heighten his esteem among Party colleagues.

When he was well enough for Gabi to wheel him outside, Jacek worked in his garden. In the beginning he did so by dragging his splinted legs from spot to spot. Later it was a form of exercising the atrophied limbs. Every day he checked under the geranium pot.

So Jacek waited.

He waited to heal. He waited for the blossoms on his fruit trees. He waited for the sun to warm his tired limbs as he sat outside on the patio. He waited for the moment when he could walk on his own, for the evening hours.

He waited for a chance to visit Izzy. He had to see her, to find out what was going on.

When neither the Party nor anyone from his station had contacted Jacek, the only conclusion he had been able to draw was that Gabi's presence in his home was only a part of the surveillance the SB had placed him under. His house must be too hot to touch.

But he still needed information.

There was so much uncertainty surrounding his current status that he had to clear up. Where did he stand with the various sectors he would be working with when he resumed his ministerial post? Had Roman left behind orders to finish off Jacek in his absence? Did the Company want Jacek to lie low or resume his normal tasks of espionage?

Finally he could walk. And when the combination of factors were all favorable, Jacek made his escape from house arrest. He did so at night, after a day when Gabi had called in sick. As he slipped out of the gate in the front garden, an unfamiliar feeling of panic came over him. He felt he was leaving a safe haven and wondered, despite himself, if he would ever return. He shook the negative thought away. It was bad luck to think of failure.

Jacek crossed the street to be in the shadow of the streetlamp. He would crisscross his way across town until he reached Izzy's back stairs. He was lucky there was no moon that night.

He heard a vehicle slowly making its way toward him. Jacek ducked into a doorway and held his breath as a milicja patrol rumbled past. Then he briskly walked by the other houses on this street and turned the corner.

Three SB agents stood there waiting, their legs wide, rifles pointing straight at him. Jacek gasped. *They knew I was coming*, he thought. Gabi's day off had just been a ploy to get him out of the house. If the SB couldn't eliminate him officially, they would do so unofficially. *Former minister found dead in Wisła. Reasons unknown.* The three men closed in on him as Jacek whirled and ran.

His legs were not what they used to be. Within three strides, one of the agents had tackled him from behind. Jacek went down with a thud, his knees throbbing. He twisted in the man's grasp and kicked his captor full in the face so that he fell back onto his comrades.

Before he was taken down, Jacek had seen one route of escape. His only hope. He stayed down and scrambled forward a few meters in the split seconds that it took his pursuers to get their balance. The men behind him were younger and running on legs that did not feel as though they would buckle with every impact. Jacek knew he would never survive a chase on foot.

Jacek saw the roadworks sign. To his right. He stumbled over the curb and grabbed hold of the top rung of the ladder leading underground. He let his legs dangle as the metal side bars slipped through his palms and he more or less fell to the bottom of the sewer opening.

"Grab him!"

"Stop!"

The last thing Jacek saw before he crawled away down the shaft were the polished boots of the man who had tackled him coming down that same ladder. He rose to his feet and ran to the right, into the stinking darkness.

Jacek had no light with him. He tripped a few times, feeling his way along the slimy walls until he came to a corner. Then he turned right, then left, then right again. Strangely, he heard nothing behind him. *They must have split up to track me.* Jacek made himself stop to listen every forty steps. His breathing was labored; he could feel his heart again. He forced himself to inhale through his mouth only, for every time the stench reached his nose he began to gag noisily.

Jacek kept to the right, fairly sure that it was the direction he wanted, leading downtown. He would not admit to himself that he could be lost. The Warszawa sewers were one part of the city that had more or less survived the Germans' brick-by-brick dismantling of the city at the end of the war. This too had all taken place under the watchful eye of the Soviet troops, who had called on the Home Army to initiate the Warszawa Rising, but then had done nothing to come to their aid. They had simply waited to take the city when the Germans were through.

Jacek's mind wandered. He lost track of time. The darkness was absolute. He heard only the sounds of his own shoes sloshing through the knee-deep filth and the scrambling of rats as they let him pass. More than once, tiny feet scratched unseen over his fingers.

Jacek tried to focus on the direction. He kept the panic at bay and thought how thankful he was that it had not rained recently. If it had, he would be up to his neck in the sludge. The fetid air hung heavy around him. Fresh air must be coming in from somewhere, since he could breathe, but he could not feel it stirring.

After what seemed an eternity, Jacek stopped yet again to listen. He heard dripping and his own heartbeat, which refused to calm. He was about to move on when suddenly there was a sound slightly out of the ordinary. He listened again.

"Jacek." It was not even a whisper.

Jacek thought the stench and time and putrid air, the darkness, were all playing tricks on him. He lifted his right foot and took a step, then stopped again.

This time it was clearer. "Jacek Duch."

A woman's voice. How was it possible? He must be hallucinating. The sound had come from somewhere up ahead. In the distorted water spaces underground, there was no telling how far away the speaker was.

He moved toward the voice, sweat pouring down his back despite the damp, both knees threatening to give way with every step. Had he been at this for hours?

"Jacek?"

"Yes?" Closer, but how close?

"Are you alone?"

He said nothing as he followed the wall curving to the right and suddenly saw a light. A figure stood a few paces ahead of him wearing a cloak, the hood covering the face.

The woman's voice again, "You found me, good. Here, I have two lights. You take one and follow me. Your legs must be killing you. Come on, we're very close to an entrance."

"Izzy?" He reached out toward the hand offering him a flashlight and grabbed hold of the wrist. Why wouldn't she lower the hood and let him see her face?

"Don't be silly. Who else would I be?" She jerked her hand up and out, shoved the flashlight into his palm, and started heading away from Jacek.

He had to get out of there. With every step, his knees were locking up. The gratitude he felt that help had shown up threatened to take his mind off the job he still had to do. He could not talk to Izzy here, though; she had already put too much distance between them. He switched on his light and followed, watching her labor through the same muck he had been wrestling with for hours.

To the right, and again to the right, and then a beam of light coming from a hole above them. Jacek remembered the moonless night and deduced the manhole must be at the foot of a streetlamp.

He shone his light at the ladder to the opening. Curiously, the manhole cover was missing, and the hole stood wide open. Then he shifted the beam downward onto the spot where Izzy's back should have been. Only the sparkle of lamplight on gleaming walls greeted him.

"Izzy?" he whispered. "Izzy, where are you?" Louder this time. He reached the foot of the ladder and looked up. She could not have climbed upward; he would have seen it. He ran his hand along the rung at shoulder length. Dry.

With the ladder at his back, Jacek swiveled the beam of his flashlight in a semicircle. Two tunnels opened up in front of him, branching off from the main tunnel he had just traversed from the left, which also continued on to the right. So she could have gone in one of three directions. "Izzy?"

Jacek cast the light down the two corridors facing him. At their junction, the light picked up some strange scratches on the wall. Despite the ache he felt to get out while he still could, he stepped up to the wall to get a closer look.

"Here we stood, the inscription went, *lived and loved, on the threshold to hell, the doorway to heaven.* Beneath the writing was a list of ten names and a date from during the war.

Jacek knew these sewers had served as a hiding place for Home Army partisans during the war. He had also heard that the sewers had provided the last remnants of the city's Jewish population with shelter and secret passageways as the Nazis systematically destroyed any sign of Jewish life in the Ghetto they had established above ground.

The Nazis had shut the gates to the Warszawa Ghetto on the rest of the world in November 1940, then used it as a collecting center for Jews from all over Poland. During the Ghetto Rising in April 1943, any Jews who had managed to survive the concentration-camp conditions and avoid the countless deportations to the dreaded camps had taken refuge in these same sewers. In the end the Nazis had sent fire bombs down the shafts to flush out like rats the last who had dared to fight. The names on this list were Jewish. Jacek was surprised the inscription had survived the charring.

Where was he, then? Jacek began to calculate the layout of the city. If he stood beneath the former Jewish Ghetto, then he had made it to the city center. That meant Izzy's place would only be a few streets away. She really was gone. Why had she left him like this? Perhaps she knew of another route home through the sewers but had figured he could find his way better through the streets.

Jacek's fatigue was starting to slow his thought processes. He could barely feel his legs anymore. An inner voice warned that he had to get out of the maze of tunnels now, before he no longer could. He reached for the ladder bars and flung back his head. The streetlamp blinded his vision. Nothing stood in its way. He stopped only once as he climbed. And at that moment, he heard the sound of a jeep coming closer.

Jacek froze, his hand on the top rung of the ladder. The light blinked out as the motor roared over Jacek's head, then its gleam resumed again. *So it's an unmarked opening*, Jacek thought. He was lucky one of the jeep's wheels hadn't landed on his head.

Very, very slowly Jacek pulled himself to the surface. The fresh air was already driving the ache from his head. He looked right and left, then crawled the rest of the way to the corner of the nearest building. Despite the warm summer night, Jacek sat huddled, his back against the brick, trembling from head to foot.

I'm too old and still too weak, he thought to himself. He looked around and recognized the street. He was indeed only a few blocks from Izzy's. He pulled himself to a standing position, stamped as much of the filth off his shoes as he could, and started shuffling his way down the street. If anyone saw him, he could pretend to be a drunk who had fallen down the hole.

As he thought about the manhole, Jacek glanced quickly behind him. To his utter astonishment, the gap in the middle of the street was gone. He stopped, catching his breath. He had stumbled over the cover when he climbed out just a few moments earlier. Someone from inside must have pulled it back over the opening. Jacek started running.

The fear took over his body, shooting adrenaline through his veins. Left, straight, the alley, the stairs. He took them in twos, then stood panting in front of the door. It was unlocked and just barely open. Izzy would be expecting him, of course.

Jacek pushed the door open and waited. No one. No sound, not even the smell of Izzy's perfume that usually hung in the air. Maybe he had beaten her back, he thought. He carefully entered and said nothing, silently closing the door behind him and locking it out of habit.

Then he stepped into the anteroom where she usually briefed him. The light was out, the window open. He heard a woman moan.

Still clutching the flashlight and not wanting to signal anyone outside who might be watching, Jacek shone the light around the room, avoiding the window. At his feet lay Izzy. His lamp picked up her legs, her dress—no sign of mud—her arms outspread, her blood-caked face.

Jacek dropped to his knees and took her head in his arms. "Who did this? Izzy, can you hear me? It's Jacek. Tell me, talk to me, stay with me, do you understand?"

One arm rose, and a red-polished fingertip motioned for him to come closer. Jacek leaned forward, only now picking up the perfume he had missed when he entered the house. Why didn't she smell as bad as he did?

"Duch." She had a coughing fit, throwing up more of the blood that already stained her neck.

"Tell me who did this, Izzy. What happened? How long have you been like this?" He rattled off the questions despite her obvious inability to answer.

Izzy's eyes rolled once so he saw the whites, then she focused again. "Gabi." With the last syllable, her head twisted and she fell away from Jacek.

"Gabi? What Gabi? Gabi did this?" Jacek would not accept that he had lost his one contact with what might be called the real world. He recognized that he was not thinking clearly. Jacek caught himself bending over and softly kissing the blood-stained lips of the woman who had died in his arms.

Then he stood with a groan. How long ago had it happened? Was her assassin still in the house? Jacek had to contact his station chief. What was the next step? *Go home.* Yes, that was it. They would know where to find him. Jacek left the house at a limping run and did not stop until he had passed through the gate into his own yard.

When he entered his home, he was surprised to see that the grandfather clock showed he had only been gone for three hours. He headed for the shower and, despite one of the few promises he had ever made to himself, poured himself a glass of cognac on the way.

Gabi?

———— ✑ ————

Jacek stood by the edge of the pond, throwing bread at the swans. He glanced at his watch. Another five minutes until he would be contacted. He could not shake the horror and confusion of what had happened a few days earlier. He had analyzed it over and over from all sides.

Gabi was gone. She had not shown up at the house the morning after he found Izzy's body. He hadn't really expected her to.

The Company still had not contacted him overtly, but they had let him know he was not alone by leaving the cigarette butt under the geranium pot again. He must be even more dangerous to approach than he had thought.

So he had made it a habit to walk in the park every afternoon and feed the swans. Yesterday he had found the time "7 P.M." inscribed on the corner of the wooden bench where he usually sat. It had not been there the previous day.

It was seven o'clock now.

"Don't turn around." A man's voice. "We are aware of the potentialities."

"Potentialities," Jacek repeated. "What about the ramifications? Izzy said Gabi's name before she died."

There was a silence, then, "You were with her when she died?"

"Yes, of course. Didn't you have her placed under surveillance?" Jacek was sorely tempted to confront whoever it was who had not sufficiently protected Izzy from their enemies. "Did one of your people mess up?"

"You need a new contact."

"What I need is a new cover. I need to get out. Or were you going to suggest we conduct business as usual?"

"Nothing of the kind. A new cover is out of the question. Damage control is imperative. Do what you have to do to restore previous status. That's an order. There will be no face-to-face for the time being. When you have a package, go to the news agent on the corner of your street. Drop a piece of wadded-up blank red paper into the garbage bin beside his stand. Wait two days and make your drop at seven in the morning in the same place."

"You've got it all figured out, don't you?" Probably some

young punk with six months' field experience, Jacek thought.

An old woman strolled into Jacek's line of vision. She walked by, nodded at him, and turned the corner. The voice behind him dropped a notch. "I've stayed too long. What we have figured out is that Isabella was a liability from the moment she turned Goleniewski. We had to let her be killed," the voice paused, *"for your benefit.* They knew you would be going there. They knew you had been visiting her for years. After your little encounter, you're hotter than you know."

The cold anger rose up in Jacek. "So she was expendable."

"No, not in so many words."

"Then I'll ask it again. I want to know where your people were when Izzy was taken out."

"Emotionally involved, were we?"

Jacek swirled, his hand already clenched into a fist. But nothing stood behind him but the trees and his park bench. He was alone again.

Stripped of the three people he had grown accustomed to, leaned on, and relied on over the years, Jacek found himself in the unfamiliar position of being on his own. Wiktor. Izzy. Gabi. Now no one. It was like the war all over again.

Jacek could not know what Izzy had revealed about him before she died, just as he would never know what his Brześć contact had revealed about him. Perhaps his enemies already held information that could condemn him, or perhaps they were watching him, waiting for confirmation.

Now, though, after receiving direct orders for the first time since being released from the questioning session, after finding Izzy's body, after what he referred to in his mind as his conversation with the invisible spook, he had the confirmation that the SB had singled him out for intensive surveillance. They were watching him even more than they watched most of the other members of the government. They would like nothing more than for him to slip up so they could take him out their way.

Jacek had his orders, and he also needed to save his neck. To prove his loyalty to Poland, he had to make a bold move.

Jacek knew he needed a bone to throw to the mad dog, something to get the SB off his trail. And living in Poland for so many years had shown him clearly the way to deflect attention from himself. He needed a scapegoat, someone he could persecute, someone else to keep the SB busy and at the same time prove Jacek's loyalty beyond a doubt.

There was no way it could be the Catholic church. The Catholic influence was far too strong in Polish politics. And Jews were now off-limits because of General Moczar's failed anti-Semitic movement.

But the Protestants—that was something else altogether. There were few enough of them in the country to make them a distinct target, and they had little power to fight back. And there was already an undercurrent of tension between the Protestants and the dominant Catholic culture.

There had been a time when the communists gave favors to Protestants, letting them build churches again. This had been sanctioned with the sole aim of weakening the Catholic church and causing resentment and friction between the two groups. The strategy had worked back then, and now Jacek had the opportunity to use the same strategy to his own advantage. He decided to publicly announce a scourge on Protestants in Poland. Jacek was pleased with his decision. The Protestants were a group most of the country could afford to blame and persecute. In the process, he could take a lot of the pressure off himself.

He introduced the new measures himself, through his ministry office, and he had his misinformation aide come up with an entire list of wrong deeds the Protestants could be blamed for.

In the weeks following the policy move, Jacek's tingling sensation lessened somewhat. Eventually Jacek felt sure enough of himself to start leaving the red paper as a signal. Soon he was delivering packages on a regular basis. The ruse had worked.

It was a certainty that the SB would be watching, and they, under the tutelage of the KGB, might even use him in the future to feed misinformation back to his own controllers. But those were all circumstances that could be contained. His data would be cross-checked with that of other agents. Misinformation was a tool of the trade, something that had always been taken into account.

No, he could actually do more damage if they were watching him. There were ways of misleading the KGB that he could only accomplish if they had him under surveillance. Everything had its use.

By Christmas 1975, in fact, Jacek felt he might even be in a better position than he had been before his "interrogation." Now no one could question his loyalties to Poland; that had already happened, and he had been cleared of suspicion. The Party had greater respect for him since he had thwarted the SB. No, all that Jacek had lost in the deal was Amy's picture.

The image of a baby, Jacek knew, could tell them nothing.

Jacek had known it was a safe thing to do, carrying that photo with him all those years.

He had known his daughter could never betray him.

29

REFINES

Revelation 3:18

1975

Jan watched Amy help Tomek blow out the single candle, his round face solemn with concentration. They had sung "Happy Birthday" to him in English and in Polish. And now the whole family sat around the table watching the little boy devour his first taste of birthday cake.

"I have an idea," Tadeusz said. He was leaning over his grandson, trying to wash the boy's face.

"Tatusiu, that's a losing battle you're waging. My son's face won't be clean until he wants it to be," Jan laughed. "What's your idea?"

"Tomorrow is Saturday. I think it's time to take Amy and Tomek to the lake Hanna once showed me, where *her* father took her to play. It's a little to the south of here."

"Oh yes!" Hanna clapped her hands like a little girl. "What a lovely idea. We could make a day of it, maybe even a day and a night and camp out if it's going to stay dry."

"Yes." Amy was smiling, too. "It's turned into such a warm week—really the first we've had this year. Let me see if I can find the weather forecast." She crossed the room and bent over to turn on the small black-and-white television. She was tuning in to the news, to which no one ever listened except for the weather, when the word *Protestants* caught Jan's attention.

"Listen to this," he called the others. His parents crowded around the set. Amy picked up Tomek, who immediately en-

311

twined his little hands in her hair.

One of the assistant ministers was talking in flawless, cultivated Polish, which was in itself unusual, thought Jan. Most of them spoke with some accent or another. The man was giving a speech or reading some sort of statement.

... These new measures will go into effect immediately. The Party has finally confirmed what have been long-held fears that a particular segment of the population was operating in a manner subversive to national security. Now it has come to light that so-called Protestant churches are in actual fact enclaves for counterrevolutionaries. They are under investigation for links with the underground. Their efforts as part of the underground to undermine the stability of the glorious Polish People's Republic will be rooted out. They will be stopped. An end will come to the lies and betrayal done in the name of God.

Jan gasped. "It's blasphemy."

Tadeusz said quietly, steel tones bracing his voice, "No, my son. It's conspiracy." He paused. "I *know* that man." He looked at Hanna, who was shaking her head back and forth, as if trying to forget a bad dream. Tadeusz leaned forward and turned off the set.

All thoughts for the family outing had fled. In their place hung an air of dread and expectation. Jan put his arm around his wife. He had hoped she would not have to witness this warped and ugly side to his country.

Jan had the distinct feeling that the storm he had almost forgotten to watch for had finally hit.

———— ∽ ————

It began two days later. As they met in the small wooden church, built according to Paweł's plans so many years ago, SB agents stormed through the door. Jan's first thought was relief that his mother had not been feeling well and had stayed home together with Amy and the baby.

He watched the men charging through the double doors toward his father as if watching a rerun in slow motion. Jan's heart froze in his throat as the agents grabbed his father and started dragging him down the aisle.

A deep, cold anger rose in him. "No!" He cried out, the authority in his voice carrying over the murmured protests of the congregation. Jan knew exactly what he must do. But it had to happen quickly.

He stepped forward, walking with bold strides down the aisle toward his father. "That is just an old man we invited to talk to us this morning. A visitor. *I* am the pastor here. If you want to arrest a church leader in this witch-hunt, you take me."

Every single person in the church knew he was lying, but no one breathed a word. Jan looked the agents in the eye, just as Aad had taught him to do with border guards. *The bolder the lie, the more believable.* He reached out for his father and thought so clearly, *I won't let it happen a second time.*

Jan said to Tadeusz, "Thank you. It looks like there's been a mix-up somehow. You picked a bad day to visit us, I'm afraid." He pushed Tadeusz aside before he could utter a protest and started outside. The two agents had no choice but to run after him so they could seem to escort him to the armored car they had parked on the sidewalk.

As Jan sat inside the vehicle, his head hitting the metal roof with every bump in the road, all he could think about was the look on his father's startled face and how he wished Tatuś didn't have to be the one to break the news of his arrest to Amy.

The dark van took Jan to the large police building near the center of town. They brought him downstairs and blindfolded him. Then the interrogations began. "Confess your actions as a counterrevolutionary!"

Jan could not believe what he was hearing. And then, "We have photos of you marching with students in the underground during the riots in 1968. Tell us their names and those of the members of your church!"

Jan was shocked. He hadn't seen Bogdan after that first day, and had always been a little afraid he had ended up in prison with so many of the other leaders of the demonstrations then.

When he said nothing, the guard continued, "We have others from your group, and they will tell us if you don't, so you had better talk or it will be hard on you later."

The interrogation seemed to go on and on. "Your wife is an American imperialist. You have a spy in your house. Did you know this?"

Silence.

"What have you been telling people about the Party?"

Here was a question he could answer. Jan said, "I only told people what was in the Bible."

"You are mad." The interrogation lasted all night, and there were repeated threats, but none of Jan's faceless interrogators laid a hand on him. By morning he was emotionally drained with the fear of what could happen, but he was starting to catch on that maybe, just maybe, this was all an act.

He must have dozed off. A rough hand pushed his shoulder and then was untying the blindfold. Jan shaded his eyes from the light as the voice said, "Follow me. We're letting you go, but don't ever let us catch you again. Let this be a warning."

He was led up stone steps, then shoved out a door that opened onto an alley behind the police headquarters. He was just a few streets away from home, so he walked the distance, humming to himself with relief that it was over so soon.

Jan would never forget the look of utter astonishment and relief on his parents' faces as he walked through the door. Of course they had been fighting old fears that he might be gone for years. Instead, it had barely been twenty-four hours. Amy flew across the room and flung herself around his neck.

"I *knew* it. I knew you'd be back soon. I *said* so, didn't I?" she said to her in-laws. But Mamusia had turned her back to them and was looking out the window. Tatuś coughed a few times, then strode over to him and enclosed them both in his arms.

"Son, don't you ever, *ever* pull a stunt like that again." Then more softly, "Thank you." Mamusia turned away from the window, and Jan saw she had been crying. She sat down heavily on one of the chairs, and he went over to her.

"It's all right, Mamusiu. I think this was just all a sham, a fake way of blaming some group or other, and we were singled out. They told me it was a warning."

Tadeusz said, "Poles are so inconsistent. They decide to persecute Protestants one day, and the next day they are busy discussing it again. This will blow over."

But in the days and weeks to come, more members of their congregation and Marek's, as well as the other Protestant churches, continued to pay the price for being different. Tadeusz told Jan, "Perhaps the police simply didn't know what to do with you during the early days of the crusade. Maybe that's why you got off so easily."

Jan shook his head. "It's hard to see the pattern. I'm worried about the hand I have in all of this. Those photos they say they took of me in Warszawa—could they be used to incriminate a whole segment of the population like this?"

"No. But it does mean they've been watching you . . . and us for years. I've often wondered if they've still had us under surveillance. If they suspected you of being part of the student movement, then that explains it."

Jan knew Tadeusz hadn't said what was uppermost in both their minds, *Piotr*. Tadeusz continued. "As far as bringing down the arrests on Protestants in general, no I can't believe you're to blame for that."

Jan was also worried that the police seemed to be holding people for longer and longer periods. "They know no one will oppose them. It's as if when we do nothing, they do more."

Tadeusz rested a hand on Jan's shoulder. "Son, at some point you learn to recognize certain things. You should have seen your grandfather when he and I were in the Soviet camp, how he inspired people. When you hear that others dare, it motivates you to do the same. The blessing is from danger. Remember this: During crucial moments, prayer *is* the blessing."

That night in bed, Jan told Amy, "We don't know what's ahead. Can you handle this?"

She nodded, her big eyes pools of warm darkness Jan could stare at for hours. "I don't think we should let what's happening inhibit us in any way," Amy said.

He swallowed. "Amy, I can't tell you how much it means to me that we are fighting this as a team."

The next day Jan went door to door, visiting members of the church, trying to convince them that they had to fight back, take the offensive. "In past battles, the best possible weapon has always been to spread the Word."

When he stopped by Marek's apartment, the door swung open on its own. The place was in total disarray—books on the floor, furniture ripped open. He ran home in fear of what he might find.

Tadeusz lay sleeping on the couch when Jan burst in the door. Relief flooded Jan even as he braced himself to break the news to his father about his oldest friend. "He's been taken away. They have Marek."

Tadeusz turned away from Jan. Jan had never seen his father look so old and sick and weak. *I have to do something. I can't just sit around and wait for them to arrest someone else.*

He went down to Marek's garage, hammered wood over the window, and slept on the floor for two nights until he had printed hundreds of fliers denouncing the persecution and explaining what they stood for—the Gospel.

On the third night, while members of the church were coming by to pick up the tracts and distribute them, Jan heard the sirens before the others did.

"Quick, lock the door, and everyone empty those sacks of coal onto the press. Cover the papers!" If there hadn't been five people there, and if there hadn't been an accident farther up the road that tied up traffic, as Jan heard about much later, they couldn't have finished the job. But they did, and by the time the two cars came screaming to a halt in front of the line of garages, the others had escaped. Only Jan stood waiting, standing at the opposite end of the row.

Jan was saddened to see they knew exactly where to go. *Who has tipped them off?* His main concern was the printing press. They had waited and prayed for it for years.

He stepped forward and shouted, hoping to distract the police from the press. *Let them take me and forget what they came for.*

One of the three men who approached Jan raised a finger and pointed, recognizing Jan. "I warned you, didn't I?" He nodded, and one of the other men struck Jan across the base of his back with a baton. The last thing Jan remembered was covering his face, and rolling in a ball, trying to protect his head from the two agents' relentless kicks.

Jan had no idea where he was. He woke in a semidark room, the only light coming through the cracks of the black-painted window. Since there were no traffic sounds, he assumed he was somewhere outside the city.

Jan groaned and tried to straighten his legs. He ran his fingers over his face, relieved to feel only a few cuts. But then he began to cough, and the bitter taste of blood warned him of other injuries.

A few moments after his coughing fit, he heard the lock slide back, and the same SB man who had ordered his beating entered the room. "You may have underestimated us, Piekarz. But that's probably my fault, since we did not communicate clearly our intentions during your last visit. I can assure you there will be no such misunderstanding this time. Let me start by suggesting that you get used to this place. You'll be here for at least a year."

The man left and another entered. Jan tried to stand, but pain shot up his spine. He looked up as the man asked, "Name the members of your church. You are all suspected of being part of the underground. We know members of your family are also involved. Tell us, or we will go after your wife. We'll have no problem proving her imperialistic leanings."

Piotr! he thought desperately. *I have to protect him at all costs.* As far as Amy was concerned, he knew they wouldn't touch a U.S. citizen. *They wouldn't dare,* he told himself. It was the one bluff he could afford to call. He raised his chin and said nothing, even as the blows began again.

Jan lost track of time as the days ran into weeks. At first the hunger pains woke him, then he felt only racking aches in his head and along his back. Then the thirst took over as he faded in and out of consciousness. Finally, he woke up to find a bowl of tepid water by his head. After that there was stale bread.

Jan held on by thinking about his family, Amy's face, little Tomek's smile, his parents' memories, their stories. He thought about his father, his father's words about enemies.

Pray for them. It had helped before, with the Russians. Jan tried again now.

He lay alone. How much time had he lain there listening to other men moan? He went over and over and over his feelings for Amy until Jan finally saw something clearly. "I am not worthy of Amy's trust." The thought hit him harder than the blows. It was the root cause of their problems. He had not been trusting her totally. He realized he was still harboring doubts about her relationship with Piotr. Was he uncertain of their love?

Forgive me. He felt wretched, inside and out. For all these two years she had been doing her best for him, while he had not been totally honest with her.

He was his own worst enemy.

Forgive me, I beg.

———— ✐ ————

He woke to rain falling on his face. He moved his legs and could feel his clothing soaked clear through. Then he opened his eyes and saw he was lying in a field somewhere.

Am I losing my mind? Have they finished with me? The thoughts hurled themselves one after the other through his mind as he carefully sat up and looked around. No one. He breathed in the fresh air and laughed out loud. "I'm out!" *Thank you.*

Slowly, very slowly, he dragged himself out of the mud to a standing position. His head throbbed, his heart beat fast, and every step felt as though his legs were made of lead. None of it mattered. A smile beamed on Jan's face as he looked around and recognized one of the roads leading into Gdynia.

The first day he was home, Jan slept. On the second day, he woke to the sounds of Mamusia and Tatuś discussing something in soft tones. They stood in the other room, but the door was open.

"How will you contact him?" Mamusia was saying.

"I think I know a way. Now that Jan is back, I have to act. Jan . . ."

"Jan what?" He sat up in bed and peered through the door opening.

Both his parents came in. "Jan is back with us." They smiled.

"In more ways than one," he answered. "Now tell me what you were talking about out there." He saw his parents exchange glances.

Then Tatuś leaned over and turned on the radio. He added in quiet tones, "I can't stand by and let this persecution escalate. You were right all along, Jan. We must *do* something to alleviate the suffering of our friends. Marek is still gone. I have no more doubt that we are being used as some sort of scapegoat, perhaps even as a distraction. And I think I know by whom."

"What do you mean?"

"Well, I think I do. I made some inquiries while you were being held and found out there's a boyhood friend of mine, someone from Łódź, who's in the government now. He's named Henio, and he used to be a carpenter. It's a long story, but I think that if I got a message to him he could contact the man we saw on TV. *If* he's responsible, then I may have a way of getting him to reverse the policy."

"What could you possibly have that he wants?" Jan asked, matching his father's whisper.

Tadeusz smiled wryly at Hanna. "Old war stories, my son. Old war stories."

Jan was afraid for his father, but he didn't know what to do. He looked around the apartment and only then noticed how quiet it was. "Where are Tomek and Amy?" he asked, concerned.

"It's all right," Mamusia said. "Amy's just taken the baby out for fresh air and to let you rest. I think that seeing the state you were in when you stumbled through that door upset her more than she let on."

Jan was quiet. He still felt quite sore from the beatings. But he wanted to find her now, to talk to her, to tell what he had discovered about himself in prison.

He thought about how they had been blessed with so much, reunited with each other and with Tomek. They had grown closer to each other, despite their cultural differences, and closer to God. They shared an intense faith, and they could handle fear and anger and doubt together. He knew they could.

But first—what was wrong with him?—first he had to ask her forgiveness. That was the first thing he had to do. He had promised himself in prison. . . .

"Is there something, Jan?" his mother asked him.

"No. It's just . . . no, nothing. No, wait." His mind was working in jerks. "There *is* something." His tone dropped again. "I've just realized—about the printing press. If it's still in one piece, then perhaps my arrest was worth it."

"No, Jan." Tadeusz shook his head. "I'm afraid that whoever informed on us was very thorough. They knew exactly which garage to go to. They still claim it's because we're part of the underground."

"I can't believe it." He got out of bed and slowly started getting dressed.

"And where do you think you're going?" Hanna asked.

"I'm all right, Mamusiu. Just a little weak. Please, I just have to see for myself. I was just a little tired. I need to move about." He gave both his parents a kiss as he passed them and was out the door, carefully making his way down the stairs before they could object.

It took Jan twenty minutes to reach the garage. He checked in his pocket, too late, and realized he had no key. But it wasn't necessary. The lock had been forced. He swung the door upward and ducked under to see the colossal chaos.

The printing press had been taken apart piece by piece and damaged beyond any hope of repair. The coal had discolored and ruined their paper supplies, all of which had been torn open and tossed around. There was nothing worth salvaging, nothing at all, unless you counted the coal.

Jan picked around the rubble, shoving pieces of metal and coal aside with his foot. He came to the base of the printing press and kicked that over. Underneath he saw a plastic bag wrapped around what looked like a large brick.

He bent over and caught his breath as the bruised ribs cut into him. So he squatted down to inspect the bag. Inside he found a package and a card in an envelope with his and Amy's name on the front. He opened it to find a wedding card with Piotr's signature on the inside.

Jan straightened up. He was remembering the last time he had spoken with his brother; on the phone he had mentioned a gift of some sort. He and Amy had thought nothing of it at the time, then with all the excitement of getting married and settled in, they had completely forgotten.

Now Jan asked himself, *Why would Marek not give it to us?* He tore open the wrapping paper and opened a wooden box. He began to read the sheaves of paper inside, beginning with one dated February 1973.

And then Jan wished with all his heart that he could hide the box all over again.

30

DESTROYS THE ELEMENTS

2 Peter 3:10

1975

The first time she lost Jan, Amy had been frantic.

The second time she lost him, she had learned to wait and pray and be stronger than she had ever thought she could be.

When she lost him the third time, Amy wondered if she had learned anything at all.

When Tadeusz came from church and told about Jan's arrest, her mind had flown in five directions at once. "What are they doing to him? Why is it taking so long?" Neither Hanna nor Tadeusz had been able to give her an answer. Instead, Tadeusz had left quickly to warn Marek. Hanna had crossed over to Amy and folded her into a long embrace, but then she had stepped back, her face stern. "Now listen. Everything will be fine. You *must* believe that. But we must also fight this. Starting with this moment, we will hold a vigil for Jan's safe return, take turns praying for him and for the others who were probably taken from other churches. Can you do this with me?"

"Yes, I . . ." Amy had choked on her tears, but she had nodded. "Yes. All right . . . Hanna, I'm not like you and Tadeusz and Jan. I'm afraid I don't really know. . ."

But Hanna knew. Amy could see in the worried eyes, the creased brow, that she knew too well. How it must hurt her to live through this once again.

So Amy had prayed and tried to be strong. And within a day Jan was home—their prayers answered more quickly than anyone had expected. What a joy that had been!

But then he had been arrested again, and the joy had been ripped away. After Amy lost Jan this second time, the waiting was so much longer, so much harder.

She could not sleep. Tomek seemed to cry constantly. And since Tadeusz refused to tell her anything about his own time in prison, Amy knew it must be bad. Very bad.

In the middle of a night like so many others, Amy paced their little room, trying to get Tomek to settle down. She heard a light knock on the door and opened it to Hanna's concerned face.

"My dear, I heard you up. Are you all right?"

Amy knew the cardinal rule in this household was not to complain, but that made it even worse. The empty weeks without Jan were taking their toll. Everything stayed bottled up. She swallowed hard. "Yes. I was just trying to calm Tomek."

"I think he misses his tatuś," Hanna said softly.

Amy felt the tears brimming in her eyes. "I'm sorry. I'm just *so* worried, so tired. . . ." She walked over to the window and stared down at the street. "I'm not used to this."

"Of course you're not, but, Amy, look at me. None of us are. This is torture, and it never gets easier." Hanna sighed and sat down on the bed. "Here, give me the baby, and you try to relax."

Amy watched Tomek fall asleep in his grandmother's arms. "I'm so tense; he picks up on that, I know. It's just all this uncertainty. . . ." She broke off and sobbed, "Oh, I'm just weak."

"Listen to me." Amy felt the older woman's hand on her arm and looked up, surprised by eyes as full of tears as her own. "Amy, I *know* the fear you are fighting. Don't be ashamed; it's a sign of your love. I don't know if it will help, but I remembered something."

They crossed over to the sofa bed and sat on the edge, Hanna holding Tomek on her shoulder and rocking him as she talked.

"When Tadeusz was arrested in the early fifties," she said, "it was such a terrible time. We were all manipulated against one another—friends, neighbors, family members—it was like some cruel game. Anyone who stood out for any reason was singled out and humiliated—at home, at work, at school. And of course our prayer meetings made us a natural target.

"And so they came to arrest Tadeusz. They came at night and just dragged him away, and I couldn't get anyone to tell me where he was or what he had been charged with or when he was coming back. I did everything I could to find out what had happened. I tried to discover who had turned him in. Perhaps it was Dorota and Henryk, our neighbors, or it could have been Jasiu's teacher or even someone to whom we had opened our home during the meetings. There was no way to tell.

"Eventually I had no choice but to accept the unthinkable, that Tadeusz would not be coming home soon. During the days and weeks it took for this to sink in, I became aware of something else—Jasiu's sadness refused to lift. On the night of his father's arrest, Jasiu changed from my clever, curious little boy into this downcast child who was always staring at his shoes. He shuffled his feet and no longer asked questions.

"Because of these two things—Tadeusz's continued absence and Jasiu's refusal to respond, I started to panic. I could feel it rising in me with each passing day. The way you're feeling now, my dear."

Amy realized that she had been squeezing Hanna's hand in a death grip, willing herself not to cry. She gave her mother-in-law a weak smile and reached over to take Tomek from her. She laid him carefully on the bed behind them, stroking his downy hair.

"You were so alone then," she murmured. "I don't know if I could have stood it."

Hanna nodded. "Not completely alone, of course. Marek and the others from the nucleus of our prayer group were helping me in any way they could. We were determined not to be scared out of our faith. And of course I knew that the Lord was watching out for me. But still I felt betrayed. Here I was pregnant and without my husband, and now I seemed to have lost my son.

"I could do nothing but wait. Wait and pray, like we're doing now. Every day I kept hoping Tadeusz would again walk through that door, that Jasiu would again smile with dancing eyes, that the baby would grow strong and healthy.

"The weeks became months. Daily I went through the trial of

passing through Henryk and Dorota's room. I felt humiliated by his gaze, but her silence stung me more. Whatever Dorota knew, it had stolen any words of comfort right out of her mouth. Whenever Henryk's brother was there, he did nothing but stare at me, even as my stomach grew. Every night I doublechecked the extra locks I had put on the door myself.

"The tension mounted until I felt I could bear it no more. And then, as I let it go, the burden was taken from me."

Amy didn't even voice her question: *How*. She asked it with her eyes, her gaze never leaving her mother-in-law's weathered face.

Hanna answered very gently. "It happened on a night when Jasiu woke up and wet the bed again, and he was crying. I sat there rocking him back to sleep, his long legs dangling against me. And then my spirit broke. Listen, Amy, I could feel it happen. Something gave way inside of me—like an earthquake, like the plates shifting and resettling along a fault. Something broke and was taken away and replaced with something else not wholly of me but truly strong.

"I prayed again, the same old prayers. And I still felt empty, but something was different now. It was as if something was making room inside of me for something new.

"The anger was gone, and the fear was less. Somehow I realized that I had to be broken before God could build me up again.

"Something in me used to cry out constantly, 'But I've already suffered so much.' But now that voice inside me was quiet. I didn't know what had happened, but I knew it was real.

"And do you know what? That next morning Jasiu smiled. I was watching him from the other side of the room, and I waited until he saw me looking at him. Then he ran over and threw his arms around my legs, and he said, 'I dreamed about angels last night.' "

Amy sighed. If only she could take this story into herself and be changed as well. Oh, how she wanted Hanna's strength. She said, "And finally Tadeusz did come home."

Hanna's eyes were tender as she reached over and pulled her daughter-in-law to her, gently stroking her hair and rocking back and forth as though she were holding a child.

"You see," she said. "Eventually you have to let go. And when you do that, God will carry you." Hanna leaned back from Amy and rose slowly, painfully to her feet. "And now," she said, "we must say some prayers and I must say good night, because I am an old woman and need my sleep."

Holding hands, they prayed fiercely, and then Hanna crossed to the door.

"Good night, Mamusiu," Amy said in a quiet voice.

"Good night, my love," Hanna answered softly.

That was two weeks to the day before Jan came home again.

———— ✍ ————

And then he was hers for one day only—the day he slept. Again and again, when she wasn't busy with Tomek or the housework, Amy would steal quietly into the room and watch him lie so still, the exhaustion too strong even for bad dreams to stir him. Silently she gazed over the scars on his battered face, the welts from the beatings, and wondered what they had done to him and when he would be able to tell her.

But she could give him time. She could wait. That much she had learned from Hanna.

The second day Jan was back, to give him more time to rest, Amy took Tomek to the park. There she reveled in the sunshine, the birds' songs, the laughter of her son as he pulled himself up on the park benches, delighted with his newly acquired skill.

"And your tatuś hasn't even seen you crawl yet," she told him. "He'll be so proud." She smiled and picked him up and whirled him around, almost giddy from the beauty around her. It was as if she were seeing colors for the first time since Jan's arrest. Oh, he was back, he was home, he was safe. Amy's heart sang with praises for the protection God had granted her.

She returned to the apartment bursting with plans for them all—time together, ways to move forward in the ministry, already treating herself to the thought that once she unlocked the familiar door, she could enter and relish in the nearness of Jan, his very presence a precious gift. But all she saw when she entered the apartment were Hanna and Tadeusz.

"Where's Jan?" Amy asked.

"He went out."

"What?" Amy said. "I thought . . ."

Tadeusz shook his head. "I know. But he seems to be rested. He had to see the printing press for himself. He'll be back soon. Hanna and I were just going out shopping. If you want, we'll stop by Marek's garage and tell him you and Tomek are back. He's probably just trying to clean up the mess."

Amy watched them leave with mixed feelings. Why didn't she just run down to the garage herself? She could help him, just be with Jan—that was all she wanted. But little Tomek's howl startled her back to the present. What had he gotten into now?

Amy ran to their bedroom and found Tomek with a red face, inhaling during an enormous pause, just getting ready for another scream. Somehow, he had pulled the tablecloth right off their small table and brought the bowl of fruit on top of himself. Amy could see the red mark where the bowl must have crashed onto his forehead.

"Oh, look at you." She scooped the baby up and held him until the sobbing softened into little gasps. Well, now there would be no going to the garage. She held a cold cloth to the place where the bowl had hit and stroked Tomek's sweaty head until he fell asleep.

After Amy had put Tomek to bed, she got out her sketchpad and tried to finish the sketch of Tomek sleeping she had begun earlier that week. She had thought it would be an easy study, with him lying still, but even in sleep he moved so much that she had to work quickly and keep starting over. Tenderly her pencil traced the roundness of his baby cheeks, the sturdiness of his little legs.

Then Amy heard the locks turning. Jan. Eagerly she set the sketchpad aside and rose to go greet him.

When she emerged from their room, she saw Jan standing in the main room with his back to her. It was almost as if he didn't know where he was. A little gasp escaped her from the pure relief at seeing him physically so near and so well.

"Jan?"

As he turned to face her, Amy braced herself for the sight of his battered face. She had promised herself not to fuss over him. He hated that. But what she saw caused her to gasp. And the reasons were not the scars and the welts, but his eyes.

"Jan, what is it?" She stepped forward, already reaching for him. He looked devastated. "You must still be so weak." But even as she said the words, she knew that what ravaged his face could not be physical pain.

Amy never reached Jan's side. He raised a hand to keep her back. Amy stood in the room with her husband and heard the neighbors' music playing next door, thought of Tomek sleeping so near, watched the dust dance in the ray of sunshine, and said one more time, "Jan? Tell me—what's happened?"

But she had lost him. Again.

She saw that much in his eyes.

———— ∽ ————

This third time that Amy lost Jan was the hardest because she couldn't imagine how or why it happened. For some reason she couldn't fathom, a chasm had opened between them, and Amy felt helpless to reach across the gap.

They went through the motions both for Tomek and for Hanna and Tadeusz, but Amy doubted they fooled anyone. Outwardly Jan was courteous and civil. But in their bedroom he would not touch her, could not seem to face her. And he would not tell her what was wrong.

Amy racked her brain to think of something she might have done, but she could think of nothing. He hadn't been home long enough for her to offend him. Then she thought that something must have happened in prison, something he couldn't bring himself to share with her. But if he couldn't tell her what was bothering him, how could they live as husband and wife? How could they live with this chasm between them?

She begged him to open up until even she tired of her pleas.

Finally, she let go of the nagging and started to wait.

The first two times Amy lost Jan, Hanna had shown her a way of waiting. This time, Amy knew, she would have to win Jan back from the place he had gone to on her own. But she didn't know who the enemy was. And she could not share this with her mother-in-law.

Amy thought of the verse Hanna had told her she discovered

the night the secret police took Tadeusz away. What was it again?—something about God's promise to be the glory in her midst. Oh, how she prayed for that now, for God's glory to return to their midst.

Night after night she prayed it fiercely, as if she were doing battle. Rallying her courage. Summoning her strength, again and again. Praying for Jan. Willing him back to her.

For Amy had known something from the first moment her husband pulled away from her—that she would do whatever it took to find him again.

No matter how long she had to endure.

This was her battle to fight.

31

REVEALS

1 Corinthians 3:13

1976

Piotr had mixed feelings about seeing his parents again. As he walked down the familiar streets of Gdynia, it didn't seem as if he had been gone for more than three years.

"Hey, want to change some money?" A man around his own age emerged from beside the *Pewex* store and waved a wad of dollars under Piotr's nose.

"No thanks. Hey, isn't that illegal?"

The man looked at Piotr, then broke out laughing.

Piotr thought, *Some things never change.* Yet he had. Unlike the lovesick boy who had left this place so confused and angry, Piotr was returning as a deeply committed force behind the new underground movement. His passion and ability to get results, as he had in the Katyń research, had catapulted him into leadership. Recently, he had helped orchestrate the last round of food riots. As a result, Piotr had been warned. The SB now had him on one of their "Wanted" lists.

He turned the last corner and entered the building, all the familiar odors of the staircase reminding him that he had come home.

———— ✑ ————

Jan had never seen his parents so nervous. The radio was blaring as Tadeusz stood very close to Jan and Hanna, trying to explain about their visitor. But he kept breaking away from them to pace back and forth, then he would return to say something more. Jan was glad Amy had gone to take Tomek to the neighbors. It wouldn't do her any good to see his father struggling like this.

"I just want to make sure we all understand what is at stake here. The fact that he's agreed to meet with us tells me we have the right man. Understand one thing." Tadeusz took Hanna's hand instinctively and turned to Jan. "This man can threaten our family, the church, our very life."

Jan thought that whoever the visitor was, he had reemerged out of his father's past like a specter in the dark. He was a danger then, and he had become more of one now. "Tatusiu, please don't go through with this. I haven't liked this plan from the beginning. Too much is at stake. This man is too dangerous."

"There's no other way, Jan."

"Then tell me what the hold is you have over him. I have to know if anything happens."

"No. I won't put you into any more danger."

"What?"

"Respect my decision, Jan, please." As Jan started to protest, his father coughed. Jan swallowed his frustration, then heard the timber of his father's voice change.

"My Hanna, to be with you all these years has been a gift in itself." Jan watched his father straighten Hanna's collar without her even noticing it. "I am so thankful we are growing old together."

"You don't need to say these things now," she interrupted.

Jan looked from one to the other, their love for each other shining in their eyes. They seemed to have forgotten he was even there. They were each other's strength, the focal point for every day.

"My old warrior," Tadeusz said softly.

Hanna smiled and stroked his face, unable to mask her concern. Jan knew what she was thinking about. Tadeusz had been too weak lately, too pale, too out of breath. And recently, Hanna's own illness had escalated.

"Fifty-six is not so old," she answered. "My joy is simply in being with you, husband. If there could be more joy, then I have that, too, in the shape of Jan and Amy's little Tomek."

Jan swallowed hard. His parents' rare show of intimacy only underscored his fear that they were embarking on a course of action they could not control.

"Son," Tadeusz said. "I have been meaning to tell you for some time now that you should be aware of the ways God has answered our prayers concerning you. Ever since I returned from prison, your mother and I have been praying for your emotional healing. Now, in the same way, I offer daily prayers for the safety of your brother. I know there has been tension between you two, but it is your responsibility to heal that. Whatever has been keeping you two so apart, you must try and remove. Do you understand?"

Jan felt as if a thunderbolt had just penetrated his most secret spots.

Tadeusz sighed. "Yes, I pray that Piotr might discover the same way of bearing his bitterness as I once did." He paused and nodded to Jan that he should turn off the radio.

Then Tadeusz said slowly, "Sometimes, like Daniel, we are called to face the lions. And now I have called a lion into our very home. If I am right, this man is using the anti-Protestant crusade as a distraction, perhaps away from himself. That the man with the power to do such a thing would be one who owes a debt to me—that is God's hand."

At that moment, they all heard a knock at the door. *The lion roars*, Jan thought.

———— ✐ ————

As Jacek stood outside the door, he heard music, then nothing. He knocked and listened to the bolts being drawn back. He did not recognize the man who opened the door.

Jacek entered and looked around the room, taking in the furniture, the two doors, the window. He peered at the man who had motioned for him to enter. Then he saw the old man in the corner and realized that the man who had let him in was a younger version of his former rescuer. Since no one had said anything, he took the initiative and crossed the room.

"So, Pani Piekarz." He extended his hand to the old man. His grip was not as weak as he looked.

Jacek suddenly felt very unsure. He had no idea what to expect, and that in itself was a dangerous state of affairs. The son went to sit beside his mother. Jacek nodded at her, thinking what a pity it was when young women grew old. Then he turned his attention to the business at hand. He must try to maintain the offensive.

"So, Pani Piekarz," he repeated, "I heard you had a message for me and that I should come here alone. This is highly irregular. Do you know who I am?"

"I have an idea," Tadeusz said.

The pause grabbed at Jacek. *What does he mean?*

Tadeusz continued, "A minister in the government."

Jacek breathed out slowly. "That's right. And that means I'm a busy man. So what can I do for you?" Jacek did not like the steely blue eyes staring him down. Two could play this game.

"I'll be frank. We have not seen each other since the war. Do you remember the circumstances?"

Jacek nodded. He had known this was coming. Why on earth would this Tadeusz be asking for a favor now. Why not earlier?

"Well, your recent measures against the Protestants have hurt a lot of innocent people, including my son, my church. I recognized you when you made the announcement on television. I had a hard time believing then that things would escalate as they have. Now I think it's time to call in a certain debt. Do I need to remind you of what happened at Wawel Castle?"

No you don't have to remind me, fool. Jacek was thinking that of all the groups he could have picked to persecute, the man who had saved his life would have to be one of their leaders. "Of course not, Pani Piekarz. I told you then, and I tell you now that I owe you one. But I think I know where this conversation is headed, and I should warn you that I have no more power than you over what's been happening. The fact that I was the one to announce the policy doesn't mean it was my idea."

Slowly, Tadeusz took two steps forward so that he was staring straight at Jacek. Surprised, Jacek had to fight an impulse to back away from him. Then Tadeusz said in a low tone that told Jacek the wife and son knew nothing of this, "I know something about you."

You know I fought in the Home Army, but that won't bring me down, not anymore. The only reason Jacek had even agreed to the meeting was just to make sure that this was Tadeusz's only hold over him.

"I heard things when you were delirious that you might not want me to advertise."

If you heard things, then I should have had you killed years ago. Even though he was desperate to find out what Tadeusz knew, Jacek still said nothing. In the hunt, waiting was everything.

"All these years I kept my silence, but now too high a price has been paid among my own people. How do you think your fellow ministers would feel about what I heard? Reverse your policy."

My policy. Jacek would not let this weak, religious fool get the best of him. If he could take on the SB, he could handle an old man. And yet Jacek could not shake the feeling that he was back to fighting a two-front war, and this time he was completely alone.

He took Tadeusz by the arm and led him into the corner away from the other two. *I will stop at nothing to silence you,* he thought, even as he said the words. "Tell me what you know."

"Tell me that you're in a position to end the persecution. That maybe this madness *is* your idea."

Had the game suddenly changed? "Tell me."

Then Tadeusz said loud enough for his voice to carry, "In which language, Polish or Russian . . ."

Jacek shook his head, confused for a split second. But then Tadeusz finished his sentence and hissed, "Or English?"

"Enough." Jacek moved to cover Tadeusz's mouth, but the son was on him before his hand had even reached its mark.

———— ⌒♭ ————

Jan watched and waited, trying to guess at what might be going on. The tension in the room cut into both his parents' faces. When he heard his father speak louder, he took it as a call for help. Then, when the stranger stepped toward Tadeusz and raised his arm, Jan flew off the sofa and threw himself at the man's back.

"No!" he roared. He had counted on the older man's being weaker, but the stranger's strength took Jan totally by surprise. He pivoted and grabbed Jan's right arm, twisting it behind his back and forcing him forward all in the same motion.

"Call him off," the man grunted at Tadeusz.

"Jan, it's all right," Tadeusz said.

The man shoved Jan back toward his mother and jeered, "This is between me and your father," but he continued in a voice they all could hear. "I acknowledge the debt I owe you," he said to Tadeusz. "And I want to be rid of it, but I really am unable to reverse the current measures. I'm sorry I cannot help you." Here he included all of them with a sweep of his arm. "You must understand, it's too late to take back the order that, for example, teachers should single out Protestant children and ridicule them. And I am so sorry that Protestants must stand in line for hours longer than others in order to obtain travel papers, but the order is out—I cannot rescind it. I beg you, come up with another favor I can do."

Something the man said struck a chord in Jan. He was thinking about this when he heard his mother speak for the first time.

"Yes, as a matter of fact, there is."

Jan saw his parents exchange one of their glances. *They already know what they're asking*, he thought.

"Our daughter-in-law has been searching for her father here in Poland. Perhaps with your connections you can help her find out what happened to him."

"During the war?"

"Yes," Hanna said. Then she stood and motioned for Jan to go get Amy, who was at the neighbor's. He crossed the room toward the door with mixed feelings of reluctance and relief. He didn't want to leave his parents alone with this stranger. But better than anyone, Jan knew how much it would mean to Amy to find out something concerning her father. He wondered though, what price would they be asked to pay?

———— ✍ ————

Jacek felt more sure of the situation when he was alone with the old couple. As Jacek watched Hanna approach, he wondered secretly how he could arrange to have them both killed.

"Do you remember when we met?" Hanna asked.

"You two know each other?" Tadeusz looked from one to the other.

"Yes," Hanna said. "This man warned us not to take the train from Kraków to Dresden."

Inside his silk suit, Jacek began to sweat. He had never dreamed that she would remember their brief encounter on the eve of the Soviet liberation of Kraków. He had watched her say good-bye to Tadeusz and recognized him as the man who had saved him after the Nazis shot Jacek during an assassination attempt. He had waited for Tadeusz to leave the train station hall before approaching the little dark beauty and paying back the debt he owed Tadeusz. He had heard Hanna say out loud that she needed to get to Dresden, a destination U.S. military intelligence had told him would soon be bombed.

"You and Helena?" Tadeusz asked.

So Jacek had simply saved Tadeusz's wife and mother-in-law. Jacek squinted his eyes at Hanna. Before their encounter today, it was much more likely that she had passed the incident off to coincidence. Jacek chided himself. Had he forgotten her?

"Yes," Hanna answered Tadeusz. "It was all very strange, if I remember right. You seemed so sure of yourself."

When Jacek still did not respond, Tadeusz said, "Yes, strange that my wife and I never put two and two together. For months I thought she died among the thousands the night Dresden was bombed. And I never told her about our little encounter on Wawel hill. She doesn't know the events of that day. I'm sure she's always wondered, but she never asked and I never told her. For her safety," he added.

"Yes, for her safety," Jacek finally said. Their two stories were harmless enough if taken separately. Together however, they wove a rope that could very well hang him. He glared at Tadeusz. Yes, the threat had hit its mark.

Hanna said, "So you see, Tadeusz, our friend has already paid his debt."

Jacek saw the old couple look at each other a certain way. As if they had just discussed something and agreed on it without even speaking the words. *Piekarz must be pleased with this ace in the hole his wife had just handed him. It's time to do a little damage control.*

Then he heard Tadeusz ask softly, "How did you know it would happen?"

Amy was pleased that she had managed to get Tomek to sleep at Iwona's. She paced back and forth, worrying about the meeting next door.

Lately, it seemed, she was wrestling with so many things. There was this two-dimensional relationship Jan had imposed on them. Then there were the changes that having a baby at thirty-five brought with it. She loved Tomek passionately, and she and Jan had wanted a large family as soon as possible. But now that she was pregnant again, Amy found herself wondering how they could possibly survive in even more cramped conditions.

It was probably because of the pregnancy, but her list of irritations grew with the day. It bothered her knowing the apartment was bugged—the phone she could handle, but their own bedroom? The hardest part had been the little things, day in, day out, like learning to start meals sometimes three hours ahead of time just because of the lack of conveniences and ingredients.

Amy's prayer every morning was for patience and understanding. She hated to complain, but she often felt like complaining. Then she felt guilty, knowing that her problems paled when compared with her parents-in-law's illnesses or the suffering of people like Marek, who had been in prison now for more than a year. And throughout it all, she wanted more than anything else to win Jan back. That desire tinted everything.

And now there was this visitor. Jan had insisted that morning that he knew as little as she did, but Amy was not so sure. She could not shake the feeling that something even more significant than an end to this wretched persecution was going on.

She tried praying, but she couldn't calm down and couldn't find the words. *I don't even know what I should be praying.* So she hoped for their safety, and then she could pray that Hanna, Tadeusz, and Jan all be granted discernment and insight.

Insight, something I never seem to be blessed with.

Then there was a soft knock at the door, and Iwona came out of the next room, where she had been ironing. Amy opened the door to Jan's taut face.

"Is everything all right?" Amy asked.

"Well, there's been an unexpected turn of events. I think you'd better join us, Amy. Can you leave Tomek here?"

He glanced at Iwona, who nodded. "Of course, of course. The boy is sleeping. Go now."

"Thank you," Amy said, "I won't be long." She hurried after Jan, who was already out the door.

He was waiting for her in the hall. "Jan, what is it? What's happened? *Who is he?*"

Jan answered in rushed whispers. "I think Tatuś was right, that this is the man who started all the arrests. But they know each other from the war, and this man owed Tatuś some sort of debt. But he refuses to rescind the order about Protestants, says it's out of his hands."

"Is he telling the truth?"

"I doubt it. At any rate, he's asked what else he can do for us instead. And Mamusia suggested he help find out what happened to your father."

Amy gasped, "Oh no. Use him for things that matter, not for my wild goose chase. Hanna said that?"

Jan took her by the arm. "Yes, and I think it's a good idea, Amy. Let's use him for whatever we can get out of him. It's all right. Mamusia and Tatuś know what they're doing."

"You don't sound convinced." She paused and looked at her husband.

Jan had come back from his stay in prison so different, more mature and, of course, so very distant. Only much later had Amy finally discovered the cause of the terrible gap growing between them after he came home. And then, the comfort of finally naming the cause had thrown them together for the first time in months, and the only time since. The result of that one night of closeness was the baby Amy now carried. The distance between them had narrowed, but Jan's continued suspicions kept it open, and Amy still had not managed to bridge the gap. She was slowly realizing Jan would have to want that as well before the healing could happen.

She wanted so badly to reach out for him now and ask, *Tell me how I can make it better.* But he would deny there was anything wrong. Instead she said, "Well, what do I have to do?"

"Talk to the man."

"He's dangerous, though, isn't he?"

"Yes. He can have anyone arrested he wants. He already knows about our belief, the ministry. We have nothing to hide, except for Piotr. He won't ask, but we need to protect Piotr. Remember that, and everything will be all right. Come on."

As Amy watched her husband walk away, she thought she heard a scuffling sound nearby. She peered into the dark hall leading to the staircase but saw nothing. She sighed. If only Tomek or perhaps the new baby could somehow help her span the remaining stretch still keeping her from Jan.

Then Amy remembered something Hanna had told her once about difficult times, something her own mother had said.

Amy thought for a moment. What was it again? She had been talking about those terrible times right after the war. "My mother would have called it a dark time, something to be outlived until light and hope could be felt again. My mother would stroke my face and say those things were always there. Just because we can't feel them, that doesn't mean that hope and light aren't with us always."

Hope and light. Amy held on to the thought as she followed Jan into his parents' apartment.

She saw the visitor standing with his back toward the door as he talked with Hanna and Tadeusz. In the split second before he turned, Amy could feel herself tensing for the encounter. She didn't like this. She didn't want to become the center of attention here.

Then, as Tadeusz looked up and nodded at Jan and Amy's entrance, he turned. Immediately, Amy saw that the man despised Hanna and Tadeusz. It was written in his eyes, still discernible from his conversation. Strangely, Amy's first impression of him was one of recognition. *It's because you saw him on TV*, she told herself.

Amy studied the stranger's face. It told a story of its own, of this she was sure. He was an old man, old not because of his stature, which was tall and lean and ramrod straight, but because of a face, scarred and ravaged with wrinkles going in all the wrong directions.

Tadeusz said to her, "This is someone we believe may be able to help you find out what happened to your father."

"Hello," Amy said. The stranger nodded. So she wasn't supposed to know his name. Well, Jan didn't know who he was, either. One of the government ministers, he thought.

"We have a few things to discuss," Tadeusz told her, "so we'll just be in the other room."

Amy shot Jan a look of desperation. He said, "We'll be right here, *with the door open*," he added, clearly for the man's benefit.

Hanna and Jan took their cue as Tadeusz turned to the man and said, "Any help you can give my daughter-in-law would be greatly appreciated. Tell him your story, Amy."

From the moment he heard her name, Jacek felt sick with premonition. Then she began talking, and her Polish, though fair, could not mask the American accent. This merely confirmed what Jacek could no longer doubt.

As Amy told him everything she had discovered in her search for her father, Jacek's mind reeled. There was no doubt whatsoever who this woman was, that he was her father. He looked at her closely, desperate to find something of Barbara in the hair, the eyes, the bearing, but instead recognized his own straight, blue-black hair, his dark eyes, his chin. His Amy.

But Amy's dead. The thought severed his consciousness as a part of him anchored itself to the tangible world, his surroundings, the low tones of people talking in the next room, just beyond the doorway. *She died with her mother in the car accident.*

The thought had barely formulated itself in his mind when Jacek knew the truth. He remembered the passion with which another agent in Berlin had warned him to drop Barbara so he could do his work better. Izzy had always told him his position was too sensitive, too crucial to jeopardize in any way. "No one can ever take your place."

And then he knew.

They lied so they could keep me here, where they wanted me. She's been alive all this time. The proof stood before him. Jacek could feel his emotions spinning out of control. How on earth had this happened? He had missed how many years with her? He had been thirty when she was born, and now he was sixty-seven.

" . . . So, once I got to Poland, a friend started helping me look up anything we could find on Jacek Skrzypek. Surprisingly, there were records of his emigration. . . ."

He had only been half listening when the sound of his real name riveted Jacek's attention back to the story she had been telling.

"What friend?" he asked, almost without thinking.

A look of fear flashed across her face before Amy continued, ignoring his question. Jacek's training told him he had hit a vulnerable spot. If it were anyone else, this would signal a point worth returning to, a weakness Jacek could exploit. Now though, everything had changed.

As Jacek listened to the trail of clues he himself had left, he thought it was amazing, really, how much she actually knew. Frightening. *She must have had help—that's what she said*. He wondered if it was her husband.

A thousand questions pummeled him. How did she ever get into Poland? She had been vague about that part of the story as well. How had she come in contact with his Tadeusz? Of all the people for his daughter to hook up with. . . . Jacek shook his head. *Who is the friend?*

Amy rattled off the litany of places where he had left behind his signature, and Jacek cursed himself for the one sentimental thing he had ever done in this job. He had always thought no one would ever be able to make the connection between Jacek Duch and Jacek Skrzypek. It had been his way of validating his existence, somehow necessary to one living so long undercover.

In those years of madness during the war, Jacek had still been suffering from his prison experience. One way to steady himself had been to hold tight to the knowledge that there really was somewhere he could go and still feel that he was real. He had also meant it as a signal to his controllers, a trail of bread crumbs in case something ever happened to him, a way to trace his movements. How was he to know that his daughter would be the only one to discern the signs?

He was safe from the SB. Jacek made an effort to remember this. The clues were worthless to anyone who did not know the key, his real name. Jacek told this also to himself in order to

quench the panic already eating away at the edges of his consciousness.

———————— ∽ ————————

Amy stopped talking. The stranger facing her seemed distracted anyway. She had just been thinking, *He's probably not even
listening*, when the front door slowly swung open. Only now did
she realize it had been left unlocked.

In the space stood Piotr.

Amy froze, hoping the man would not notice. She looked in
Piotr's eyes and caught herself fighting an irresistible force drawing her toward him. *You've changed so much*, she thought. *Harder,
older.*

Amy shrank from the tenderness and remorse radiating from
his face. *Oh, Piotr. Not still.*

She glanced quickly toward the other room and saw only Jan's
back, partially obscured in the doorway. No one but she had noticed Piotr. Then she caught the eye of the stranger. So he *had* been
listening, and now he was watching her. His eyes instantly bright-
ened with understanding as he spun around.

The sudden transformation of Piotr's face took Amy's breath
away. In the next second, he had ducked out the door and was
gone again.

Amy's first impulse was to run after him, to call, but the stranger's eyes boring into her anchored Amy's feet. The sure knowledge that Piotr still loved her, had never stopped loving her, cut
into Amy like a knife. She felt confused, distrustful of her own
responses.

And only then did she wonder, *Should I tell Jan?*

———————— ∽ ————————

At first, Piotr could not tear himself away. He had not known
himself that he was so deeply in love until he saw her and felt her
presence rip into him. He knew the man whose back was turned
to him posed a grave threat, but once he saw Amy, Piotr could not
move.

You are so beautiful. He had forgotten—how was it possible? He
had forgotten her grace and her beauty, her tender dark eyes.

How, *how* had he let her slip through his fingers—how many? Three years ago? It felt like an eternity.

Piotr had heard most of the encounter. He had arrived shortly before Tadeusz sent Jan to fetch Amy and had stood outside the door as the meeting between his parents and the stranger was in progress. At first Piotr had thought his parents were betraying him, turning him in to the secret police. Then, as what he heard began to settle into a shape he had caught sight of before, new realizations sent a chill running down Piotr's spine.

When he heard Jan step toward the door, Piotr hid behind a column and waited as Jan left the apartment and brought Amy out of the neighbor's. He had even overheard bits of the ensuing conversation between his parents and this man. Then he ducked into the shadows a second time and eavesdropped on Amy and Jan. Piotr had thrilled to hear Amy's voice again in the dark. Tuned in to her with every cell of his body, Piotr had picked up on the tension between Amy and his brother.

As Jan and Amy had entered the apartment, Piotr had caught hold of the door before it closed all the way. Amy and Jan were so focused on the visitor that they hadn't even noticed. He held the door open just a crack. Now he could hear everything.

Piotr listened closely as Amy started her story and then grew afraid. She was going into too much detail. *She'll give me away and not even know it.* Any mention of Katyń would arouse the wrong set of suspicions. He had to stop her. When Piotr heard Amy approach that stage of their search, he silently pushed the door open and entered the room.

The sight of her filled him with longing. His heart leaped toward her. Now more than ever, he knew her as his only love.

Piotr was thankful he never told Amy what else he found out in his investigation of the Katyń massacre. In fact, he had discovered yet another of her father's signatures and had since come to believe that he was indeed the one who escaped Katyń before the killing. Since that breakthrough, he had known he must protect Amy. It was one of the reasons he had come to the apartment that day, to check on her and see how best he could shield her from the knowledge of who her father really was.

Jacek recognized the dark young man who entered the apartment so quietly. Even in the few seconds that he stood there, Jacek could see clearly that this was one of the men thought to be responsible for the riots in June, a leader in what the government propagandists liked to call the counterrevolutionary movement.

Jacek had been watching Amy, trying to come to grips with the concept that this woman was his daughter, when he saw a look of such undeniable love cross her features that at first it struck him dumb. Then, in a flash of understanding, Jacek knew that whoever had caused that expression on Amy's face was the accomplice he sought.

It was there for all to see. His daughter loved another man. This man. Jacek's uncanny skill at reading a situation, honed over the years, his ability to sense what people were really feeling—all this had revealed a dilemma to him. It was scant comfort, for this was something Jacek wished he never knew.

When the younger man left again without signaling anyone but Amy, Jacek understood enough. *Outlaw and outcast.* The fear on this man's face when he saw Jacek also told Jacek he would have to find and silence him.

After that, Jacek had to struggle to maintain his mask of indifference.

"Is everything all right? Has Amy told you everything?" Tadeusz reentered the room.

Not quite, I think, Jacek thought. He was extremely curious about Amy's next move. It would reveal a great deal about her.

"Yes," she said, "we're finished. It was kind of your . . . friend to listen to me ramble on like this."

Well done, girl. "No trouble at all, believe me," Jacek said. "I will remember the names you told me. . . ."

"Name," Amy corrected him as the others looked sharply at them both.

"Yes, what was it again, Skrzypek? Fine. Now, I think my business here is ended. I must be going."

"Yes," Tadeusz said. He picked up Jacek's coat and held it for him, then walked alone with him over to the door. "This is the least you can do for us. But I must insist you do the other thing for all the rest like us. Do we have an understanding?"

Jacek tried to stare him down, but the upheaval inside separated him from his usual calm. *I have to get out of here, at any cost.* "Yes, of course. But you must *never* contact me like this again. You will not see me again."

As the door closed behind him, Jacek let the full impact of what he had just undergone wash over him in one great, tumultuous wave. He put out a gloved hand to steady himself against the wall. Even now, the web of lies he had so carefully spun prevented him from telling her who he was. But he would protect her in any way possible.

He thought back to her reaction to this man, clearly her partner in crime. He had hit a raw nerve with his questions. *If it were anyone else, I'd now know where to hit. Now that I know you're my daughter, it means I've found out the part of you in need of guarding.*

Jacek had the distinct impression that all his debts now remained unpaid. He could feel his world crashing around him, reality smashing down the gates he had erected, the explosion all the greater because of all the years spent constructing his false reality.

As he found his way down the stairs of the Piekarzs' apartment building in Gdynia, Jacek suddenly thought he saw a woman reappear from somewhere and stand before him in the dark corridor. Monika, his former landlord's daughter? Ina ... Izzy? Amy's mother, Barbara? The ghosts had returned.

Betrayer, betrayed, Jacek now feared he must pay the highest price of all for the choices he had made.

———— ✧ ————

Piotr waited, wondering if he was doing the right thing. He had to be sure. The shapes kept shifting. And he had not heard all of what was said, just enough bits to think he could put together a pattern.

When he heard the footsteps descending the stairs, he readied himself. As the man turned the corner, Piotr leaped at him, pulling his head back by the hair and forcing him under the bare lightbulb on the landing.

"I thought so," he said out loud. This was no less than one of the assistant ministers in the Party government—very powerful, very high up, very vulnerable. Piotr held him for a few moments, then let the man go, surprised by his lack of resistance. He had not even tried to counter Piotr's attack.

"I don't know what exactly your name is." It was time to spring his trap. "But I do know who you are, Mr. Assistant Minister," Piotr said. "Amy's father."

"You're out of your mind," the man said. "I don't know what you're talking about. You think you have the upper hand here, but *I* know who *you* are, terrorist. What did you think, that I was blind? After your little entrance back there," the man breathed. "I know you are this Amy's lover."

Piotr tried to ignore the remark. He had to stay focused. What he did next could either sign a death warrant for Amy and the rest of his family or set them free.

"We will make a deal," Piotr said. He backed into the shadows, hoping to mask his fear, summoning up all the training he had received in the underground these last years.

"Two things," he said, "or I will give away your secret. You will call off the SB from these Protestants." Piotr was counting on this man not knowing that Piotr also belonged to the family. He had Jan to thank for that. "And you will call off your hunt for the instigators of the riots."

"I'm not responsible . . ." the man started to protest.

"No, of course not. But you know who is."

"Even if I did," the old man hissed, only now waking up enough to trace Piotr's steps into the shadows, "why should I do you any favors?"

Piotr didn't like the edge in the man's tone. He sounded dangerously close to losing control. "Because I overheard what the old couple said to you."

When the man opened his mouth, Piotr held up his finger in the dim light. The sweat poured down his temples. He could hear his heart pounding in his ears. "Do you want to know why I had no lines during my little 'entrance,' as you called it?" Piotr took a deep breath. "Because, assistant minister, that apartment is bugged by your own secret police."

Piotr watched the devastation his words caused in the face so close to his own. *One more, to be safe.*

"And," he swallowed, praying the truth he had just hurled at the man would mask his next move. He was guessing, but if he really was Amy's father, then maybe this was also true. One maybe and a little confusion was all Piotr needed to make his bluff work. "I know the secret that pastor overheard when you were raving.

"I know what you really are."

32

BURNS THE CHARIOTS

Psalm 46:9

1976

Jan tossed and turned in bed that night, troubled by the knowledge that something was deeply wrong. He could not rest. His thoughts raced from one problem to the next.

The meeting with the minister had not gone as his father had hoped—that much he knew. And there was not much the man could do for Amy. It seemed that dashed hopes were the order of the day.

For some reason, Jan had been thinking about Piotr all day. He was in trouble—Jan knew this, too. Even when they were boys, he had had a sixth sense about Piotr. Although Jan had not seen his brother since before the wedding, he had a feeling Piotr had been involved in the June riots. And if that was true, then Piotr was a hunted man.

Before that, ever since he found Piotr's wedding gift, Jan had been wrestling daily with the wrenching emotion the letters had stirred up in him. It was not jealousy—for that he could have put behind him—but the sure knowledge that he was the one who had stolen his brother's joy. Again and again, Jan had blamed himself for ruining his brother's life and probably his wife's as well. If he had not stood in the way, Amy might have been used to bring Piotr to the Lord. And the two would be together, where they belonged. Jan had tried to suppress the dread, but it had taken him over, coloring every view he held.

Ever since that week following his release from prison, he had often thought of how for these two years he had basked in the full blessing and happiness of being with Amy, blindly innocent of the cost his act had exacted from his own brother.

Piotr's last letter in the wooden box mentioned a visit he had made to Amy around Christmastime, not long before the wedding. Piotr wrote of loving Amy, of losing her to Jan. Why hadn't Amy told him about the visit?

In the months since Jan had found the letters, this question had been the one that tormented him the most. In his agonizing search for an answer, he had been able to think of only one reason why: His wife was still in love with his brother.

When Jan could no longer bear the tortured spell his doubts had cast upon him, he had confronted Amy with them. But confronting her had not answered his questions. Was that because there were no acceptable answers?

———— ⟳ ————

Now Jan sighed and sat up in bed, swinging his feet onto the floor and leaning over to cradle his aching head in his hands. How often had he gone over that conversation? A thousand times a thousand? What had he done? Instead of asking Amy's forgiveness for not trusting, as he had sworn he would do in prison, he had accused her.

"So *do* you still love Piotr?"

Her look of dismay should have warned him instantly, but now Jan realized he had numbed himself to anything but his own fears. She had told him, "No. I don't understand, Jan. Why do you need to hear this? Why now again?"

Without a word he had placed the wooden box on her lap. She looked up at him. Her expression was so troubled that for a split second Jan had been tempted to forget the whole thing, to snatch the box back, to slay the dragon his action had just breathed into life.

Instead Jan had done nothing. He had stood by and waited in judgment. *But what was there to judge?* And when he had seen the recognition of Piotr's handwriting dawn on her face before she even started reading, he had known enough.

She had read a few pages, skipped to the last letter, then looked up at him, her face imploring. "Jan, I had no idea he had kept these. He wrote them before we were married. Jan, listen . . ."

But he had cut her short in a voice that choked on each word. "You told me he didn't still care."

"I thought he didn't. *He* was the one who would not see *me*. Piotr broke it off, Jan."

"Then why didn't you tell me he came back that Christmas to mend it? What else haven't you told me?" The words, once out, had seared like fire, burning him in the saying and her in the hearing. Jan had seen the damage in the way Amy looked at him.

"You don't trust me," she had murmured, incredulous. "Oh, Jan, you *must* believe me. *I didn't know.*"

"You did know. And you said nothing. You let me marry you. My brother still loved you, and you said nothing." He almost hadn't dared to ask the next question. Why had he asked it? "Did you still love him?"

"I'm sorry, Jan. I swear to you there's nothing else. You know everything about Piotr now. There aren't any secrets between us, and there won't ever be, Jan. You can't keep bringing this up; it's destroying us. You have to put this behind us, Jan. *I love you.*" She had reached out to touch him.

And he had stepped away. "Do you still love him?"

"How can you ask that? Jan, we've been married more than two years. We have a child. Doesn't that count for something?"

She doubts. She's covering it up, but she doubts herself and me. He had shaken his head and said only, "I don't know, Amy. You say you want to put this behind us. All right. We won't ever, ever bring it up again. Throw these letters in the fire if you must, but you can't lie anymore to yourself or to me."

Then Jan had turned his back on Amy and left her alone in the room with his brother's wedding gift.

———— ❧ ————

That night, perhaps because of the relief of finally bringing the problem out in the open, Jan and Amy had found each other in bed and been together. But afterward, by the next morning already, the distance had descended again. And the doubts had never really gone away.

Now, still caught up in his memories, Jan heard Amy stir. In her sleep, she reached for him. He watched her hand curl, palm upward, on the place beside her. The place where he should be.

Jan sighed. It was so hard to trust. Ever since the day he confronted Amy with Piotr's letters, he had been running away from his own doubt. *What if Amy still loves Piotr?*

Would she tell him so? Would she tell him if she saw Piotr again?

What if she doubts our love?

He sighed, countering his own thoughts: *As I doubt.*

Jan's tired mind leapt from one thought to the next, resolving nothing, unsure, incessant.

Then he stopped as something fell into place. He thought of Piotr, of his beloved violin gathering dust just behind the door. He thought of the torture he had been putting himself and Amy through in these past weeks. And he thought of stolen joy. *The joy we steal from ourselves.*

Amy sighed in her sleep. Jan looked from her to his son and back again. Like a promise in the dark, they'd been given a second child to be born later that year.

And then Jan found he was looking at them all with different eyes, as if he was suddenly able to take a step back and see what he had been doing to his own family. What had he been thinking? That he could leave them, desert them, send her away? The thought itself caused him to shake his head involuntarily.

A love so real it hurt welled up in Jan. He lay back down and curled his body around Amy's back, smelling her hair. God had given this woman to him. Jan remembered that now, as if somehow he had been blinded to the knowledge before. And now he saw.

Despite the uncertainty of the day, Jan sensed the resolve move in his heart as quiet and steady as his wife's sleeping breath. He was strong enough to resist the doubts, his own and Amy's, if need be. He would do so and God would strengthen him. *Oh, stand by me in this*, he prayed with all his heart.

Holding Amy in prayer, asking forgiveness, half asleep, Jan found himself returning yet again to the events of that day. And then he knew what is was that had bothered him so about his conversation with the visitor.

At some point the man had referred to the government measures to single out Protestant children in the schools. What was it again? He had heard them talking about the order against children.

And then, without warning, Jan felt it descending again, the deep sadness that had scarred his own childhood.

Jan saw a little boy holding up his arms, waiting to be taken away by the trees around him. He was that boy with his face in the mud, sobbing.

He was that boy who looked toward the light and lay his fear and anger and betrayal down like so many slaughtered lambs.

But then there was the rushing sound of strong, beating wings, and powerful feathered forms rising as easily as sparks in a dancing fire.

Beautiful.

And wild. Yet somehow comforting.

Then he saw something else. He saw his mother the night they took his father away, the night his own ongoing persecution began, that same persecution that resonated to the new persecutions. *It goes on and on. But there is healing. Courage, courage.*

She had knelt, her hair falling in her face. Jan had watched her with ice in his throat, terrified that his shattered world would never be restored. Her hands had danced over the floor, nervously skipping from one page of the broken Bible to the next. And then she had stopped and read out loud the promise he had carried in his heart all his life:

> " 'For I,' declares the Lord, 'will be a wall of fire around
> her, and I will be the glory in her midst.' "

As he let go of consciousness, Jan's last thought was of the fire. It had done all these things, mostly unseen, sometimes not.

The wall remained, God's glory in their midst remained.

The fire still burned.

And this was where.